ADJACENT *but only* JUST

the PENN-LEITHS of
THISTLE MUIR
BOOK TWO

NICHOLE VAN

Fiorenza Publishing

Published by Fiorenza Publishing
Print Edition v1.0

ISBN: 978-1-949863-16-1

To those who grieve,
Light will return.

To Dave,
For holding me through my grief.

God answers sharp and sudden on some prayers,
And thrusts the thing we have prayed for in our face,
A gauntlet with a gift in it.
                    —*Elizabeth Barrett Browning*

Ah, but a man's reach should exceed his grasp,
Or what's a heaven for?
                    —*Robert Browning*

PROLOGUE

Viola Brodure could not scoff in the face of Death.

But then, she struggled to speak in her actual Life, so the realization was hardly a surprise.

The destitute woman seated before her, however, scoffed and spoke with ease.

"I hope I die with grace," Martha chuckled breathlessly, rocking her sick babe in her arms. "Heaven knows I have a dreadful lot to atone for." She spared a glance for Viola as if anticipating words of comfort.

Viola's tongue froze, anxiety and asthma tightening her breathing and choking off any reply.

"Hopefully death shall not visit you anytime soon, Martha," Mrs. Eloise Carpenter, Viola's cousin, soothed before the silence stretched too thin.

Today, Viola and Eloise had ventured into the heart of the ironically named 'Angel Meadow' slum of Manchester, wishing to further Eloise's charity work.

"Aye, we're no' dead yet." Martha touched her babe's fevered cheek. "'Tis a fine line around here between life and death. And we walk that line like Mr. Fredericks from downstairs after a bottle of gin—none-too-straight with mounds of off-key singing."

Again, she glanced at Viola. Again, anticipating a reaction. A smile. A chuckle. *Something.*

But the caustic coal smoke combined with Viola's asthmatic lungs and shy nervousness ensuring her lips remained shut.

Granted, the dingy sleeping mat on the floor and solitary table piled with dirty crockery already spoke volumes. Despite the forced cheerfulness of Martha's words, Death hovered in the corners and lurked outside the flat's rickety door.

Giving Viola a tight, understanding look, Eloise turned back to the baby in Martha's arms, pressing a hand to his forehead.

Shame flushed Viola's skin, which only served to bind her chest tighter and stuff her mouth full of cotton.

Oof.

Her asthma and anxiety were a vicious cycle.

Just speak, she pleaded with her brain. *Simply open your mouth.*

If she were sitting at a desk, the words would flow easily from her pen.

But even then, mere words felt hollow in the face of Martha's suffering, a woman whose husband had abandoned her and their *five* children—children who crouched around their mother and stared at Viola with sunken eyes. Their mean circumstances were a far cry from Viola's own at the vicar's manse in Westacre, the rural Wiltshire village where she lived with her father.

Viola's visit with Cousin Eloise was to have been an uneventful one—a relaxing holiday enjoying the social whirl of Manchester. But Eloise was passionate about addressing the ills of the Poor Laws. And so, instead of making morning calls and attending garden luncheons, Viola trailed her cousin through crumbling tenements and rookeries. Two of Eloise's sturdiest grooms accompanied them, ensuring their safety.

Before this week, Viola had understood that abject poverty existed. That at times, people had to make difficult choices to survive.

But nothing could have truly prepared her for the harsh reality of Angel Meadows—rats feasting on the body of a dead man, a woman screaming in agony as a man beat her, rag-clad children who snatched chunks of bread from Viola's hand with skeletal fingers.

The touted Poor Law Amendment of 1834 had failed them all.

"More must be done, Cousin," Eloise had said just that morning. *"Consider using your voice to advocate for true change. Your readers will listen, just as Mr. Dickens's do. I am sure of it."*

As if picking up the thread of Viola's thoughts, Martha smiled tentatively at her. "I cannot wait to tell my neighbors that the famous Miss Brodure visited me today."

Viola's breath hitched, her fingers knotting. Every eye in the room turned to her. Watching. Waiting.

She implored herself to say something—a simple phrase like, *Martha, I admire how you confront your struggles with such grace.*

Instead, she stood motionless, a frozen rabbit of a person.

It was intolerable. Unconscionable.

"You've read my cousin's works then?" Eloise asked.

"Aye," Martha nodded. "Mr. Fredericks downstairs has a copy of *Little Lottie.* And he can read, he can. He's already read it to us twice."

"Cor, Lottie was right plucky, standing up to her wicked aunt like that," a girl at Martha's shoulder said, gaunt eyes wide.

Eloise gave Viola a look that said, *Say something! You cannot disappoint a child!*

Viola swallowed. "Th-thank you," she managed to stammer. "That is v-very kind."

Viola wrote moralizing stories about pious orphans and virtuous maidens who held to their principles even under trying circumstances—characters who saw the world in crisp shades of black and white.

But after everything Viola had witnessed this week, writing about pious orphans felt ridiculous.

Orphans, she knew now, did not have the luxury of piety.

In the tiny tenement room, hung with filthy linen and stinking of unwashed bodies and mildew, Viola faced the reality of her own inadequacies.

Not just her asthmatic lungs and nervously stammering tongue.

No.

It was her silence—spoken *and* written.

Her inaction.

Because even though her prim tales were beloved the country over, they did nothing to measurably improve the lives of others.

Abruptly, she saw herself from above—a mute, marble statue in the center of the room, silence and indecision damning her.

Eloise, however, had scarcely ceased moving. Touching the babe. Laughing with Martha. Smiling at the other children. Speaking gentle words of comfort.

Shame flooded Viola's chest.

She needed to *act*.

She should be writing stories that *mattered*. Stories that challenged traditional notions, not reinforced them. Stories that demanded change.

Resolve burned within her—a primal vow beating in time with her heart.

Never again would she be a rigid bystander.

Never again would she remain silent in the face of another's suffering.

UPON RETURNING TO Eloise's townhouse, Viola retreated to her bed chamber.

But the elegant room was too much. Too lovely with its fine linens, Italian wallpaper, and velvet curtains. Too warm with its cheery fire. Too comfortable with its feather-stuffed cushions, thick Savonnerie carpet, and pillowy bed tick.

Unable to face her own hypocrisy, she slid down the wall beside the bed, sinking onto the hard floor, her head resting against the wooden paneling. Her lungs felt tight. She bit her trembling bottom lip and stared up at the pretty yellow chintz bed curtains.

After a moment, her eyes drifted to the book of poetry on her bedside table.

Poems from the Highlands by Ethan Penn-Leith.

Though they had never met, Viola admired Mr. Penn-Leith intensely. He was one of the most celebrated poets of their day, praising the moors and braes of the Scottish Highlands with such skill that even the Queen lauded his work.

His first and only book accompanied Viola everywhere, a comforting symphony of rhythm and profundity.

Her hand reached for the slim volume, the well-loved pages opening to her favorite poem—

"Adjacent But Only Just."

> I am adjacent,
> But only just
> A falcon's flight away
> From feral moor and heather'd scent,
> A prisoner of the malcontent
> Of life lived in delay.
> I am adjacent,
> but only just . . .

Viola reread the familiar words, a fingertip tracing over the lines.

The poem described Mr. Penn-Leith's life as the son of a Scottish gentleman farmer, a man working in the shadow of the Highlands, adjacent to wildness but never part of it. The lines were heralded as a metaphor for modern life—the separation of humans from the natural world, a desire to seek truth *in* Nature instead of simply living in sight of it . . .

Adjacent, but only just.

Mr. Penn-Leith's poem profoundly summarized Viola's life.

A native shyness, anxious nervousness, and unpredictable asthma caused her to approach life with too much temerity.

Adjacent, but only just—

Adjacent to action and true living.

Adjacent to revolutionary ideas and words.

Adjacent to marriage and children.

Hers *was* a 'life lived in delay.'

Viola was so very weary of it.

Of spending her days metaphorically immobile in the center of a room, knowing she needed to act—to do, to move—but somehow . . . *not.*

She swallowed and looked back up at the bed curtains, their sunny lemon cheer taunting her newfound sense of purpose, reminding her that other forces also influenced her pen . . . her father and his reliance on the Duke of Kendall foremost among them.

The elderly, tyrannical Duke of Kendall would be apoplectic were he to learn of Viola's current mindset. And given that Kendall funded her father's living as vicar of Westacre . . .

Well, to incur the wrath of her father's employer would be the very height of folly.

But . . . surely there was *something* she could do. Some way to untether the fierce creature that stretched restless inside her.

An idea formed in her head. *Two* ideas, actually.

Viola pushed up from the floor, slowly standing.

Did she dare?

She darted another glance at Mr. Penn-Leith's book of poetry.

Why, yes. She rather thought she did.

She crossed the room to her small desk and reached for her pen and notebook.

Gentle Reader, we here at *The Tattler* have one burning question: Will Mr. Ethan Penn-Leith and Miss Viola Brodure make a match of it?

Few can dispute the popularity and romanticism of Mr. Penn-Leith, our own Highland Poet. Why, just last month, he strolled down Bond Street in his customary great kilt, turning heads and causing several young ladies to swoon. Is it any wonder he is often compared to Lord Byron?

Similarly, all of London is well-acquainted with the popularity of Miss Brodure's novels. Speculation continues regarding her latest book, *Polly Pettifer*, and its now infamous chapter eleven in which Miss Brodure, using Polly as her mouthpiece, proclaims the brilliance of Mr. Penn-Leith.

Now that Mr. Penn-Leith has returned home to Scotland to complete his second book of poetry, we wait with bated breath to see if he will reply to Miss Brodure's overtures in a similarly literary fashion.

On this Valentine's Day, when we celebrate love, we hold out hope that the two literary giants of our age will write a romantic tale of their own.

Viola had not anticipated that her marriage would be decided by committee.

Namely—

An autocratic duke.

An elderly baroness.

And her father.

All ruthlessly plotting Viola's nuptials and writing career over the *fish* course, of all things.

"An August wedding, I should think," Lady Whipple was saying from one end of the dining room table, leaning sideways as a footman slid a generous slice of trout in aspic onto her plate. "With her fair coloring, Miss Brodure should be a summer bride."

"An excellent suggestion," Dr. Brodure replied at Viola's side. "Though September might be better for my Viola to wed Mr. Ethan Penn-Leith. There is much to accomplish between now and then."

Her father shot her a quick smile. His gray hair stuck out in soft tufts above his ears, lending him an owlish appearance that tugged at her heart.

Viola attempted a weak smile in return. Her own face surely looked akin to a blacksmith's forge—fiery red and scorching. Her heart certainly picked up the metaphor, hammering in her chest with punishing force.

Worse, her lungs threatened rebellion, her breathing tight. As usual, nerves and tension aggravated her asthma, and her current situation was the definition of nerve-wracking tension.

Taking in a shallow breath, Viola gathered her courage and steadied her shaking hands.

"If I m-may offer an opinion," she said, attempting to control the wheezing warble in her voice, "I should prefer to actually *meet* my prospective groom and, well . . . become acquainted, c-conduct a courtship, ascertain if we have affection for one another, and so forth . . . *before* planning our n-nuptials."

Her halting words dampened the enthusiasm in the room for approximately four seconds.

"September is an excellent month for a wedding," the young Duke of Kendall intoned from the head of the table, swirling his wine glass and nodding toward his aunt, Lady Whipple. "Miss Brodure should marry Mr. Penn-Leith then."

Though tall and imposing, His Grace had inherited his late father's propensity to gray early in life. His salt-and-pepper hair more closely resembled a gentleman in his sixtieth year of life, not his twenty-third.

Viola found the contrast between the duke's gray hair, dark eyes, and youthful face rather unnerving.

Granted, *everything* about dining at Hawthorn was unnerving—from the lavishly-gilded mirrors on each wall to the eight footmen in starched livery standing at attention behind her dining room chair.

Even the fish on her plate—the trout's glassy eyeballs jiggling in their jelly casing—disconcerted her. Viola had a strong aversion to aspic. It felt unnatural to suspend an entire fish in gelatin, hovering in midair, fixed and unmoving.

Much, she supposed, as her life at present—

Frozen. Caught in a net. Only *some* of which was of her own making.

"I hear the Queen herself has given her seal of approval to a match between Miss Brodure and Mr. Penn-Leith," Lady Whipple said, poking at her own fish with a fork. Her ladyship had been in residence at Hawthorn—seeing to the duke's household and acting as hostess—for as long as Viola had lived in Westacre. "Lady Portman said as much at the Duchess of Buccleuch's soiree, and as Her Majesty's Lady of the Bedchamber, Lady Portman would certainly know."

The *Queen* was in on this plot, too?!

Viola pressed a hand against her stomach, her lungs spasming.

What was she to do?

Truly, she should have foreseen this. The broadsheets *loved* Ethan Penn-Leith—the sweeping romanticism of his poetry, the handsome virility of his person. The papers regularly printed a lithograph portrait of him—a large man in a great kilt, square-jawed with tousled curls, a glint of humor in his eyes.

Was it any wonder the Scot was so celebrated?

Was it any wonder her own fingers had penned Polly Pettifer's tribute to him?

Any woman with a beating pulse would wish to know him better . . . herself included, obviously. To count him a friend and perhaps—slowly, over time—see if something more might evolve.

But befriending a gentleman was a far cry from matrimony, no matter how much Kendall and Lady Whipple tried to equate the two.

Moreover, there was still one rather large obstacle . . . well, another obstacle in addition to Viola having never met Mr. Penn-Leith, ascertained their suitability as a couple, determined his interest in herself as a prospective wife . . .

She placed a hand on her rambling thoughts.

Swallowing, Viola lifted her eyes from the trout. "You do not c-consider my age to be an impediment, Lady Whipple?"

Her ladyship frowned, reaching for her wine. "Whyever should it be, Miss Brodure?"

By *soon* she meant *later.*

Much, much later.

As in . . . most likely never.

"I had hoped that you might be farther along the path by now, Miss Brodure," Kendall frowned. "We first spoke of this before Yuletide last year."

Yes, and Viola had been dodging the issue since then.

"I am still trying to find my m-muse, Your Grace." How she hated the nervous stammer in her voice. "The story is proving difficult to pin down."

Kendall's frown deepened. "Even a short story printed in a popular publication like *The Gentleman's Magazine* would be effective. And surely such a paltry thing could be written quickly, don't you agree Miss Brodure?"

Viola took in a slow breath and nodded her head. What other response was left her, after such a manipulative question?

"I shall consider it done then, Miss Brodure." Kendall studied Viola for another heartbeat—as if assessing her acquiescence—and then turned to her father. "In the meantime, I feel that a sermon on this very subject next Sunday would be advisable, Dr. Brodure. Perhaps your words will inspire your daughter." His eyes dipped sideways to her.

Dr. Brodure agreed to Kendall's request, accepting the duke's demands with a nod.

Everyone in the room understood that her father, as the fourth son of Viscount Mossley, had his ambition firmly fixed on being appointed a bishop.

Viola supported him wholeheartedly in his goal. As a vicar, her father rushed to comfort a grieving father or assist a hungry child. She could only imagine the greater good he could do as a bishop.

But, as with everything, being elevated to a bishop required Kendall's help and support. And so Viola and her father bowed to the necessary evil of his demands.

When the elder Duke of Kendall had died on the heels of Viola's trip to Manchester, Viola's father had hoped for a possible improvement in his own fortunes. The old duke had been reluctant to use his clout to

Viola barely stifled a (somewhat) hysterical laugh.

Because at thirty years of age, I passed the gates into spinsterhood an eon ago, she nearly replied.

But, of course, did not.

Because . . . shyness.

Her bashful tongue had always hampered her ability to converse with the opposite sex. As a younger woman, just the thought of speaking with a gentleman had sent Viola into a full-blown asthma attack. Even now, when faced with a man she admired, words caught in her mouth and her asthmatic lungs rebelled.

Viola Brodure had never quite blossomed into a prize-winning rose. In fact, some might describe her as the most wallflowerish wallflower who had ever wallflowered.

But after the upheaval of those days spent with Eloise last summer, Viola had realized that she needed to not only take risks in her writing but in her personal life as well.

And so in an effort to no longer live *adjacent* to life, she had put her admiration of Mr. Penn-Leith into the mouth of one of her characters.

And if Mr. Penn-Leith replied to her indirect compliments, Viola had reasoned, then she could respond back. From there, a dialogue could ensue—a comfortable, *written* communication of ideas between like-minded people.

That had been her sole intention—to secure a pen pal. A charming, literary Scottish pen pal whose dashing appearance regularly caused even London's finest roses to swoon, but still . . .

Then *Polly Pettifer* had become a runaway success; it was already onto its second printing.

And in light of the novel's popularity and Mr. Penn-Leith's fame, a London gossip rag had seized on Viola's homage to him and constructed a narrative—

Viola Brodure and Ethan Penn-Leith were destined to fall in love and marry.

Heaven help her.

Kendall, of course, had picked up the narrative thread as a means to fuel his own political ambitions. He intended to harness Mr. Penn-Leith's fame and the elevated popularity of Miss Brodure's work to garner public support *against* amending the callous Poor Laws.

Her cheeks pinked and her breathing constricted further at the thought.

"What say you to September for the wedding, Aunt?" Kendall asked Lady Whipple, cutting his trout into neat, square pieces. "It would be the perfect culmination of the parliamentary session and could buttress my defense of our current laws for assisting the poor."

Viola all but squirmed at His Grace's comment, his aims being the precise *opposite* of her own.

Unfortunately, in the eight months since those pivotal weeks in Manchester, Viola had found paltry few ways to express her views to the empire's masses.

After all, her father's employment as vicar of Westacre depended entirely upon the patronage of Kendall—a man who preferred to 'stoppeth his ears at the cry of the poor,' as Proverbs so eloquently put it.

Viola found it a terrible disappointment. The new duke had spent most of his formative years away from Hawthorn and Westacre, so she had been cautiously hopeful that his political opinions might *not* align with his gray hair.

But in that, she had been mistaken.

Kendall most definitely displayed the politics of an elderly man—a nostalgia for eras past, an instinctual distrust of progress, and a hostility toward the working classes. All opinions he had, no doubt, inherited from his recently-deceased father.

Though Viola did not like speaking ill of the dead, she had nothing kind to say about the previous Duke of Kendall. He had been a convicted bigamist who had ruled his dukedom like a tyrant—that is to say, ruthless, with no tolerance for dissent.

But the old duke had been enamored of Viola's writing—commending the humility of her characters and their praise of the upper classes. His Grace's support had been crucial to her success, and so she had adhered to writing on the topics he dictated.

Consequently, the current duke considered Viola and her novels to be an extension of his political views. Though young, Kendall was fiercely ambitious. He reportedly aimed for nothing less than the Prime Minister's seat.

Viola, dearest, you could be Virgil to Kendall's Augustus, if you so wished it, her father had remarked only the day before.

So tonight, like most evenings dining at Hawthorn, was rather a fraught dance—Viola taking what rope she could, attempting to assert her own wants and needs, but constantly chafing against the tight pull of Kendall's leash.

Viola gritted her teeth and poked at the trout on her plate. The fish stared belligerently back at her.

"September would also be excellent for the wedding." Lady Whipple sent her nephew an approving look. "There is much groundwork still to do if we wish to stave off further erosion of the Poor Laws. Unfortunately, Mr. Dicken's novels have been remarkably effective at swaying public opinion against our aims."

Yes. A feat Viola herself wished to emulate.

"Agreed," Kendall said, tipping his glass toward Viola. "Which is why we have Miss Brodure to advocate for *us*. It is bad enough that the Whigs managed to pass the Poor Law Amendment Act a decade past. The poor must work harder to escape their straitened circumstances, not look to the government to provide relief *gratis*. And now that Miss Brodure has used her pen to essentially summon Mr. Penn-Leith to her side, we can use her heightened fame to draw attention to her tales that, in turn, support our goals."

"Yes," Lady Whipple nodded in approval and motioned toward Viola. "My nephew tells me that you have begun a new novel to address this very thing, Miss Brodure. An *anti-Dickens* novel."

Viola's throat closed further. She had only given token responses to the duke's suggestion that she write such a novel. No inspiration had come to her yet, for obvious reasons.

She had plenty of ideas for stories that *supported* Mr. Dickens's ideas, however. Some stories . . . she might have even written.

Lady Whipple looked at her expectantly.

"Yes, I hope to b-begin in earnest soon." Viola swallowed, prevaricating.

see Dr. Brodure elevated. The new Duke of Kendall, however, appeared more amenable.

But Viola had returned from Manchester full of revolutionary zeal. She longed to act, now, now, *now*.

Dr. Brodure, to his credit, had not been dismayed at the change in her political leanings. Instead, he had listened as she told him about her new ambitions for her writing and then had urged her to proceed carefully.

"We rely too much upon young Kendall's grace to upset the cart," he had said, head shaking. "If you deviate too sharply from His Grace's strictures, I might be relieved of my duties as vicar and have to seek another living. I certainly would lose the opportunity to become a bishop. Either of those outcomes would grieve me. That said, I do understand your wishes and desires, daughter. Perhaps we can find a compromise that will allow us both to achieve our aims?"

If her father had become angry and dismissive, Viola could have perhaps felt justified in writing something revolutionary anyway. But anger was not her father's way. He had reached out to her in love, asking for her understanding.

And she *had* understood.

He proposed she delay publishing anything too incendiary. Just long enough for Kendall to put forth Dr. Brodure's name to Queen Victoria for appointment to bishop.

Once Dr. Brodure was a bishop and no longer reliant upon Kendall's patronage, Viola would have the freedom to publish what she liked, including stories that opposed the duke's parliamentary goals.

And so, Viola promised to bide her time and carry out Kendall's decrees.

Or, rather, she *tried* to. Truly, she did. Granted, there *might* have been (translation: there absolutely were) one or two notable exceptions, but—

"As Miss Brodure writes, we must plan." His Grace's words pulled Viola back to the dinner table and the unappetizing trout still staring up at her. "I shall instruct my secretary to contact the editors of *The Gentleman's Magazine* immediately and have them prepare for Miss Brodure's work. Then, she and Mr. Penn-Leith will embark on a courtship. Once that occurs, the broadsheets will be full of Miss Brodure and Mr. Ethan

Penn-Leith's romance. This will ensure that Miss Brodure's short story is widely read, further cementing public opinion in our favor. From there, we can use the added publicity and support to stave off those who attempt to reform the Poor Laws."

Viola had to give the duke some credit. His plan was actually rather ingenious. Diabolical . . . but ingenious.

Granted, there was one rather gaping hole.

"Though I do sincerely appreciate your concerns for my m-matrimonial happiness, Your Grace," Viola began, poking at her trout with a trembling fork, "I must point out, once more, that I am entirely unacquainted with Mr. Penn-Leith. I haven't the foggiest n-notion how I shall 'begin a courtship' with him."

She had absolutely no experience in matters of courtship. Hence her thirty-years-old-spinster-wallflower status.

"But you have corresponded with the man, have you not, Miss Brodure?" Lady Whipple asked.

"I have recently received a few kind lines from Mr. Penn-Leith thanking me for my homage in *Polly Pettifer*." *Deep breath.* "Hardly enough to term a correspondence."

And yet, even that was a lie, was it not?

Much of his letter had felt like more than mere correspondence, the words humming a merry tune in Viola's memory.

> *Thank you for your expansive praise of my humble poems. I find the creative turn of your mind most fascinating. I do not wish to seem impertinent, but I beg you to indulge me—from whence do you draw your inspiration?*

Viola had not yet responded. The very thought made her hands shake. With nerves? Anticipation?

"Nonsense!" Lady Whipple harrumphed. "A man replying at all is always a sign of interest. Gentlemen are lazy correspondents. You have him on the line, girl, best to reel him in." Her ladyship cut into her trout, as if the metaphor needed more emphasis.

Flummoxed, Viola wheezed for breath, mouth agape and, well, fishlike.

Viola barely stifled a (somewhat) hysterical laugh.

Because at thirty years of age, I passed the gates into spinsterhood an eon ago, she nearly replied.

But, of course, did not.

Because . . . shyness.

Her bashful tongue had always hampered her ability to converse with the opposite sex. As a younger woman, just the thought of speaking with a gentleman had sent Viola into a full-blown asthma attack. Even now, when faced with a man she admired, words caught in her mouth and her asthmatic lungs rebelled.

Viola Brodure had never quite blossomed into a prize-winning rose. In fact, some might describe her as the most wallflowerish wallflower who had ever wallflowered.

But after the upheaval of those days spent with Eloise last summer, Viola had realized that she needed to not only take risks in her writing but in her personal life as well.

And so in an effort to no longer live *adjacent* to life, she had put her admiration of Mr. Penn-Leith into the mouth of one of her characters.

And if Mr. Penn-Leith replied to her indirect compliments, Viola had reasoned, then she could respond back. From there, a dialogue could ensue—a comfortable, *written* communication of ideas between like-minded people.

That had been her sole intention—to secure a pen pal. A charming, literary Scottish pen pal whose dashing appearance regularly caused even London's finest roses to swoon, but still . . .

Then *Polly Pettifer* had become a runaway success; it was already onto its second printing.

And in light of the novel's popularity and Mr. Penn-Leith's fame, a London gossip rag had seized on Viola's homage to him and constructed a narrative—

Viola Brodure and Ethan Penn-Leith were destined to fall in love and marry.

Heaven help her.

Kendall, of course, had picked up the narrative thread as a means to fuel his own political ambitions. He intended to harness Mr. Penn-Leith's fame and the elevated popularity of Miss Brodure's work to garner public support *against* amending the callous Poor Laws.

Her cheeks pinked and her breathing constricted further at the thought.

"What say you to September for the wedding, Aunt?" Kendall asked Lady Whipple, cutting his trout into neat, square pieces. "It would be the perfect culmination of the parliamentary session and could buttress my defense of our current laws for assisting the poor."

Viola all but squirmed at His Grace's comment, his aims being the precise *opposite* of her own.

Unfortunately, in the eight months since those pivotal weeks in Manchester, Viola had found paltry few ways to express her views to the empire's masses.

After all, her father's employment as vicar of Westacre depended entirely upon the patronage of Kendall—a man who preferred to 'stoppeth his ears at the cry of the poor,' as Proverbs so eloquently put it.

Viola found it a terrible disappointment. The new duke had spent most of his formative years away from Hawthorn and Westacre, so she had been cautiously hopeful that his political opinions might *not* align with his gray hair.

But in that, she had been mistaken.

Kendall most definitely displayed the politics of an elderly man—a nostalgia for eras past, an instinctual distrust of progress, and a hostility toward the working classes. All opinions he had, no doubt, inherited from his recently-deceased father.

Though Viola did not like speaking ill of the dead, she had nothing kind to say about the previous Duke of Kendall. He had been a convicted bigamist who had ruled his dukedom like a tyrant—that is to say, ruthless, with no tolerance for dissent.

But the old duke had been enamored of Viola's writing—commending the humility of her characters and their praise of the upper classes. His Grace's support had been crucial to her success, and so she had adhered to writing on the topics he dictated.

Consequently, the current duke considered Viola and her novels to be an extension of his political views. Though young, Kendall was fiercely ambitious. He reportedly aimed for nothing less than the Prime Minister's seat.

Viola, dearest, you could be Virgil to Kendall's Augustus, if you so wished it, her father had remarked only the day before.

So tonight, like most evenings dining at Hawthorn, was rather a fraught dance—Viola taking what rope she could, attempting to assert her own wants and needs, but constantly chafing against the tight pull of Kendall's leash.

Viola gritted her teeth and poked at the trout on her plate. The fish stared belligerently back at her.

"September would also be excellent for the wedding." Lady Whipple sent her nephew an approving look. "There is much groundwork still to do if we wish to stave off further erosion of the Poor Laws. Unfortunately, Mr. Dicken's novels have been remarkably effective at swaying public opinion against our aims."

Yes. A feat Viola herself wished to emulate.

"Agreed," Kendall said, tipping his glass toward Viola. "Which is why we have Miss Brodure to advocate for *us.* It is bad enough that the Whigs managed to pass the Poor Law Amendment Act a decade past. The poor must work harder to escape their straitened circumstances, not look to the government to provide relief *gratis.* And now that Miss Brodure has used her pen to essentially summon Mr. Penn-Leith to her side, we can use her heightened fame to draw attention to her tales that, in turn, support our goals."

"Yes," Lady Whipple nodded in approval and motioned toward Viola. "My nephew tells me that you have begun a new novel to address this very thing, Miss Brodure. An *anti-Dickens* novel."

Viola's throat closed further. She had only given token responses to the duke's suggestion that she write such a novel. No inspiration had come to her yet, for obvious reasons.

She had plenty of ideas for stories that *supported* Mr. Dickens's ideas, however. Some stories . . . she might have even written.

Lady Whipple looked at her expectantly.

"Yes, I hope to b-begin in earnest soon." Viola swallowed, prevaricating.

By *soon* she meant *later.*

Much, much later.

As in . . . most likely never.

"I had hoped that you might be farther along the path by now, Miss Brodure," Kendall frowned. "We first spoke of this before Yuletide last year."

Yes, and Viola had been dodging the issue since then.

"I am still trying to find my m-muse, Your Grace." How she hated the nervous stammer in her voice. "The story is proving difficult to pin down."

Kendall's frown deepened. "Even a short story printed in a popular publication like *The Gentleman's Magazine* would be effective. And surely such a paltry thing could be written quickly, don't you agree Miss Brodure?"

Viola took in a slow breath and nodded her head. What other response was left her, after such a manipulative question?

"I shall consider it done then, Miss Brodure." Kendall studied Viola for another heartbeat—as if assessing her acquiescence—and then turned to her father. "In the meantime, I feel that a sermon on this very subject next Sunday would be advisable, Dr. Brodure. Perhaps your words will inspire your daughter." His eyes dipped sideways to her.

Dr. Brodure agreed to Kendall's request, accepting the duke's demands with a nod.

Everyone in the room understood that her father, as the fourth son of Viscount Mossley, had his ambition firmly fixed on being appointed a bishop.

Viola supported him wholeheartedly in his goal. As a vicar, her father rushed to comfort a grieving father or assist a hungry child. She could only imagine the greater good he could do as a bishop.

But, as with everything, being elevated to a bishop required Kendall's help and support. And so Viola and her father bowed to the necessary evil of his demands.

When the elder Duke of Kendall had died on the heels of Viola's trip to Manchester, Viola's father had hoped for a possible improvement in his own fortunes. The old duke had been reluctant to use his clout to

Metaphor, indeed.

Mr. Ethan Penn-Leith currently resided in rural Scotland, nearly the entire length of Great Britain away from Hawthorn and Westacre. How was Viola expected to 'reel him in'?

"I can see your point, Miss Brodure. A visit must be arranged," Kendall said, tone decisive. "It will also give you time away to write the short story we require."

"A v-visit?" Viola detested the breathy quiver in her voice. "Surely, continuing our correspondence is best, not presenting myself on Mr. Penn-Leith's doorstep?"

Until that very moment, Viola had not realized that a person could literally die from embarrassment. She pressed a hand against her stomach, her lungs closing further, her asthma looming.

Yes, she did want to know Mr. Penn-Leith better.

But not like this.

Not offered up to him on a platter, like a trussed Christmas goose.

Not face-to-face where she would have to talk and converse and somehow not be so hopelessly . . . hopeless.

Viola drew in air, trying vainly to keep her panic at bay.

"We will do both." His Grace's voice was that of a general briskly marshaling his troops. "You will continue to write the man, Miss Brodure. Dr. Brodure, do you have any contacts in the area where Mr. Penn-Leith resides?" He looked to Lady Whipple. "Where *does* the man reside, Aunt?"

"Scotland?" Lady Whipple said, with a shrug. "On a farm?"

"Fettermill, Your Grace," Dr. Brodure replied. "I believe I am acquainted with the vicar there, one Dr. Ruxton. We attended Oxford together. Perhaps he would welcome a guest preacher in his parish this summer. My curate would have Westacre well in hand here."

"Excellent," Lady Whipple smiled. "And if you hare off to Scotland for the summer, what else can you do but bring your devoted daughter along?" She raised her wine glass in Viola's direction. "Miss Brodure will be assembling her bridal trousseau before the summer solstice, mark my words."

Viola closed her eyes, chest heaving, panic gripping her lungs in a steely vise.

To those in the room, Viola Brodure and Ethan Penn-Leith were destined to become another Percy and Mary Shelley, a celebrated couple of the *literati*.

Viola did not necessarily disagree with that goal, per se. She simply wished to pursue it in her own manner. Her own *written-from-hundreds-of-miles-away* manner.

Wrapping an arm around her mid-section, Viola tried to breathe in deeply, but the air would not come. A muscle constricted at the back of her throat.

Finally, her father noticed her labored breathing and high color—signs of an imminent attack.

"Do you need air, daughter?" His voice was soft.

Mutely, Viola nodded.

As if from the end of a long tunnel, Viola heard her father apologize to Kendall and Lady Whipple. Then, his steady hand was on her elbow, helping her through the large doors and into the garden, leading her to a bench near a burbling fountain.

The clean, humid air immediately went to work, soothing her lungs.

Viola concentrated on taking in slow, measured breaths, anything to force back thoughts of the momentous conversation in the dining room.

Her father waited patiently beside her, his hand covering hers.

"Better?" he asked after a few minutes.

She nodded. "I'm terribly sorry I caused a scene. But you know how my nerves can be . . ."

"Yes, particularly when Kendall gets a bee in his bonnet of this magnitude." Her father paused for a long moment. They both stared at the duke's lavishly-maintained garden, the daffodils bobbing cheerily in a crisp spring breeze. "Do you like the idea of Mr. Penn-Leith, Viola?" her father asked softly. "Do *you* wish a further acquaintance with him?"

And there it was.

Despite the panic humming in her blood, the embarrassment that had so thoroughly constricted her lungs, Viola *did* wish it.

You began all this with the hope of forming an acquaintance with Ethan Penn-Leith, remember? Does it matter how it all comes about from here?

Like that moment in Manchester with Eloise so many months ago, she abruptly saw herself from above—once more frozen, hesitating, too *anxious/worried/indecisive* to reach for what she truly wanted.

Enough.

If Viola intended to truly live physically and not just in her head—if she ever wished to marry and have children—she needed to break out of this statue-like existence.

Sitting at her desk all those months ago, she had harnessed the courage to set these circumstances in motion. Now, she would take another step forward.

With a fortifying breath, she looked straight into her father's eyes. "I do. I do wish a further acquaintance with Mr. Penn-Leith."

"Well, then," her father glanced back toward the dining room doors, "let us see the matter settled."

2

Malcolm Penn-Leith had been many things in his life: husband, widower, farmer, businessman.

But until now, he had never been a matchmaker.

Granted, if anyone would drive him to such mawkish heights, it would be his wee brother, Ethan.

"Ye need tae pen a reply, Ethan." Malcolm clasped a length of thick metal chain in his left hand. "This is Miss Viola Brodure, need I remind ye? One of the most celebrated writers of our age. She is hardly some obscure English miss."

"I am a rather famous poet myself, in case ye forgot," Ethan said, cuffing his sleeve up his forearm.

Stripped down to shirtsleeves and kilts, the brothers stood in the pasture opposite the front drive of Thistle Muir, the family farmhouse in rural, northeast Scotland.

"That's hardly the point. When a lady like Miss Brodure writes ye a letter, ye pay it the attention it deserves," Malcolm grunted. "I've given ye my truth."

He motioned for his brother to stand back.

Ethan sighed and walked ten feet to Malcolm's right, stopping atop a low boulder jutting out of the ground and folding his arms across his chest.

Malcolm whistled for Beowoof to come. The dog bounded forward, tail wagging, tongue lolling, curly hair flopping into his eyes. With his free hand, Malcolm scratched the hound's ears and then motioned for the dog to go stand beside Ethan.

Malcolm drew the metal links taut. At its opposite end, the chain knotted and looped around a thirty-pound boulder, holding it tightly.

Taking in a deep breath, he backed up three paces to stand behind a wooden toe-board laid in the turf. The heavy stone dragged behind him, its weight gouging a dark slash in the wet grass.

Standing behind the board, Malcolm clutched the chain with two hands and spun in a circle—his kilt swirling around his knees, the world swinging on its axis.

Once. Twice.

Malcolm released the chain and sent the stone flying across the field. It soared a solid ten feet past Ethan's previous mark, landing with a satisfying *thud*. Beowoof barked and gave chase, dancing around the rock as it rolled.

"Hah!" Malcolm ran a hand over his bristly beard. "That will be a challenge for ye tae best."

"You're becoming cocky in your dotage," Ethan scoffed. "I am still warming up."

"Good. That means more truths for ye tae spill."

The chained-stone throwing had become a ritual for Ethan and Malcolm. The goal was simple—whoever hurled the stone the farthest won.

It was, of course, a traditional form of Scottish male bonding, and therefore, competitive as hell. Many a night's drinking at the Lion Arms ended with men spilling into the street, three sheets to the wind and attempting to roll a mill stone or lift the blacksmith's forge.

Naturally, in the vein of that competitive spirit, the brothers had added truth-telling to their stone-hurling.

Before each throw, they had to first tell a truth.

Today, Malcolm intended to drag as many confessions as possible from Ethan . . . before soundly trouncing him.

Ethan hadn't a prayer of beating Malcolm. Not today. Malcolm had an inch, twenty pounds of bulky muscle, and a head full of steam on his younger brother.

Malcolm watched Ethan walk across the field, kilt swinging, to retrieve the stone. Even dressed casually for sport, no one would mistake Ethan for anything other than a refined gentleman. Tall and lean, he walked with a casual elegance, his light-brown hair curling over his ears in the first stare of London fashion.

Scratching at his beard, Malcolm knew that his own out-sized body and unruly dark hair only required a battle axe to complete a Viking-pillager look.

But then, Ethan had been raised to the life of a gentleman, having been fostered by their aristocratic uncle in Aberdeen when he was only ten years old, returning to Thistle Muir only intermittently.

Four months ago, however, Ethan had come for an extended stay.

His publisher had been pressuring him to produce a second book of poetry, but Ethan was struggling to find the words. And so he had come back to Fettermill to seek inspiration from the Scottish glens and braes that had made his first book of poems so popular.

Ethan marked the distance of Malcolm's throw with a stick and dragged the boulder back to the throwing line, Beowoof prancing at his heels.

"Miss Brodure is not your typical admirer, Ethan," Malcolm said, steely patience in his tone. "Her attention to ye is *flattering*. She replied tae your letter most promptly—"

"*Too* promptly, I ken," Ethan countered, dropping the chain and fiddling once more with his shirtsleeves. "The ink had scarcely dried on my own letter and, *poof*, hers arrived in reply. Such eagerness smells of desperation."

"A timely reply tae your letter is a mark of courtesy and a nod to Miss Brodure's well-bred upbringing. She is simply being polite."

"Well, here is my truth then." Ethan grasped the chain and waved Malcolm to stand back. "I wrote my first letter merely to thank Miss

Brodure for her kind words in *Polly Pettifer*, nothing more. I dislike being badgered into a correspondence with the lady."

Sighing, Malcolm stepped atop the low boulder and whistled for Beowoof to sit.

With a deep breath, Ethan spun quickly in place, kilt flaring, the tethered stone spinning in a dizzying arc around him. He released the chain, sending the rock flying, landing just short of Malcolm's mark. Beowoof yipped in excitement, tearing after the stone.

It was Ethan's turn to grunt. He fell into step beside Malcolm as they walked to inspect the throw.

"Just because I am a poet, and Miss Brodure is an authoress," Ethan continued, "it doesn't follow that we're a matched set. That we need tae be paired together like fussy Sèvres china."

Malcolm begged to differ. From what he knew of Miss Brodure, the lady seemed nearly perfect for his wee brother—a refined, English gentlewoman to match Ethan's refined, Scottish gentleman-ness.

For all that Malcolm and Ethan were brothers, a vast ocean of experience and education separated them.

Their mother, Isobel, had been a wealthy Leith from Aberdeenshire with family connections to the Earl of Aberdeen. Isobel's betrothal to Mr. John Penn, a gentleman-farmer well below her station, had upset her genteel family. As a condition of her marriage contract, Grandfather Leith had required the new couple to combine their surnames into Penn-Leith. But the lowliness of Isobel's marriage had always rankled her family.

Their mother's brother, Uncle Leith, had been determined that at least one of his sister's children would escape the taint of their birth. Initially, Uncle Leith had set his sights on Leah, the brothers' much older sister. But she had proven recalcitrant, and so Uncle had shifted his focus to Ethan.

Malcolm, with his reticent tongue and watchful eyes, had been utterly overlooked.

So while Malcolm worked the farm alongside their father, Ethan went to live with Uncle Leith in his fine house in Aberdeen. Ethan attended the same grammar school Lord Byron had frequented, took a Grand

Tour of the Continent, and graduated from Oxford with a first. All the trappings of a gentleman.

Moreover, last year, after the untimely death of Uncle and Aunt Leith's only daughter, Ethan had been named their sole heir. Eventually, he would inherit a sizable estate, making him a gentleman in every possible sense.

So much had been presented to Ethan, wrapped in a silken bow atop a golden platter. But the glittering fame of Ethan's poetry was all his own, the result of hard work, charisma, and relentless dedication.

Malcolm's chest ballooned with pride when he thought of all that Ethan had accomplished.

"I will reply to Miss Brodure when the Muse strikes me," Ethan continued, stabbing a stick into the soft earth to mark the position of his throw.

"This is a letter, Ethan, not an epic poem, for heaven's sake."

"Aye, but I read ye that snippet from her last letter, right? She intends tae come for a visit."

Malcolm nodded. He recalled the letter easily, probably because he had sneaked into Ethan's desk to reread it a time or three:

> . . . *Your letter has lingered with me these past few days, particularly as my father is prone to asking prying questions. He keeps speaking of possibly visiting Scotland, so please consider yourself forewarned.*

"She merely said that her *father* may contrive a visit," Malcolm said. "That is hardly the same thing as Miss Brodure presenting herself on our doorstep."

Ethan scoffed. "It is precisely the same thing and well ye know it." He picked up the chain and began dragging the rock back to the throwing line.

Malcolm kept silent as he followed in Ethan's wake. His brother was likely correct. Though, unlike Ethan, Malcolm would welcome Miss Brodure visiting Fettermill.

Whether he realized it or not, Ethan needed a lady like her.

Malcolm had noted the tautness around Ethan's eyes that never quite subsided. The jittery bounce to his brother's knee. The late nights spent slumped over the desk in his bedroom, pen scritching.

Yes, Ethan had achieved remarkable success, but that success came with its own weight—the never-ending letters from his publisher, the heavy expectations of being Uncle Leith's heir, the endless stream of correspondence from enthusiastic readers demanding his attention.

Ethan had returned to Thistle Muir ostensibly to find the inspiration and quiet needed to finish his next book of poetry. His publisher had set a deadline and Ethan was floundering to meet it, claiming his well of poetic inspiration had dried up.

But Malcolm wondered if there wasn't more to it than that.

He had never considered that fame would be isolating. That Ethan, having risen to heights that paltry few did, would find life at the top so very . . . lonely.

But . . . how could Ethan not? Everyone demanded something from him—*Play the Highland Poet! Entertain us! Write faster!*

It had to be exhausting.

To Malcolm's purview, his brother needed love, trust, and long-lasting support in order to successfully navigate his future.

In short—Ethan needed a wife.

Though Malcolm's own marriage had ended far too soon, he knew the soul-satisfying bliss of sharing life with a partner—the strength and comfort that such a bond could give. How his wife, Aileen, had rubbed his back as he wept over the death of a farmhand. How, on a cold winter's night, she would giggle helplessly as her cold feet chased his warmer ones under the counterpane. How she would pause her sewing, lift her head, and listen to him blether on about drainage problems in the north pastures.

A similar relationship, particularly with a lady so well-acquainted with Ethan's world, would help him navigate the ups and downs of life and fame.

Miss Viola Brodure fit the bill in every sense.

Honestly, if the woman decided against a visit to Fettermill, Malcolm would be sorely tempted to journey to England and plead with her in person to reconsider.

"The more I write her," Ethan said, pulling the stone to rest at the throwing line, "the more I appear to wish a deeper friendship. I do not want to give rise to false expectations where Miss Brodure is concerned." He squinted at Malcolm. "Why are ye so insistent on this point?"

"I dinnae like ye disrespecting Miss Brodure with your silence," Malcolm lied with straight-faced aplomb.

"A delay in replying is hardly silence, brother. Besides," Ethan gave Malcolm a wry side-eye, "if you're going tae be so bizarrely insistent upon this, perhaps *ye* should write Miss Brodure. Tell her how much ye admire her writing and strike up a friendship. Ye know ye would enjoy sparring wits with her."

Malcolm's breath froze in his chest.

The very thought was so . . . . so . . .

"Your answer tae that can be your next truth," Ethan smirked at him, every inch the taunting wee brother. "Go on then. Throw the stone."

Gritting his teeth, Malcolm stared down at the chained rock.

He hated that Ethan knew him so well. That he had easily intuited Malcolm's deep admiration of Miss Viola Brodure's work.

Yes, the snippets of her letter to Ethan were charming, clever, and shrewdly insightful. Yes, her novels of pious orphans and clever servants were beloved the kingdom over.

But it was the lady's possible hidden depths that fascinated Malcolm most.

Several months ago, *The Rabble Rouser*—a liberal journal Malcolm subscribed to—had published a story written by one Mr. Oliver Aubord Twist. The story itself, *A Hard Truth*, detailed the plight of a poor mother living in the slums of Manchester and scathingly attacked the inadequacy of the Poor Law reformation.

He had not admitted as much to his brother, but Malcolm had read enough of Miss Brodure's novels to recognize the voice of her writing. And *A Hard Truth* sounded more like Viola Brodure than . . . well, Viola Brodure. When he had looked at the author's name again, Oliver Aubord Twist, he wondered if the surname *Twist* was a prompt to do precisely that—twist all the letters around.

And so, Malcolm had.

Oliver Aubord; Viola Brodure.

If it truly was her work, Miss Brodure was destined for literary immortality.

Even if the author of *A Hard Truth* proved not to be Miss Brodure, Malcolm still couldn't imagine writing her himself. His words would surely sprawl his admiration of her across the page much like Beowoof before the parlor fire on a chilly evening, brazenly demanding pets and affirmation.

Malcolm cringed at the image.

Besides, writing an unmarried lady felt like crossing an invisible line.

Romantic love was an emotion he had buried alongside his wife and their stillborn bairn. The horror of those last hours of Aileen's life, her blood spilling out . . . and himself, helpless to do anything other than cradle her in his arms until the bitter end.

He would never remarry. How could he move on and leave Aileen behind? The thought of cultivating tender affection for another woman roiled his stomach.

So . . . no. Malcolm would never write an unmarried woman, no matter the lady or how often Ethan pestered him.

Besides, *Ethan* was the one who needed a wife, not Malcolm.

"Writing tae Miss Brodure would feel too much like a courtship, Ethan." The words scraped Malcolm's throat, emerging raw and gruff. "And ye ken well that I will never court another woman."

"Court, is it?" Ethan chuckled. "Now ye are finally telling truths in earnest, brother. Despite all your fine words about friendship, ye mean for me tae *court* Miss Brodure, not simply write her. Admit it!"

Malcolm grunted, testing the heft of the chain, and then scanned the field.

Cows lowed in the distance.

Sparrows quarreled.

"Ah." Ethan threw up a hand. "Now the famed Malcolm Penn-Leith reticence arrives."

"Ye need a wife, Ethan." Malcolm whistled for Beowoof.

"Why?" Ethan stepped atop the low boulder, scratching Beowoof behind the ears as the dog sat at his feet.

"Because life is less lonely when it's shared, Ethan. Because my greatest happiness was having Aileen by my side. Not only because she gave her love tae me, but because I gave my love tae her. Ye deserve such a love, too, ye *bawbag*. That is my truth."

Malcolm grunted and swung the stone in a circle, sending the boulder flying across the pasture. This throw landed even with Ethan's previous one.

Ethan whooped.

"What did I tell ye?" he said, grinning widely, green eyes lit with delight. "You're growing soft in your dotage."

Malcolm couldn't help but give a reluctant grin in return. Ethan was just so damn likable.

How his sunny, earnest brother had become a celebrated poet, Malcolm would never know.

Weren't lauded poets supposed to be a sulky, self-centered, moody lot? He would have thought it required a significant amount of zeal to take one's self so seriously.

And yet, Ethan remained stubbornly guileless, producing works of profound depth while retaining an infectious *joie de vivre* all his own.

Was it any wonder everyone loved him? Ethan was impossible not to adore.

Surely Miss Brodure would adore him, too. And provide his brother with the support he needed to navigate his fame.

Malcolm simply had to motivate Ethan to communicate with her.

"Write the letter, Ethan," Malcolm muttered. "Even if Miss Brodure never visits, it's the right thing tae do. As a man in his dotage, I can tell ye with authority, tackling onerous tasks is the final step that takes a lad into manhood."

Ethan rolled his eyes and then paused.

"*Tackling onerous tasks is the final step that takes a lad into manhood . . .*" he repeated. "I quite like that. May I use the idea in a poem?"

This had been Ethan's way since returning home—extracting snippets of their conversations to use as ballast for his writing. Malcolm had no idea if it was helping or not, but he would always do what he could to assist his brother.

"Of course." Malcolm stared down at the stone. "I'm right tired of throwing this blasted rock. Let's go cut down a tree and make a caber. I'm hardly soft yet. And maybe tossing something more properly Scottish will give ye poetic inspiration."

3

Viola stood in the middle of the road, staring at the rutted tracks disappearing into the roiling fog of the Scottish countryside.

She had been stranded for nearly two hours now, pacing up and down the narrow, tree-lined lane. Their gig rested behind her, its single axle listing at an unnatural angle. Her maid, Mary, was curled up sound asleep on the carriage seat, having grown weary of waiting.

The series of events that had landed them here, waiting on a foggy lane, was a scene from one of Viola's own novels.

As promised, the Duke of Kendall and her father had contrived an invitation for Dr. Brodure to preach in the parish of Fettermill. Her father would spend the summer discussing arcane doctrinal points with the local vicar, his old acquaintance Dr. Ruxton, leaving Viola free to write and, 'make friends with the local population.'

And by *local population*, Dr. Brodure meant Ethan Penn-Leith.

Viola blushed whenever she pondered her father and Kendall's scheming—machinations, she acknowledged, that she had readily accepted eight weeks ago.

But since that time, Mr. Penn-Leith had made only two replies to Viola's overtures of friendship. And now . . . she worried.

Did his silence indicate indifference? Worse, had she placed the man in a difficult position—not desiring a deeper correspondence but also not wishing to offend her?

Or was it as Lady Whipple had said: men were simply lazy correspondents?

Regardless, due to his lack of reply, Viola had not informed Mr. Penn-Leith of her impending arrival in Fettermill. She feared the words would echo and clang if dropped into the well of his silence.

The journey north had been typical of any long journey: tedious, jolting, and muddy, if generally uneventful. That was, until the last few hours.

After the stagecoach deposited them in Brechin, her father had hired a horse and gig to take them into Fettermill to the west. However, the older carriage had been unequal to the badly rutted road, its axle cracking before their little party reached the country cottage Dr. Brodure had let.

Consequently, he had unhitched the horse and pulled himself onto its back, riding to fetch help.

And now, Viola stood in the middle of a rural lane awaiting her father's return, the silent mist swirling about her.

No sound reached her ears at the moment. Perhaps the mist had silenced the birds?

And yet, the countryside burst with life, glimpses of vitality shifting in and out of the fog—the vivid yellow flowers of prickly gorse, new lambs clambering in the field. Branches arched over the lane, their leaves just beginning to sprout despite it already being May.

Spring came late this far north, Viola supposed.

Wrapping one arm around her waist, she sucked in a deep lungful of air and released it slowly.

She had worried that the endless greenery and animal dander of Scotland would act as irritants to her lungs, exacerbating her asthma.

But instead, Viola found the air and fecundity oddly soothing. As if the thousand shades of green around her—from the yellow-green of newly-sprouted ferns to the dusky green limbs of Scots pine—hung with breathy anticipation.

Scotland hummed with promise, as if Change itself were hidden in the whisking fog.

This! This was what she had wanted. A sense of transformation. That she could move on from living adjacent, frozen in place, afraid to act.

She would meet Ethan Penn-Leith, open her mouth, and converse with him. They would exchange ideas and critiques. Perhaps he could even advise her on how to proceed with this dreadful short story Kendall demanded she write.

And of course, if Mr. Penn-Leith were to find her just as compelling as she did his poetry and person . . . well, she wouldn't say *No* to more than mere conversation.

With each breath, a fierce creature stretched inside her, testing the humid Scottish air, reaching for something entirely . . . *new*.

The fog continued to flow around her, eddying across the road, trees rustling in the wind. Though how wind and fog could coexist remained a puzzle. Why didn't the wind simply blow the fog away?

In her experience, fog was a creeping thing born of coal smoke, settling into her lungs with a muffling heaviness that triggered her asthma.

This Scottish fog seemed made of purer forces. It swirled and blew, filling her lungs with dense, wet air that soothed and calmed.

A paradox.

Or, at the very least, another metaphor portending change.

She paused to savor the sensation—the electric hum in her veins, the whoosh of blood in her ears. As a writer, she hoarded such moments, tucking them away to be remembered weeks or months later.

Viola pulled her cloak tighter around her shoulders.

A shape loomed out of the fog.

She nearly sighed in relief. At last! Her father had returned—

But, no . . . a large dog loped up the road, tongue lolling, tail wagging.

Viola froze, breath catching in her throat.

The dog seemed exuberantly friendly, with a cheerful face and curly, honey-colored hair. She adored dogs. Unlike cats or horses, dogs were living sunshine, endlessly happy with themselves and the world.

But dogs, in particular, triggered her asthma.

This dog, of course, was oblivious to her worries. He wandered right up to where she stood in the grassy middle of the lane, nuzzling her skirts with an amiable sniff.

Viola lifted her hands above her head, looking up to the swirling fog and taking in shallow breaths, terrified that even studying the animal might trigger an asthmatic fit.

A loud whistle sounded.

Viola turned her head toward the noise.

A burly Scot strode out of the mist, kilt swinging, looking far too much like a mythical hero of a lost age. A medieval laird, intent on vanquishing his rivals. Or a Scottish knight off to court his lady fair.

The russet-and-blue tartan of his kilt wrapped around his waist and crisscrossed his broad chest, an enormous pin holding the heavy wool in place at his shoulder. A more modern jacket and waistcoat rested underneath; a jaunty tartan cap sat atop his head.

But it was the man who wore the ensemble—with his dark hair and dark beard under even darker eyes—that ensnared her.

He was not classically handsome, she supposed. The lines of his face were too defined for mere prettiness—the slash of wide-set cheekbones, the expanse of forehead, the formidable brow ridge. He was more elemental than pretty. Unbreakable iron forged of metal from Scottish mountains.

He met her gaze, igniting a fizzing firecracker *pop* in her blood.

Gracious.

Here was a *man*.

He seemed accustomed to carrying heavy burdens atop his broad shoulders—whether the weight be a dragon's treasure, a woman's tears, or chopped firewood.

He came to a stop several yards in front of her, his kilt swaying. Viola had to tilt her head up and up to look at him, as he easily had a foot of height on her own. She knew herself to be petite, but surely this man was part giant. *Did* he raid dragon gold in his spare time?

His gaze darted past her, frowning at the broken carriage, before coming back to her.

"Madam." He nodded.

"Sir," she replied with a hesitant smile.

He said nothing more for a moment, his attention turning again to study the gig listing at an angle, the maid sleeping. Viola sensed that few details escaped his notice.

She waited for her breathing to hitch. For her body to freeze and her nerves to assert themselves.

But no . . . her typically-fretting brain chose to feel safe and calm. Or perhaps it wasn't her brain at all, but her body—her bones, her very skin—soaking up comfort. As if this man could not only hold back marauding pagan hordes, but an asthmatic wallflower's paralyzing jitters.

Was this what others meant when they called Scotland a land of contrasts? Liberating fog and soothing Highland warriors?

Finally, the man brought his eyes back to hers, hitching his thumbs into the leather pouch—a *sporran* she had heard it called—that hung from his belt.

"Please tell me yer husband has taken the horse and gone for help?" His brogue rolled over her, a rumbling wave of shivering delight.

Viola's smile grew.

Heaven help her, but she loved a competent man, one who moved past self-evident matters and asked the most pertinent question.

No restating the obvious. *Stuck, are ye?*

No manly posturing. *Stand aside, lass. My muscles and superior knowledge will right your predicament in no time.*

No. Just simple, straightforward competence.

Perhaps it was his sense of strength that emboldened her tongue.

Or perhaps it was his friendly dog.

Or maybe it was the surreal hush of the rushing fog and humid Scottish air.

Regardless, her debilitating shyness had yet to make an appearance.

And that simple fact was . . . bloody *marvelous.*

Viola wanted to laugh in astonishment.

"Yes, in a way," she replied without a hint of a stammer nor a twist of her fingers. "I haven't a husband, but my father returned to the inn in Brechin from whence we hired this wretched vehicle." She motioned at the gig behind her.

Speaking with the Scot felt comfortable—almost akin to talking with her father—but simultaneously charged, like a shower of starlight cascading to kiss her skin.

He nodded, gaze meeting hers and then moving away.

As if he, too, were . . . shy. Or, perhaps, simply reserved.

A sense of kinship nearly shimmered between them. An explanation, perhaps, for her ease in his presence.

Was he a local gentleman farmer? A laird's steward?

And the crucial question every spinster asked—

Was he married?

His dog shuffled forward again, whining and sniffing at her hands. Startled, Viola raised them skyward.

"He willnae bite ye," the Scot said. "He's right friendly."

Viola looked into the dog's eyes. The poor thing's longing to be petted reflected her own wish to pet him.

"Oh, I would love nothing more than to touch him." She looked from the dog to the Scot. "But I fear I have a severe sensitivity to dogs." She waved a hand in front of her face.

"Ah." The man rocked back on his heels, expression still pensive.

He seemed to have trouble *not* looking at her. Over and over, his eyes would slide away only to return to her, as if they were disobeying him.

Viola found it curiously endearing.

Of course, she also noticed that his eyes were warm like a pool of molten chocolate, and two freckles punctuated the corner of his left eye, as if waiting for a third to make an ellipsis.

His dog continued to nuzzle at her skirts, head swiveling between his master and her as if to say, *why won't she cuddle me?*

"If ye would like tae pet him," the man continued, swallowing hard, "he likely willnae irritate your senses, as he doesnae shed. 'Tis some oddity in his breeding."

Viola hesitated. How she longed to touch the dog, but to potentially risk an asthma attack . . .

She met the man's gaze, her hesitation surely evident. His eyes pinned her in place, dark pools of calm.

"It's true. Ye can trust me." The quiet assurance of those words rumbled over her.

And . . . she believed him.

She looked down at the eager dog. As if sensing that a good scratching might finally be in the offing, the animal wagged his tail more vigorously, nudging his body closer to hers.

Heavens. He was a handsome pup.

She took a fortifying breath.

Life was to be lived, was it not? Surely, this was part of her commitment to no longer exist adjacently.

Tugging off a glove, she bent forward, holding out her hand.

"There now," she crooned. The dog ecstatically communicated his delight, sniffing her hand. Smiling, she cautiously scratched behind his ears as she had seen other dog-lovers do.

Gracious! His fur was warm and soft, curling around her fingers. The dog angled his head, granting her better access.

Nothing in the motion appeared to aggravate her senses, as her lungs would normally feel the irritation immediately.

Crouching on the grass that ran down the middle of the lane, Viola rubbed the dog with both hands.

She took a deep breath.

And . . . nothing.

No tickle at her throat. No tightening of her airway.

Nothing at all.

How many times had she longed to own a pet? To bury her face in a dog's side and simply relish in sharing air with another living creature?

Laughing in wonder, she lifted her gaze to meet that of the Scot.

"How utterly marvelous!" she exclaimed, the astonishment in her voice as clear as birdsong drifting from the mist-shrouded trees.

MALCOLM STARED AT the unknown woman as she scratched Beowoof's ears, her smile an electric zing of happiness.

Utterly marvelous, indeed.

The woman, to put it bluntly, stunned his senses. His very bones vibrated in their sockets as if struck by a brass gong.

That initial glimpse of her . . . so wee and fey, standing alone on the lane, slowly coming into focus out of the fog like a dream. He had nearly thought her a kelpie, a mythical beast said to haunt Scotland's rivers and lochs, luring men to their dooms.

And when their eyes had met . . .

She had wrenched the breath from his lungs as thoroughly as any Highland gale.

Silvery blond curls framed a dainty oval face and achingly-blue eyes, the graceful silhouette of her body outlined against her dark blue cloak.

Her accent proclaimed her to be English and highly-born at that. A genteel traveler, most likely visiting a friend for the summer. She nearly thrummed with bewitching energy, her expression full of child-like wonder.

Malcolm's blood thumped in his veins in response, sending prickles of awareness across his skin and heat coiling in his chest.

He recognized the sensations for what they were—physical attraction.

Malcolm hadn't felt attracted to a woman other than Aileen since . . .

Since . . .

Never . . . he realized.

And he had never been smitten with a lady at first glance. Not once.

Even his affection for Aileen had crescendoed slowly from childhood friendship to desire to romantic love. And since his wife's death, no woman had elicited a second look.

But this . . . this apparition, this sprite, this lady . . .

He couldn't stop staring—at the sensual bow of her top lip, the sloping curve of her waist, the spark in her blue eyes. Wee details ensnared him. The indent of a small chicken pox scar beside her left ear. The high arch of her fine eyebrows.

Helpless. He was simply helpless against the onslaught.

No matter how stringently he ordered his eyes to *stop staring like* glaikit *fools!*, they refused to obey.

How could a pixie of a woman scramble his wits so?

So . . . this must be infatuation, a bemused part of him realized.

It was a rather uncomfortable paradox of an emotion.

As wee boys, he and Ethan had lashed logs into a raft and sailed it down the River North Esk. The ride had been a heady mixture of exhilaration and terror and had ended with them both being *dooked* in the frigid water. They had emerged dripping wet, shivering, and racing to do the whole again.

Watching the woman ruffle Beowoof's jowls, Malcolm realized his current state was similar to that—jubilant, thunder-struck, breathless.

Naturally, Beowoof basked in her attention, the wretch.

Was it not enough for this woman to overwhelm himself? She had to go and capture his dog, too?

The lady, still grinning, buried her face in Beowoof's fur, before raising her gaze to Malcolm's once more.

"I can scarcely believe it." She sounded amazed. "His fur doesn't irritate my lungs. What is his name?"

The shameless beast shot Malcolm a smug look, as if to say, *O'course, the lovely lass prefers me.*

Malcolm grimaced. *Traitor.*

"Beowoof," he answered the woman.

Her eyes glowed. "Beowulf? How charming."

Och.

He hated having to correct her, but . . .

"Actually, it's Beo*woof*." Malcolm stressed the final syllable.

Her gaze dropped to his dog. "Beowulf?" she repeated.

Drat his thick accent.

"Beo*woof*," Malcolm clarified again, detesting the blood he could feel rising to his cheeks.

First, infatuation.

And now . . . blushing.

What other nearly-forgotten sensation would this lady inspire before the hour was over?

Her fair brow continued to pucker in confusion.

Blast it all.

How was he to help her understand?

"It's Beo*woof*—" He paused, rolling his hand . . . and then rolled his eyes over what he was about to say, cheeks burning hotter. "—as in what a dog says . . . *woof, woof.*"

Thank goodness Ethan wasn't here to witness this.

Malcolm would never live it down—how he was reduced to literal barking in front of a beautiful, sophisticated English lady.

"Oh!" Her face turned incandescent with understanding. The joy of it battered Malcolm's chest. "*Woof!* Beo*woof!*" She rubbed the dog's jowls, clasping his face between her palms, her voice sing-song. "Who's the hero of the Geats? Who defeats Grendel? You do. Yes, you do, you excellent beast."

Beowoof was ecstatic, his entire body quivering in fervor to get closer.

Malcolm understood the feeling. The blood in his own veins thumped in time with his dog's wagging tail.

The lady cuddled Beowoof for one more moment and then pushed up to her feet, cheeks brimming with happiness. She brushed her hands down her skirt.

"I should commend you on your excellent taste," she said, her smile soft. "Calling one's dog after a great hero of Anglo-Saxon literature displays a certain amount of verve. Are other animals in your care similarly named?"

No ignorant miss, this lady. The more he spoke with her, the older she seemed. She was too self-possessed, too mature. Was she close to his own thirty years?

"Aye," he said, short and staccato.

He intended to stop talking there. After all, he had answered her question.

But the curious, expectant look on her face demanded more. And Malcolm found himself powerless to refuse.

He rubbed a hand across the back of his neck. "We have a cat named William Shakespurr . . . and there is Coolius Caesar, my prized Highland steer."

The lady laughed, a joyful song burst of sound.

He appreciated the laugh lines at the edges of her eyes. They spoke of years lived and wisdom gained.

Even more, he liked that he had made her laugh.

Malcolm permitted himself a wee grin.

"Shall we introduce ourselves?" she asked. "This is no fine London drawing room, so I suppose we needn't stand on ceremony."

Oh.

Yes.

Introductions.

He likely should have thought of that before now.

"Mr. Malcolm Penn-Leith, at your service, madam." He sketched a loose sort of bow. Proper formalities were not his forte.

Her dazzling smile froze.

"Malcolm Penn-Leith?" she repeated.

Ah.

He heard the recognition in her voice, and therefore, could nearly recite the next sentence for her.

"Are you a relation of Mr. Ethan Penn-Leith, by any chance?" she asked, a sort of hesitant eagerness in her tone.

"Aye." Malcolm beamed with pride. "Ethan's my wee brother."

Again, she laughed, as if he had said something absolutely astonishing. Heaven help him, but her delight poured across his chest like golden sunshine.

Malcolm wanted to make her laugh again. Immediately.

"*Wee* brother?" she repeated. "Does Mr. Penn-Leith prefer to be called that then?"

Malcolm couldn't help his own wide grin, the motion pulling at his cheeks and reminding him that he did not smile often enough.

"Aye," he replied.

Again, silence hung. The lady paused, her body canting toward his, as if waiting for him to finish some thought.

Malcolm's brain scrambled, trying to find purchase, to remember what they were talking about.

Oh, right. Introductions.

"And your name, madam?" he asked.

A small hesitation and then, "Miss Viola Brodure."

Malcolm could not stem his startled inhalation. "The authoress?"

She ducked her head in apparent bashfulness. "The very same."

Malcolm's mind hummed in stunned silence for a moment.

This was Viola Brodure? The woman of Ethan's letters? This sunny, effervescent creature?

Foolish of him not to make the connection immediately. How many other English ladies did he anticipate would be summering in Fettermill?

Malcolm had known it was a possibility that she might arrive here.

And yet . . .

Why would he have supposed this woman to be Viola Brodure?

His brain sputtered, scarcely able to reconcile the whole of it. To merge his fierce admiration for Miss Brodure's writing with the striking woman before him. The one who had set his heart to beating out a rapid tattoo. The one who stirred longings he thought long buried in the kirkyard of the Fettermill parish church.

Miss Brodure looked away, as if embarrassed or, more likely, finally realizing the distance between their stations in life.

Malcolm was little more than an uneducated farmer.

Viola Brodure was a gentleman's daughter and a celebrated novelist.

More to the point, she was destined for his own *wee brother*.

"Why does it behave like this?" she asked after a pause.

The abrupt change in topic had Malcolm scrambling. "Pardon?"

"The fog," she clarified. "How can it be windy and foggy at the same time? I find it most puzzling."

Oh. *That* he could answer.

He surveyed the humid mist. "The fog is called *haar*, and it blows in off the North Sea in early summer, though it usually doesnae reach this far inlan—"

The sound of an approaching carriage stopped him short.

"That must be my father." Miss Brodure turned toward the noise, giving him one last chance to stare at her unashamedly.

She was lovely. Enchanting. A vivid sunrise over a glassy sea.

But two facts Malcolm understood clearly.

One, Miss Brodure obviously held some affection for his brother. She had written to Ethan. Her journey to Fettermill had a purpose.

Two, knowing his brother as Malcolm did, Ethan was going to adore her. She was too lovely, too vibrant, too eloquently charming not to love.

Viola Brodure and Ethan Penn-Leith were destined for one another.

And that was . . .

That was . . .

. . . precisely what Malcolm wanted.

Yes.

Yes, that was it.

Miss Brodure would be perfect for Ethan.

Malcolm had treasured his slice of heaven with Aileen. Ethan deserved to have the same. His brother needed to settle down, marry, and anchor his life so that the whims of fame and popularity didn't set him utterly adrift.

Surely, as Malcolm watched Ethan charm and woo Miss Brodure, his initial attraction to the lady would fade into something more appropriately sibling-like.

Because any other path . . .

Well, any other path was simply unthinkable.

4

"How fares your asthma, daughter?"

At her father's question, Viola looked up from her writing. She took in a deep breath, testing her lungs.

"'Tis fine, Papa. Why do you ask?"

Viola and her father sat before the fire in the parlor of the country cottage they had let for the summer. The house was small compared to their vicarage in Westacre, but Viola already adored its coziness, the sense of home.

The parlor itself exuded Scottish charm: from the stag horns mounted over the door, to the russet and blue tartan of the drapes framing the bow window, to the sofa and pair of wingback chairs before the fire. And even though daylight hours lingered this far north, she appreciated the cheerful fire in the grate taking the chill from the air.

Viola sat curled into one of the wingback chairs, a notebook and pencil in her hand. Across from her, Dr. Brodure rested in the matching chair, hunched over his traveling lap desk, attending to his correspondence.

"I am writing a letter to Kendall and wished to inform him of your health." Her father pushed his wired spectacles up his nose, dipping his quill in the small inkwell inlaid along the edge of the lap desk. "His Grace, of course, will also want to know how your work on his short story progresses."

Of course, he will, Viola suppressed a sigh. She had yet to write a word of the dreaded tale.

"I am slowly crafting the story," she hedged—praying God did not strike her down for lying—and then changed the subject. "And please tell His Grace that Scotland agrees with me very much."

That, at least, was the truth.

Viola's unexpected meeting with Malcolm Penn-Leith the day before lingered—a morsel of sweet toffee that stuck to her teeth and gums and commanded her attention. The rumble of his Scottish brogue. The rueful twist of his mouth as he repeated Beowoof's name. The quiet reassurance of his gaze.

And still, a full day later, she marveled how calm she had been in his presence. None of the shy anxiety she normally experienced with strangers had emerged.

Was it a Scottish phenomenon? She crossed the border into this wild, untamed country and her social nervousness decided to holiday elsewhere?

Surely, the elder Penn-Leith was similar to his younger brother. If she felt so at ease with Malcolm Penn-Leith, certainly conversing with Ethan would be comfortable.

And what a delicious thought that was, to speak freely—to be her truest self—with the handsome poet whose words had inspired her own courage.

Perhaps stepping from the shadows of her life—moving from two-dimensional words to the three-dimensional world—would not be as trying as she had supposed.

A hopeful sort of giddiness bubbled in her chest.

Feeling her father's eyes upon her, Viola lifted her head from her notebook.

"You needn't pursue this acquaintance, you know." He peered over his glasses. "If Mr. Ethan Penn-Leith isn't to your liking, no one will force you into a courtship that—"

"Please set your mind at ease, Papa. I am genuinely interested in becoming better acquainted with Mr. Penn-Leith. You haven't cajoled me into being here." Viola laid her notebook and pencil down. Sliding from her chair to the floor, she took his hand and pressed a kiss to the back of it. "I am glad we are come."

So *very* glad.

Dr. Brodure clasped her hand in his. "You are the best of daughters, Viola. I know that this arrangement with Kendall is not entirely to your liking, no matter how brave a face you put on it. But I appreciate your sacrifices for me." He patted her cheek and pulled off his spectacles, polishing them with a handkerchief.

Viola rose to sit on the edge of her chair.

"Nonsense, Papa." She would find a way to write something for Kendall, truly she would. After all, she couldn't remain a lying liar forever. "We are partners, helping one another to reach our aims."

"I would like to think so, yes."

"Kendall wishes to harness public interest in my potential courtship with Mr. Penn-Leith to gain public support for his own aims in Parliament. And you, dearest Papa, appear well on your way to securing Kendall's help in petitioning Her Majesty to appoint you as a bishop."

"Yes. I am hoping His Grace will see the matter settled come autumn."

"Precisely. Once that happens, I will have more freedom to publish as I wish. We all achieve something we want."

Compromise, particularly in this instance, was a necessity.

No matter her own desires, Viola wanted her father to realize his goals, too. He sought to be appointed bishop of a diocese—not just for himself and all the good he could do in such a position—but for his mother and grandfather, to honor a family legacy.

Viola's grandmother, Lady Mossley, had been the daughter of the Bishop of Gloucester. Her dying request had been for her fourth son, Charles Brodure, to pursue the same profession as her father.

Dr. Brodure had taken his mother's wishes to heart, and Viola would do anything in her power to assist him.

Viola's own mother had died when Viola was yet a babe. Her father had never remarried. Every memory she had of parents and family involved only her father—just the two of them united against the world.

It had been her father who held her when she crawled into his bed at night, terrified of the scratching bats in the attic. He had nursed her through measles and influenza, scarlet fever and chicken pox.

When a doctor recommended that they move from London to improve Viola's asthma, Dr. Brodure hadn't hesitated. He had quit his prominent post as a Mayfair vicar—a position perfectly situated to an appointment as bishop—and had immediately removed to Wiltshire.

Dr. Brodure had encouraged her tentative attempts at writing and had doggedly pursued selling her first manuscript to a publisher.

And even now, he supported her desire to write more politically charged stories, despite the threat it posed to his own livelihood.

No one believed in Viola more than Charles Brodure.

And for that, she owed him everything.

Her conscience twinged at all the ways she had *not* supported her father.

"I received a letter from Mossley this morning." Her father shuffled the correspondence on his small desk.

"What does your viscount of a brother have to say?" Viola asked.

Her father pulled out the letter. "He states that although he has no power to assist my appointment to bishop—that requires an aristocrat of Kendall's clout—Mossley has been laying a foundation that might see me appointed as a Lord Spiritual should Her Majesty approve my suit."

"That's marvelous, Papa." Viola beamed at him. "You will do wonders if granted a seat in the House of Lords."

And he would. The Lords Spiritual were taken from a select group of bishops, ensuring that religious voices and concerns were heard alongside political ones in Parliament.

Her father would be a diligent defender of the faith were he appointed.

"Thank you, child. In the meanwhile, Mossley bids us to enjoy our holiday, so I say we do precisely that." Her father tucked his brother's letter away. "In fact, I believe Dr. and Mrs. Ruxton will call upon us tomorrow."

"Excellent. We shall enjoy our time here in Scotland, you and I."
Viola stood and pressed a kiss to his weathered forehead. "Just you wait
and see."

OVER THE ENSUING days, Malcolm reflected that only the arrival
of Queen Victoria herself could cause more uproar in Fettermill.

Unfortunately, he found the furor over Miss Brodure's visit highly
irritating.

Why any part of Miss Brodure's presence should be irritating, he
couldn't say. Had he suffered a blow to the head?

The irrationality of the emotion naturally led to more irritability, then
on to frustration . . .

In short, Malcolm was finding Miss Brodure's appearance in the
neighborhood to be something of a trial.

It was simply . . .

He had never experienced attraction like this before. That a mere half
hour spent in a lady's company could invade his thoughts so thoroughly.

Miss Brodure popped into his mind at the oddest moments.

For example, while walking the south pasture with his overseer,
Callum Liston, Malcolm noticed that the summer sky was the precise
color of her eyes. Would Miss Brodure have a clever name for the new
calf that had been born overnight? Would she enjoy the pork roast Mrs.
McGregor, his housekeeper, made for dinner as much as he did?

His fascination with Miss Brodure was as unexpected as it was
unwelcome. His one and only experience with similar attraction had led
to his marriage with Aileen.

But, of course, the thought of Malcolm marrying someone of Miss
Brodure's class and elegance and education . . .

He blushed with mortification just mentally positing the idea, it was
simply *that* ludicrous.

Besides, Malcolm never intended to remarry. Not because he felt guilty or believed Aileen would be angry with him were he to bind himself to another woman. He recognized that his wife would be grieved if she knew he planned to spend the rest of his days alone.

But the thought of another wife felt . . . impossible.

Malcolm recalled how Ethan loved to tell the story of hiking the Rhône Glacier in Switzerland while on his Grand Tour. His brother related the tale with hands waving, his voice deepening into German-accented English as he repeated the words of his alpine guide: 'You must valk in my feet, ya. Zee ice, it is not your friend.' As Ethan explained it, a crevasse could open at any time, tumbling the unlucky traveler into its vast sky-blue depths, never to be seen again.

Aileen's death had been an unseen crevasse in Malcolm's life—an unexpected calamity that had abruptly opened at his feet and sent him plummeting into a fathomless chasm.

Initially, the shattering plunge—the grief, the pain—had been all Malcolm could feel or see. But over time, he became familiar with the new landscape at the bottom of the abyss. The idiosyncrasies of grief, its ebb and flow like the cavernous walls around him.

More to the point, Malcolm didn't have the strength, will, or desire to climb out of his chasm now.

Not even for a woman as remarkable and lovely as Miss Viola Brodure.

Not even if she matched his station in life.

Not even if she wasn't destined for his brother.

Unfortunately, *knowing* any deeper relationship with Miss Brodure was impossible did not stem his infatuation.

He attempted to talk some sense into his muddled brain.

Miss Brodure is a refined, cultured lady.

Ye arenae a refined, cultured gentleman.

She has journeyed tae Scotland in pursuit of your refined, cultured brother.

Ye encouraged this, as ye would like them tae marry and have refined, cultured children.

Your brother needs *this woman.*

She is not for you.

Cease thinking upon her in this fashion.

But, of course, *knowing* a thing was quite different from feeling it.

And as everyone in the village wished to discuss Miss Brodure's arrival, putting the lady from his mind proved difficult.

If one more person started up a conversation with the words, 'Have ye heard about Miss Brodure?', Malcolm feared he couldn't throw a stone large enough to exorcise his aggravation.

All in all, it made a man downright *crabbit*.

Mrs. Clark and Mrs. Buchan—Fettermill's indefatigable 'walking heralds'—wasted no time in cornering Malcolm as he walked by the dairy stalls on market day.

"Miss Brodure has us all aflutter," Mrs. Clark declared, clutching a basket of fresh *baps* and gooseberry preserves to her hip.

Malcolm nodded a greeting and shifted the wheel of cheese in his hand. Farmer McCray made an excellent Dunlop that Malcolm liked sliced atop hot oatcakes.

"Aye. We are all breathless anticipation for her tae meet your brother," Mrs. Buchan agreed stopping beside her friend, the feathers in her bonnet bobbing in time with her nodding head.

"Assuming they havenae already met?" Mrs. Clark added, eyes looking slyly in Malcolm's direction. "Mrs. McGregor wouldnae say a word when we asked her."

Malcolm likewise said nothing. Mrs. McGregor's ability to hold her tongue was one of a thousand reasons why he treasured the woman as his housekeeper.

"They say Dr. Brodure is tae preach a sermon on Sunday," Mrs. Buchan said, "so we shall at least meet Miss Brodure then."

Both women frowned slightly at Malcolm's silence.

But, truthfully, everyone knew that Malcolm Penn-Leith kept his own company. Words were not trifles to be wasted. Perhaps that was why he valued the measured, sparkling thoughts of Miss Brodure's writing so highly.

"Will your brother be attending the service with yourself, Mr. Penn-Leith?" Mrs. Clark asked far too innocently. "Will he take a fancy to her, do ye ken?"

"We shall see," Malcolm replied, refusing to say anything further.

But Mrs. Clark's question remained in his head for hours afterward:

Would Ethan take a fancy to Miss Brodure?

Everything within Malcolm said, *Yes.* Yes, he would.

And that was . . . excellent.

Ethan needed to be settled, to find his own measure of happiness and ease the tension that clung to his eyes.

What did it signify that Malcolm felt unnervingly attracted to the woman?

He had experienced—and lost—his one great love.

There would be no other woman for him.

Viola Brodure was meant for Ethan.

The sooner they met, fell in love, and began their happily ever after—leaving Malcolm to his habitual, solitary existence —the better.

"I FIND THIS entire situation alarming," Ethan said the next day, tossing a letter down on the table beside his chair. "I'm fearful of setting foot outside the house. The village nosy *nebbies* have been terrifyingly persistent."

Ethan relaxed into Malcolm's favorite wingback chair before the fire in the front parlor of Thistle Muir, reading a bundle of correspondence from his publisher.

Malcolm sat at the desk beside one of the large windows, petting William Shakespurr on his lap with one hand while reviewing plans for his cattle herd and drafting a letter to his business partner, Sir Rafe Gordon, with the other.

Unlike typical Scottish farmhouses, Thistle Muir was an elegant, modern dwelling with symmetrical windows, a wee triangle pediment over the front door, and generous panes of glass that let in cheery, warm sunlight. The large sash windows overlooked a graveled drive to the front and a courtyard ringed with the dairy and wash house in the back.

Their father had built the house for their wealthy, aristocratic mother—a home worthy of the fine lady she had been.

Not that either brother could summon a single memory of her. She had died shortly after giving birth to Ethan, when Malcolm had been scarcely three years old himself. Both brothers had only heard stories of her from their much older sister, Leah, who had raised them.

Ethan slumped further in his chair. "I wouldn't put it past Mrs. Buchan tae force me into a compromising position with Miss Brodure just so she could set up a stall on market day and charge her neighbors a tuppence tae hear the tale. And now I've received this—" He tapped a finger on the letter he had just set down. "—a letter from His Grace, the Duke of Kendall."

Frowning, Malcolm set his pen in the inkwell perched on the desk. "Ye correspond with the Duke of Kendall? Truly, Ethan, ye do nothing by halves, do ye?"

William Shakespurr butted Malcolm's free hand, demanding another stroke. Malcolm obliged. White and impossibly fluffy, the cat was a bit of a *prima donna*, not unlike his namesake. His sire, Mr. Dandylion McFluffles, lived with Leah and her husband, Fox, and was every whit as tyrannical.

"That's just it, Malcolm," Ethan said. "I believe His Grace and I were introduced at Mrs. Armand's evening soiree earlier in the year, but we didn't speak more than five words to one another. We are scarcely acquainted."

"So why is he writing ye?"

Ethan rolled his eyes and picked up the letter. "His Grace says, 'It would please me greatly to hear that you are courting Miss Viola Brodure in earnest.'"

"Pardon?" Malcolm's eyebrows lifted. "Why in heaven's name should the Duke of Kendall care who ye court?"

"How the hell should I know."

Malcolm's eyebrows inched higher. He glanced down at his own correspondence. "How odd that ye mention Kendall. I am currently writing Sir Rafe Gordon to arrange a visit next week."

"Ah. I had forgotten that Sir Rafe is assisting ye with your coos. I cannot imagine he has any hand in Kendall's meddling." Ethan set the duke's letter down. "They may be half-brothers, but I have never heard tell of Kendall or Sir Rafe spending time in one another's company."

"Aye, but after the old duke's death last year, perhaps young Kendall has decided to step out of his father's shadow? Mend family fences?"

The scandal surrounding the previous Duke of Kendall had become the stuff of legend. Even nearly twenty-five years on, people still spoke of it in hushed tones. How the prior duke had been a bigamist, resulting in Sir Rafe's illegitimacy. Desperate for a legitimate heir, the old duke had remarried a young Italian noblewoman, legally this time, and sired twins—Kendall and his sister—not even a year later.

"Having met both the elder and younger duke, I must disagree with ye," Ethan said. "The present duke appears tae be cast from the same mold as his father."

"*Och*, the letter in your hand would disabuse that notion. Seems a wee bit romantic for an overbearing duke." William Shakespurr seemed to agree, as he meowed and hopped down from Malcolm's lap.

"Or perhaps it is the behavior of an aristocrat who believes he can force the entire world to obey his every whim. Though why Kendall should care about Miss Viola Brodure, I cannot say."

Malcolm shrugged in agreement.

"As I keep saying, just because I'm a poet and Miss Brodure is an authoress, it doesn't follow that we will be suited," Ethan continued, running a hand through his brown hair. "I will not be thrust into a relationship simply because some *bampot* duke and the village gossips think it a romantic idea. No matter that the lady has journeyed the entire length of Britain to meet me, despite the tale that they are merely on holiday to visit the Ruxtons."

Malcolm tugged at his beard, pivoting back to his desk and the letter to Sir Rafe. He declined to state the obvious to his brother. That anyone who had met both Ethan and Miss Brodure correctly assumed that they were, in fact, perfectly suited.

His brother would realize this soon enough.

After a moment, Ethan said from behind, "I am half tempted to write Kendall and tell him *he* may have Miss Brodure, if he is so enamored of the lady."

That . . . Malcolm could not let pass. He dropped his quill, rotating to look at his brother directly. "Miss Brodure is a person, Ethan, not a parcel tae be passed about."

"Aye, but I dislike my hand being forced like this. I'm going to arrive at church on Sunday, and half the congregation will be expecting Miss Brodure and myself tae tie the knot then and there."

"*Och*, now you're being a wee bit hysterical. Ye will simply meet Miss Brodure on Sunday, nothing more. I promise no one will force ye into matrimony." Malcolm couldn't keep the sarcasm from his voice. Though truly, Miss Brodure was so unutterably lovely, he couldn't imagine any man not securing the vicar's services on the spot. "Besides, you'll have reinforcements. Leah sent word from Laverloch Castle that they will be attending Sunday services, as well."

Their sister, Leah, had married Captain Fox Carnegie five years before. Given that Leah had been nearly forty at the time, her abrupt plunge into matrimony had raised some eyebrows. But her marriage to Fox had proved a happy one. Malcolm could not have conjured a better husband for his sister. They had two children—an adopted daughter, Madeline, and their own wee boy, Jack.

"Leah's coming? No wonder Mrs. McGregor has been up baking shortbread and meat pies since dawn. I would have thought our older sister too sensible tae be caught up in the fervor around Miss Brodure."

"She is," Malcolm said with a grin. "Fox, however, is a devotee of Miss Brodure's work. Leah says he is quite beside himself in eagerness tae meet her."

Leah's husband, Captain Fox Carnegie, seemed the least-likely person in Britain to read and admire Miss Brodure, but Malcolm supposed it spoke to the long reach of the authoress's captivating novels.

Silence rested between the brothers for a moment. Malcolm knew better than to assume that Ethan was done with the matter.

After a pause, Ethan sighed again. "I suppose there is no help for it. Wee Tam Farquar saw Miss Brodure driving with her father two days ago and said she's as fine a bird as he's ever seen. And despite all his faults, Wee Tam isn't the sort tae give such praise lightly." Ethan lifted a foot atop Malcolm's favorite footstool.

"I am sure Miss Brodure is more than the sum of her outward graces," Malcolm said, swallowing back a jolt of that ever-present irritation. Why was Wee Tam looking at Miss Brodure anyway? "Like any woman, she contains a soul and heart and mind that should be carefully explored.

I fear ye are behaving like a hunter—viewing her as a thing tae be bartered—when you should be donning the hat of an intrepid explorer."

Ethan stilled, his eyes getting that far-away-pondering look. "*Ye are behaving like a hunter, when you should be donning the hat of an intrepid explorer . . .* I quite like that. May I use it?"

"Of course. And as for the rest—even with Kendall's pressure and the relentless gossips—do not disparage the chance to get to know Miss Brodure."

"Aye." Ethan agreed, picking up the duke's letter again. "Only a child refuses something simply because others wish him tae have it."

That was a startling bit of self-awareness from Ethan.

"Besides, it helps that someone—" Ethan looked back to Malcolm, a teasing glint in his green eyes. "—has been encouraging me tae take the final step into manhood. Perhaps I will give it a try."

"Do that. How goes the poem writing, anyway?" Malcolm asked.

Ethan groaned, sank back into the wingback chair—footstool scuffing the floor—and pressed the heels of his hands to his eyes. "As ye can see, I'm struggling tae find inspiration. Perhaps one book of poetry has simply dredged all the possible ideas out of me."

"Ye will find your muse." Malcolm turned back to his letter. "Perhaps it will even be Miss Brodure herself."

"Hah!" Ethan chuckled. "If only I could be so lucky."

Well . . . *yes.*

That was precisely how Malcolm wanted the situation with Miss Brodure to play out. She would help Ethan through his literary slump; they would fall in love and marry. Then Ethan and the new Mrs. Penn-Leith *née* Brodure would rise to even loftier heights of fame, supporting and loving—and, who knew, possibly editing—one another along the way.

Surely, any attraction Malcolm felt for the lady would die a cold death long before then.

He would see her at church—see her together with Ethan—and Malcolm would forget entirely that, for one brief, flitting instant, he had imagined himself as a different man.

A man who had never faced devastating loss.

A man who would consider winning Viola Brodure for himself.

G od appeared to smile upon Malcolm's plan, as Sunday dawned to
  encouragingly blue skies.

As promised, Leah and Fox along with their children, Madeline and
Jack, made the long journey down the glen from Laverloch Castle to join
Malcolm and Ethan for worship services.

They made a merry band, walking from Thistle Muir to the parish
kirk, four-year-old Jack stopping every fifth step to pick up a rock that
he insisted on dropping into the sporran hanging from the belt of
Malcolm's kilt.

They had intended to arrive early at the church, only to find that most
of the parish had awakened with the same idea.

The kirkyard overflowed, villagers *blethering* with one another in their
colorful Sunday finery—top hats, feathered bonnets, and lacy parasols
bobbing amongst the tombstones.

Malcolm frowned at the agitated thump of his heart as he scanned
the gathered crowd, ostensibly *not* searching for Miss Brodure, but in
truth hoping to spot her blond head.

Och, this had to stop.

She is but a woman, ye eejit, he told himself. *Ye arenae infatuated with her.*

His wayward heart simply beat faster.

Malcolm found it bloody annoying.

Finally, Mrs. Clark and Mrs. Buchan turned to greet Leah, affording him a view of the church door.

Ah. At last.

There she was.

Miss Brodure.

She was every bit as beautiful as Malcolm remembered. Perhaps even more so. Ethereal, fey, and petite, she appeared as luminous as a fine-boned porcelain plate.

His breath lodged in his throat and his ears rang with what he feared was angel song.

Did she have to be so absurdly lovely?

She stood between the vicar, Dr. Ruxton, and her father, all three welcoming parishioners as they entered the church.

It was an unusual circumstance, to be sure, but gracious of Miss Brodure to greet people personally, as if she recognized that the entire parish fairly hummed with the hope of meeting her.

Her silvery-blond hair peeked out from under the wide brim of her straw bonnet, while her dusky blue gown cinched her trim waist and complemented her fair complexion. Malcolm was sure Leah would educate him on the intricacies of it later: *Did ye see the Dutch lace trim along her sloped collar? Most charming. And not an ounce of puff tae her sleeves. Thank heavens that ridiculous fashion is firmly behind us—*

Why was he so smitten by *this* woman?

She was nothing like Aileen. Malcolm's wife had been tall, dark, and strong. A miller's daughter accustomed to the physical demands of country life. A woman who tackled the world directly, chin high.

By contrast, Miss Brodure ducked her elegant head and blushed becomingly when introduced to Lord and Lady Hadley, her eyes modestly averted.

Such bashfulness was unusual. Lord and Lady Hadley were so gracious and kind, they readily setting others at ease.

Malcolm found it humorous that Hadley—the most Scottish Scotsman Malcolm had ever known—was, in fact, an English earl. Sir Rafe had recounted more than one tale of Hadley throwing his Scottish roots in the faces of other Peers in Lords. And though Hadley was old enough to be Malcolm's father, he counted the earl a friend.

Malcolm and his party waited patiently for their turn to greet the authoress.

At his side, Ethan frowned, leaning to the side, trying to glimpse Miss Brodure between Mrs. Clark's feathered bonnet and a tall obelisk grave marker. Just as Ethan raised a hand to ward off Mrs. Clark's lofty plumage, the crowd parted, affording a clear view of the church door.

Ethan's slack-jawed reaction was everything Malcolm had predicted.

"Well," his brother said faintly, angling his head for a second . . . and then a third glance. "I fear I may owe yourself, Kendall, and the entire village of Fettermill an apology. I should have listened sooner. She is magnificent."

Malcolm nodded tersely as his brother was absolutely correct.

Ethan and Miss Brodure were headed straight for marital bliss.

Others in the parish clearly thought the same. The elderly Fredericks sisters openly studied Ethan. Isla Liston, a hand on her pregnant belly, nudged her husband, Callum, and discreetly pointed toward Miss Brodure. Lady Stewart whispered something to her other half, Sir Robert Stewart, causing the man to immediately whip his head around to stare at the authoress.

At last, Malcolm's party reached the church door, Leah and Fox in front, Ethan behind.

A hush settled over the crowd.

Or perhaps the ringing in Malcolm's own ears had turned the world silent.

Miss Brodure darted a glance in their direction, looking first at Leah and Fox before moving on to Malcolm.

Their gazes tangled for the briefest of moments.

The force of her eyes, wide and cobalt blue, punched the air from his lungs. Then, just as she had with Lord and Lady Hadley, she flushed and demurely lowered her head, fingers twisting her reticule strings into knots.

Dr. Ruxton made introductions. Malcolm, Leah, Fox, and the children bobbed their heads in murmured greetings.

Miss Brodure did the same, but her eyes remained fixed on the ground. She seemed utterly different from the engaging woman Malcolm had met along that foggy road.

He frowned.

Where was the charming lady who had laughed in delight over Coolius Caesar and William Shakespurr? The one who had petted Beowoof with such happy abandon? Where was the revolutionary who had possibly written *A Hard Truth*? Though given Miss Brodure's hesitant behavior, perhaps Malcolm was mistaken in that.

Frown deepening, Malcolm stepped aside, following Leah and Fox.

Ethan took their place before Miss Brodure.

The assembled villagers canted forward, eager to witness the celebrated Scottish poet greet the famous English novelist.

"Miss Brodure." Ethan offered her his most charming smile. The one that Malcolm had dubbed *The Swooner*. The one that had caused many an unsuspecting lass to buckle on the spot; Malcolm had witnessed it.

"Mr. Penn-Leith," Miss Brodure replied. Her low cultured voice barely carried to Malcolm's ears.

She raised her head and met Ethan's gaze briefly, before blushing and looking down at her folded hands nested like a pair of doves at her waist.

They made a striking couple—Ethan with his wind-swept, Highland gallantry and Miss Brodure in her refined, ladylike reserve.

Malcolm was sure this moment would be retold over hearth fires for years to come. Without a doubt, he would read about it in some magazine—'The Highland Poet Meets Miss Brodure'—printed alongside a lithograph of Ethan in kilt and cap, bowing extravagantly over Miss Brodure's hand, just as he was at present.

"Miss Brodure, permit me tae say," Ethan lifted his head, "how ardently I admire your writing. Ye grace our kirkyard with your presence."

A sigh ran through the crowd.

"How romantic," a female voice murmured somewhere near the entrance gate.

Miss Brodure clearly heard the woman, as her blush deepened, eyes remaining downcast. "Mr. Penn-Leith, you are too kind."

Miss Brodure curtsied, still not raising her head fully to look at Ethan, as if she were . . . *shy*.

Malcolm nearly grunted in surprise.

Was Miss Brodure shy?

She certainly hadn't seemed shy during their conversation on the lane. But given the number of people waiting to speak with her, he supposed it would be natural to feel overwhelmed. After all, she was such a wee wisp of a woman—the top of her head didn't quite reach his shoulders—the gathered crowd likely felt akin to a colossus looming over her.

And yet . . . the thought of Miss Brodure being shy was an ill-fitting shoe, rubbing and chafing the inside of his chest.

VIOLA FORCED HERSELF to take in a deep, slow breath.

Her lungs resisted, hardening and tightening in her ribcage.

Ethan Penn-Leith continued to grin at her, his wide smile nearly bludgeoning in its force.

Mmmm, the broadsheets certainly had not exaggerated the magnetism of his person. *Lord Byron reborn*, she remembered a newspaper article declaring.

Ethan was rather alarmingly handsome, with a roguish lock tumbling across his brow and framing a pair of startling green eyes.

"I cannot imagine I could ever be too kind when it comes tae praising your writing, Miss Brodure," Ethan said, his smile so bright-edged it felt positively lethal.

Gracious.

He should be careful where he pointed that thing. It was liable to take out an unsuspecting debutante. Case in point, Viola caught two young ladies earnestly fanning themselves out of the corner of her eye.

"Thank you," she managed to say, voice entirely too breathless.

Why was it so difficult to maintain eye contact with the man?

She dropped her eyes to her hands and took in another slow lungful of air.

The specter of asthma and anxiety had reared its ugly head today, exacerbating her shyness to debilitating levels.

She felt helpless when her body betrayed her like this. When she could scarcely speak for stammering. When every breath brought her that much closer to an asthmatic fit.

And now, she faced the weight of Ethan Penn-Leith's attention.

Viola waited for excitement to flood her. To feel a rush of exhilaration and giddiness. For her agonizing self-consciousness to flee, just as it had on the lane with Malcolm Penn-Leith.

After all, she had been anticipating *finally* meeting Ethan Penn-Leith for over a year now.

But at the moment, her hammering heart and sweating hands drowned out all finer emotions.

Granted, in all her imaginings—and there had been embarrassingly far too many—she had never considered that she would exchange her first words with Ethan in front of an entire *village*.

Without asking permission, her wayward eyes lifted and moved to the left of Ethan, unerringly finding Malcolm Penn-Leith's dark gaze.

He contemplated her with a quiet intensity, one hand leaning on his walking stick, a bastion of calm in the teeming churchyard.

In the days since their first meeting, Viola wondered if she had exaggerated her sense of initial attraction to Mr. Malcolm Penn-Leith. Surely her feeling of bewildering electric calm had sprung from the exhaustion at finally—after five days of jarring roads and lumpy inn beds—arriving in Scotland.

But, no . . . she had not.

Staring at him now, she acknowledged that he was every whit as compelling.

And similar to that moment along the foggy road earlier in the week, some pressure eased in Viola's chest. A thought that, perhaps with Malcolm's stalwart presence at her side, she could manage her shy tongue and begin a friendship with Ethan.

If only her hands would stop shaking.

IS MISS BRODURE SHY?

The question would not leave Malcolm be.

He pondered it as Ethan and Miss Brodure finished their conversation, as Malcolm and his party entered the church to sit in their respective pews, as Dr. Brodure delivered his sermon.

Miss Brodure sat close to the lectern, her body angled toward the congregation, enabling him to study her profile during the long, often tedious discourse. She repeatedly ducked her head, as if the press of so many eyes upon her was a physical burden.

Again, after that first meeting, *shy* was the last word Malcolm would have used to characterize her.

Joyful. Effervescent. Enchanting. Intelligent.

Those were the words he would choose. Not shy. Not bashful. Not retiring.

Granted, pondering the discrepancy between the woman he saw now and the woman he met on the road was, truly, none of his affair.

His entire goal was to promote the lady to his brother and encourage a courtship between them. Surely, as Ethan and Miss Brodure deepened their acquaintance, any stirrings of attraction Malcolm felt would dissipate. The last thing he wished was to wade farther into the waters of . . . of . . .

Mmmm, what exactly were these waters he was treading? Affection? Romance?

Och, it hardly mattered. He was capable of none of it.

And yet, as he watched Miss Brodure tuck a stray wisp of hair behind one ear with fingers that actually trembled, Malcolm's own palm ached to reach for her hand and soothe away her nerves.

Ridiculous impulses, the lot of them.

He was a lowly Scottish farmer, for heaven's sake. Socially, he and Miss Brodure inhabited different universes.

Ever the pragmatic sort, he forced himself to envision it. To test the possibility of turning his back on Aileen's memory and embracing a future with Viola Brodure.

Images drifted through his brain, a sort of foul-tasting physic to set his thinking straight.

Him, dressed in fashionable finery, sipping tea at a London soiree. Or, ever more preposterous, making idle conversation over port with the likes of the Duke of Kendall.

Malcolm could more readily imagine himself moving his farm to the moon than hobnobbing with the *haut ton* of society.

But then, the reverse was just as absurd. Miss Brodure stomping through the fields as Aileen had done, skirts ringed in mud, intent on helping him milk a cow or birth a calf.

The images accomplished what Malcolm intended—they plunged his thoughts into the bracing cold of Reality.

Viola Brodure was an enchanting pixie who set the world aglow with her clever brilliance.

Malcolm was an uneducated, grief-broken widower who never intended to remarry.

When he had fallen in love with Aileen, he had pictured himself literally stowing his own heart within her chest. But in the end, her body hadn't been strong enough to defeat Death. When Aileen had died, she took most of his heart with her.

And now, Malcolm simply wasn't brave enough to place what remained of his fractured heart in another's frail body.

Worse, he could imagine the pity dripping from Miss Brodure's gaze if she ever learned of his misplaced devotion, the kind timbre of her voice as she informed him that such regard on his part was as laughable as it was unwanted.

Yes, his embarrassing infatuation had to end.

Right now. Today. In this pew.

Malcolm tore his eyes away from her and spent the rest of the sermon staring firmly at Dr. Brodure, the stained-glass windows, the ancient carvings on the lectern.

Looking anywhere but at the fine slope of Miss Brodure's nose and the plump pillow of her lips.

AFTER THE SERVICE, Viola stood with her back nearly touching the stone fence which encircled the churchyard, her gaze fixed on the church door, praying her father emerged soon.

Around her, parishioners chattered—bonnets bobbing and beaver top hats nodding—the occasional glance or head turning her way.

Swallowing, Viola fought to keep her breathing slow and steady.

Breathe in. Breathe out. One. Two.

Picture your lungs as airy as gossamer.

She clung to the image.

Her hands had trembled throughout her father's sermon, the scrutiny of literally every eye in the church rendering her chest as tight as hardened pitch.

At least outside in the fresh Scottish air, she could breathe more easily under the collective weight of the townspeoples' regard. Now if only the shaking of her limbs would cease.

"Miss Brodure, I have decided we must invite you for dinner." Lady Hadley appeared at Viola's side, her husband not far behind. "The gardens at Muirford House are so lovely in the summer. You must see them."

The countess was beautiful, the gray threading through her auburn hair only adding to her unaffected loveliness. Lord Hadley stopped beside his wife, regarding her with a fierce happy fondness.

"*Och*, ye know we are for England and Hadley Park tomorrow, *mo chridhe*," Lord Hadley reminded her gently.

Lady Hadley laughed. "Yes, well then, Miss Brodure must promise to remain here until we return." Her ladyship pinned Viola with a hopeful look. "Am I cruel to extract such a vow?"

"Not at all, my l-lady." Viola bobbed her head, heat growing like tendrils up to her earlobes and entangling her words. "I believe my father intends to r-remain here until the end of summer. We would be m-most honored."

"It is settled then." Lady Hadley nearly beamed with kindness. "We shall dine in midsummer when we return."

Lord Hadley nodded his agreement and reached for his wife's hand, wrapping it possessively around his elbow as they turned to greet another couple. Would that Viola could find someone who, after twenty years of marriage or more, regarded her as fondly as Lord Hadley looked upon his wife.

Would Ethan Penn-Leith be that man?

As if sensing her thoughts, Ethan emerged from behind a pair of burly laborers to the left of the church door and threaded his way through parishioners and tombstones to where Viola stood against the stone fence.

Yes, he was still every whit as handsome as he had been two hours previously. And yes, her nerves still vibrated with a disquieting agitation in his presence.

"Miss Brodure, what a pleasure it has been tae find such a fair English rose amidst the bonnie hills of Scotland." Ethan bowed, low and elegant, that same lethal smile upon his lips.

Viola longed to ask if he found her arrival unwelcome, if his lack of reply to her letters was deliberate or simply a hiccup in his busy life.

But her hammering heart stemmed the questions.

All she could manage was a curtsy and a stammered, "The p-pleasure has been all mine, Mr. Penn-Leith."

Viola swore half the kirkyard—Lord and Lady Hadley included—turned toward herself and Ethan in that moment, eyes eager, bodies leaning as if watching a Punch and Judy Show.

Did the entire parish anticipate Viola and Ethan making a match of it, then? And did Viola find that thought exciting? Or terrifying?

Her lungs seemed to have their own suffocating answer.

Change. You want change, she reminded herself. *A life no longer adjacent.*

She had journeyed a great distance to meet Ethan Penn-Leith.

What did others' hopes matter in this instance?

She had not come this far to only come this far.

And so she smiled at Ethan, took a step away from the stone fence, and ordered her anxious tongue to unknot.

"I have greatly enjoyed my first few days in Scotland." Her words came out without a stammer. Thank goodness for small miracles. "Your descriptions of your homeland do the landscape justice . . . if just barely."

"*Och,* I cannot accept such high praise, Miss Brodure." Ethan returned a positively incandescent smile. "My modest attempts tae capture Scotland's magnificence often frustrate me with their inadequacy."

"You are far too humble, sir."

Ethan's frank admiration was everything Viola could have hoped for when she left Wiltshire for Scotland.

Again, she waited patiently for a rush of excitement or enchantment or *something* to follow—

"Ah, Malcolm, excellent tae see ye!" Lord Hadley's voice interrupted her thoughts.

Viola turned to see Malcolm Penn-Leith striding toward them, shoulders back, walking stick swinging, red-and-blue kilt swishing with each step.

Gracious.

Just the sight of him set heat prickling along Viola's skin—the *good* kind of heated skin prickles. Why her body responded this way to him was just as inexplicable as the onset of nerves or asthma.

Malcolm Penn-Leith was unmarried, that much she had managed to ascertain when Dr. and Mrs. Ruxton had called. Though Mrs. Ruxton had hinted that Malcolm was perhaps a widower. Their conversation had flowed so organically—and Mrs. Ruxton so thoroughly enjoyed talking—Viola had been unable to steer it elegantly back to Malcolm.

It seemed nearly impossible that he did not have an adoring wife and big brood of children counting the minutes until he returned home. The man appeared a ready-made *paterfamilias*—a scion of responsibility.

Malcolm paused at Ethan's side, shaking hands with Hadley and bowing over Lady Hadley's knuckles before turning to Viola with a rumbled, "Miss Brodure," that rolled over her like warm summer sun. And similar to a sunflower, her face instinctively rotated toward its comforting heat.

But as had happened earlier at the church door, Malcolm quickly retreated into the background, merging in with his neighbors ringed around. At some point in the last five minutes, the villagers had all stopped pretending to be discreet in their gawking and now watched Viola and Ethan with avid interest.

Lord Hadley asked Ethan about his recent trek into the Cairngorms.

"My pilgrimage to communion with Mother Nature, ye mean?" Ethan said affably, taking a step closer to Viola and placing a hand on the wall beside her.

Needing no further encouragement, he launched into a detailed story about tracking a pair of capercaillie across the moor to Loch Muick, telling the tale for all to hear.

Ethan Penn-Leith was a born storyteller.

And Viola, a natural-born storyteller herself—on paper, at least—admired that about him. Truly, she did.

His words wove through the crowd—hands gesturing, face emotive—as he leapt atop the stone fence to mime watching the sun rise from the top of Ben Tirran.

He was . . . well, what she had expected him to be . . . silver-tongued, captivating, a bit overly enthusiastic in evangelizing himself and his ideas.

And yet Ethan, for all his magnetism, was not the Penn-Leith who held Viola's attention.

Malcolm Penn-Leith stood unmoving to the right side of the gathered villagers, his left shoulder nearly touching the base of a lichen-covered memorial, jaw firm beneath his beard, a slight breeze stirring his kilt. He gave the impression of steadfast immovability. As if he would face a raging inferno, a blood-thirsty vampyre, or one of Lady Jersey's gossipy London soirees with the same unflappable *sangfroid*.

Both brothers had a similar look; anyone could see they were related. But as any good writer knew, the small details told a larger story.

Malcolm rested his palms atop his well-worn walking stick. He wore no gloves. Thin, white scars crisscrossed his knuckles, a silent testament to years of hard labor, of determination and focused duty. Of a life not bound by custom and endless etiquette.

Ethan's hands, however, were encased in supple kid-leather, protecting his skin from the harsh conditions of life. Such gloves were the mark of a gentleman, of refined manners and a genteel upbringing.

Before this moment, Viola would have said gloves were a necessity, a trait of true gentility. After all, a similar set of soft gloves covered her own hands. A lady always protected her skin from exposure to the sun and elements.

Why, then, did her gloves abruptly feel like a token of her confinement?

A symbol of her life adjacent? That instead of allowing her hands to become dirty—worn and used and scarred from the heavy business of *living*—she chose to remain unscathed. Sheltered. Pampered, even.

As in that squalid room with Eloise in Manchester, Viola wanted to cease existing in indecision. She needed the gloves to be stripped from her life, both metaphorically and literally.

As Ethan's story wound down, Viola squirmed in her silence.

Abruptly, her shyness itself seemed a cage, just one more intangible glove smothering her, causing her to retreat instead of engaging with life.

So despite the press of the people, despite the staring eyes that rendered her nervous and threatened to trigger her asthma—she forced her tongue to speak.

"Your story is most c-captivating, Mr. Penn-Leith." *Heavens!* How could her voice still be so breathless? "Was it during your hike that you realized the Cairngorms could be a metaphor for our modern life? That we have removed ourselves from Nature, and therefore, perhaps lost some of our humanity in the process?"

She *had* to know, she realized. She had to see the flashes of genius that glimmered like moonbeams in his poetry.

"That is a most perceptive question, Miss Brodure." Ethan gave her his signature entrancing smile. "I should love tae call upon ye and recount the whole of my artistic process. I adore nothing so much as communing with a fellow writer."

A female voice sighed behind Viola and someone else murmured, "What a perfect couple they make!"

"I should be most honored, Mr. Penn-Leith." Viola curtsied. "P-please call at your leisure."

6

E than Penn-Leith made good on his promise to call upon Viola. The man appeared in her front parlor the very next afternoon, his sister, Mrs. Leah Carnegie, on his arm. They burst into the entryway in a bustle of hats and overcoats and walking sticks, stripping off those ever-present gloves and handing all to Mary, who hovered in the hallway.

Viola ushered her guests into the parlor, willing her blushes and stammering to remain at bay . . . with only marginal success.

Just as on the day before, Ethan's exuberance tangled her tongue. His blinding smile and high spirits were a bit like stepping from a dark room into vivid sunlight. Viola expected it to be warm and welcoming, but it mostly left her blinded and blinking.

Regardless, she stuttered her way through inquiries about the weather and Captain Carnegie's health.

"Malcolm rarely makes social calls," Mrs. Carnegie said when Viola inquired after the third Penn-Leith sibling.

Viola took an instant liking to Mrs. Carnegie. Though significantly older than her brothers, humor sparked in her hazel eyes. Mrs. Carnegie seemed an eminently sensible woman, the sort who could be relied upon, no matter the situation.

"Besides, Malcolm is off tae Perth at the moment," Ethan added. "Something about his coos."

"His . . . coos?" Viola asked.

Mrs. Carnegie smiled. "His prized cows."

"*Och*, don't get Malcolm started in on coos." Ethan gave a crack of laughter as bright as his grin. "It is the one topic upon which our brother will wax eloquent."

"W-whyever for?" Viola asked, fingers fisted in her lap.

The thought of Malcolm Penn-Leith harboring a passion for cows seemed . . . incongruous.

And possibly a bit adorable.

Not that Viola was contemplating Malcolm Penn-Leith's adorableness.

Mrs. Carnegie exchanged a glance with Ethan before speaking. "'Tis no great secret, I suppose. As ye may have heard, Malcolm's wife passed away in childbirth nearly five years ago."

Oh.

So he *was* a widower. A man who had, once upon a time, had a wife.

"They were a love match," Mrs. Carnegie continued, "and Malcolm, as ye can imagine, has found the loss of his wife and babe . . . difficult."

"Aye. Bit of an understatement, actually." Ethan's sparkle dimmed. "Aileen was a lovely woman. We all miss her. Malcolm was, understandably, in a bad way after her death. Leah, here—" He lifted his chin toward his sister. "—and her husband lived at Thistle Muir for almost a year afterwards, didn't ye?"

"Aye. Malcolm could scarcely eat, much less keep track of the house and farm. Someone needed to ensure he didnae hurt hisself." Mrs. Carnegie—Leah—blinked back emotion.

Viola pressed a hand to her sternum, swallowing around an ache in her throat. To think of Malcolm, losing both his wife and baby in one harrowing day, drowning in the depths of grief and despair, . . .Well.

"Before Aileen's death," Ethan said, "Malcolm had spent years breeding a new type of coo from the native cattle here in Angus. An animal that is longer through the body and produces superior beef. After Aileen's passing, he dove headlong into promoting his new breed."

"He has been remarkably successful," Leah added, "attracting investors and shipping coos all over the world."

"Did ye know he is now working with Sir Rafe Gordon on developing a similar type of Highland cattle?" Ethan mused to his sister. "That's why he went off tae Perth."

"Fox mentioned as much. Apparently, the queen herself has made overtures tae purchase cattle for the royal herds."

"In short," Ethan turned to Viola, "our brother doesn't have much time for afternoon visiting hours, even if he were a dedicated conversationalist."

Viola nodded and knew she should let the topic go—that her odd interest in the elder Penn-Leith brother was unhelpful—but she had to ask one more question.

"Does Mr. Malcolm Penn-Leith not t-talk much, then?"

"Nae," Leah shook her head, "he has never been one to gnatter on, even as a wee boy."

"Aye." Ethan waved a dismissive hand. "I cannot imagine Malcolm in a parlor, sipping tea, and settling in for a *blether*."

Hmmm. Neither could Viola, she supposed.

Instead, her mind supplied an image of her own timid self climbing the rugged moor above Fettermill, Malcolm reaching out a hand to help her up the steep path.

She shook the idea away.

Enough.

Ethan Penn-Leith was here.

The Highland Poet himself. In her front parlor.

Focus on the handsome man in front of you, Viola.

They spoke of inanities after that.

Or rather, Ethan and Leah discussed Dr. Brodure's sermon the day before, the departure of Lord Hadley for his estate in Sussex, and the prospect of picnicking in a folly near the Rocks of Solitude west of Edzell.

Mary arrived with a tray, and Viola poured tea, nodding at the appropriate times. But her words became more reticent, not less, the longer she listened.

This needed to cease.

She liked Ethan Penn-Leith. Truly she did.

She admired the philosophical clarity of his poetry. Surely she would adapt to the charisma of his personality given time.

And so as she had the day before, Viola placed a firm hand on her nerves and opened her mouth.

"I have l-long appreciated the ingenious turn of your mind, Mr. Penn-Leith. As an author myself, I find it fascinating to discuss writing endeavors with a f-fellow writer. What is your process for composing a new poem?"

"An excellent question, Miss Brodure." Ethan stretched his feet out before him.

Leah sipped her tea and smiled, obviously enjoying the tableau before her.

"Before beginning any new poem," Ethan continued, "I must find a suitable subject."

The appreciative gleam in his eyes suggested that *Viola* was his subject of the moment.

Ah. He was flirting with her in earnest now.

That fact should cause her heart to skip and dance. The man was exuberance and enthusiasm personified.

Who didn't adore an exuberant enthusiast?

Something must be wrong with her.

"After securing a subject, then what do you do?" Viola gave Ethan what she hoped was an encouraging smile.

His returning grin turned self-deprecating. "And then I think and walk and study the world around me. It is all about allowing time for images tae accumulate and coalesce into cohesive ideas."

"Ye also make endless lists of rhyming words," Leah added.

"That, too. Though my poetry does not rely heavily upon rhyme as much as rhythm and meter."

That was true. "And depth of thought," Viola added.

"I thank ye for the compliment, Miss Brodure. It all takes time, much pondering, and endless revision. Things I am sure ye must do in spades."

Viola gave a rueful laugh. "Indeed. Revisions often feel never-ending. When I am in the midst of a book, I frequently despair that it will ever come out right."

"I understand that pain all too well." Ethan set down his teacup and leaned forward, eyes intent. "In fact, allow me tae recount an anecdote that happened while sailing from Montrose tae Arbroath last September that I think exemplifies my process . . ."

He spoke on and on, hands waving, his handsome face flitting from excitement to surprise to awe.

And yet . . .

No deeper emotions surfaced from the depths of Viola's heart.

Ethan did not bore her, to be sure. And she had liked his notion that pictures could accumulate into ideas.

But she felt none of the giddy fervor of a lady being wooed.

Mmmm.

She searched for the right metaphor to describe it.

Once, many years ago when she had been wrestling with a particularly thorny plot problem, she had taken a hackney cab to Westminster Abbey. There, she had spent the afternoon sitting on a bench in the Poet's Corner. Surrounding oneself with the graves of dead literary greats—Chaucer, Spenser, Dryden—seemed a rather morbid way to seek inspiration, and yet, the experience had been transcendent. The moist air of the abbey soothed her lungs. The cathedral's quiet hush allowed the energy of the place to penetrate her soul. It had been a silent conversation of sorts, a rejuvenation, filling her mind with ideas and renewed zeal for her project.

Viola had supposed that spending an afternoon with Ethan Penn-Leith might be a similar experience. That they would feed off one another's creativity, practically finishing each other's sentences in the race to connect their thoughts. That with Ethan, she would feel alive and *living.*

But that wasn't quite how the afternoon went.

To be sure, Ethan Penn-Leith was interesting and handsome and beautifully mannered—the exact gentleman Viola would have scripted for a suitor.

And yet, as she listened to Ethan talk of *his* interests and *his* writing and *his* work, Viola felt as if she were standing on a street corner, watching another's world stroll by.

How could Ethan Penn-Leith *himself* make her feel adjacent to living?

Was that not the pinnacle of all ironies?

After Ethan and Leah finally took their leave, Viola was left with one lingering thought—

Would she have felt the same lack of connection had Malcolm Penn-Leith accompanied his brother and sister and spent an hour conversing with her about his coos?

"THIS YEAR'S CALVES are among our best yet," Sir Rafe Gordon said, handing Malcolm a finger of whisky.

Malcolm nodded at his host and business partner. "Aye. We've done well. We cannae keep up with the demand for them."

Sir Rafe snorted. "I received a letter from a French *comte* just yesterday offering me an absurd sum of money for three heifers."

"We cannae be selling on our breeding stock."

"*Och*, that's precisely what I told our French *aristo*."

Malcolm smiled.

Sir Rafe raised his glass. "To our continued good enterprise."

"To your willingness tae take a chance on a Highland farmer." Malcolm lifted his own glass in return.

Sir Rafe grinned at that. "Ye did come highly recommended. And Hadley has never led me astray."

Hadley being another man to whom Malcolm felt indebted.

After Aileen's death, Malcolm had poured his energy into improving his cattle, but he had needed more capital in order to scale up his breeding operation. Hadley had recommended him to Sir Rafe Gordon, a fellow Scot, as a partner.

Together, Malcolm and Sir Rafe had built his wee cow herd into something of an empire.

Best of all, Malcolm now counted Sir Rafe as a close friend.

The man appeared younger than his fifty-odd years. Tall and lean, his dark eyes always brimmed with mirth, as if Sir Rafe were accustomed to laughing at life's foibles. Given what little Malcolm had seen of Sir Rafe's relationship with his bonnie wife—Lady Sophie Gordon—he didn't doubt that the man was content.

"Do ye have many dealings with your late father's family?" Malcolm asked, changing the subject.

"With Kendall? My wee brother?" Sir Rafe sat back, brows drawing down. "Nae, we don't speak with one another. Our father cut me off completely after his bigamy trial, thank goodness. Then he remarried some Italian noblewoman and sired the twins—the present duke and his sister, Lady Allegra. I believe Lady Allegra and her mother have lived in Italy for the past decade; the duchess somehow managed to break free of my father's chains. As for young Kendall, I have crossed paths with him in London but have never exchanged more than a dozen words with the lad. Why do ye ask?"

"Kendall has been writing Ethan."

"Whyever for?"

"As best I can tell, Kendall is playing matchmaker."

Sir Rafe scoffed at that, sipping his whisky. "My ducal brother would be more likely tae take a role in a Covent Garden pantomime than play matchmaker. He is cut of the same cloth as our sire—autocratic, self-interested, and not given to flights of romantic whimsy."

"Precisely my own assumptions. But I understand Kendall has taken a lively interest in Ethan marrying Miss Viola Brodure."

"The authoress?"

"The very same."

Malcolm tossed back the rest of his whisky. It seemed the only appropriate response when thinking upon Miss Brodure—use every means possible to obliterate her from his mind.

Perhaps that was why he had brought up Kendall. Another physic to remind himself of all the forces drawing Ethan and Miss Brodure together. Forces much higher and more powerful than himself.

Sir Rafe snapped his fingers. "Her father is the vicar at Westacre, is he not?"

"I cannae say," Malcolm said.

Sir Rafe's gaze went hazy. "I am almost sure he has the living at Westacre. I seem tae remember someone mentioning it in a letter tae me . . . that Dr. Brodure replaced old Mr. Samuelson."

Malcolm raised his eyebrows. "That seems an uncannily specific thing tae know."

Sir Rafe shrugged. "The living is held by the Dukes of Kendall. 'Twas the parish church where I grew up. If that is the case, I can see why Kendall might take an interest. He perhaps wishes his vicar's daughter tae marry well. Or, more likely, tae harness her popularity for his own gain."

Did knowing that Kendall was Dr. Brodure's benefactor make the duke's meddling letters to Ethan more or less understandable? Malcolm was unsure.

"Or perhaps I am wrong," Sir Rafe shot Malcolm a wry grin, "and my wee brother has taken an interest in romance. If so, he might be better suited for a Drury Lane farce than I had supposed."

Malcolm nodded in agreement, though secretly he wondered if he, himself, in the throes of this gauche infatuation with his own brother's intended, was the *glaikit* fool destined to enact a melodrama.

MALCOLM ARRIVED HOME the next evening in time for dinner and to receive a moment-by-moment recounting of his sibling's visit with Miss Brodure the previous day.

He stripped off his coat, washed his hands, and joined Fox, Leah, and Ethan in the dining room just as Mrs. McGregor set hot dishes on the tabletop.

Leah and Fox had decided to stay a few extra days, both to keep Ethan company and for Fox to conduct business with his solicitor in Brechin. They would be returning to Laverloch in the morning.

"Are ye sure ye didnae need me tae come back to Thistle Muir sooner rather than later?" Leah asked for approximately the twelfth time, passing a bowl of roasted tatties to Fox. "I ken Mrs. McGregor's daughter is set tae have her baby soon and will certainly need some time away tae tend to her."

"Nae, Leah." Malcolm shook his head, reaching for the platter of Yorkshire puddings. "As I keep telling ye, the midwife thinks it will be perhaps even a month or more afore Isla has the babe. Mrs. McGregor has been spending her free-day with Isla and Callum, preparing what she can in advance. But as this is Isla's fourth bairn, I think she kens well what tae do. I spoke with Callum about it just yesterday, and he seemed at ease. Ethan and I can manage here, Leah. We didnae need yourself to travel clear down the glen tae wait upon us bachelors."

Across from Malcolm, Ethan nodded in agreement. "Besides, I intend tae spend as much time as possible with Miss Brodure. I take back any abuse I have dealt in my refusal to come to know her. She was utterly charming, Malcolm," he said around a mouthful of Mrs. McGregor's excellent roast beef.

Malcolm grunted his agreement, slathering butter onto a warm bap.

"Aye, she and Ethan rubbed along brilliantly." Leah grinned far too widely, spooning tatties onto her own plate.

"I regret that I was unable to accompany you on your morning call." Fox gave his wife a doting look. "I should have liked to better make Miss Brodure's acquaintance."

"She is quite perfect, I think," Ethan beamed.

Malcolm couldn't let that comment pass. "No one is perfect, Ethan. 'Tis unfair to place perfection upon the lady—"

"Bah!" Ethan wiped his mouth and held up a staying hand. "Ye may have your grumpy opinions, Malcolm, but I beg ye tae make them silent ones."

Malcolm let it drop. His stupidly infatuated heart unhelpfully pointed out that Viola Brodure *was* rather close to perfection.

"I'm fair on my way tae falling for her, I ken," Ethan continued, reaching for the gravy.

He spoke the words with his typical bonhomie, much as one would declare, *This meal has been delightful*, or *Ye should pop by on a Tuesday*.

"What do ye like about her?" Malcolm had to ask, wondering if his brother saw the same strength and joy in her that Malcolm did.

The question pulled Ethan up short. As if he hadn't pinpointed what, precisely, he liked about the lady.

"Miss Brodure is . . . decidedly lovely," he said after a hesitation. "And she has the most beautiful . . . manners."

"Very gracious," Leah agreed.

"Aye," Ethan nodded, warming to the topic. "She has this delightful way of cocking her head and looking inquisitive as she listens. She isn't one of those women who revels in the sound of her own voice."

That's it? Malcolm felt like asking. *That is why you're fair on your way tae falling for her?*

"Did she discuss her writing?" he asked instead.

Ethan frowned. "No . . . we never quite got around tae it. She asked how I write my poems, and I told her about that boat trip from Montrose to Arbroath last year."

"The one with the aggressive seal that ye shouldnae have pestered?" Malcolm squinted his eyes at his brother.

"*Och*, I didn't pester the creature." Ethan paused under the weight of Malcolm's stare. "Or if I did, it makes for a good story. Very inspiring. Miss Brodure even laughed in a place or two."

Malcolm gritted his teeth, reading between the lines to what Ethan hadn't conveyed. His brother had barreled into the Brodure's parlor and prattled on about himself instead of endeavoring to know the lady.

Miss Brodure deserved songs of praise or bouquets of flowers or—

"Ye should write Miss Brodure a sonnet, telling her what ye like about her," Malcolm said.

A brief silence ensued as Ethan pondered this, chewing his roast beef slowly.

"Aye," his brother said after swallowing, expression a trifle glum. "I suppose I *should* write a sonnet about her."

"Why the dour face then?" Malcolm grunted in reply. "Surely, Miss Brodure rouses your poetic faculties."

"Will she pull ye from your writing doldrums, do ye ken?" Leah asked, sopping up gravy with her Yorkshire pudding.

"Possibly. It's hard to say at the moment." Ethan tossed his fork down, shrugging. "I just wish I could dredge more concrete ideas from my brain."

"They will come," Leah said softly.

"Perhaps." Ethan loosed a self-deprecating laugh. "Though I

suppose I should simply recognize that it's generally more enjoyable tae bask in the fame of being hailed a celebrated poet than tae actually do the work required to *be* one."

Malcolm felt his eyebrows fly nearly to his hairline.

That was likely the most self-aware statement his brother had ever uttered.

Leah chuckled as she patted Ethan's hand. "Ye are far too hard on yourself. Ye were born for greatness, but like everything one aspires to, it must be reached one slow step at a time. Now, how can I help your suit with Miss Brodure?"

Ethan brightened. "We had mentioned the possibility of organizing a picnic in the folly along the Rocks of Solitude. Would ye be willing tae take that in hand, Leah?"

"Of course. Leave it with me. I will plan a lovely afternoon out." Leah sat back in her chair, nursing her wine glass. "We can invite the usual array of characters, as well as Dr. and Miss Brodure." She turned to Malcolm, motioning with her glass. "And you, brother. I should like tae see ye there, too."

Malcolm chewed his roast beef, already manufacturing ways to bow out of attending, no matter Leah's—

"Quit your plotting, Malcolm. I can practically hear ye thinking." She pointed a finger at him. "You'll be coming tae the folly picnic, too. Ye need tae get out in society more. I'll hear no arguing."

"Leah's right," Fox added quietly. "You should venture out into society more, Malcolm."

"Aye." Ethan added. "The picnic will be the perfect thing for ye."

Malcolm sighed and nearly threw down his napkin.

He *liked* his solitary, un-venturesome state.

"And between now and then, Ethan, you can further woo your Miss Brodure." Leah's face beamed with a smile.

Malcolm managed a strained smile of his own.

For his own sanity, his brother's wooing couldn't happen quickly enough.

7

E than Penn-Leith's social call left Viola feeling off-kilter.

Fortunately, her father was ecstatic enough for the both of them.

"Mark my words, my dear," he said over tea two days later. "This is just the beginning. Mr. Penn-Leith means to court you in earnest. Did I mention I received a letter from Kendall earlier today? He is very pleased that we have arrived safely, and I have already penned him an update about our—or rather, *your*—progress with Mr. Penn-Leith."

"Gracious, Papa." A blush scorched Viola's skin, surely turning her cheeks as red as the velvet fabric of her chair. "It is very much early days yet."

"Yes, I know, daughter, but I cannot help but think upon it! A marriage to Mr. Penn-Leith would cement your position among the greatest novelists of our age—"

"I thought my *writing* would do that, not my choice of husband," she countered, tone as dry as the Sahara.

"Of course, you are quite right, my dear." He laughed good-naturedly, reaching for a piece of shortbread. "But you like Mr. Penn-Leith, do you not?"

Viola shook off a sigh as she poured her own tea.

She *did* like Ethan.

Or, rather, she *wanted* to like him.

So why, as she stirred sugar into her cup, was she wondering if Malcolm Penn-Leith took time out of his busy day for tea?

She supposed it was because . . . well . . .

Malcolm appeared to have an intensity, a *gravitas*, that she had yet to see in Ethan. As if all those hours with his coos were spent pondering the breadth of the universe.

And yet, . . . she could not simply abandon Ethan after two lackluster encounters.

The very thought was absurd.

Particularly as her father's ambitions and Kendall's plans relied on her engaging Ethan Penn-Leith's interest.

Surely her lack of immediate connection with Ethan stemmed from the intense pressure surrounding their possible courtship. Viola merely needed to relax and form a true friendship with him.

To that end, she smiled at her father and took a sip of tea. "I *do* like Mr. Penn-Leith"—*both of them*—"I simply wish to allow our acquaintance to progress at its own pace."

But, of course, in that wish, Viola was utterly thwarted.

Just like Kendall, the townspeople of Fettermill pushed Viola and Ethan to make a match of it as quickly as possible.

In the days that followed, every social call Viola received, every call she returned, someone wished to discuss where she and Ethan were on the path to their own timeless literary romance.

Dr. Ruxton regaled Viola with stories of Ethan as a wee lad, how he used his glib tongue to talk Mrs. Ruxton out of shortbread, which given his wife's volubility, was no mean feat.

Mrs. Clark and Mrs. Buchan offered Viola a rather shocking amount of unsolicited advice on married life.

Lady Stewart invited Viola and Dr. Brodure to her garden party in two weeks' time, where she would ensure that Viola learned "everything needed to fix your heart upon Ethan Penn-Leith."

But, inexplicably, the more others pushed her toward Ethan, the more Viola thought of Malcolm.

How the quiet gruff of his laugh along that foggy lane had pooled in her stomach like warm honey.

How his wide shoulders appeared ready-built to heft a hay bale, carry a laughing child, or support a lover's head.

How, unlike Ethan and every other eligible man on the Isle of Great Britain, Malcolm eased her shyness and anxious stammer.

Unfortunately, all these thoughts of Malcolm were hampering her potential relationship with Ethan.

Simply put, they had become an *obstacle*.

The answer to her conundrum was rather clear—

Thirty minutes of dialogue along a misty lane ten days past had landed her in this mental quagmire.

Ergo, a second similar conversation would likely provide the clarity she sought.

After all, Viola shunned novelists who regularly employed miscommunication as a plot device. Any problem that could be solved through a five-minute conversation was hardly a novel-worthy conflict.

Why was she tolerating similar behavior in her actual life?

The simplest solution was to call upon Ethan and Malcolm.

But when Viola and her father *did* venture to Thistle Muir, Malcolm was nowhere to be seen.

"*Och*, Malcolm is never at home during the day," Ethan said over tea, shooting her his infamous smile. "The farm requires his full attention, particularly during the summer months."

Disappointment was a lead weight in Viola's chest.

Finally, in desperation, she realized she would need to orchestrate the meeting with Malcolm herself.

And so, she resorted to the best tool in a woman's arsenal—

The subterfuge of planned coincidence.

Ethan had mentioned that Malcolm kept several prize Highland cattle—Coolius Caesar among them—in a small glen on the edge of the

Thistle Muir farmlands. Most evenings, Malcolm checked on his cattle before returning home along a quiet country lane not too far from the Brodure's rented cottage.

So the evening after her visit to Thistle Muir, Viola crossed the meadow behind her cottage, stepped over a small stile, and made her way down the deserted lane.

Sadly, she did not know the precise time at which Malcolm would be coming *up* the lane, so she had crafted a stratagem straight from a hackneyed tale.

All she needed was a place to sit down.

Thankfully, midway down the road, she encountered a swing just a few steps off the path—a broad slab of glossy oak suspended from a sturdy birch by two thick ropes at each end. With its fine workmanship, the swing seemed almost incongruous hanging in such an unfrequented place.

But when she perched atop it, Viola realized she could see a distance down the lane in each direction—from the bend that led toward her cottage on her left to the tree-shrouded hollow that ran to Thistle Muir's fields on her right.

Perfect.

Bending down, she partially unlaced one of her half-boots.

The entire scenario made perfect sense.

Malcolm would come up the lane, and he would find her sitting on the swing in the process of retying her shoe, making it seem as if their meeting were entirely happenstance.

Heavens, the lengths she went through to speak with the Penn-Leith men.

First traveling to Scotland for Ethan, and now this.

Truthfully, if one of her heroines behaved so ridiculously, Viola feared her readership would rebel at the sheer idiocy.

And yet, *sheer idiocy* now appeared to be a theme in her life.

Fortunately, it was a lovely evening in early June, the sun lingering long in the sky.

Unfortunately, Malcolm was not quick to appear.

A half-hour passed.

Viola rocked slowly back and forth on the swing, and then began twisting one way and then the next, the two ropes crisscrossing above her head.

A pair of red squirrels darted up an oak on the opposite side of the lane, chittering at one another.

Another quarter-hour passed.

In the distance, cows lowed. A soft breeze rustled through the ferns to her left.

Finally, Viola slumped against one of the swing ropes. Her left leg had gone quite numb, and her head was rather dizzy from the spinning.

Was Malcolm not coming, then? Had he returned home along another path? Or was Ethan's knowledge of his brother's habits faulty?

Obviously, she could not remain here all night.

Viola arched her back, stretching her sore muscles.

That initial encounter with Malcolm had likely been an anomaly.

Finally, after another quarter-hour and no sign of Malcolm, Viola bent down to retie her shoe in truth.

He would not be coming. The entire idea had been a mistak—

Beowoof abruptly appeared, rising from the tree-shrouded dip in the lane, loping toward her at a good clip.

Viola sat up higher, watching as Malcolm's form slowly emerged from the same hollow.

Her heart panged in her chest.

Somehow, he appeared even taller than she remembered, broader in the chest, his ever-present great kilt wrapping across one shoulder and swishing as he walked.

And in that moment, she had an answer to her question—

Why did *this* particular man dominate her thoughts so?

Because he was simply . . . a *man*.

A *mature* man, burnished and tattered from life's heartbreaks but still striding forward.

In comparison, Ethan appeared a glass-house orchid. Lovely and exotic, to be sure, but temperamental, finicky, and perhaps a little too aware of its own beauty.

Malcolm was hardy heather, able to bloom and thrive in the harshest of conditions.

He stared at the ground, appearing lost in thought. But as if sensing her gaze, he raised his head.

That first lock of their eyes. The giddy butterflies winging through her chest.

Oh!

Faint lines radiated out from his eyes, and his dark hair ruffled in the slight breeze. His beard appeared particularly bushy, as if he had been running his hands through it, and that small fact endeared him to her.

Seeing Malcolm . . . it was like surfacing from underwater. Suddenly, for the first time in days, she could breathe again.

But with that breath came an almost overwhelming thrum of tingling awareness—her skin, her scalp, the palms of her hands.

During their encounter beside her broken-down gig, speaking with him had felt effortless.

Would that hold true given her present feelings?

MALCOLM NEARLY STUMBLED when he realized that Miss Brodure was sitting atop his swing, retying her boot. A lock of her pale hair had escaped her bonnet to tumble across her cheek, a ribbon of summer gold.

Beowoof had barked and run ahead, alerting Malcolm to someone's presence—someone the dog knew.

Viola Brodure had been the last person Malcolm expected. And yet, the air in his lungs felt abruptly lighter for seeing her twenty feet ahead of him.

Oof. He was an utter *eejit.*

The lady had traveled the length of Great Britain to make Ethan's acquaintance. The entire *village* was working behind the scenes to ensure that Ethan Penn-Leith and Viola Brodure plighted their troth before summer's end.

Ethan, himself, appeared well on his way to falling for the lady. Just that morning, his brother—still in a banyan and nursing a cup of tea— had declared that Miss Brodure's eyes were the color of bluebells under morning's first light.

And yet none of this had deterred Malcolm's pulse from hammering away at the sight of her elegant neck stretched long as she bent over her boot.

Ye've had your love. Ye will never remarry, he reminded himself. *She is meant for Ethan. Ye must cease gawking after his fine lady like a green lad.*

Miss Brodure finished tying her shoe and stood to greet him, a tentative smile on her lips. She tucked that errant lock of hair behind her ear—a delicate shell of an ear, Malcolm helplessly noted.

Honestly, he needed to haul himself into the courtyard behind Thistle Muir and pound some sense into his thick skull. Preferably with a wooden mallet.

"Miss Brodure." He bowed, which immediately felt too formal beside the swing under a birch.

"Mr. Penn-Leith." She nodded her head at him, biting her bottom lip before dropping her gaze to Beowoof.

The poor pup remembered only too well Miss Brodure's affection from the previous week. He waggled his tail and nudged at her skirts, whining.

Smile blooming, she sank down into the grass in front of the swing, scratching the dog behind his ears with her gloved hands.

"Your animal is utterly shameless, Mr. Penn-Leith." She gifted him with a wry look, her blue gaze scattering what remained of his wits.

Huh. Ethan had the right of it. Her eyes truly *were* the color of bluebells at first light.

How was Malcolm to rein in this infatuation? Miss Brodure had already monopolized an embarrassing amount of acreage in his brain.

Why just that morning, Malcolm had completely forgotten to post two letters and pick up a packet from the apothecary for Mrs. McGregor.

Instead, he had walked the breadth of his western fields, wondering if Miss Brodure thought about her novels as he thought about his harvests—endless months of work and planning all with the vague hope that something fruitful would arise from the effort.

"Beowoof is a bit of a flirt, I am afraid," he said. "Like most Scottish men, he likes the lasses."

Malcolm spoke without thinking, but given how quickly Miss

Brodure's eyebrows flew to her hairline, she read more into the words than he had intended.

Like most Scottish men, he likes the lasses.

Instead of saying flirtatiously in return—*Indeed, and do you like the lasses as well, Mr. Penn-Leith?*—Miss Brodure buried her face in Beowoof's fur as if embarrassed.

As if . . . *shy.*

That trait surfaced again.

Miss Brodure was truly *shy.*

Why had no one else in the village noticed this?

But asking the question, Malcolm knew the answer. Most were so overwhelmed to be in her presence—to actually speak with the lauded Miss Brodure—they neglected to see the woman ducking her head behind her words.

An aching sort of tenderness swelled in Malcolm's chest. Shyness, a reticence to speak, was something he understood well. There had been a time when his younger self had struggled to even form sentences when talking to a stranger, particularly a woman. His mouth would feel stuffed with cotton and buzzing would fill his ears.

But even then, Aileen had been at his side. Vibrant and outgoing, his wife had been his mouthpiece, before and after they wed. She had chitchatted with visitors and asked questions that his tongue was too knotted to form. Her easy friendliness was one of a thousand things he missed about her.

His old nervousness rarely surfaced now. Maturity had helped.

But the reticence to speak still remained. Malcolm wasn't like Ethan—delighting in being the center of his own world. He had no desire to dazzle with charm and make small talk for hours with patrons and admirers.

Malcolm had never bemoaned the lack of those skills in himself. He had never wanted them.

Until now.

Until her.

Would that he could summon light words to set Viola Brodure at ease.

"Beowoof appreciates your attention." Crouching beside her, Malcolm ran a hand over Beowoof's back. "And I appreciate that he doesnae appear tae irritate your senses."

Miss Brodure—Viola, in his heart—gave him a glance. Despite her momentary retreat, her breathing appeared calm, her color even.

"I never imagined that there would be a dog I could touch so readily. You said it was something in his breeding that prevents him from shedding?"

She didn't stammer around him, Malcolm noticed. No hesitancy or breathiness, as he had seen in the kirkyard.

"Aye. His story is a bit unusual, tae be honest. Beowoof was actually a gift for Ethan from Her Grace, the Duchess of Buccleuch."

This admission startled a laugh from Viola. "Ethan? And . . . a duchess?"

She stood and sat on the swing, gently rocking back and forth, eyes so expectant and bright and interested that Malcolm *wanted* to tell her more.

If Viola looked at his wee brother like this, no wonder Ethan did most of the talking when visiting her.

Malcolm rose to his feet and leaned a shoulder against the trunk of the birch, crossing his arms over his chest.

"Oh, aye. The duchess is quite enamored of our Ethan, she is. She wrote three or some odd years back, intent on gifting him one of the duke's prized Labrador Retrievers."

"A Labra . . . what?"

"A Labrador Retriever. 'Tis a new breed of dog His Grace has been developing for the past decade or so. We Scots are always casting about for dogs tae withstand the marshy hunting grounds of the Highlands. To that end, the duke brought over some water retrievers from Newfoundland and bred them with his favorite hunting dogs here tae create an entirely new breed."

"And Beowoof is one of those dogs?"

"Nae, actually, he's not." Malcolm smiled. "Ethan doesnae like dogs all that much—"

"He doesn't like dogs?" Viola paused her swinging to bend down and place her hands over Beowoof's ears, as if to prevent him from hearing the words. "How can anyone not like dogs? What's not to love about a dog?" She slid her hands down to Beowoof's jowls and touched her nose to his, her voice going husky and low. "How can anyone not love you, you adorable thing?"

Beowoof wagged his tail in joy, clearly thinking that Viola herself was the most adorable thing.

Malcolm could not agree more.

He swallowed, floundering over what to say next. Surely this fine lady did not relish talking about dog breeds.

"So how did you end up with Beowoof?" Viola asked, raising her head and grasping the swing ropes.

A breeze tangled in the curls framing her face, sticking one to her lips.

Viola tugged it free with a solitary gloved finger.

Malcolm stared as the curl slid away, dragging across her mouth before slipping across her soft-looking cheek.

He slowly blinked before *finally* remembering she had asked him a question.

"Like yourself," he replied, "Ethan told the duchess that he had a sensitivity tae dogs—even though he doesnae—thinking that would end the exchange. Not even a week later, Beowoof showed up on our doorstep in the arms of one of His Grace's grooms." Viola's expectant gaze encouraged Malcolm to continue talking. "Apparently, His Grace's prized Labrador Retriever had escaped his pen and enjoyed a—shall we say romantic?—encounter with Her Grace's favorite French poodle. Beowoof and his sibling puppies were the result. Surprisingly, the puppies retained some of the best qualities of both dogs—the loyalty and energy of a water retriever mixed with the tighter fur of a poodle, which reduces sensitivity."

And . . . Malcolm was now talking about canine husbandry with Miss Viola Brodure.

Yes, someone truly did need to haul him into the courtyard behind Thistle Muir and pound some sense into his thick skull.

Or, at the very least, a crash course in polite manners.

Burning heat climbed his cheeks.

Fortunately, Viola appeared not to notice.

Instead, she laughed in delight and reached past the swing rope to pat Beowoof's head. "How very clever of you, you darling dog." She looked back up at Malcolm, eyes glowing. "Let me guess how the rest played out. Ethan could not refuse the gift of a puppy at that point, obviously."

"Obviously." Malcolm couldn't quell the answering grin on his face.

"And you were, therefore, happy to claim Beowoof as your own."

Malcolm nodded.

Silence settled between them, but it was not an uncomfortable thing.

Finally, she spoke, voice quiet, "The truth . . . well . . . I experience a bit more than just nasal irritation with dogs." She waved a hand over her face. "I suffer from asthma, and animal dander can be a catalyst. It's why I have always fastidiously avoided dogs. I cannot describe how lovely it is to pet Beowoof."

Malcolm's chest tightened at the admission. "Has asthma always plagued ye?"

She sighed, slowly rotating the swing side to side. "Yes. We lived in London until I was about fifteen. Papa was a vicar in Mayfair and determined to curry the favor necessary to be elevated to a bishopric. He was well on his way when I suffered a severe asthma attack after inhaling coal smoke near Bond Street. Our doctor recommended we remove to the countryside immediately for my health. Papa didn't hesitate. He left his position in London, took a new post with the late Duke of Kendall in Wiltshire, and set aside his ambitions for the sake of my well-being."

"Dr. Brodure is a good father to ye," he said.

"The best. He sacrificed his every ambition for me."

"Any loving father would do so," Malcolm added and then mentally winced. *Och*, why had he said that? He had only intended to agree with her, not imply that her father's devotion was nothing extraordinary.

But Viola continued on, as if she understood the intent of his words. As if she understood . . . *him*.

"Yes. He has always been loyal to me. Thankfully, my asthma improved as I aged," she said. "I only rarely have severe fits now."

"And is it coal smoke and animal dander that triggers them?"

"Yes." She hesitated for a moment and then took a deeper breath, as if the next words were a confession. "Nervous worry—the sort brought on by having to interact with strangers—can also provoke an attack. Truth be told, it's lately been the primary trigger for me." Her lips twisted in a rueful smile.

Ah.

The admission illuminated an entire facet of her personality.

No wonder she had seemed so distressed during the church service on Sunday. The entire situation must have been a tightrope walk between speaking with people and attempting not to succumb to her asthma.

Pushing off of the birch tree, Malcolm placed a hand on one of the swing ropes, wishing there was some way he could quickly communicate that he valued the trust she placed in him. That he felt honored to be a confidant.

Something of his thoughts must have whispered through his movement because she continued, "When life or situations become too overwhelming, my body reacts by attempting to strangle me." She gave a cheerless smile. "'Tis why I normally avoid crowds and struggle to speak at times. My shy tongue ignites my nerves and then next thing I know, my throat has closed off and I'm struggling to breathe."

"And yet, here ye are, interacting with the good people of Fettermill and going out of your way tae make others feel at ease."

She looked away, a blush flooding her cheeks anew at the compliment.

Malcolm felt his own skin burn in response.

"Come, Miss Brodure." He extended his hand to her, wishing to help her off the swing. "Allow me tae escort ye tae the meadow behind your cottage. Ethan would never forgive me if some harm came to ye."

He *had* to say the words. To remind himself—and her, he supposed—that everyone viewed her as his brother's territory.

Given the way Viola's expression dimmed, she did not miss his implication.

Regardless, Viola placed her gloved hand in his, her slim fingers sliding over his gloveless ones. He was a farmer, after all. A gentrified one, but a farmer nonetheless. He had never bothered with gloves.

But now, the contrast spoke of everything that stood between them.

Her hand resting overtop his, fingers sheathed in elegantly-stitched kid leather, buttery soft. Beautiful. Protected.

His palm was like a rough-hewn oak, clean but nicked and worn in places. Rugged. Calloused.

She stared at their hands too, her breath hitching, as if the moment were significant . . .

Or perhaps she was simply appalled at his lack of decorum in offering her his bare hand.

He was no London dandy, no rarefied rake to charm and dance attendance.

Some flickering emotion he didn't understand flitted across her face.

And then . . . her fingers tightened around his. Not gently. Not shyly. A vise of a grip. Nearly a claiming of a sort.

The heat of her hand burned where it touched him, the light weight of her fingers scalding his blood. His stomach swooped and his heart soared, drumming helplessly in his chest.

He should never have assumed that Ethan had rights of refusal on this woman.

Viola Brodure would never be anything but her own independent self.

Malcolm responded in the only way he could—

He tightened his grip and pulled her to standing.

She wobbled slightly, and his free hand grasped her elbow, steadying her.

"Thank you," she whispered.

The husky timbre of her tone made her gratitude seem like more than mere words, more than his hand raising her up.

He felt as if she were thanking him for being . . . himself.

Which, as a thought, was quite absurd. Why should Viola Brodure be grateful for *him*, of all people? He was merely the brother of her intended. A widowed farmer who had twice detained her on a solitary road.

But at the moment, he only cared that he stood near her. So close he could see himself reflected in her eyes. How else was he to learn that all the glorious blue was edged in soft gold?

She possessed a touch of the angelic, it seemed. A ring of angel dust rimming her pupil.

Hah! Poetic that.

Ethan couldn't have that thought. Malcolm wanted it for himself.

If he wasn't careful, he would want this woman for himself, too.

And even Malcolm knew that path led to disaster—conflict with his brother and another deep fissure in his own heart.

Because Viola Brodure would never stoop so low as to consider the likes of him.

8

Staring up at Malcolm Penn-Leith holding her hand along the lane, Viola realized that her lungs ached.

And not from an incipient asthma attack.

No, her shortness of breath was entirely due to Malcolm's nearness. Being with him was . . . effortless.

She had experienced a brief moment of trepidation when he stopped before her on the lane. A flitting panic that he would see her machinations written in pen across her face.

But just as before, once words were spoken between them, all her self-consciousness vanished, like fog thinned away by daylight.

Speaking with him felt paradoxical. Like the warmth of a homecoming and the exhilaration of beginning a journey.

Attraction was such an odd phenomenon, she decided.

Malcolm—broad, dark, serious—set her heart to stampeding.

Whereas handsome and charming Ethan elicited nothing deeper than polite interest. Not once had she pondered what it might feel like to hold Ethan's hand.

But now, standing and holding Malcolm's, she could think of nothing else. The strength of his fingers pressed against hers. The leashed muscle tensing in his arms.

And then, the natural progression of female thought—how those same fingers would feel wrapped around her waist. Or pressed to the small of her back as he lifted her up to place a hungry kiss—

Viola blinked to stop the image right there, terrified that her salacious thoughts might tumble from her head to his feet like spillikins.

And why, in all her scheming to arrange this moment, had she not considered that she might find Malcolm *more* attractive?

Unfortunately, Viola realized she had been holding the man's hand—staring into his chocolate brown eyes while mentally rambling—for far longer than was polite.

He likely thought her the veriest nutter.

Let go of the delectable man, Viola ordered her fingers.

They did so . . . if only reluctantly.

"Thank you," she repeated, stepping back.

"'Tis my pleasure." He doffed his hat to her, his expression giving away nothing of his thoughts.

But then . . .

. . . he offered her his arm. As confidently as any fine gentleman.

Viola watched as if through another woman's eyes as her own gloved hand slid around his elbow, marveling at the flex of tendons underneath her fingertips.

Malcolm whistled to Beowoof to attend them. The dog loped out of the woods.

"Would you be so kind as to tell me about the life of a Scottish gentleman farmer?" she asked as they began to walk, her skirts brushing against his kilt. "I have only ever lived in England, and I wonder how very different things are here."

Beowoof trotted ahead of them before stopping to sniff at something beside the bend in the lane.

"Indeed? And how are ye finding *here* then? Is Scotland too wild for your tastes?"

"Quite the contrary. I am starting to believe that I never took a true breath of air until arriving in Fettermill."

"Is that right?"

"Oh, aye." She drawled the word just as he would.

He laughed. "We'll make a Scot of ye yet, Miss Brodure."

They rounded the bend, the tree-lined lane stretching before them. Beowoof barked at a squirrel.

"So tell me about your life, Mr. Penn-Leith," she repeated.

"I will happily, Miss Brodure." He shot her a look from the corner of his eyes. "But when your eyes glaze over as I discuss corn shares and planting schedules, I willnae apologize. Ye have been duly warned."

She laughed, surely too long and giddy.

And yet, she couldn't help herself.

Malcolm Penn-Leith's sly, self-deprecating wit caught her unawares in the most delightful ways.

He spent the rest of their walk up the lane describing his take on crop rotation, the reasoning behind the animals he bred, the endless worry of pests and weather.

And though the topics held the potential to turn mundane, when discussed with Malcolm Penn-Leith, Viola found them fascinating.

Thankfully, in all their conversation of potatoes, coos, and fickle rain, Malcolm neglected to ask the most obvious question:

What had brought her besotted self to the lane in the first place?

THE NEXT DAY, Malcolm tried to not think about Viola Brodure *every* passing second.

But as he helped his men repair a stone fence, consulted with Callum, his farm manager, on drainage in the east pasture, and prepared the barns for shearing, his brain harbored images of only one subject—Viola.

Viola, crooning to Beowoof, her eyes lit with joy.

Viola, tilting her head, face pensive as she asked after future plans for his cattle.

Viola, laughing as he told tale of Coolius Caesar breaking loose from his pen and rampaging through a line of fresh laundry.

Why Malcolm had prattled on about that particular memory, he winced to think upon. But, no . . . he *did* know why. He had simply wished to hear the timbre of her honeyed laugh.

Conversation with Viola was effortless. Easy in a way he hadn't experienced since . . .

Well, since Aileen.

But he and Aileen had been childhood sweethearts, and Malcolm had always assumed that the closeness between them—how they had practically raced to finish one another's sentences—was the product of years of shared history.

He had never thought it possible to experience the same thing with another woman, particularly so quickly.

And yet, here he was . . . experiencing it.

Before Viola's arrival, he would have described his existence as . . . well, not *content* exactly. Comfortable, perhaps?

Living in the crevasse of his grief was not precisely a happy existence, but it was, at the very least, familiar. Manageable. Predictable.

For example, he knew the places where he could relax and the ones to be studiously avoided.

Case in point, Malcolm always took the long way round from Fettermill to Thistle Muir, bypassing the bend in the River North Esk where the water swirled into a lazy pool.

The very place where Aileen had loved to dip her feet on a warm summer's day.

The same spot where he had first kissed her over a decade ago. That day, his hands had trembled as he reached for her waist—nerves vibrating his bones in their sockets—but then Aileen had smiled and, rising to her tiptoes, whispered 'Go on, then. I shallnae bite ye,' and his immediate mortifying thought as he lowered his mouth to hers had been, '*Och*, more's the pity.'

Years on, he had recounted that moment to her—late on a winter's evening, when they were curled around one another in their bed. Aileen had laughed until she wheezed, tears rolling down her cheeks. Chuckling, Malcolm claimed she had lied to him because she did, in fact, like to give his shoulder a wee nipping bite on occasion. Then Aileen had proven his point by rolling onto him and ensuring their winter bedroom was heated indeed.

So, yes . . . he avoided that bend in the river.

And the path behind the kirkyard.

And the oak swing along the lane . . . the same one where he had come upon Viola retying her boot. Obviously, he couldn't escape walking past it—the lane was the artery between Thistle Muir and his far-flung pastures—but he could avoid looking at the swing . . . the swing he had hung in anticipation of becoming a father, a place for his children to play as they grew.

Malcolm had carefully fashioned the seat, smoothing the rough oak with a handful of horsetail and rubbing the whole with linseed oil until it gleamed. Aileen had grinned when he showed it to her, a hand pressed to her swollen belly as she rose on tiptoe to kiss him soundly.

And yet, not one of those memories had surfaced when he saw Miss Brodure sitting on the swing yesterday evening.

His head had been full of only her . . . of Viola.

And somehow, that was the most awful part of all. The most unbearable.

That seeing the swing—and, even now, remembering moment after moment with Aileen—did not send heartache crashing over him.

Malcolm faced a difficult truth:

Living in the abyss of his grief was no longer comfortable.

Since Viola's arrival, his chasm home had begun to feel somewhat . . . confining. The walls loomed too high and narrow, the space too dim. He would study that sliver of sunlight far above and wonder . . .

What would the world look like from up there? And did he care enough to pull himself out of his crevasse to see?

He pondered this as he headed toward Thistle Muir after his habitual evening survey of his prize coos. Beowoof snuffled through the grass lining the lane, the sun slowly turning to amber treacle as it descended toward the horizon.

Just as it had yesterday.

In fact, every moment furled out as it had the previous evening when he had stumbled upon Viola Brodure swaying on his oak swing.

Of course, she would not be waiting for him again today. The very idea was absurd.

And yet, his stupid heart still hoped, leaping at the possibility.

No wonder poets wrote ridiculous words when in the throes of infatuation.

The emotion was as irrational as it was uncontrollable. It was an eager puppy of a feeling—ecstatic and lunging at the leash and Malcolm helpless to know how to tame it.

Puppy love, indeed.

So when Beowoof barked and set off down the road, Malcolm had to forcibly stop himself from chasing after.

Was she there? Had she come?

He willed his feet to walk at a normal pace, ignoring the *whoosh-whoosh* of blood through his veins.

He came up the low rise . . .

And indeed . . . there she was, sitting on his swing and rubbing Beowoof's chops.

An errant ray of sunlight broke through the trees, rimming her head in golden light—as if some mischievous angel needed to add a *hosanna* to the jubilation chorusing in Malcolm's chest.

And yet . . . even the melodramatic sentimentality of his thoughts did nothing to dim his joy.

She *had* come.

By coincidence again?

Perhaps.

"Miss Brodure." He nodded his head, halting before her.

"Mr. Penn-Leith." She stood and dipped a small curtsy, the low timbre of her voice curling around him.

"What brings ye past my swing on this fine day?"

If Viola found the question intrusive, it didn't show.

"I missed seeing my favorite dog," she said, patting Beowoof's head.

"Truly? I would have thought my discourse on the differences between Highland and Angus cattle yesterday would have put ye off both Beowoof and his owner."

"Nonsense. I find cattle endlessly fascinating." Viola's answering grin did alarming things to Malcolm's breathing.

"Now I know ye be bamming me. *No one* finds coos fascinating."

"Are you quite sure?" She squinted up at him, mirth dancing in her eyes. "You were rather emphatic on the topic yesterday. I think you are a bit of a coo evangelist, Mr. Penn-Leith."

"Nae, coos dinnae comprise their own gospel. They're merely useful."

"Mmmm." She tapped a gloved finger to her chin. "I must disagree. Your sermon on them had the feel of a tent revival meeting. I'm fairly certain I heard *hallelujahs*. In truth, I was rather converted to coos after our discussion."

Malcolm couldn't control his startled guffaw of a laugh. The sound felt rusty, like shears left too long in the rain.

He hadn't laughed in a lifetime.

Laughter belonged to his younger self, the one who had loved Aileen. Since her death, there had been too little humor in his life.

And yet, even after only a few interactions, Viola lightened his heart in ways he could scarcely articulate.

In ways he was *afraid* to articulate.

He had never anticipated meeting a woman like this. Someone he not only liked but also admired with a bright intensity. Someone who challenged his wits and offered up intelligent, effortless conversation.

But why had Viola been waiting on the swing today? Despite her teasing, Malcolm doubted she had an overwhelming interest in cow husbandry.

Perhaps she sought him out because, unlike the rest of his neighbors, he placed no expectations on her. That with him, she could just be . . . Viola.

Or . . . did her interest in him possibly go beyond that?

"Come," he motioned, still smiling. "Allow me tae escort ye home."

"Thank you."

"Dinnae thank me quite yet, lass. I have stipulations."

"Stipulations?"

"Aye." He crossed his arms over his chest. "I dinnae wish to speak of cows."

After his monologuing over Coolius Caesar, Malcolm felt compelled to redeem himself. Or, at the very least, find a topic of conversation that wasn't quite so embarrassingly banal.

"No cows? Are you quite sure?" *But they are your favorite topic,* her expression said.

He chuckled again. "No coos. And nary a word about feed or beef or market prices. Chickens, pigs, sheep, and other barnyard animals are also prohibited topics of conversation."

Viola affected a put-upon sigh. "I suppose goats, ducks, and swans are also forbidden?"

"Ye suppose correctly. Might as well throw in all crops, as well. Barley and oats and such."

"Even potatoes?"

"*Particularly* potatoes. A wretched business . . . potatoes."

That piqued her curiosity. "Truly?" She tilted her head at him. "Why are potatoes wretched?"

"Have ye not heard? They say there is a blight affecting them in Ireland at the moment, though it hasnae reached this part of Scotland as of yet—"

"How dreadful!"

"Aye, it is. I cannae think what we'll do if—" He stopped midsentence, wagging his finger. "Hah! I see what you're doing there, lass. I willnae be distracted into discussing tubers."

"You misunderstand, sir. I am sincerely interested—"

"Nae. I'll have none of it. I will not be accused of turning farm life into a religious experience again. 'Tis nearly blasphemous tae contemplate."

She laughed as he intended. The merry sound bounced off the surrounding trees and set Beowoof to barking in happiness.

"I wish tae know more about your writing," he continued.

As he had yesterday, he offered her his arm.

"Sincerely?" Like yesterday, her small fingers slid around his elbow. "I fear I shall bore you."

"Nonsense." *Impossible,* he wanted to add.

They began to stroll down the lane. Beowoof bounded ahead of them, darting through the ferns lining the road.

"What would you like to know about my writing?" she asked.

Mmmm, what *did* he wish to know? "How do ye create a vivid, memorable character?"

"That is an interesting question." She tilted her head, pondering. "So what would be my process were I to create someone like, say, yourself as a character?"

"Me?" Malcolm asked, surprised.

"Yes. You." She darted a look his way. "In order to do that, I would first need to think of a sentence that describes your defining characteristic."

Malcolm wanted to tell her nevermind, that he was hardly a worthy topic. But he was abruptly desperate to know—how *did* she see him with her writerly eyes?

"So what would it be, that sentence?" he asked.

Viola paused in the road, pulling back slightly and making a great show of raking him from head to toe. Everywhere her eyes touched tingled—ears, lips, sternum . . . even his kneecaps, for pity's sake.

He had never been so grateful to have a bushy beard that hid his surely formidable blush.

A smile tugged at her mouth. "I fear I am gravely tempted to say something about coos."

"*Och*, nae. That topic is forbidden, remember?"

Her smile drifted into something softer, more seeing. "Then I think I would describe a man with the gift to find light in even the darkest of circumstances."

His breath caught at her words.

That was how she saw him?

And how bitterly ironic, as he chose to dwell in those shadows.

The silence stretched between them.

"I would have said *purpose*, myself," Malcolm finally said. Was his voice a wee bit hoarse? "A man who can find purpose, even when all reason has been lost."

She nodded. "That would work, too."

How achingly lovely she appeared in that moment, pert chin tilted upward, intelligence thrumming in her gaze.

"And then what would ye do?" he asked. "Tae turn that recognized desire into a character?"

"That is quite a lengthy discussion, I fear."

He waved them forward along the lane again. "Then we shall walk slowly."

Malcolm listened as they strolled along, adoring the featherlight weight of her hand in his elbow, the rustle of her skirts against his calves.

Yes, indeed, Viola Brodure was a light beckoning from overhead, tempting him to climb upward and behold the brilliant luminosity of a world outside his grief.

Religious experience, indeed.

Aileen would not want him to stay in his shadowed chasm, hidden away, his existence narrowed to this wee space of living. She would berate him and insist he leave his abyss once and for all.

He knew this.

And yet . . . even if his crevasse was no longer entirely comfortable, it was *safe*.

After all, what further depths could loom ahead for him? In losing Aileen and their child, Malcolm had suffered the worst catastrophe. He already dwelled at the bottom.

It was only if he climbed out, if he reached for that sun-drenched world, that he risked falling again.

And he simply didn't have the courage to face that possibility.

VIOLA STARED DOWN at the letter she had just received, her heart hammering so hard, she feared the entire household could hear it.

She darted a glance across the parlor to her father, blissfully reading before the fire. Morning light streamed through the bow window at her back, rimming his gray head and gleaming off the pages of his book.

Without a doubt, Viola was the worst of daughters.

First, her secret infatuation with Malcolm Penn-Leith.

And now . . . this.

Seated at a desk to the right of the window, she closed her eyes for a brief moment and plead for divine forgiveness. Opening them, she looked down at the letter that had come in the bundle of correspondence from her solicitor in London.

. . . the power of your story, Mr. Twist, cannot be denied. Our jour-
nal has received copious correspondence regarding A Hard Truth.
I have taken the opportunity to transcribe some of our reader's com-
ments for your perusal . . .

Viola had already scanned the enclosed snippets. Some praised her writing, her insight, her courage in speaking out. Others, in shaky unschooled penmanship, told of living through years of similar hardship. Like her characters, these readers had been forced to make unspeakable choices in order to survive. Each one thanked her for addressing such urgent issues.

The editor continued:

Our readers are clamoring for more tales like A Hard Truth, *Mr. Twist. I recognize that you write these stories under a pseudonym and wish to hide your identity, and therefore, might be loathe to continue writing for us. But we must advocate for change, to improve the lives of our fellowmen. Please consider submitting further items for our consideration.*

Swallowing, Viola looked out the window to the front garden of the cottage and shifted in her chair.

What was she to do?

She had known that writing *A Hard Truth* could not be kept a secret forever. That there would be difficult decisions in her future because of it.

And yet, the guilt of betraying her father's trust hadn't stopped her from writing the story either.

After the events in Manchester last summer, Viola *had* to do something to bring attention to the plight of women like Martha. Yes, she had promised her father to wait, but the old Duke of Kendall was not budging on seeing Dr. Brodure appointed to bishop. It could be *years* before anything changed.

God had gifted her with an outsized voice, Viola had reasoned. It felt nearly sinful not to use that talent to affect real change *righthisinstant*.

A Hard Truth had effortlessly spooled from her pen.

Thankfully, not even the editor of *The Rabble Rouser* had realized that 'Oliver Aubord Twist' was actually Viola Brodure.

But after seeing *A Hard Truth* through to print, she had stopped pursuing such stories. The remorse of keeping the secret from her father was simply too heavy. And then the old duke had died, giving Viola hope that her father would *finally* realize his professional goals and free her to write as she wished.

She could wait a little while longer to continue her fight. She could be patient.

The problem, of course, was that the new Kendall wanted her to write something that would be the exact opposite of *A Hard Truth*.

She had struggled for months to come up with a plotline that would meet with the duke's approval. When she pondered the story he requested, her mind devolved into a vast, barren sea with no ideas in sight, the kingdom of her inspiration utterly vanished.

But now, faced with *The Rabble Rouser* editor's request, idea after idea raced through her head, a vivid landscape of scenes, dialogue, and plot all aimed at condemning the current Poor Laws and advocating for change.

If she wrote any of these stories—if she put them forth for publication—it would be one more betrayal to her father.

If he found out, he would be devastated.

If Kendall found out, she and her father could both be ruined—cast out of their home and her father left without employment.

She pressed a shaking hand to her forehead and licked her dry lips.

Yet, it felt nearly sinful not to use that gift to do what she could to better the lives of millions.

Unfortunately, this was the logic that had led her to submit *A Hard Truth* for publication in the first place.

What a dreadful mess she had made of things.

"You seem contemplative, daughter," her father said from his seat by the hearth. "Is all well?"

Viola startled, nearly dropping her letter to the floor.

She shot her father a reassuring smile. "All is well, Papa. Just a mound of correspondence to address."

"Would you like some assistance? I know His Grace is keen to see a draft of the short story you have promised him. We must ensure you have adequate time to write."

Occasionally, when the letters from Viola's admirers became too much, she would solicit her father's help in penning replies. That, of course, was the last thing this current situation needed.

"You are too kind, Papa, but it is not too much at the moment."

"Well, please let me know if that changes."

Her father beamed at her and went back to reading his book.

His hair had receded another inch this year, Viola noted, slowly transforming from gray to white. One of a thousand reminders that her father would not always be with her.

Yes, she truly was the most traitorous of daughters.

She *had* to tell the editor of *The Rabble Rouser* that she would not be submitting further work at this time.

One story could go unnoticed. However, if Mr. Oliver Aubord Twist continued to write, he would gain notoriety. The anagram of her name was not so well hidden. Someone of import would make the connection eventually.

Viola Brodure would be exposed.

And that fact would wound her father more than she could bear.

No matter her personal goals to live no longer adjacent—no matter the greater good she might do—Viola could not devastate the very person she loved most.

She picked up her quill and began to pen a polite refusal to the editor.

M alcolm did his best pondering among the tombstones in the kirkyard.

After all, the inhabitants were utterly silent and not bothered by the clamor of his thoughts.

Today, his feet took him unerringly through the graveyard's soft grass, weaving in and out of markers to the wee corner behind the church.

The one place that Malcolm both loved and hated in equal measure.

He stared down at the tombstone.

Sacred to the memory of
Aileen Penn-Leith
Beloved wife of Malcolm Penn-Leith
Buried here with their stillborn son
July 19, 1839

Nearly five years since the day his reality had been forever altered.

He liked to come here. To be with Aileen and, in a way, exist with her in the confines of his grief-carved crevasse.

Sitting down on the sun-warmed grass beside her grave, he stretched out his legs, tilting his face toward the sky.

And yet, the moment didn't soothe as it once had.

Even before Viola Brodure's arrival, Malcolm had found himself going whole days, perhaps even a week, without thinking about his wife, without the horror of her loss cutting him down at the knees.

It was awful, that Aileen had somehow . . . faded.

As if her death had happened a lifetime ago to another person.

And in a sense, Malcolm supposed it had.

Just the thought swamped him with a wave of fresh sorrow.

Ah, Aileen, he thought. *How have we come tae this, my love?*

And yet . . . they had.

Because no matter how hard he resisted, his thoughts repeatedly drifted to another woman.

Four evenings now, Viola Brodure had been waiting for him at the swing. Four evenings of sparring wits and discussing increasingly philosophical ideas.

Their conversations along the lane refused to let him be.

The quickness of her mind, leaping from idea to insight. The laughter in her eyes as she teased him. The gentle kindness radiating from her person.

He had never expected to be in this situation—sitting with one woman while contemplating another.

"She is utterly different from yourself, Aileen." He glanced at the grave beside him. "She is just a wee sprite of a woman. She spins tales out of fairy dust and sends her words into the world. And then she turns around and teases me in one breath before arguing philosophy with the next. Can ye imagine it?"

Malcolm could practically hear Aileen chuckling over his conundrum.

Aileen, for all that Malcolm adored her, had never enjoyed discussing intellectual topics. She had always attentively listened to him *blether* on about Dr. Adam Smith's take on the accumulation of capital or Kant's theories of *a priori* knowledge. But she didn't engage with his opinions. She was a miller's daughter, after all, and wasn't given to reading, preferring instead to focus on more practical matters.

Because of this, no matter how close they became, there had always remained a wee hiccup between Malcolm's intellectualism and Aileen's pragmatism.

"Miss Brodure has fair bewitched me," he continued, "which is unfortunate, as she is intended for Ethan."

Viola might ask polite questions about Malcolm's life as a gentleman farmer and discuss esoteric philosophy with him, but it did not follow that she thought of him as anything more than the elder Penn-Leith brother.

She had traveled to Fettermill for Ethan, after all.

And just as Malcolm had anticipated, Ethan was utterly taken with Viola Brodure. He had already cornered Malcolm twice that morning, wanting images he could use to describe devotion. Usually, Malcolm was content to offer Ethan what insight he could. Ethan didn't get all his ideas from Malcolm, after all. His brother was a brilliant thinker in his own right.

Yet in the matter of Viola Brodure, Malcolm was less than helpful.

It was one thing to watch Ethan woo Viola.

It was something else entirely for his brother to expect Malcolm to actively participate in said wooing.

Ethan could damn well court his own lady love.

"Ye always said I had a thick head, Aileen," he said with a sad smile. "So, aye, this whole situation is a bit of a laugh. I *want* Viola tae marry Ethan. They would be good together."

But the idea also rendered Malcolm a wee bitty nauseous.

The snick of the church door had him looking to his left.

Viola strolled around the corner of the parish kirk, as if he had somehow summoned her.

Fairy dust, indeed.

Like him, she had removed her bonnet.

Unlike himself, she had yet to see him.

She paused and turned her face to the June sunshine.

Malcolm drank his fill, disliking how his heart ballooned at the sight of her pert, upturned nose. Her pale hair shimmered in the noon sun, adding to the sense that she was part fey. Her rose-colored pelisse cinched in her tiny waist above the volume of her skirts and matched the ribbons dangling from the bonnet in her right hand. How could a woman be so small and yet so perfectly formed?

Viola lowered her face, her eyes swinging to his. If his presence startled her, she covered it well. Instead, she raised a hand in greeting.

Malcolm pushed his way to standing, watching as she threaded her way through grave markers to reach his side.

"Miss Brodure." He bowed, hands clasped behind his back.

"Mr. Penn-Leith," she returned, bobbing a wee curtsy. "How lovely to see you. My father is in an earnest *tête-à-tête* with Dr. Ruxton, and as much as I enjoy discussing Aristotelian logic in the Pauline epistles, the day seemed too fair to remain inside. What brings you here on such—"

She broke off abruptly, her eyes dipping to the tombstone beside his right knee.

"Oh." Her soft exhalation captured a myriad of emotions—realization of what he had lost, empathy for his grief.

Malcolm watched it all flicker across her face as she read the engraved lines.

Her eyes raised to his, tinged with understanding.

"Would you like me to leave you in peace?" Her quiet consideration erased his good sense.

"Nae," he said, voice perhaps gruffer than he intended.

They stood, staring at one another, listening to the breeze that rustled the birch trees and tugged at Viola's skirt.

He couldn't pretend like being here with Aileen was of no import.

Her gaze said she understood this.

Finally, she looked away, chest rising and falling on a deep breath.

"I cannot imagine what it would be like to lose a child and my spouse in one dreadful day," she said.

"I hope ye never do," he replied. "'Tis a hellscape I wouldnae wish upon my most spiteful enemy. It's the sort of pain ye never recover from, I ken."

Aileen's screams of agony still haunted his dreams. Or worse, the unearthly silence that had followed. When Malcolm had clutched her still body to his chest and howled his pain into her hair.

No. Those memories had no place in this sun-drenched place.

He studied Viola, memorizing the creamy skin of her cheekbones, the ethereal brightness of her pale hair.

"Would you . . ." She paused on a swallow, returning her eyes to his. "Would you tell me about her? About your wife? I would like to hear."

The kind compassion in Viola's expression battered his chest.

But her kindness also, perversely . . . *irked* him.

A rather immature sliver of his heart wanted Viola to dislike hearing him speak of another woman.

Did she see him in a fraternal light? As merely Ethan's older brother and nothing more?

And why was he chafing against that very idea? It wasn't as if Viola Brodure would ever see him as *more* than that. Even if Malcolm wished it.

Which, he reminded himself for easily the thousandth time, he emphatically did not.

"What can I say about my Aileen?" he began, shifting his weight from one foot to the other. "She was nearly the opposite of yourself. A miller's daughter with very little education beyond basic reading and writing. We were friends as children and that friendship developed into a deep love as we grew older. I never even glanced at another woman. My Uncle Leith in Aberdeen—the one who fostered Ethan from an early age—was nearly apoplectic when I married her. It was already bad enough that my father was a mere gentleman farmer, but for me to sink even lower and marry a woman whose father was a common laborer . . . well . . ."

Malcolm didn't know why he said the words as he did. Maybe to remind himself how ridiculous his infatuation with Viola Brodure truly was, how utterly unequal they were in social class. Her uncle was Viscount Mossley, for heaven's sake.

If Viola sensed any of Malcolm's self-doubts, her expression did not show it.

"She must have been remarkable, to so capture your heart," she said.

Silence for the space of three heartbeats.

"Aye." Malcolm cleared his throat, but words stacked up on his tongue, demanding an outlet. "Aileen *was* truly remarkable. Clever, despite her lack of book learning. Quick tae laugh. Even quicker to defend a friend or solve a problem. She was brave and strong and I loved her with everything I had. Her loss is a heaviness that never ends."

He looked away, swallowing against the hard knot of *grieflongingsadness* lodged in his chest.

A pair of robins quarreled in the tree above his head, their bickering echoing through the kirkyard.

Viola regarded him with those bluebell eyes of hers. As if seeing *into* him.

"Ethan wrote a poem about that once, did he not? About grief?" she asked.

Malcolm nodded, as he didn't quite trust his voice at the moment. Ethan's words were blazoned on his soul.

> I bear with me always a weight.
> It rests, a heavy knot of stone
> Upon my neck, sinking down straight
> Into the memory of you now gone.

"*I bear with me always a weight*," she whispered, repeating the first line. "That poem was about you."

He nodded again.

Ethan, for all his endless cheerfulness and unflappable eagerness, could be deeply empathetic and profound. His words had acted like honey on a burned finger, soothing the wound of Aileen's loss.

Viola glanced again at the tombstone. "I recognize the futility of what I'm about to say—that it is too little far too late—but I am truly sorry for your loss. For the painful weight of it."

"As am I," he managed to say.

And those spare words, a concession to the ache inside him, breached any remaining hesitance to speak. He felt words rushing upward, spilling out, compelling him to confess the most painful irony of all.

The one that he scarcely admitted to himself, much less anyone else. Until now.

"Loss is a terrible thing . . . *grief* is a terrible thing." He looked up at the puffs of clouds chasing one another across the blue sky. "Not only does it hurt more than ye think ye can bear. But . . . it changes ye beyond recognition."

He blinked, hating the moisture gathering in his eyes but helpless to stem it.

Viola took a tentative step closer to him. As if wishing to lend him the support of her person.

"How so?" she asked.

"Because—" His voice broke.

Malcolm paused, releasing the air in his lungs, breathing through the pain of speaking aloud words he never imagined saying.

"Because," he repeated. "I am no longer the Malcolm who loved Aileen."

Viola studied him, bonnet dangling from its ribbons between her clasped hands, her beautiful face brimming with compassion.

"What do you mean?" she asked. "That you are no longer the Malcolm who loved Aileen?"

How remarkable that he had garnered the attention of this extraordinary woman. He felt compelled to share his deepest thoughts with her, as if she alone could untangle them.

"Just that," he said. "The pain of losing Aileen as I did . . . the relentless grief . . . it changed me. Imagine it like a flood. How at first, the water simply surges in, obliterating everything in its path. But as the floodwaters recede, ye see that the land is forever altered. New channels have been carved where none existed, new formations revealed."

"And that is what happened to you?"

"Aye. It is the most bitter irony of all. Aileen died and, in a sense, the Malcolm she loved died with her. The anguish of losing her has shaped me into a different man."

"*Oh.*" Viola appeared to be blinking back tears.

"'Tis the final injustice of her death. That if Aileen and I were tae meet now, I cannae say that we would be taken with one another. She would see me as too stern, too serious. And she would be correct. The man who loved her was less careworn, less philosophical. A more optimistic, buoyant human being."

Malcolm dashed a wrist across his eyes, attempting to banish the wetness there.

"As for myself," he continued, "I would probably see her as not serious enough . . . too eager to take risks, too carefree for the man I've become." He dragged a shaking hand over his beard. "I hate that grief and loss have forced me, in a sense, tae outgrow her. That we lost the chance to age together. It's the final, awful blow."

Viola pressed a gloved hand to her waist.

Malcolm disliked that even in this moment, a flame of heat licked his veins as he envisioned stepping forward, wrapping his hand around that wee waist, and tugging her against him.

It was insufferable. To be standing beside Aileen's grave and wanting another woman.

A woman who was not even destined for himself, but for his brother.

Yet . . . the pull of her was unrelenting, a ceaseless ache.

"I have never been in love," she said, voice low and tender, "so perhaps I should not offer words beyond a simple, 'You have my deepest compassion,' and yet . . ."

She hesitated.

He felt desperate for her words.

"And yet?" he prompted.

"And yet, I wonder if love is not the greatest act of exploration, both of another and yourself. That in loving someone else, you uncover pieces of your own soul that you never understood existed."

Malcolm found himself nodding. "Ye love another for the bits of ye they unearth. For the person they help ye become."

"Yes. Exactly. The pain of Aileen dying forced you to uncover new elements of your soul without her. But those elements no longer have a home, a loving hand in which to entrust them. So they tumble free, cutting and hurting in their loosened state. And grief begins anew."

He smiled faintly at that.

"Have ye considered becoming a writer?" he asked. "Ye have a brilliant way with words, Miss Brodure."

She laughed just as he had intended she would, the sound rueful and tinged with melancholy.

It felt unconscionable, that he could live his life without the daily sunshine of Viola Brodure's presence.

She turned his blood effervescent.

Without conscious thought, he stepped toward her.

As if every one of those jagged, unmoored pieces of him called out for her, and he helpless against the tumult.

"Miss Brodure—" he began.

"Viola, love, there you are!" Dr. Brodure's voice carried over the kirkyard.

She turned away from Malcolm at the sound, raising a hand against the sun and squinting at her father.

Dr. Brodure and Dr. Ruxton crossed the churchyard to where Malcolm and Viola stood, nodding greetings to them.

"Delightful news, daughter," Dr. Brodure beamed. He had left the parsonage without his hat and his gray hair stood at attention around his ears. "I just received a letter from Kendall. He declares that the Duke of Westhampton speaks highly of Fettermill."

"Kendall? Fettermill?" Viola paused and then asked, "Whyever would the Duke of Westhampton know this area?"

"That's just it." Dr. Brodure's eyes gleamed with excitement. "Captain Fox Carnegie is related to Westhampton through marriage, so His Grace has visited here in the past. And now, Kendall says he must see the area for himself. His Grace has decided to holiday in Fettermill this summer and has already made arrangements to let Fettermill Castle. Is that not delightful?"

Malcolm suppressed a grimace. Kendall certainly seemed the meddling sort. First, he wrote Ethan, all but ordering him to court Viola. Now, the man was coming to visit in person?

Fettermill did not need more imposing dukes. The Duke of Westhampton, whom Malcolm had met, was more than enough.

Unfortunately, Viola had her back to Malcolm, so he couldn't see her expression to determine how she felt about this turn of events. But her voice was genial and cheerful.

"That is, indeed, delightful news, Papa. His Grace will be most welcome."

"'Tis a pity that Lady Stewart's luncheon garden party is nearly upon us," Dr. Ruxton added with a wry grin. "Her ladyship will be crestfallen that she didn't hold out for Kendall's arrival."

Malcolm excused himself from the small group, not wishing to listen to more of Dr. Brodure's raptures over Kendall. Or to ponder the duke's possible motives for coaxing a courtship between Viola and Ethan.

How was Malcolm to suffer through it?

Because one awful, terrible thought coalesced as he walked down the road toward Thistle Muir.

Despite the differences in their upbringing and social stations—

Despite the loyalty and love he felt for Ethan—

Despite his own belief that he would never remarry, never fall in love again—

Malcolm Penn-Leith wished to pursue Viola Brodure for himself.

10

The next morning, Viola sat at her desk in the front parlor, staring at the purple foxglove and cheery daisies blooming in the front garden.

Ostensibly, she was writing a short story for Kendall.

But in actuality, she was trying to understand how every word she exchanged with Malcolm Penn-Leith expanded in her mind like a balloon, engulfing all other thoughts.

Did Sir Isaac Newton have a law that explained such a phenomenon? Or was the problem less a law of physics and more a neurosis?

Regardless, seeing the anguished twist of Malcolm's mouth as he candidly discussed the depth of his grief, the harsh reality of it . . .

It had been humbling. Overwhelming.

She had wanted to gather him into her arms and soothe his pain. To somehow take his burdens upon her own small shoulders.

An absurd thought, given that he was easily three times her size and could speak to a stranger without devolving into a stammering, asthmatic shambles of a person. He clearly did not need a mere wisp of a woman to hold him.

And yet, the impulse had remained.

Worse—or was it better?—she longed to answer his confidences with her own. To lay her conundrum with *A Hard Truth* at his feet and together work toward a solution. If one was to be had.

She frowned and looked down at the starkly blank page before her. Kendall's expectations weighed heavily, particularly as the duke was supposedly wending his way north at this very moment.

Ethan, the wee brother, had become more and more forward in his attentions. He visited nearly daily, ensconcing himself on the velvet sofa at Viola's back and talking endlessly.

Viola found Ethan . . . perplexing.

On the one hand, he was a skilled conversationalist. He could monologue for hours on just about any topic. The unkind part of her wanted to ask him something absurd—*Tell me, Mr. Penn-Leith, what do you think about the mating habits of the Southern Andian finch?*—just to see what he would say.

On the other hand, as a shy person, she preferred listening to talking anyway, and so she couldn't say, in all truthfulness, that she disliked Ethan's visits.

Moreover when she did speak, their conversations veered toward writing—the difficulties inherent with publishers, adoring (and not-so-adoring) readers, and so on. And *that*, a friendship between like-minded writers, she enjoyed immensely.

Ethan had sent over a poem two days past. Viola touched the foolscap where it rested beside her blank notebook page. The poem was clever, written in Ethan's bold handwriting, the words comparing friendship to exploring a foreign land:

> Carry onward, bold soul, to that heart-land
> Of ready marvel and mystery,
> Where gorse lies waiting to understand
> Why you lay no flag of victory.

Ethan Penn-Leith may not set her blood to singing, but he knew his way around poetry. Yet when she asked him how he conceived his touching metaphors, Ethan had chuckled and made a joke about communing with the Goddess of Inspiration and listening to her dedicated Muse.

Viola had laughed, assuming it to be a jest, but the whole did leave her somewhat puzzled.

In her experience, writing was more hard work than meditation and lightning bolts of genius. Perhaps this was why Ethan had been struggling to write his next book of poetry. He was waiting for divine intervention to bestow the words upon him.

Malcolm certainly didn't need any heavenly assistance. He spoke of life and death as though the subjects were always with him, ready to be lifted out and examined.

Regardless, one thing she did know—

She absolutely did not wish to marry Ethan Penn-Leith.

There.

She had admitted it to herself.

Ethan Penn-Leith, she had realized, was rather like a Claude glass.

About five years past, she and her father had taken a small trip to Weymouth to celebrate the publication of her second novel. They had walked the seashore and driven their gig up the coast to Abbotsbury to see the ruins of the ancient abbey there. Viola brought her mother's Claude glass along—a black convex mirror set in a mother-of-pearl case. The Claude mirror cleverly reduced an entire landscape into one image—flattening contrast, enhancing color, and rendering the whole more beautiful than it looked to the eye. It was a favorite tool among artists and travelers alike.

Viola had spent the trip with her back to sights, preferring instead to view them reflected in the Claude glass.

Ethan Penn-Leith was similar, in a sense.

Viola liked the idea of him, the reflection of what she thought him to be. But when faced directly with Ethan, the view just wasn't the same.

He simply felt like so much surface.

And, consequently, her heart held nothing beyond a sisterly, writerly sort of affection for him.

She suspected that Ethan probably *did* hold unplumbed depths— wells of sagacity that he himself had yet to unearth.

But for her part, she simply had no desire to go foraging further.

Unfortunately, this knowledge left her in a bit of a muddle.

She had traveled to Scotland to meet Ethan.

Her father, the Duke of Kendall, and an entourage of aristocrats had plotted it.

The entire village of Fettermill was practically pushing them through the church doors to be pronounced man and wife before the vicar—

Scratch that—

If the *London Tattler* was to be believed, the whole of Queen and country wished Viola and Ethan to marry.

Perhaps even Ethan himself anticipated they would wed.

And now Kendall was coming in person to ensure their courtship met its proclaimed end.

Her lungs hitched painfully as she contemplated all the eyes, literal and figurative, turned expectantly her way.

Oh, heavens.

She rested her forehead on her hands, massaging her temples.

How could she extricate herself at this point?

Until Ethan said or did something to indicate he wished for a more formal courtship—like ask her father for permission to pay his attentions to her, for example—it wasn't as if Viola could preemptively tell him, *Oh, by the way, I don't wish to marry you.*

Such words would be the height of presumption.

For a shy, cautious, God-fearing woman, she had somehow managed to create an unholy tangle of her life.

Of course, none of this stopped thoughts of Malcolm from pinging through her poor muddled brain.

Any formal courtship between them was impossible with so many eyes fixed upon herself and Ethan.

And yet, she longed for it.

Being near Malcolm was more than mere chemistry or animal attraction. As they had discussed in the graveyard, she continually uncovered new treasured pieces of herself in his presence—teasing humor, confidence, an ease in speaking—bits of her soul that she hadn't recognized until he had shined a light on them.

Peering down at the still blank notebook page, Viola faced another truth—

She was nearly desperate to see Malcolm again.

THE NEXT DAY, Viola thought about Malcolm during Lady Stewart's garden party, disappointed that he had not been in attendance.

She thought about him again as Dr. Ruxton and his wife accompanied her father and herself home following the party.

And after Mrs. Ruxton's not-so-discreet hinting resulted in Dr. Brodure inviting the Ruxtons in for tea, Viola fretted over missing an encounter with Malcolm along the lane. But ever the dutiful daughter, she shed her bonnet and gloves and requested a tray be sent to the parlor.

Through a small miracle, she managed to curtail Mrs. Ruxton's tongue and send the couple off after only an hour's delay. Her father, thank goodness, was quickly tucked into his study.

Even so, Viola knew she would be too late to catch Malcolm at their swing.

Heart heavy, she nonetheless hurried out the door—bonnet forgotten, gloves abandoned—down the narrow path, across the meadow, and onto the lane that led to Thistle Muir's far fields.

She walked quickly, fearing that the exertion of running would be too much for her lungs.

But, oh, how she longed to sprint!

Had she already missed him?

Please be there.

Please wait for me.

She hoped against hope that perhaps Malcolm might have already passed the swing but would still be walking up the lane.

But he was nowhere to be seen.

No bark from Beowoof. No whistle from Malcolm.

Chest heaving, she continued on. Just a little farther. Just to the swing. Then she would know for certain that she had arrived too late.

She rounded the last corner, steeling her heart to find an empty road.

Beowoof's joyous bark greeted her instead.

Viola's stomach flipped with joy.

There he was.

Malcolm.

Standing tall, shoulder leaning into the birch beside the swing, a slight breeze ruffling his kilt. His gaze met hers.

Oh, heavens.

Gracious.

Electricity crackled between them. The very air vibrating with a buoyant sort of wonder.

In that look, she saw it—

He *knew*.

He knew she had been racing to see him.

And . . .

Now *she* knew.

He had been waiting for her.

He had hoped she would come.

Jubilation thrummed in her chest.

Slowing her pace, Viola stopped a few feet in front of him, a helpless, giddy smile on her face.

He gazed back at her for a long moment before a quiet grin stretched wide, stacking up wrinkles at the corners of his eyes.

It was quite like a sunrise, luminous and full of promise.

His eyes darted over her person—noting her missing bonnet, her absent gloves, her laboring lungs—surely understanding precisely how eager she had been to meet him.

Viola should have been chagrined, at the very least.

But instead, all she felt was freedom. That she was, *at last*, alive and truly living.

"What brings you along the lane today, Miss Brodure?" he asked, that grin still tugging at his mouth and rendering it endearingly lopsided.

"I m-missed Beowoof," she replied, trying to slow her breathing.

That same electricity bounced between them, snapping, growing in portent.

He did not ask the obvious question: *Are ye sure it wasn't myself ye missed?*

And she did not give the clear answer: *Of course it was you.*

"Ye should catch your breath before I walk ye back up the lane."

He motioned toward the swing beside them. "I should hate for ye to exacerbate your asthma."

Tucking her skirts beneath her, Viola sat on the swing, glad of the reprieve for her lungs. Beowoof sniffed the grass at her feet. Bending, she gave him a brief scratch behind his left ear.

"I trust ye have had a lovely day." Malcolm leaned his shoulder into the birch once more, arms folded across his chest.

Beowoof loped off into the woods, sniffing through the leafy underbrush.

Viola grabbed onto the ropes holding the swing, her arms outstretched.

"As well as could be expected." She kicked her feet, setting the swing to a gentle glide. The resulting breeze whispered over her skin. "Lady Stewart held a garden luncheon."

"I've heard tales of her gatherings."

"But you do not attend them?"

He shrugged. "In the past, I was never invited to such affairs. One of the many prices I willingly paid when I married Aileen. Since her passing, I have been occasionally invited to genteel gatherings but havenae developed a habit of going."

It was the most opaque reference Malcolm had ever made to the difference in social status between them.

"Would ye like a wee push, Miss Brodure?" He lifted his hands, palms out.

Viola nodded, perhaps a tad over-enthusiastically.

"Well, you missed quite the hubbub in Lady Stewart's garden today," she said, head turning as he walked behind her.

"Aye?" The word hummed in her ear as he bent to gently wrap his enormous hands around her waist.

Viola inhaled sharply at the touch. At the sensation of his breath rolling across her neck. Gooseflesh flared to life along her arms.

She could feel every searing point of contact between them—all ten fingertips, the palms of his hands.

Viola swallowed.

He pushed her away from him, the lightest motion.

What had she been saying?

Right.

Lady Stewart's garden party.

"It was a scene fit for a Punch and Judy show." Viola's voice turned breathless. "Lady Stewart had the luncheon set up on the south lawn, not the conservatory, as the day was sunny and lovely."

"Aye, we've had a spell of nice weather lately." Malcolm's words whispered over her neck as his hands gave another gentle push. Viola longed to lean back into his touch.

"All was well and good at the outset. Ethan was in fine form, you will be pleased to hear." Viola looked back at Malcolm. "He regaled us all with tales from his Grand Tour year abroad. Apparently, pickpockets in Rome are particularly vicious."

"Ah, yes, I've heard that story a number of times. The one with the monkeys and a lemon?"

Another breath across the back of her neck.

Another push.

Focus on the story.

"Yes, precisely," she continued. "Ethan's tale, though humorous, was not the pinnacle of hilarity. No, that moment came when Sir Robert Stewart's prize sheep escaped his pen."

"Fergus?"

Viola coughed a laugh. "I see Fergus's reputation precedes him."

"He has a habit of sticking his nose where it doesnae belong, but as he is a fine Scottish blackface ram and useful for improving all our breeding stock, we put up with him."

Malcolm pushed her again, his strong palms engulfing her waist and his thumbs pressing into the small of her back.

Viola soared higher, thrilling as the wind tugged at her hair.

"Well, you will perhaps be delighted to know that Fergus has taken a rather strong liking to your Ethan."

"How's that?" The broad smile in his voice echoed her own.

"Ethan had just finished enacting the monkey bit of his story—"

"With all the screeching?"

"And flapping of his arms," Viola giggled. "Perhaps Fergus mistook it for some sort of sheep mating cry, I cannot say. Regardless, one moment Ethan was mid-monkey call and the next, Fergus had tugged him out of his chair by his tailcoat."

Malcolm laughed, a crack of sound so bright and free that Viola felt her own heart take flight along with her body.

She half twisted to see him grinning behind her, his teeth flashing white against his dark beard.

Dragging her feet on the ground, Viola slowed her swinging. Malcolm rested a firm palm against her spine, slowing her further and setting her heart to racing.

"You laugh," she pointed a finger at him as the swing came to a stop, "but that was only the beginning of the madcappery. Ethan flailed to free himself, tugging on his coat, but the dratted sheep would not let it go." She mimed a frantic pulling motion. "So Ethan twisted out of his coat—truly, he is to be commended on his quick thinking and flexible elbows—but the moment he freed himself, Fergus dropped the coat and went after Ethan himself."

Malcolm sagged against one rope of the swing, shoulders shaking with mirth, head bowed as he gasped for air.

Viola giggled uncontrollably. "It was the best entertainment I've had in years. Ethan streaking across the Stewart's back garden, shrieking at Fergus to, 'Lay off, ye daft *eejit*!' Naturally, Lady Stewart's butler and two footmen joined in the pursuit. They made quite the merry band—servants chasing Fergus chasing Ethan. Fergus is astonishingly swift for a sheep, I must say. The beast would latch onto an article of Ethan's clothing as he ran, so your brother was obliged to contort himself to strip out of it. I had no idea his brogue could be so thick. Ethan gave the lot of us a rather eye-opening glimpse into his Scots vocabulary."

"He is a p-poet, after all," Malcolm wheezed. "Words are his p-profession."

"Well, he was a credit to you all in that regard. Lady Stewart fainted right about the time Ethan climbed the garden wall and stood atop it, cursing both Fergus's manners and parentage in an astonishingly creative manner. By that point, Ethan had lost his waistcoat, neckcloth, half a shirt sleeve, and his right shoe to the beast's apparently amorous pursuit. The poor sheep merely pawed at the stone, bleated his thwarted displeasure, and head-butted every servant who attempted to wrangle him away."

That was the final straw. Malcolm bent down, hands on his knees, tears streaming down his cheeks and into his beard.

Seeing Malcolm Penn-Leith doubled-over in laughter was as breathtaking a sight as the aurora borealis, though perhaps even more rare.

Surely laughter had been sparse in his life since his wife's death. But, oh, he was a man born to laugh. To soak up life's joys.

His cackling, wheezing mirth was contagious. Viola leaned on the swing's rope, gasping for air herself.

Malcolm collapsed onto the swing beside her, as if his legs were no longer up to the task of holding him upright.

"Oh, oh!" he panted, wiping tears off his beard.

Viola laughed with him, surprised that they both fit on the swing and all too aware of how close they were. Her legs faced one way, his the other. But they now touched from hip to shoulder, her side pressed against his. If she tilted her head a scant few inches, she could rest her cheek on his shoulder.

Malcolm swiped at his eyes. "I cannae wait to tease Ethan. I shall never let him live that down."

"You cannot! 'Twould be cruel. Poor Ethan was beet-red and mortified."

"*Och!* Ethan's never been mortified a day in his life. He was merely red from exertion, I am sure. Trust me, he'll be telling the tale with gusto outwith a week. It will be my own pleasure tae remind him of his humiliation for the next fifty years of our lives. 'Tis how we show our love."

"I will never understand men. Or brothers, for that matter."

He pressed a hand to his side. "I needed that laugh, but I fear I may have strained a stomach muscle."

Running his thumbs under his eyes one last time, he turned to her. And froze.

As if finally realizing that there was scarcely a whisper of space between them. That with the slightest dip of his head, they would be kissing.

His eyes danced over her face, emotions flickering so quickly— humor? longing? alarm?—she couldn't identify them clearly.

Without seeking permission, her gaze focused on his lips. Something dipped low in her stomach, heat spooling through her veins. How would it feel to kiss a man with a beard? But not any man, she supposed. *This* man. This tender, unyielding force of a Scot.

Viola didn't move. She scarcely breathed.

Don't go, she wanted to murmur. *Stay here for a while.*

Canting an inch closer to him, she willed him to dip down, to kiss her.

His nostrils flared as his eyes found her mouth.

Lifting upward, Viola closed the distance, lips trembl—

Woof!

Beowoof's cold nose abruptly appeared between, nuzzling at Viola's hands and yipping excitedly.

The tension between herself and Malcolm evaporated like so much morning mist, leaving Viola to wonder if perhaps the moment had been in her head all along.

Malcolm swallowed, a long slide of his Adam's apple, and bent to pet his dog.

"Well," she finally said, "we shall simply have to ensure that you laugh more often, Malcolm Penn-Leith. Accustom those muscles to the exercise."

He glanced up at her, his dark eyes wells of chocolate, warm and delicious.

"Aye, Viola Brodure, that we will. That we will."

IN THE YEARS to come, Malcolm would remember the weeks that followed as snippets of conversation with Viola.

Every day, if possible, one or the other of them would be waiting at the swing. He would leisurely walk with her along the deserted lane, leaving her at the edge of the meadow that backed the Brodure's cottage. It wasn't precisely proper perhaps, but as they were outdoors and along a public lane, the situation was hardly compromising should they be seen together.

Their conversations covered a wide range of topics—from Voltaire to labor reform to bonnet styles—almost all involving laughter and teasing.

Most of all, however, Malcolm loved hearing Viola talk about herself.

"Why did ye decide to become a novelist?" he asked her one evening as they strolled arm-in-arm up the lane.

It wasn't quite the question he wanted to ask—*Are ye the author of* A Hard Truth?—but it was a step closer.

She smiled and shrugged. "To be very honest, I cannot actually remember a time when I did *not* wish to be a novelist."

"Aye?"

"Aye," she said back, causing him to smile.

He did that more nowadays, Malcolm realized, particularly anytime the thought of Viola Brodure passed his mind.

In other words, a smile rarely left his face.

"I fear storytelling is in my blood," she continued. "Our last name, Brodure, comes from the French *brodeur*, or embroiderer. As a family, we have always loved to embellish things. My father said that I came out of the womb spinning yarns and never stopped. My mother was apparently the same way."

"She was?"

"Well, my father says so. She died of a fever when I was just a babe."

"I'm sorry ye never had a chance tae know her."

"So am I, but I did have my father growing up. He is everything to me."

"I can well understand that. My mother died when I was only three, so I know what it is tae only have one parent. My father passed when I was twenty-two. I suppose ye dinnae truly become an adult until ye bury both your parents. That's when true adulthood arrives."

"Are you implying that I still have some growing up to do, Mr. Penn-Leith?"

"Perhaps," he grinned at her teasing. "But I wonder if it isnae time for ye to call me Malcolm?"

She tut-tutted her tongue. "Such informality, Mr. Penn-Leith. What would all my genteel acquaintances say to such a thing?"

"That ye count me a friend, Viola?"

"Well . . . Malcolm." She paused, a soft smile upon her lips. "I suppose I do."

11

As much as Malcolm enjoyed his evening strolls with Viola, he did not relish keeping his feelings for her from Ethan.

Naturally, Malcolm had told Ethan about that first meeting with Miss Brodure along the lane.

The conversation with his brother had been decidedly anticlimactic.

"I encountered Miss Brodure as I was walking back from the south fields last night," Malcolm had said over breakfast.

"Did ye?" Ethan had said, reading the *Edinburgh Chronicle* and scarcely glancing up from his black pudding and eggs. "Isn't she the loveliest creature? I am so glad she has come to Fettermill."

Malcolm had agreed and that had been that.

But as time passed and Malcolm continued to meet Viola along the lane, he felt like he needed to say more. Particularly as his brother spoke of the lady almost incessantly.

"Miss Brodure is simply charming," Ethan said one Tuesday morning over breakfast. "I marvel every time I am in her company."

Malcolm grunted, reaching for another slice of black pudding.

His brother looked happier than he had in months, the tension around his eyes easing, his smile appearing more readily.

It made the guilt sitting on Malcolm's own shoulders feel all the heavier. He didn't want to disturb Ethan's newfound contentment.

Because even though Viola accepted Ethan's attentions, she did nothing to seek them out. She certainly did not race to meet him along a lane, a welcome smile on her lips.

Furthermore, she did not confide in Ethan. Whenever Malcolm asked Ethan questions about Viola—*What happened to her mother? Has Miss Brodure always wanted to be a writer?*—Ethan could answer none of them.

But when Malcolm had waited for Viola along the lane, she had come. As if as desperate to see him as he was to see her. And then there had been that moment sitting beside her on the swing, when time had slowed like spreading treacle and Malcolm had, for a brief second of insanity, contemplated kissing her.

Ye cannae be that enamored of her, ye eejit, a voice at the back of his mind rumbled. *Because ye know where that will lead. Are ye truly considering climbing toward the light? Tae attempt a romantic relationship again and risk hurting your brother in the process?*

That was the question now, was it not? Because with every passing day, Malcolm edged a wee bit closer to deciding *aye*—aye, he did wish tae climb out of the dark and into the blinding light, even knowing the risks to both himself and Ethan.

Not that he had made such a decision . . . yet.

"Did ye know the London broadsheets are saying we'll make a match of it?" Ethan said, delight in his voice. "A university mate of mine sent up a clipping from *The Tattler* or some such. And now the Duke of Kendall has arrived."

"His Grace certainly has taken an interest in your courtship of Miss Brodure." Biting into his bacon, Malcolm stared ahead, unseeing. "Is he here tae usher ye both to the altar? Stand by with a shotgun while ye say your vows?"

"Ah-ha!" Ethan brightened, either missing or ignoring the sarcasm in Malcolm's words. "I was wondering what would finally get sound tae come out of your mouth."

"Ethan," Malcolm began, sagging back in his chair.

"Leah invited Kendall tae her picnic." Ethan pointed his fork at Malcolm. "Just think, on Thursday ye will dine with a duke along the River North Esk. You're going tae have tae talk then."

"Well, if I must speak," Malcolm began, "I understand there is a rather diverting story about Fergus and an amorous pursuit . . ."

Ethan froze, a forkful of eggs halfway to his mouth. He set it down with a *clank*. "Who told ye that? Was it the servants?"

"Far be it from me tae name my sources."

Ethan's eyes narrowed. "I want names."

"Not a chance in hell," Malcolm grinned, just a shade shy of wicked. "I protect my informants."

"Malcolm," his name a warning.

"Dinnae *fash* yourself. I promise tae make ye seem a hero to His Grace."

"Leah will eviscerate you if ye make a scene at her party."

"Aye, but the look on your face says my death might just be worth it."

"That's it." Ethan pushed out of his chair. "We need tae throw stones."

"Whyever for? I have no truths tae tell." Or, rather, none that Malcolm *would* tell. Not yet. Not until there was definitively something *to* tell.

"Ye may keep your truths today. I simply need ye to remember that I can out-throw your sorry arse."

"Like hell, ye can." Malcolm stood, tossing his napkin on the table. "Ye have yet tae beat me."

"Haven't ye heard the fable of the Tortoise and the Hare?"

Malcolm rolled his eyes. "Ye might be the first person on this planet who has compared me to a rabbit."

"Persistence, Malcolm. Just watch me. I always win out in the end, due to sheer, stubborn persistence." Ethan slapped the door lintel on his way out.

Malcolm followed him, tongue tight in his throat.

Because Ethan was not wrong.

He *was* persistent. He *did* always get what he wanted in the end.

Malcolm had never begrudged Ethan his successes.

But at the moment, Malcolm struggled to summon the enthusiasm required to cheer his brother across the finish line.

"HIS GRACE DOES us all such an honor by this visit," her father said at Viola's side as they climbed a small knoll to the folly. "He dined with the Queen last week, and now, *poof*, here he is, gracing us all with his presence."

"Indeed, Papa." Viola knotted her hands together.

Her father glanced down at her twisted fingers.

"Come, daughter." He took one of her cold hands in his. "Kendall is pleased with you. Nothing about this situation should afflict you with such nervousness."

"I cannot help it, Papa," she said softly as they walked. "My shy tongue will always tremble in the company of imperious dukes. It is a fact of Nature as irrefutable as gravity or taxes."

Her father laughed at her weak jest, but it did little to ease the tension twisting in her chest.

The Duke of Kendall's presence underscored the mountain of expectations currently facing her—*Marry Ethan Penn-Leith! Write me a short story!*

The repercussions of not summiting the mountain would be dire.

Viola mentally pushed aside that fact, as the more she imagined it, the more agitated her nerves became, and she simply could not withstand more anxiety at the moment.

The folly came into view, a romantic jumble of unroofed, crenelated towers around a circular keep. It gave every appearance of a centuries-old ruin slowly crumbling into the forest floor. Even its position was charming—one side nestled against trees, while the other descended on a steep slope to a dramatic gorge. The far-off murmur of a waterfall hovered in the air.

Servants bustled about, setting up a picnic atop blankets spread on the flagstone floor.

Ethan, Captain Fox Carnegie, and the Duke of Kendall all looked in

Viola's direction as she and her father approached. The weight of their eyes stifled Viola's urge to stand on tiptoe and search out Malcolm.

As usual, the duke was an aquatint fashion plate come to life—immaculate cravat under a green silk waistcoat and superfine day coat, his trousers pressed to perfection. Even his gray hair lay perfectly pomaded, despite (Viola was quite sure) having been under a hat at some point in the day.

Even at his young age, the man dripped power and condescension the way a spinster exuded desperation—it was the first and only thing one noticed.

Viola couldn't imagine a scenario that would ever ruffle a man like Kendall. Truthfully, she was rather surprised his hair had dared to gray so early. Or that His Grace had somehow lacked the authority to command it to obey him.

"Dr. Brodure. Miss Brodure," Kendall greeted them with an exquisitely calibrated bow. Say what you would about the duke—and, heaven knew, Viola could say *much*—his manners were flawless.

Viola curtsied low, stammering a greeting.

Captain Carnegie thanked Viola and her father for attending.

Ethan gave her a warm smile and bowed lavishly over her hand.

His Grace merely nodded and then turned to stare off into the half distance, as if questioning his decision to travel into the wilds of Scotland, and thereby, forcing him into close quarters with lesser mortals.

It was all unbearably awkward.

As her father spoke with Ethan and Captain Carnegie—Kendall's haughty silence a millstone around their conversation—Viola's eyes drifted toward the other guests.

Lady Stewart chatted with Leah and Mrs. Ruxton.

Finally, Viola spotted Malcolm well behind the ladies, hovering at the edge of the crowd, listening to Sir Robert Stewart.

Malcolm seemed out of place in his pressed kilt and bushy beard. A raiding wolf amid a flock of fluttery geese.

Viola was sure he had only come today because his sister and brother-in-law were hosting the picnic and, therefore, his absence would have been conspicuously peculiar.

It felt odd to see Malcolm among the aristocracy.

When speaking with him privately, she never felt the social distance between them. They were equals in every way that mattered.

But here today . . .

She saw it clearly for the first time:

Malcolm Penn-Leith truly was not a member of her world.

He held himself apart, eyes wary, bowing stiffly when Mrs. Ruxton approached.

By contrast, when Viola turned back to Ethan, she noted how the younger Penn-Leith brother laughed and spoke easily with her father and Captain Carnegie. Ethan Penn-Leith's impeccable manners had clearly been polished and honed against the blade of the *ton*'s fascination with him.

Case in point, he even skillfully attempted to draw Kendall into conversation. Ethan's friendliness seemed to remind Kendall that he needed to be civil if he wished the poet to go along with his aims. The duke tilted his head toward the poet.

"Malcolm!" Ethan eagerly called just as Kendall drew breath to speak.

His Grace winced, brow furrowing.

Ethan gazed beyond Viola's shoulder, flashing his signature knee-weakening smile.

Viola turned to see Leah approaching with Malcolm at her side. He met Viola's eyes for one fleeting moment, before shifting his eyes away.

"Come meet His Grace," Ethan continued, waving his brother over. If he noticed or cared about the difference between his own refined deportment and his brother's more uncertain bearing, it didn't show. Viola liked Ethan all the more for it.

Malcolm's expression, however, turned stoic, as if to mask his discomfort.

Viola's heart panged in her chest.

"Your Grace," Leah said politely, giving Ethan a quelling look, "I do not believe ye have had the opportunity tae make the acquaintance of my other brother, Mr. Malcolm Penn-Leith."

"Your Grace." Malcolm bowed. It was a credible bow, but even Viola noted that it lacked Ethan's polished finesse.

Kendall surveyed Malcolm with a cool eye before nodding his head—the barest of acknowledgments.

Viola could practically see the gears turning in Kendall's brain. Clearly, the duke disliked having to accept an acquaintance with a man of Malcolm's lowly status. But he also needed Ethan to fall into line with his matrimonial plotting, and therefore, being impolite to the poet's older brother seemed ill-advised.

A gleam lit in Malcolm's eye, as if he, too, had reached the same conclusion.

"It's a right pleasure tae have ye here, Your Grace. Did ye have a fine journey north?" Malcolm asked with uncharacteristic chattiness.

The two men stared at one another, looking similar to a pair of bulls facing off.

"Yes. It was . . . tolerable," His Grace said.

"Aye, 'tis lovely weather we've been having," Ethan added.

Silence descended on their group, Kendall's aloof presence chilling the words on Viola's tongue.

Unlike his older brother and the duke, however, Ethan struggled to dwell in that silence.

"Malcolm has been developing a new breed of Highland cow, Your Grace," Ethan offered. "Even Her Majesty has expressed an interest in them."

"Indeed." Kendall's tone implied a vast sea of indifference when it came to cows. His gaze flicked over Malcolm. "So, Mr. Penn-Leith, unlike your renowned poet of a brother, you are a . . . farmer?" His Grace imbued the word *farmer* with several hundred years of autocratic disdain.

Malcolm's eyes tightened, the tiniest twitch of emotion. He stared at the duke with unrelenting calculation.

"Aye, Your Grace. I consider it my civic duty tae improve the quality of my cattle tae help feed our nation, something *some* noblemen see the importance of. I've been breeding the coos with the assistance of Sir Rafe Gordon."

Kendall's nostrils flared.

Malcolm's expression said he clearly understood he was now baiting his fellow bull.

Viola frowned. More was being said here than she understood. Who was Sir Rafe Gordon? The name sounded vaguely familiar.

"I see," Kendall narrowed his eyes. "I would be mindful of the company you keep, Mr. Penn-Leith."

"Oh, aye, that I'm doing," Malcolm replied with uncharacteristic breeziness.

Kendall froze further, if it were possible.

But, of course, no one could out-duke a duke.

"Well, I am sure that is an interesting . . . enterprise." Dipping his head in the barest of nods, Kendall turned to Dr. Brodure, leaving Malcolm with a direct view of his shoulders.

Viola could scarcely contain a gasp. Leah's eyes widened at the slight.

It was not precisely the cut direct, but it was a snub. A very ducal way of saying, 'I do not wish to be rude to my hosts, but I am not pleased with your presence.'

Malcolm caught Viola's eye. His expression had not changed, but Viola felt the weight of it. Of the social chasm wide and yawning between them.

But before she could so much as blink, he had rotated back to his sister.

Viola pressed a trembling, gloved hand to her forehead.

Heavens, why must her nerves be such a restless jumble?

TWO HOURS LATER, Viola was unsure if her body was capable of absorbing any more tension without collapse.

The guests were seated upon colorful tartan wool blankets, dining on a repast of roast beef sandwiches, crowdie cheese on oatcakes, scones with bright strawberry jam, and treacle tarts, all washed down with an excellent Spanish white wine.

After an hour of stony silence, several solicitous questions from the vicars present and two glasses of fine *rioja* finally succeeded in loosening Kendall's tongue.

Too loose, perhaps.

So far, the Duke of Kendall had pontificated about the price of corn shares, the role of a true gentleman in animal husbandry, the possibility of Ethan being invited to dine with the Queen, the encroaching nature of unwanted and illicit relatives, the corruption of breeding stock by ignorant farmers, and the chaotic disorder of London's street traffic.

In that precise order.

Kendall was an insufferable ass.

There.

Viola had admitted it.

Yes, he was a duke.

Yes, he was one of the wealthiest, most powerful men in the kingdom.

Yes, he had grand ambitions and gave every appearance of assisting her father in his career.

And, yes, he had Viola by her pen, steering her writerly and romantic choices.

None of those things automatically made Kendall an ass.

That particular attribute, unlike nearly everything else in his life, sprang, fully-formed, from his own psyche.

Why had the man bothered traveling all the way to Fettermill if he was merely going to be unpleasant?

The small exchange with Malcolm earlier had likely been the catalyst for the duke's ill-tempered behavior. As if Kendall had been trying to play nicely with the other privileged children, but then Malcolm's rough-edged words had pricked him, reminding His Grace that he was a duke and didn't have to share or play nice with anyone.

Regardless of the cause, the man's barbed comments were undoubtedly aimed at Malcolm Penn-Leith.

Viola's hands trembled with suppressed outrage, her lungs tight.

The old duke had often behaved like this, cracking the whip of his scorn at those beneath him simply because he could. Kendall clearly had learned the behavior from the master.

Even jovial Ethan grew quieter and more tight-lipped the longer His Grace spoke, darting glances at his older brother.

For his part, Malcolm bore the indirect assault with his usual stoic verve. He sat as far as possible from Kendall, his back against the side of the folly, arms folded, legs stretched out before him and crossed at the ankles.

"Furthermore," Kendall was saying, "once Parliament has addressed the issue of merchant wagons choking London streets, they will need to turn their attention to the blight of the urban poor."

"Blight?" Dr. Brodure murmured. "Not . . . *plight*, Your Grace?"

Kendall scowled at the older man. "No, why would I not say precisely what I mean? *Blight*. Poverty is no excuse for a degradation of morals. It is why literary works like your daughter's are of the utmost importance. Miss Brodure captures the suitable humility and goodness that the impoverished must demonstrate in order to deserve the charity of their betters."

Viola's father barely stopped a wincing grimace.

"Is that so, Your Grace?" Ethan's baffled expression stated he was as flummoxed as everyone else over the duke's bitter verbosity.

"Yes." Kendall gave a decided nod of his head. "In fact, when I arrange for you and Miss Brodure to dine with the Queen, you should remind her of these truths. Her Majesty will be most eager to discuss the subject, I am sure."

Gracious.

Did Kendall expect Viola to *converse* with the Queen on these matters? Her lungs constricted tighter.

Abruptly, the muscles in her neck tightened, sending tingling shocks down her spine.

No.

Oh, please no.

How could she have been so careless? She had been so intent on Malcolm and Kendall's boorish behavior—on the realization that she might have to dine with royalty—that she had neglected to listen to the panicked cues of her own body.

She could not bear having a full-blown asthmatic fit in a folly in front of a crowd of people—three of whom were a pontificating duke, the poet everyone expected her to court, and the man *she* hoped to court—

If she wished to avoid an attack, she had to leave. Now.

"I c-cannot feel worthy of such t-trust, Your Grace. If you will p-please excuse me."

Palm pressed to her chest, she stood.

The gentlemen scrambled to their feet around her. Her father touched her elbow.

"Are you unwell, daughter?" Concern tensed his face.

"Humid air," she struggled. "I need calm and moist air."

"Allow me. I know just the place." Leah leapt to her side, placed a hand around Viola's waist, and led her away from the picnic.

"Whatever is the matter?" Kendall asked behind Viola.

"'Tis nothing to worry upon, Your Grace," Dr. Brodure replied. "Just the same touch of asthma that my daughter experiences from time to time."

Kendall's reply was lost as Leah led Viola toward a path that angled along the gorge. They walked through the trees to the edge of the ravine. The sound of rushing water, leaves rustling, and the smell of damp, green ferns and sycamore trees engulfed them.

Leah urged Viola to sit on a seat cut into a rocky outcropping. Viola did so with relief, hand pressed to her chest, eyes closed.

The air hung with humidity this close to the river. She took in deep, measured breaths.

Slowly . . . the crushing tightness in her lungs eased, the symptoms of an imminent attack retreating.

Thank goodness she had acted in time.

"Better?" Leah asked.

Viola nodded.

"How goes it?" A familiar voice asked.

Viola opened her eyes to see Malcolm walking toward them, kilt swaying, concern pleating the corners of his eyes.

The sight of him loosened the vise banding Viola's chest that much more.

"I'm much improved." She smiled weakly. "Just doing my best impression of a fainting wallflower."

That earned her a grimacing grin.

Leah frowned at her brother, peering at the path behind him. "Where's Ethan? I would have thought he would come to assist Miss Brodure."

"*Och*, Kendall's got him cornered, demanding his opinions on the *blight* of the poor and how, if Her Majesty were to knight Ethan, he would use his position to further Kendall's politics."

Malcolm's scathing tone and the twist of Leah's mouth left no doubts as to their feelings on Kendall's 'politics.'

Voices rose from the folly up the path.

"How did this entire picnic go sideways so quickly?" Leah asked, and then snapped her fingers. "That's right. A duke is involved. And I thought Westhampton was bad. I owe that man an apology."

"Go on back tae your guests, Leah. Ye are needed there." Malcolm nodded toward the folly. "I will ensure that Miss Brodure comes tae no harm. We are out in the open here where anyone can see us, so there will be no scandal in me remaining here."

Which is how after a whispered exchange between the siblings, two *are ye sures?*, and a lingering concerned glance from Leah, Viola found herself in the sole company of Malcolm Penn-Leith.

12

Malcolm stared down at Viola. She sat on the rock bench, pale but breathing more easily.

He hated that Kendall's tactless words and the anxiety of so many eyes watching had landed her here.

Witnessing Viola struggle to breathe had filled him with an almost unholy terror. His heart had raced and his hands had shook until he had all but chased after her and Leah, unable to sit still a moment longer.

And that had been only five harrowing minutes. Imagine a lifetime of watching a woman he loved battle such an infirmity.

Because even if a person seemed hearty and hale, none was robust enough to escape death.

Malcolm had well-learned that bitter truth.

He ran a hand over his nose and beard.

Viola took another lungful of air, the lovely pink of her cheeks brightening a wee bit.

"Well, I fear I have officially used up my allotment of histrionics today," she said on a sigh.

"Nae, lass. Give yourself more credit than that. The day is yet young, and I'm sure Kendall has another barb or two tae lob in your direction."

She smiled at his gentle teasing.

Malcolm held out a hand and helped her to her feet.

She stared at their joined hands for a moment, at her gloved palm resting in his bare one. Turning her head, she studied the path leading upstream away from the folly.

"Does this path wind to somewhere lovely?"

"Aye. It follows up the river to a ravine with stately steep cliffs on each side and a waterfall tumbling down from a wee burn. The Rocks of Solitude, it's aptly called."

"I think I have recovered enough to be equal to it. May we?"

Malcolm nodded and tucked her hand into his elbow, the slight weight already familiar . . . as if it should always belong precisely there.

He took in a slow breath, fighting the dread coiling under his sternum.

It was one thing to contemplate climbing out of the comfortable walls of his grief.

It was something else entirely to ponder love and marriage—in both sickness and health—with a woman who was not Aileen. To stow, once more, his heart in another's fragile body.

If only Viola didn't feel like a missing piece of him, a lost bit of a puzzle, just waiting to be slotted into place and kept at his side.

Assuming she even *wished* to be kept, that was.

Och, what a *fankle* he had gotten himself into.

"I can practically hear the heft of your thoughts," Viola said.

"That obvious, am I?"

"No. But I feel I am coming to know you."

The truth of her words landed hard.

She *was* coming to know him.

And the thought filled him with . . . *grief*, of all things.

Why was that? Was he so used to dwelling at the bottom of his pit, that the very essence of hope felt like a loss before it could even draw breath?

"And what do my thoughts say?" he had to ask.

"That I, Viola Brodure, am a hypocrite."

Her answer startled a *hah!* out of him.

"Ye couldnae be farther from the truth, lass."

She walked silently for a moment, her hand pressing on his elbow, her skirts occasionally brushing that bare strip of skin between the bottom of his kilt and the top of his stockings.

The river to their left burbled as it rushed over rocks.

"What if I told you, with all honesty, that I do not like my own writing?"

"How can ye not like yer own writing?" Malcolm huffed in astonishment. "Why . . . it's fair brilliant."

That got her attention. Viola stopped abruptly, her skirts swaying. She angled her head, eyes scrutinizing.

"You've read my work?" she asked. "Why have we never discussed this?"

"Because I thought it obvious that I had read ye. Every last story."

"Truly?"

"Aye. I enjoyed *Polly Pettifer*. Those descriptions of London." He shivered. "I could practically feel the creeping fog."

He paused, hesitating to ask the presumptuous question that had lingered in his mind for weeks, fearing it might reveal too much of his own heart.

But she had lifted back the curtain a wee bit on her own desires. Couldn't he do the same?

"Please forgive me this next question, but I have long wondered— are ye the pen behind the scathing revolutionary Oliver Aubord Twist?"

As he was already staring at her, he didn't miss the panicky surprise that lit in her eyes.

She swallowed.

"How . . ." was all she managed to gasp.

"Hah! So I am correct?"

Viola nodded, a tightly controlled motion. "But how did you . . . ?"

Now it was Malcolm's turn to squirm.

"As I said, I ken your writing. I know your ways of turning a phrase, of expounding scenes and personalities. And so when I read *A Hard Truth*, well, it just sounded like yourself. I cannae explain it. But I looked harder at the pen name of the author and realized that *Oliver Aubord* was an anagram of *Viola Brodure*. But I honestly didnae know for sure it was yourself until this moment."

She took a minute to absorb his confession, head shaking ever so slightly. In wonder? Bewilderment? Betrayal?

"*A Hard Truth* was printed in the most obscure political journal," she finally said. "You, Mr. Penn-Leith, have been hiding the vast reach of your intellect."

As usual, she surprised a laugh out of him. "That's your conclusion, is it?"

She nodded, a smile hovering on her lips. But the emotion didn't quite reach her eyes.

"Well, I am honored to finally meet the authoress of *A Hard Truth*," he said. "The world ye created in that story . . . well, I felt like I could ride tae Manchester and find it there, waiting for me."

"Thank you. Such words are a balm to a writer's soul."

Malcolm waved them forward along the trail.

The gorge narrowed further here—a steep cliff extending up to their right, another falling off to their left—both covered in dripping moss and tenacious trees determined to hold on to the mountainside. However, the river didn't rush along, despite the strait walls of its channel, choosing instead to flow with a calm solemnity.

Malcolm helped Viola to sidestep a large boulder in the path.

"As far as I know," she said, "you are the only person who has uncovered that I am the writer of *A Hard Truth*. No one else knows."

"No one?"

"No one," she repeated. "Not even my father."

Abruptly, Malcolm felt the magnitude of what he had discovered.

"Why?" he had to ask.

"In case you somehow missed the overtones of the earlier discussion"—she glanced from the ravine walls to the path behind them—"Kendall sees me as his mouthpiece. He wishes me to be Virgil to his Augustus. I had hoped that he might be less arrogant than his father, but today has confirmed, once and for all, that the Dukes of Kendall are an eerily similar breed."

"So the old duke told ye what tae write, too?"

"Yes, after a fashion. He *was* encouraging and his support helped my father to sell my first book to a publisher. And initially, I didn't necessarily find fault with what Kendall recommended. I was simply ecstatic to have people reading my novels. It was only last year, after a trip to Manchester, that things changed."

In halting words, she told him of her visit with Cousin Eloise, the Duke of Kendall's expectations, her father's hopes, and her own ambition caught in the middle. Of Kendall's demands that she write a short story according to his dictates. Of the pact she had made with her father to hold her tongue and wait to publish her more radically reformist ideas. Of how *A Hard Truth* broke that promise.

"Papa would be devastated if he knew I had broken our agreement," she said on a sigh. "That I did not keep my promise to support him in his pursuit of a bishopric."

"But I ken your reasons, lass. Staying silent in the face of such injustice can be impossible, particularly as ye feared the old duke would live on, thus stilling your pen for years. I saw traces of your reformist spirit in *Polly Pettifer*, in the passages describing Polly's living situation. But *A Hard Truth* brought it all into sharper focus. The story is aptly named, as it lays out the terrible choices women must make to survive, particularly when every last bit of their existence is a commodity for purchase—virtue, body, and soul."

"Yes! Evil and abuse thrive when we, as a society, refuse to discuss such things openly." Her voice rose, vibrating with passion and conviction. She stopped to face him. "And knowing this, how can I write this wretched story for Kendall that ignores truth and glosses over injustice?"

Ah.

She stared down at the dark flowing river, clenching her fists over and over, as if the flood of emotion scouring her matched the torrent below.

Viola Brodure and her magnificent heart.

This, right here, was why Malcolm was falling for her. Why against his better sense, society's opinions, and his own fears, he kept seeking her company.

Though their lives differed vastly, there was a sameness in the way they saw the world.

A harmony of thought.

And by meeting now, at this juncture of their lives—with his brother adoring her and the entire kingdom urging her toward that adoration—they inhabited the same sphere.

Adjacent but only just.

He smiled at the thought.

But the insight was not wrong.

Malcolm studied the gorge. At the jagged slabs of rock pushing up from the earth, as if the ground itself had once cracked in this very place.

And he rather supposed it had.

This was the precise dividing line between the Lowlands and the Highlands, after all.

Like the precise line dividing the social class, breeding, and education that separated himself from Viola.

How long could they walk this line before one or both of them tumbled off the edge?

They resumed strolling and soon reached the end of the path. The cliffs stretched around them, a waterfall cascading down the wall opposite. The air felt laden and green . . . the scent of possibility.

Abruptly, Viola turned to him, skirts whirling. "*Oof!* I am so heartily sick of gloves!"

That had Malcolm rearing back his head. "Pardon?"

"Gloves!" She raised her hand, brandishing her fingers in their kid leather as if it were a taint upon humanity.

Frowning, she tugged at her fingertips, vehemently stripping off her gloves, one at a time.

Free of their shield, her hands appeared pale and fragile-boned. *And likely impossibly soft tae the touch*, an unhelpful part of his brain noted.

A lady's perfect hands.

Malcolm stood in perplexed silence. "Why would ye remove your gloves? Your lovely hands should be protected."

"Hah!" She shook the gloves at him. "That is precisely the point! I am so tired of metaphorically covering my soul in gloves." She slapped said gloves against her palm. "My sheathed silence feels complicit. I cannot write what Kendall demands." She huffed a disbelieving laugh. "There. I have said it. I've made a decision. I will *not* write his blasted short story."

She stared at him, wide-eyed, chest heaving.

Taking a chance, Malcolm reached out and plucked the gloves from her hands, tucking them into his sporran.

He then held out his hand, palm up.

An invitation. *Take my hand.*

Viola bit her lip and lifted her right arm.

She paused and then smoothed her palm across his.

Just as on that day along the lane, the contrast between their hands astonished him—her porcelain fingers resting atop his weathered brown ones.

But this time, he could *feel* the velvet softness of her skin, the warmth of her fingers that sent electricity arcing up his arm.

And like before, she wrapped her hand around his and held on tightly—claiming him—the firmness of her grasp mimicking the fierceness of her heart.

"If I could offer a word of advice . . ." He trailed off.

"Please."

"I admire that ye wish tae use your hands for good. To earn dirt under your nails and scrapes across your knuckles."

She said nothing for a moment, eyes blinking rapidly, her left hand wrapping around her waist, fingers fidgeting. But her hand in his held true.

He pressed her palm to his chest, wanting her to feel the steady beat of his heart, the truth of his words.

Dimly, some part of him recognized that such impulses would be his downfall. That the more time he spent with Viola Brodure, the more of himself he stowed within her fragile body.

"Ye have so much fire, lass." He held her hand steady to his heart. "Ye practically *burn* with it. It's a conflagration of ideas and passion inside ye." He thumped his free hand against his sternum. "But I fear for ye, too."

She bit her lip. A tear dropped from her eye.

"You do?" The barest whisper.

She leaned forward, pressing against the hand he held to his chest, as if bracing herself.

"Aye. Such fire . . . 'tis a dangerous thing, I think. If ye dinnae let it go, it may very well incinerate ye. Put another way . . . ofttimes literal death isnae the way we die most."

She absorbed this with an audible inhalation.

He lifted her hand from his chest, pressing a kiss to her knuckles, the tender impulse so natural it terrified him. And just as he had suspected, her skin *was* impossibly soft under his lips. His thoughts careened off course, contemplating the texture of other places he longed to kiss—her cheek, the nape of her neck, that wee hollow between her shoulder and clavicle . . .

"Take on the world's ills, Viola Brodure," he urged. "Shed your gloves. Sing your heart. People *will* listen."

She nodded her head, tears falling in earnest. Pulling her hand out of his, she rummaged in her skirt pocket for a handkerchief.

Malcolm retrieved his own from his sporran. She took it with a watery smile.

"Consider speaking with your father," he continued. "I know ye feel a shame in betraying him, but I guarantee, he sees the intent of your heart. Secrets should not be allowed to fester. Tell him that ye have written *A Hard Truth*. Discuss solutions to Kendall's demands for a story. If nothing else, doing so will ease the burden of your guilt."

"How did you become so wise?" she sniffled, dabbing her face.

"Farming in rural Scotland, o'course." He grinned, cheeky and mischievous. "Have ye not heard? All the greatest poets are doing it nowadays."

Malcolm was entirely too proud of her watery giggle.

May the Lord have mercy on him.

He was already in love with the trilling lilt of her laugh.

13

In the week after the folly picnic, Malcolm's words would not leave Viola be.

She had stripped off her gloves and nearly thrown them at him, and instead of recrimination, he returned with . . .

I understand.

I see.

Poor Ethan had never stood a chance, had he?

Ironically, she felt like Malcolm had the true heart and soul of a poet.

Literal death isnae the way we die most.

Had he known how thoroughly those words would resonate within her?

Over and over, they spun through her mind, an endless wheel looping round. She had a vision of herself stuffed inside a glove labeled with expectations and etiquette and the scores of things society demanded from a woman—body and soul restricted to the point of suffocation, the words she wanted to say lacking the breath required to live.

A death in truth.

Malcolm was correct. She *did* need to speak with her father, to confess her betrayal and clear the air between them.

After all, the dear man still thought she might marry Ethan Penn-Leith.

"He is simply the most marvelous gentleman," her father said as the door closed on yet another visit from Ethan.

Ethan had called upon them dressed for travel, as he was departing immediately for a visit to his Uncle Leith in Aberdeen and would be gone for a week.

He had taken her hand at the door, bowing over her knuckles. "I shall feel bereft without our discussions while I am away. Please save some thoughts for me when I return."

Though Viola had murmured something suitable in reply, she herself felt nothing but relief at Ethan's leaving. She had been granted a week's reprieve to ponder a way to approach the relationship with him. Or rather, to inform Ethan of the *lack* of a true relationship between them.

Which only left confessing to her father.

"Mr. Penn-Leith is to be commended," her father continued, leading the way back into their small front parlor. "What a dedicated and devoted suitor he has been to you, daughter."

Viola paused in the doorway. The air sat heavy with warm humidity, the sort that promised rain by evening. But for now, the large bow windows were pushed open wide, allowing the room to air.

The caretaker of their cottage must have felt the urgency of the impending rain, as two gardeners worked away in the front garden, their shears *snicking* and scythe *shushing* as they trimmed bushes and cut the lawn. The sound carried in through the open windows.

"Mr. Penn-Leith has never professed to be my suitor, per se," she hedged, stepping into the room.

"Bah! The man can scarcely tear his eyes from you." Her father waved a hand. He sat in his preferred tartan wingback chair beside the cold hearth, picking up a book from a side table. "Though you likely should be more obviously doting, if you wish to bring him to the point."

Oh, dear. This was precisely what Viola feared.

She had to tell her father . . . now.

The sound of shears snipping hung in the room as she fought to suppress a wave of anxiety, her stomach quivering.

Glancing toward the open window, she took a few steps closer to her father.

"Papa," Viola began, voice low to prevent the gardeners from overhearing. After all, gossiping tongues were everywhere when it came to herself and Ethan. "Though I do like Mr. Penn-Leith as a friend and fellow writer, I cannot say that I wish for a further measure of his regard."

"Pardon?" Her father shut his book, angling his ear toward her.

Her father was not typically hard of hearing, but Viola *was* speaking quietly. She took a step closer and sat in the wingback chair opposite her father. "I do not wish to marry Mr. Ethan Penn-Leith, Papa. His friendship is sufficient for me."

This time, her father heard her clearly. His brows drew down as he absorbed the news.

The shears continued to snip away in the front garden. One of the gardeners called something to the other.

"I thought you liked Mr. Penn-Leith," her father finally said. "Why have you not said anything before now?"

"I did like him. Or rather, I do . . ." Viola floundered, wondering how to explain. "I appreciate his companionship, but I do not wish for a greater measure of his regard. Friendship is sufficient for me."

"I see." Dr. Brodure set down his book, expression falling and abruptly appearing so . . . weary.

Viola leaned forward and took his worn hands in hers.

"I am sorry, Papa. I know we journeyed to Scotland specifically for this. Truly, I wanted to like Mr. Penn-Leith. But I find that my affections . . . they cannot be forced."

Leaves rustled in the front garden. A lazy bumblebee bobbed past the open windows. The gardeners' voices continued to rumble back and forth, the hiss of the scythe acting as punctuation.

"Does . . . does Mr. Penn-Leith know this?"

"No," Viola said on a sigh. "But I must tell him. I simply need to find the appropriate words."

"Yes. You do need to speak with him before his feelings grow any deeper."

"I will," she promised. "As soon as he returns from Aberdeen."

And she would. She absolutely would.

"I want what is best for you, Viola. I always have." Her father patted her hand. "But as your father, I must confess my worry, as well. Your determination to refuse Mr. Penn-Leith's attentions will certainly raise Kendall's displeasure. He could choose to harm your writing endeavors. You are a woman writing in a man's world, after all."

"Yes, I am well aware of that fact."

"And so I would urge you to think carefully on this decision."

"I *have*, Papa." Viola's voice rose. "I have known for weeks that I do not wish Mr. Penn-Leith as a suitor."

Mr. *Ethan* Penn-Leith, that was. Viola did not add that distinction.

"Though I do not wish for you to marry where you do not love, I also worry for your future, my child." Dr. Brodure held up a conciliatory hand. "That Kendall will be punitive and, therefore, ensure your brilliant writing is not remembered for generations to come."

"I *do* recognize what you are saying, Papa." She sat back in her chair. "But please put your mind at ease with regard to my ambition. I do not want to rule the literary elites in London or be lauded as another Shakespeare. I do not wish for greater renown or fortune—"

"Truly?" Her father frowned.

"Yes. Truly. I do not need fame—" She took a fortifying breath. "—but I *do* need to make a difference." She continued on, forcing the words past her numb lips. "I know we have touched on this in the past, but Papa, I cannot write the moralizing tales that Kendall wishes me to write . . . nary a one."

"Daughter, the duke has made his expectations clear." Her father's words reverberated with agitation. "I thought *you* had agreed to them, as well. You cannot renege on your promise. Kendall will retaliate in earnest if you do."

Her father's raised voice and implied accusation had Viola darting a look toward the window. It was eerily silent outside. Had the gardeners gone off to lunch? Or were they now listening?

Her lungs tightened.

"What else am I to do, Papa?" She tried to speak quietly, but her words emerged high and strangled, growing louder as she spoke. "I have tried to write this ridiculous story, but the words simply won't come. I have realized that I can only write about the true woes of our society. To expose the wretched conditions of the working class that many, like Kendall, would prefer to ignore. I want to be remembered as a woman who braved criticism and censorship, not one who hid behind moralizing platitud—"

Tap, tap, tap.

The sound of someone rapping on the glass behind Viola sent her leaping from her seat, her heart a frantic rabbit in her chest.

She whirled and met the gaze of the Duke of Kendall standing outside the open window. As usual, His Grace appeared immaculately turned out in a top hat and green coat.

"Good afternoon. Dr. Brodure. Miss Brodure." The duke tipped his hat as calmly as if encountering them upon a street in Mayfair.

"Your Grace!" Dr. Brodure moved past Viola, face wreathed in a nervously welcoming smile. "How kind of you to call upon us. Please, do come in!"

As if that were all the coaxing he needed, His Grace removed his top hat, folded his tall body, and stepped through the open window into the parlor.

Viola took an involuntary step back. Her father kept a strained smile on his face. Clearly, neither of them had expected Kendall to just pop through the window, though it was certainly large enough to be a makeshift door.

She didn't think she had ever encountered Kendall in such a small space. His broad shoulders and humorless eyes desaturated the room, rendering the space as leaden as his gray hair.

More to the point—

How long had the duke been standing at the open window?!

Viola's rabbity heart thumped and lurched.

"To what do we owe the pleasure of your company, Your Grace?" Dr. Brodure motioned for the duke to be seated.

Kendall ignored him, preferring instead to spin in a slow circle, surveying the room—the cold hearth, the stag horns, Viola's writing desk to the right of the window. With two measured steps of his long legs, he crossed to the desk and surveyed her open notebook.

Her *blank* notebook.

"Pray tell me, Miss Brodure . . ." Kendall began, words falling in a measured cadence. He tapped the notebook with the tip of one gloved finger. "Tell me about these moralizing tales you now refuse to write."

The duke fixed Viola with his dark gaze. The tense set of his eyes and the tick in his clenched jaw told her all she needed to know—he had overhead much, if not all, of her conversation with her father.

Oh.

Her hands starting shaking in time with her frenzied heartbeat.

"Uhmmm," her father whirled on her, expression frantic.

"Do not bother lying," Kendall continued, voice like a winter wind and just as breath-stealing.

He waved a hand toward the window, indicating that he had heard all while standing there. Anyone else would feel chagrined at eavesdropping on a private conversation, but not a duke.

Kendall merely considered it his right.

"Miss Brodure," he continued, "it appears that you do not wish to proceed with our plan. That you have not, in fact, been working on the story I requested of you. The one you *agreed* to produce."

Viola placed a shaking palm atop the wingback chair to her right.

Her breath felt caught in a giant's vise, her father's worry and her own agitation constricting her lungs. But this confrontation had been too long in coming. She swallowed, forcing herself to take slow measured breaths.

"You heard c-correctly, Your Grace," she said, cursing her stammering tongue. "I cannot do it. The words are f-frozen inside me. I need to write stories that f-focus more fully on societal ills. Stories that m-may not—" *deep breath* "—that may not conform with your ideals."

There.

She had said it.

Facing Kendall in this moment . . . well, she now knew how to describe the sensation of a doomed man looking down the barrel of a rifle. The mad heartbeat, the perspiring palms, the sense of surreal calm . . . they all had to be similar.

Kendall stared at her, the *thwap thwap* of his hat against his thigh echoing loudly in the silence.

"I have invested significant time in this political maneuver, Miss Brodure. I will not have it upended at this juncture due to female vacillation and hysteria. Too much is riding on your commitment."

"Your Grace," her father stretched out a placating hand, "I am sure with some discussion we can reach a compro—"

"Save your conciliatory speeches, Dr. Brodure," Kendall snapped.

Her father flinched, retreating back.

Viola experienced a flash of anger over the duke addressing her father so.

"I face strong opposition from the Whigs," His Grace went on. "Periodicals like *The Rabble Rouser*—a publication I shudder to call anything other than a putrid cesspool of typescript—are gaining traction with their melodramatic stories of woe. We need Miss Brodure's tales to counteract their message and ensure that my rivals are unsuccessful in their attempts to reform the Poor Laws. Our current laws are already sufficient."

Viola's lungs tightened.

Yes.

Definitely the sensation of imminent death.

She closed her eyes, praying for divine guidance, *anything* to help her understand how to proceed.

"And then there is the matter of Mr. Penn-Leith."

Viola's eyes flew open. "Pardon?"

His Grace tossed his hat atop a side table. "I overheard talk about your relationship with Mr. Penn-Leith."

"Mr. Ethan Penn-Leith?" Viola asked faintly. Just for her own clarification.

"Of course Mr. Ethan Penn-Leith. What other Mr. Penn-Leith is there?" Kendall's frown deepened, as if she were the veriest simpleton.

Right.

Viola took in a slow breath, pleading with her lungs and nerves to *please cooperate just this once.*

"I cannot say that I consider Mr. Ethan Penn-Leith to be anything other than a f-friend, Your Grace."

"I am hardly convinced that is the truth, Miss Brodure," Kendall said. "From an outsider's view, you seem to enjoy Mr. Penn-Leith's company."

"But—" Viola began.

"No. I will not argue this point. You will carry on as you have." Kendall held up a staying hand. "You do not have to actually marry Mr. Penn-Leith, Miss Brodure. Simply become betrothed. Write the story. *The Gentleman's Magazine* will run your tale. *Everyone* will read it because your name will already be in every newspaper due to your betrothal. Then once the vote has been defeated in Parliament, you may quietly cry off. I fail to see why this process remains so difficult for you to follow?!"

Anger and outrage filtered through Viola's anxiety.

Oh! The audacity of this man!

How could he stand there, gray-haired and looming, and propose such unconscionable scenarios as if they were commonplace?

"B-because it would be hurtful to Mr. Penn-Leith to lead him on so. Because it is my own reputation, Your Grace, and I do not wish to be labeled a jilt—"

"Pardon? Your reputation is already in jeopardy. You have led Mr. Penn-Leith to have expectations." Kendall began to pace the room, a concession, Viola supposed, to his agitation. "Everyone anticipates you two will marry. The Queen herself awaits it. Whether you refuse him now or in a few months' time, the damage to your reputation is already done."

Viola inhaled—a sharp, staccato sound.

Surely she hadn't raised Ethan's expectations to that point. She had been so careful in her visits with him.

Kendall was simply attempting to tie her in mental knots.

That he was marginally succeeding only stoked the toxic mix of *angerfrustrationanxiety* roiling under her sternum.

"B-but that is others' behavior, others' wishes, not m-mine," she argued, hating how Kendall's needling tangled her tongue. "I haven't encouraged him."

"Won't you please be seated, Your Grace?" Dr. Brodure tried again, motioning toward the sofa opposite the bare hearth.

But Kendall was still pacing, jaw clenched. Were he a lesser man, he would likely be raking a hand through his silver hair in frustration.

Viola watched him, her fingers trembling more and more with each passing minute.

Heavens above! Why must so much of her life hang on this one aristocrat?

"I can only be so lenient, Miss Brodure," Kendall finally said, turning hard eyes back to Viola. "My goals and aims remain the same. I cannot have you speaking in direct opposition to them. I cannot have a vicar tied to my estate," he pointed at Dr. Brodure, "who is not in harmony with my own principles. Her Majesty certainly will not take kindly to a bishop who does not display those ideals, as well."

The duke went back to his pacing, eyebrows bunching like a thundercloud.

Viola swallowed.

So.

Here it was.

The moment she had always feared would come.

And . . .

Yes, it felt as knife-in-the-gut awful as she had imagined it would. She wanted to double over from the pain and scream her rage and dismay.

"I have valued my relationship with you both." Kendall paused in his pacing, his dark eyes glittering in the light. "Please do not force me to take actions against you, to see yourselves tossed out of house and home. I do not wish to be cruel, but you are rapidly leaving me with little other choice."

Viola's throat seized up; spots hovered in her vision and the room darkened at the edges.

Her father instantly noted her troubled breathing. Reaching out, he cupped her elbow.

"Viola and I are always at your service, Your Grace, as we have ever been." Dr. Brodure led Viola to the sofa and helped her sit. "Please forgive us. My daughter's asthma is often triggered by stressful conversation."

"I will be f-fine, Papa—"

"Hush, child."

"*Please remove him*," she mouthed to her father, eyes flicking to Kendall. She couldn't endure another moment in the duke's presence.

Her father nodded. "Stay here, child. I will speak with His Grace in my study. I'll have the maid fetch some coffee for your throat. Your Grace?"

Her father left the room, Kendall at his heels.

Viola dug her fingernails into the velvet of the sofa, her eyes stinging and lungs laboring to breathe.

What was she to do now?

Kendall's voice rose from the next room, her father's a low murmur. Dr. Brodure would placate the duke. For better or worse, her father always knew the right thing to say to a Duke of Kendall.

The maid brought in some black coffee. Viola sipped the bitter brew, willing the tightness in her chest to ease.

A Greek chorus of *whatshouldIdo* shrieked in her head.

She realized she couldn't simply ignore Kendall's demands. To do so would leave her father unemployed and find them both cast out of their home. Where would they go? Throw themselves upon Lord Mossley's magnanimity? And with all his other concerns, would her uncle help his younger brother defy a duke as powerful as Kendall?

She doubted it.

And if Viola and her father were utterly cut off from friends and family, what would become of them?

Briefly, she pictured herself like one of her own desperate characters, living in a fetid room, cooling her father's fevered head with a wet cloth.

No. She could not permit events to become as dire as that.

But at the same time, she could not continue like this . . . to bite her tongue and play the demure lady and pretend that she didn't long to scream her own truth.

Literal death isnae the way we die most.

Malcolm.

Just the thought of him scorched all other images from her mind. All she could see was his strong body standing tall beside their swing, head lifting to look at her.

With Malcolm, she could breathe.

He didn't care if she came to him bare-handed and bonnetless. Thank heavens, she currently wore shoes.

Because as Kendall's voice rumbled behind the closed door, Viola simply . . . snapped.

Crossing the room, she gathered up her skirts and, sitting on the sill, dropped to the ground outside, startling the two gardeners snipping back roses who had, yes, been eagerly listening at the window.

She had nodded a greeting to them and disappeared down the lane long before her father and Kendall returned.

14

Later, Viola would marvel that she managed to walk the long distance to Thistle Muir.

Her corset restricted her ribcage, and her asthma threatened to overwhelm her. But, as usual, the damp air of Scotland eased her breathing, opening up her lungs just enough for her to move onward— one step, two, another step. The wind had picked up, darker clouds menacing on the horizon. Viola could practically feel the promised storm nipping at her heels.

She wiped tears as she walked, Kendall's words like circling black ravens, swooping round and round in her head.

Her father would talk Kendall down from his outrage. She knew this. For better or worse, placating irrational aristocrats was a political game at which Dr. Brodure excelled.

One of the many reasons why he would make a superb bishop.

Was there a path out of the duke's shadow? A way for her and her father to reach their aims without his assistance?

And even if Dr. Brodure left Kendall's employ—if Papa could find another suitable patron—would the young duke retaliate?

His sire, the former Duke of Kendall, certainly would have. Viola didn't know this Kendall well enough to predict his reaction.

And it wasn't as if she could ask him outright—*I say, Your Grace, if I directly oppose your political aims in a decidedly vocal, public way, will you be a good egg and let it slide?*

Even as she had the thought, Viola knew her father would never agree to leave Westacre in disgrace. Dr. Brodure loved his parishioners. He loved greeting people on a Sunday—complimenting Mrs. Bell on a new hat, asking Mr. Wright if his mother's health had improved. He loved marrying the children he had watched grow from babes, of being a ferryman of sorts in the ebb and flow of life.

Another reason why he would make a remarkable bishop.

She skirted the edge of the village, not wanting to be seen in her bonnetless, gloveless state. No need to provide yet another scandalous detail for the gossips to bandy about.

Thankfully, she only glimpsed Mrs. Buchan from a distance and narrowly avoided Mrs. Ruxton as the lady walked up the path to the vicarage. Passing the kirkyard, Viola rounded the final bend to Thistle Muir.

The house appeared in storybook parts—chimneys rising toward the sky, symmetrically placed windows peering out into the green landscape, the white front door standing at attention.

A wide pasture stretched to the left of the house.

A familiar figure bent over the gate leading to the field.

Oh.

Malcolm's broad shoulders flexed, his back to her as he latched the gate shut. The wind ruffled the hair poking out from underneath his tartan cap, sending the heavy weight of his great kilt swaying.

Beowoof sat beside his master, tongue lolling. He let out a joyous woof when he saw Viola, instantly loping across the garden to her side. The dog's unfettered happiness made her vision go blurry again.

Malcolm pivoted with Beowoof's movement, his eyes meeting hers.

His gaze swept her body. And somehow . . . he knew.

In that single, simple glance, he understood the depth of her despair. The pain that had chased her to his door.

His brows furrowed and he strode toward her, a towering thundercloud gathering.

"What is it, lass?" His concerned voice undid her. "What has happened?"

Viola pressed her palms to her face in an attempt to prevent more tears.

Gently, his warm fingers engulfed her wrists, pulling her hands from her cheeks before sliding to cup her jaw. The rasp of his work-worn palms sent electricity coiling in her belly.

He leaned closer, chestnut brown eyes searching her face.

"*Och*, you've been *greiting*," he said on a whisper, thumbs stroking her cheeks. "I see it in your red eyes."

Oh, this impossibly precious man!

Viola closed the remaining distance between them and threw herself upon his chest, weeping. Her arms wrapped around his waist, her face pressed to his sternum, her nose buried in the wool of his great kilt.

The motion felt impossibly right, as if Malcolm's body had been created simply to bear the weight of her tears.

His arms banded tightly around her, pulling her close.

Viola rested everything upon him: arms and chest, hopes and fears.

He bore the burden with comforting ease.

"There, lass," he murmured against her hair. "There, there. Has someone died?"

Viola shook her head.

"Ah. Then I only have one other question—" He paused to push back her hair, his rough hand cradling her face again. "Who do I need tae give a good thumping?"

That was the last straw—the final thing that sent Viola tumbling head-over-heels for Malcolm Penn-Leith.

How she adored him!

Unfortunately, the realization was one incident too many.

Kendall's pressure and her own fears for her future.

Her long walk taken much too quickly.

Malcolm's kind words and patient understanding.

The longings of her own heart.

Her poor body was not up to the task of actually *breathing* through it all.

Her chest spasmed and her throat constricted until Viola was gasping.

Malcolm instantly noticed the change in her breathing. He pulled back.

"Breathe, lass." His rich bass rumbled over her. "Deep and easy."

Viola concentrated on sucking in steady lungfuls of air.

Malcolm's brow knit in concern.

Before Viola could utter a sound, he swept her up into his arms—surely she appeared a mass of billowing white petticoats and blue skirt—and effortlessly carried her the remaining steps to the front stoop of Thistle Muir.

Viola clasped her hands around his neck, resting her cheek on his shoulder, eyes closed, mind focused on the simple act of moving air in and out of her lungs.

Of course, as her nose was all but pressed into Malcolm's throat, she caught a heady lungful of *him*, too—man and wool, woodsmoke and hay.

The scent instantly calmed her, the seeping heat of his body easing the tightness of her throat. As if the warmth of Malcolm's touch soothed the very strands of her soul.

He shifted her to open the door, and then she was in the dark interior of Thistle Muir. If he found her weight burdensome, he showed not a hint of it. His heart remained a slow, steady thump under her ear.

Instead of setting her down as she expected, Malcolm ordered Beowoof to stay outside and shut the door behind them with his foot.

He strode into the parlor, sinking onto a sofa with Viola still in his arms. His muscles flexed, as if tensing to move her off his lap. Viola clung to him with a mewl of protest, refusing to relinquish the comfort of his hold quite yet. His rumbled assent vibrated through her sternum. He settled back. Her body relaxed into his strength, her breathing easing.

How glorious to be in this place—curled upon his lap, her nose nestled into his throat, his beard tickling her forehead. She figured if she died here and now . . . cradled in the arms of Malcolm Penn-Leith would be an acceptable way to go.

And so, even though the worst of the attack had passed—she certainly did not need his physical assistance any longer—she could not bring herself to move.

His arms wrapped gently around her, holding her in place—firm but not constricting, supporting but not binding. She knew he would loose her the second she asked. And would hold her again just as quickly.

Tears pricked once more.

How could any woman—any human being, for that matter—want more from life than this? To have another person who supported you just as you were?

Malcolm did not require her to hide parts of her soul—her ideals, her aspirations, her regrets. With him, she could be her most true self.

More to the point, she liked the person she was in his eyes.

Would that this could be the rest of her life. That she could remain here with Malcolm at Thistle Muir, curled into the comfort of his strong arms, adored simply for being . . . Viola.

They rested in silence, the ticking of the clock on the mantel counting their synchronized breaths.

With each passing tick, Viola became more physically aware of the mountain of intoxicating male underneath her. Somehow, her heartbeat had migrated to the places they touched—shoulder, hip, arm—and now her very skin pulsed as if alive.

Her breathing picked up again. His throat was mere inches from her lips. She would only have to shift the tiniest bit to press her mouth against the tendons flexing in his neck.

And if she did, how would Malcolm respond? Would he turn his head and capture her lips with his?

A wave of longing flooded her cheeks.

Abruptly, she understood all too well why women and men found themselves in compromising positions. Because if Malcolm kissed her right now, she instinctively knew she would only want more and more.

But would he find her kisses as intoxicating?

She knew he liked her as a person. As a friend.

But did he wish for more than that?

Finally, Viola's thoughts became too loud, too shouty to easily push aside. And lying scandalously curled against Malcolm in no way helped to clarify her thinking.

With great reluctance, she pulled back.

"Better?" Malcolm asked.

Nodding, she slid off his lap and onto the sofa beside him.

He met her eyes, but the carefully blank expression in his own gave away nothing.

Viola blushed in earnest, tucking a stray strand of hair behind her ear. Worried that her eyes would betray her own longings, she looked around the room.

She had visited Thistle Muir once before, but at the time, she hadn't thought of the parlor as Malcolm's home.

As a place that would tell her a story of him.

Now . . . she studied the space with different eyes.

The room appeared well-loved . . . in the best sense of the word.

It shone in the rubbed nap of the fine Aubusson carpet.

In the foolscap piled and stacked atop a desk before one of the tall windows.

In the chipped *cloisonné* on a sideboard, brimming with foxglove and peonies freshly cut from the garden.

In the worn leather footstool before the fireplace, a stack of loosely piled journals atop it—*The Atheneaum, Tait's Edinburgh Magazine,* and even one dog-eared corner of what had to be *The Rabble Rouser.*

The room rang with the laughter of a thousand conversations, with whispered late-night confidences and cozy discussions before the fire.

I could spend my life in a room like this, Viola thought.

It was a room not unlike her own parlor in the vicarage in Westacre, smelling of linseed oil and lavender.

And now that she knew Malcolm, she saw him everywhere.

The wingback chair before the hearth sagged in his shape. The literary journals, of course, were a nod to his well-read mind. Beside the desk, there was a bookshelf piled with leather-bound books, sometimes two-deep. The titles leapt across the room—*Paradise Lost, The Rights of Man, Hamlet, Candide.*

She rose from the sofa, one book lover eager to peruse the library of another.

"Could I offer ye some tea?" Malcolm's voice came from behind her.

Viola startled and looked over her shoulder at him—standing so broad and bearded.

Goodness but he saturated the air of every space he inhabited.

"Tea?" she echoed.

"Aye, tea. I hear it's all the rage with ye English." He smiled, further obliterating her wits. "Ethan may be on the road to Aberdeen, and my housekeeper and maid may have their afternoon off today—Isla Liston is 'great with child' as the Bible describes it, and Mrs. McGregor is tending to her—but I can boil water for tea."

Viola blinked at all the information.

No wonder the house felt so still. It was just herself and Malcolm within its walls.

Up to this point, they had skirted the bounds of propriety but hadn't crossed them. Not until today. Until this moment.

Thank goodness no one knew she was here. If they were found together like this, she and Malcolm would likely have to marry.

Hmmm.

That idea worried her . . . not at all.

If anything, it caused a knot of yearning to tighten in her abdomen.

"Thank you." She smiled at him in return. "But I think my English soul can manage another hour or two without tea."

MALCOLM WAS ABSOLUTELY, utterly sure that his actions of the past half hour had been a monumental mistake.

He should not have scooped Viola into his arms.

He should not have brought her into his home, completely unchaperoned, without asking her permission.

He should not have compounded the lot by then holding her on his lap for far too long.

But she had been so fragile in his embrace, a hummingbird of a woman—wee, yet vibrating with life.

The soft curves of her body remained branded on his hands and chest—a heavenly torture. Viola might be small, but she was perfectly formed.

He had held her for far longer than was wise. How could he not?

In an hour of crisis, she had come running to him for comfort. He didn't know what had caused her distress, though he presumed the Duke of Kendall was likely involved.

But until she confided in him, Malcolm contented himself with watching her explore his space, moving from fireplace to bow window with unabashed curiosity.

Currently, she was bent down, running a fine-boned finger along the spines of the books on his bookshelf. The position did rather thrilling things to her anatomy that Malcolm was man enough to notice. But being a gentleman, no matter his birth, he kept his eyes firmly on her profile.

She was a dreadful mess—her cheeks tear-stained and splotchy, bonnetless, her hair bedraggled with pale locks sticking to her temples. His Viola would never have a good *greit* without it being painfully obvious.

His Viola.

Och, when had he become comfortable with putting a possessive pronoun before her name?

She was not *his* . . . anything.

Desperately, he attempted to visualize his well-worn chasm of grief, needing its familiarity and comfort.

Only . . . the image slipped through his fingers, lost in the rushing happiness of Viola Brodure opening his copy of *Gulliver's Travels* and grinning as she read his notes in the margin.

Helplessly, he noted that her pale pink lips turned into wee clouds when pursed.

He was desperate to kiss her, Malcolm realized. But he knew that one kiss would never satisfy.

No. He would want a lifetime of kisses, a lifetime of her with—

Bloody hell.

He ran a hand over his beard, eyes closing as he faced the stark truth:

His comfortable crevasse of grief was no more.

Every look, every thought, every step toward Viola had been like a foothold climbing upward.

And now he stood in the sharp, blinding light of an unfamiliar terrain, facing an unknown future.

But . . . he also knew too well the pain of tumbling down a deep chasm of loss. The knowledge had ceased to be theoretical.

And therein lay the rub—the source of the maelstrom of terror currently roiling his chest.

He didn't understand how to battle this fear. The worry of giving his heart to Viola and then losing her just as suddenly as he had Aileen.

Not that Viola *wished* to be his.

How would a fine lady like Viola fit into your sorry life anyway?

He glanced around the parlor.

The red velvet of the sofa was faded and rubbed to the warp in places. Soot from the fire darkened the marble mantelpiece. The leg of the sideboard had been broken and repaired in at least two places. The entire room desperately needed new drapery and a fresh coat of paint.

This was what he had to offer her. A shabby house in rural Scotland. His hard-working, calloused hands. A herd of cows.

In short, nothing of real value to a refined lady.

And yet, he couldn't ignore the fact that she appeared comfortable in his space. As if being here, with him, were as natural as breathing. Nor could he deny that he felt the same, in return.

Setting down *Gulliver's Travels*, Viola moved on to study a daguerreotype portrait of Leah and Fox with Madeline and wee Jack. Malcolm's nephew had tried valiantly to sit still, but his right foot was a blur of movement.

"Do ye wish to discuss what so upset ye?" Malcolm asked after a few minutes of watching her poke through his things. "My fists stand ready to knock sense into someone's thick skull. Or, at the very least, to teach ye how to throw a solid punch yourself."

That at least had Viola turning back to him, blue eyes lit with a soft smile. She shook out her skirts, smoothing the worst of the wrinkles, before heaving a sigh.

"'Tis only what we have already discussed." She clasped her hands before her. "I am afraid that physical punishment will do no good, unless you wish to organize a militia to combat the Duke of Kendall."

Malcolm snorted. "I would actually take great pleasure in doing that, lass."

Her smile grew, true mirth touching her expression.

The rain that had been threatening all day finally announced its arrival, pattering the front bow window with a bracing *ratatat*. Though the parlor sported four large windows, the dark clouds left the interior dim.

Malcolm stirred the banked fire to life as Viola recounted the conversation with her father and Kendall. The duke's threats to withdraw his support from the Brodures. Viola's worries about her own future and her father's employment.

"And so, I am at a loss." She stopped her perusal of the room, standing before him. "I cannot write the drivel that Kendall demands. It feels so . . . dispiriting." She waved a hand toward his copy of *The Rabble Rouser*. "Particularly when all I want to do is write more stories like *A Hard Truth*."

Hands on his hips, Malcolm looked at Viola, wishing there was someone he could pummel, anything to wipe the bleak look off her face.

Well, he supposed he could bloody Kendall, as she had joked. But it would do no good. The man would still be a powerful duke, no matter how battered and bruised.

"I hate that ye are not even allowed the luxury of silence," Malcolm said. "The simplicity of inaction."

"Yes." She pressed shaking fingertips to her forehead. "I cannot see any solution other than giving in to Kendall's demands. Of figuratively donning gloves once more."

Unbidden, both their eyes dipped to her bare hands. Rain lashed the windows, filling the room with the sound of rushing water.

Malcolm longed to open his arms once more, to pull her against him and soothe away her hurt.

Something of his desire must have shone in his gaze, as Viola took a half-step toward him.

"A piece of me feels like I have betrayed your trust," she continued.

"Me?" He laughed in bafflement.

"Yes. You. Malcolm Penn-Leith."

He stilled, liking his full name on her lips, the sound of it in her proper English accent.

She wasn't done. "You have listened and encouraged me these past few weeks. You have been so patient and wise. And now I will return all that care by doing absolutely nothing with all my fine words. It grieves me." Viola bit her lower lip. "When Kendall snaps his fingers and I betray myself by racing to his call like a dog, will I still be able to call you my friend?"

"Always."

Just like that moment when they had sat, side-by-side, on the swing, her eyes focused on his mouth.

Malcolm's heart constricted.

Yes. Yes, he would love nothing more than to kiss Viola.

But . . . she had experienced a difficult day. Her normal defenses were lowered. He should not take advantage of her vulnerable state.

Or rather . . . *further* advantage.

And yet . . .

He found himself halving the space between them. She matched his movement, stepping closer until her skirts brushed his kilt.

Her gaze went hazy.

He stared at her mouth, the perfect rosebud arch of her upper lip, the plump pout of her lower.

Heaven's above, the woman was made for kissing, for risk and passion.

He found himself listing forward.

Her eyes fluttered shut.

She rose on her tiptoes.

He leaned down.

Close . . .

Closer . . .

Eager tae watch this woman die too, ye eejit?

To drag her down into your lowly life?

The thoughts ricocheted like cannon fire through Malcolm's brain.

He jolted upright, panic thrumming along his skin.

Terror flooded his veins.

He took a step back, chest heaving. Viola's eyes flared open, brow puckered.

Abruptly, he turned and poked at the fire.

Her confusion battered his shoulders.

Silence rang, filling the room.

"A good friend recently encouraged me to figuratively 'shed my gloves.'" Her voice reached him from behind. "I understood that to mean, among other things, that I should stop muffling my words. That when I felt or thought something strongly, I should speak."

And then, maddeningly, she said nothing more for a beat.

Malcolm slumped, returning the fire poker to its stand.

"Viola." He turned back to her.

That was an absolute mistake.

Her summer-blue eyes glittered even in the dim light. A blush scorched her skin, painting color across her cheekbones.

"Please, Malcolm. I trust you, of all people, not to toy with me." She wrapped her arms around her ribcage. "I cannot help but think you were just about to k-kiss me, and yet . . . and yet, you pulled away."

The fire popped in the hearth.

Rain pattered against the window panes.

Viola licked her lips.

Malcolm couldn't stop himself from staring at her mouth.

"Why?" she finally breathed. "Why did you not kiss me?"

15

Viola's words froze Malcolm in place.

Her direct question merited a direct answer.

But what was he to say?

One man has already overset ye today. I dinnae wish tae be a second.

Aileen's death nearly destroyed me. I cannae risk feeling such grief again. Not with a woman I could love so well as yourself.

Our stations in life are too disparate to forge a life together, and so, why begin?

"Malcolm?" she prompted, her blush turning splotchy and pained.

His answers choked him, as he recognized them for what they were—excuses.

In truth . . . he was afraid.

Afraid to offer his heart to another again.

Afraid to confront the agony and horror and grief of his past.

Like a red deer stag caught in the stark flame of a stalker's torch, he blinked into the light, frozen and surprised, slowly understanding that his very indecision would be his downfall.

Tightening her arms further around herself, Viola turned her head to the right, gazing at the *dreich* landscape out the window.

Silence hung.

The mantel clock ticked in time to the rain.

"Everything between you and me has, from the moment we met, been so open . . . a book easily read," she whispered, clearly not misreading his hesitation. "And so, I had assumed us to be of a similar mindset with regards to . . ." She motioned to the space between them. "But I was apparently wrong." Head high, she turned for the door. "I apologize if my forward behavior caused—"

"Viola." Malcolm intended merely to stop the thread of her thoughts. To assure her that she was not to blame for his reaction.

But her name came out in a pained rasp. Laden with his longing, with anguish at the distance between them.

Startled, her eyes snapped to his. He hated the confusion and hurt he could see in their depths, pain he himself had caused.

"Why?" she repeated. "Help me understand. Have I misunderstood what was happening between us? Do you dislike the thought of kissing me?"

No. Quite the opposite.

She had not misunderstood.

Malcolm swallowed, his fingers flexing against the urge to reach for her.

His brave, fierce lass.

He had to meet her courage with his own.

"Nae." The sound came out hoarse. "I would love nothing more than tae kiss ye. Ye were made for kisses, Viola Brodure."

Relief washed her face. She took three eager steps toward him.

He stopped her with an outstretched hand.

"But, lass, there is simply too much between us. Ethan . . ."

Viola flinched at the sound of his brother's name.

"What about Ethan?" she asked. "I am hardly a thing to be fought over, like hounds with a bone."

"I ken that."

"I do not wish a future with Ethan."

Malcolm's every muscle froze at her admission.

Not only that she definitively did not wish a relationship with his brother.

But because every minuscule gap of space in her words implied that she was open to the possibility of a true romance with him—Malcolm.

Why?!

Of all the men in Great Britain and beyond, why would Viola Brodure set her lovely sights on him?

Yes, he knew they were becoming good friends.

Yes, he found her beautiful, inside and out.

But to think of that attraction being returned in full measure . . .

"Actually, I lied," he continued. "I dinnae see. I dinnae ken why ye would like tae . . ."

Tae kiss me.

He couldn't finish the sentence.

For the first time in forever, Malcolm felt the telltale warmth of a searing blush.

Viola cocked her head at him, as if he had said something impossibly adorable. "Are you truly asking me *why* I want to kiss you?"

Malcolm nodded, ears crimson red and burning.

VIOLA WAS TORN between collapsing into hysterics of laughter or climbing Malcolm Penn-Leith's muscled body like a tree and forcing his gorgeous mouth to hers.

Unfortunately, neither option was appropriate for a gently bred lady. More's the pity.

Had he truly asked why she wanted to kiss him?!

Did the man have a mirror? One that would show not only his physical appearance but his soul as well?

He was . . . well . . . simply put . . .

Stunning.

In every sense of the word.

The sheer masculinity of him pummeled her senses. His mind blinded hers with its keen insights. His calm heart settled her agitated nerves.

"Ye seem tae be thinking about this a wee bit too hard." Malcolm's eyes narrowed.

Viola laughed at that. A snorting guffaw of sound that she instantly stifled behind a hand, which somehow made it worse.

"Again, ye aren't making a case for me here," he continued.

"Oh! I'm trying to find words that aren't entirely gauche, you wretch." She gave a helpless laugh, feeling her cheeks warm. "Why do I want to kiss you? Well, for all the obvious reasons, I suppose. You are an interesting, charming, and intelligent gentleman, and I admit to finding you unbearably . . ."—heavens, this blush would be the end of her—". . . attractive."

There.

Fortunately, Malcolm didn't look as horror-stricken as he had earlier, in the moment of their almost kiss.

That look . . .

It had nearly curdled her stomach.

"*Gentleman*," he said, lingering on the word. As if *that* were the most significant thing she had said. "Many would argue against ye applying that label tae myself."

Viola let out an exasperated puff of air. "You *are* a gentleman, Malcolm."

"Nae, I'm not. Not by any measurable standard."

"I disagree. You are kind, gentle, and sensitive to the needs of those around you. Noble things that the lofty Duke of Kendall is not, no matter his vaunted pedigree."

"But . . . doesnae it bother ye? The difference in our stations?"

"I've spent considerable time with your brother these past weeks. I don't see why you are so dissimilar."

Malcolm snorted at that. "Ye know that tae be stretching the truth a wee bit, lass. Yes, Ethan and I are brothers. But he is my uncle's heir and has been raised tae the life of a gentleman. We are anything but the same, blood notwithstanding."

"I disagree!"

This darling man was going to send her mad, talking round and round. All Viola wanted was to be welcomed back into the circle of his arms, pressed once more into the heat of his chest.

"You mentioned that Aileen was of a lower social station than you. Did that ever give you pause when you courted her?" she continued.

"O'course not. I never thought about it. She was my equal in every way."

"Well, there you are."

"Aye, but Aileen sensed the difference. I only see it now, at a distance, how she always felt less-than."

Oh.

"And do you feel . . . less than?" Viola had to ask.

Malcolm stared at her for one breath. Two.

And then looked away.

Viola's spirits sank.

"Your grandfather was a viscount," he said, as if *that* were his answer to her question. "Your uncle, Lord Mossley, *is* a viscount."

"Balderdash. The Earls of Aberdeen grace your own family tree—"

"Aye. Distantly. Through my mother, who stooped far beneath herself when she married my father."

"This is all a humbug, Malcolm. As if I care for such things. And even if I did, you have elevated your own social status through your diligence and hard work. Your business ventures are thriving. You are well-read and take time to educate your mind. You count a baronet and a high-ranking earl amongst your close acquaintance."

He pivoted away from her with a scoff.

"No." She darted around him, forcing him to look at her. "I will not permit you to brush off my opinion. Ethan is a bright star rising in part because of his dedication to his craft, but also because he was given an enormous boost by your uncle's generosity. You have had no such advantage, and yet you have succeeded despite it."

Malcolm raked his palm through his hair, mussing the whole and tempting Viola's own fingers to smooth it to rights.

Why were men always so cavalier about alluring states of *dishabille?* She was quite sure it was a conspiracy aimed at coaxing women down the path to ruin.

In Malcolm Penn-Leith's case, it was decidedly effective.

She wanted this man just as mussed and unsettled and *wanting* as she was.

If she thought for even one moment that he wasn't interested in kissing her, she would back away. But she had seen the heat, the yearning in his gaze.

Malcolm *did* want to kiss her. It was just a misguided apprehension over the differences in their social status that had him hesitating.

Or was something else stopping him, and he was using their social differences as an excuse?

And since she was trying to be more assertive in her life, she asked the question directly, "Are the social differences between us your true reason? Or is there something else, Malcolm?"

The rain outside made itself known once again, sending sheets of water against the front windows.

He glanced toward the sound, a frown on his brow.

"I simply cannae see how a relationship between us would be," he finally said, meeting her gaze. "Ye are far too fierce and beautiful tae consider tethering your life tae the likes of me."

At that, he studied the rain another moment . . .

. . . turned . . .

. . . and walked out of the room.

Viola stared after him for the space of three heartbeats.

Thump.

Thump.

Thump.

Had he just . . .

After saying . . .

OH!

"No!" She stomped after him. "No, no, no!"

His back was retreating down the central hall, deeper into the house.

"With the rain chucking down, I have tae check the barns," he called.

No, they were having this out.

Now.

Clearly *something* more was holding him back—something paralyzing—and he *would* speak with her about it.

"Malcolm Penn-Leith! You cannot call me fierce and beautiful in one breath and then walk off in the next!" Viola followed him through the house. Such brazenness displayed a terrible lack of propriety, but she was beyond caring. "You aren't the only one who gets to make decisions about us."

Malcolm crossed through the scullery, out a door, and into a courtyard at the back of the house. Work sheds and a smaller barn lined the perimeter.

The rain soaked him to the skin almost instantly.

Viola followed him out, joining him in the courtyard, water drenching her.

"Go back inside, ye wee *eejit*." His voice rose over the rain and wind. "You'll catch your death in this weather."

"You cannot run away from this!"

"Run away? From what?" he snapped, water already pouring down his face.

"From yourself. From us. From this!"

Viola Brodure, for the first time in forever, tamped down her doubts and fears and reached for what she wanted most.

She crossed the five steps between them.

Rose to the tips of her toes.

Grabbed the back of Malcolm's head.

And pulled his mouth down to hers.

Viola had been kissed in the past—an overeager swain who had stolen a quick brush of her lips at a ball.

But that was precisely it—

She *had been* kissed. Passive tense.

She had been the one receiving the action. It had not been her choice, her doing.

This, however.

This was her own claiming. Her own action.

Viola was not simply being kissed.

She was kissing.

Malcolm's lips were soft and warm, his beard a tickle.

He responded without hesitation, his hands banding around her waist and half lifting her off the ground.

Viola arched into him, head tilted back, rain water cascading down her face.

"Viola," he rasped, lips moving from her mouth to her jaw, lighting a trail of sparks in his wake. She angled her head, desperate for the feel of his touch.

He paused, dragging his nose along her throat, pressing murmured words to her skin.

"Nae," he whispered in her ear. "This willnae do. Ye're drenched tae the skin, lass."

He set her down. Viola whimpered in protest, but Malcolm's eyes burned with nearly unholy heat.

Lacing her fingers through his, he pulled her back into the house.

Their clothes dripped, making a merry puddle on the flagstone floor of the scullery. Before Viola could voice an opinion, Malcolm wrapped his large hands around her waist once more and deposited her, soggy skirts and all, atop an enormous wooden worktable.

She landed with a squeak.

Malcolm threaded one hand into her hair, pressed the other into the small of her back, and stepped into her skirts.

And then—

Viola ceased to be the kisser.

In one breath, she became the *kissee*. The one being devoured.

But it didn't take her more than a heartbeat to meet Malcolm's plundering with a greed of her own. Her perch on the high table evened their height, enabling her to reach him without cricking her neck.

It was the veriest madness.

She hadn't known it could be like this.

That the touch of his calloused thumb on her cheek could send shivers of sensation skittering down her arms. That her very skin could feel so awake, as if her body had simply been sleeping until this moment finally (finally!) arrived.

They kissed and kissed, heads angled this way and then that, twisting in an effort to be even closer.

He ran a reverent hand along her body, palm caressing from ribcage to hipbone.

"Why did you resist?" she whispered against his mouth.

"My truth? Ye are so wee. I'm afeart I will break ye," he murmured trailing kisses in the space below her ear. "Ye are the finest porcelain, and I'm not gentleman enough tae know how to care for ye."

Viola was shaking her head before he even finished speaking.

She would not allow him to give up on them because he worried about her lack of strength. Because in this moment, arching into the scrape of his teeth along her throat, hearing the low growl of his desire, she felt powerful. Indestructible.

"Someone told me recently that I'm fierce." She running her palms across his chest, loving that she had permission to touch him, to explore the hard muscles of his body. "I may be small, but I am made of steel, strong enough for the likes of you, Malcolm Penn-Leith. Test me and see."

Malcolm huffed a soft laugh.

Viola captured it on a kiss.

16

Malcolm walked through the next day in a blur.

Over and over, he relived those moments with Viola and the glory of kissing her lush mouth.

How was he to manage this? His adoration of Viola was just so much *more* than he had ever expected to feel.

It wasn't that she had replaced Aileen in his affections. The love and loss he felt for his wife was still very much present.

But Viola had taken up residence inside him, in cells and hollows he had never known existed. She had begun to remodel his thinking—expanding a room here and knocking down a wall there—until her presence felt so much like a homecoming, he floundered to accommodate the shift in his reality.

Viola—the famous, brilliant, talented, Miss Brodure—gave every indication that she might be willing to leave her comforts and literary friends, travel hundreds of miles north to rural Scotland to join him, and live and write as a farmer's wife in Thistle Muir.

Even giving mental space to the thought felt absurd, and yet, part of him ached for just such a life.

He finally resorted to visiting Aileen's grave in the kirkyard, hoping to bludgeon some sense into his addled brain.

"What am I tae do?" he whispered to her tombstone as he sat in the sun-warmed grass.

He got nothing in reply, not even a flutter of Aileen's presence.

His first marriage had been a content one, but he instinctively knew that marriage to Viola—and was he truly contemplating that?—would be entirely different.

Viola would challenge him in ways that Aileen never had. She would force him to change and morph and strive to meet her on equal footing, both intellectual and social.

Yet in the same breath, imagining Viola attempting to step into Aileen's life . . .

It felt impossible.

Yes, the farm was certainly more prosperous now. Viola certainly wouldn't be needed to help run things as Aileen had done.

And what about children?

A picture flashed through his head. Viola—wee, fey Viola—swollen with his child, her tiny body writhing in the agony of labor—

He recoiled from the scene, memory merging with his vision and sending nausea clawing his throat.

Aileen, with her sturdy, braw frame, hadn't been able to bear his child.

How could he even contemplate making a child with Viola?

Well, the *making* of the child . . . that he could imagine in excruciatingly delicious detail.

But the bearing of his child?

It would kill her.

Malcolm pressed a shaking hand to his forehead.

I'm no' strong enough tae endure that again.

Losing Viola would destroy him, of that Malcolm had no doubt. Just thinking of the possibility threatened to tumble him into madness.

And there was still Ethan to consider. Thank goodness, his wee brother was visiting Uncle Leith for the week. Malcolm would need the time to gather his thoughts, to muster his words into orderly, logical rows like good little soldiers.

"I'm in a right *fankle*, Aileen," he sighed, pinching the bridge of his nose.

And though a gentle breeze rustled through the tree above his head and a pair of robins quarreled, Malcolm still felt no answers.

He pushed to his feet and headed for the north pasture, his coos, and a discussion with Callum Liston about how to rotate grazing this winter. After all, Malcolm wasn't quite a gentleman—despite Viola's assertion to the contrary—and he had work that needed to be seen to.

But then, trudging up the lane at the end of the day, there she was.

His Viola.

Sitting on the swing, bonnet dangling from her fingers, her face turned toward the sun.

All of her rimmed in golden light.

He had kissed those soft lips. His hands still thrummed with the memory of her body under his palms.

Beowoof barked and raced to her side.

She turned and locked eyes with Malcolm. The radiance of her smile threatened to crack his heart wide. A helpless wing of affection that battered his ribcage with wild feathers.

What was he to do?

This wasn't some tepid emotion, easily managed and categorized.

No. What he felt for Viola Brodure was more akin to a tidal wave, scouring everything in its wake, dredging up the flotsam of his soul and forcing him to feel so very alive.

Because as he closed the distance between them, with so much *lovehopeadoration* roiling in his chest . . . he struggled to care about words like *duty* or *loyalty* or *consequences*.

She laughed and all but raced into his arms, face tilting upward, hands reaching for his head.

And Malcolm forgot everything but the pleasure of kissing Viola Brodure.

FOR VIOLA, THE week passed in a whirl of dizzy happiness.

She felt as she had as a child, tilting her head toward the sun and spinning in circles until she collapsed on the grass, joy a riot of champagne bubbles in her veins.

Such were the hours spent with Malcolm Penn-Leith.

She met him every day at their swing. But now, in addition to intellectual discussions—for example, Mr. Disraeli's new novel, *Coningsby*, and its scathing rebuke of the Whig Reform Bill—they spent much of their time in one another's arms, kissing and, well, kissing some more.

So much lay unresolved—Kendall's threats and her father's career, Ethan's absence and the difficult conversation she would need to have with him, the potential loss of Kendall's patronage and her own professional desires.

Her burgeoning relationship with Malcolm Penn-Leith simply added one more knot to the tangle.

And yet, despite the misery that awaited, Viola permitted herself this small space in time where she could race down a tree-shrouded lane, launch herself into the arms of a Scottish bear of a man, and greedily nip at his lips.

Like a child with toffee bonbons, she would devour the sweet joy of his company.

Insatiable was the only word that adequately captured her feelings.

No amount of time with him was enough. Not their stolen hours. Not a day or a week. How many years would be sufficient? She hardly knew.

She had never been in love before, but the emotion she currently felt did rather mimic all the excellent (and sometimes dreadful) poetry on the topic she had read over the years.

The day before Ethan's return, Viola called upon Thistle Muir.

Malcolm was all smiles when he came to the door after the maid answered.

"Miss Brodure," he said, darting a side-eye to the maid still standing behind him, "tae what do we owe the pleasure?"

Viola knew Malcolm would be balancing accounts, and so, she had seized the opportunity to return a book Ethan had lent her—*The Sonnets of William Shakespeare*—many of which Viola had taken great delight in rereading while pondering Ethan's older brother.

Truly, she was the fickle sort of woman that the Bard had also immortalized.

Regardless, she handed the book over to Malcolm. "Merely returning this. Please tell Mr. Penn-Leith I greatly enjoyed it. Shakespeare is always a favorite."

They stared at one another for a long moment.

Viola turned to leave.

"Wait," he said. "Allow me tae accompany ye to the end of the drive, at least."

Viola nodded, hoping her answering smile didn't seem too eager to the hovering maid.

Malcolm returned not even a minute later, hat on his head.

He offered her his arm.

Viola took it, wrapping her fingers firmly around the corded muscles of his forearm, wishing she could also claim a kiss, but aware that the servant's eyes would still be upon them.

"You must know how much I dislike this dissembling. I want us to be open in our affection for one another," she said once they were a few steps away from the house.

"What about Kendall and his demands?"

"I don't know," she answered truthfully. "He will be angry and likely retaliatory. Regardless, we must tell Ethan. It is cruel to allow him to go on like this."

"Aye. Ethan needs to know. It pains me to keep this from him. We can speak to him when he returns tomorrow. Will ye be attending the dinner at Muirford House tomorrow evening?"

Viola nodded.

Lord and Lady Hadley had returned from England and made good on their promise to have Dr. Brodure and Viola dine at Muirford House.

Malcolm and Ethan were to join them tomorrow night, along with Kendall, Dr. and Mrs. Ruxton, as well as Captain Carnegie and Leah, if the weather proved favorable for a drive down the glen from Laverloch. Malcolm had even mentioned that Sir Rafe Gordon and his wife would likely be in attendance. Sir Rafe was a close friend of Hadley's, so the men regularly visited one another. Though who knew how Kendall would react when faced with his half-brother.

The evening certainly wouldn't be boring, at least.

Viola and Malcolm passed onto the lane that approached the house from the main road. Trees lined the left side, while a fenced pasture bordered the right.

Malcolm looked toward the field beside them and then slowed to a stop.

"That is a reminder of our problem." He pointed toward a boulder-ish thing sitting in the middle of the pasture.

"What is it?" Viola squinted, shading her eyes.

"Come." He turned them toward a small gate in the fence leading into the field. "Permit me tae show ye."

Opening the gate, he motioned Viola to pass through in front of him before offering her his arm once more. They strolled, arm in arm, through the grass, and the details of the boulder-ish thing slowly came into focus.

"To be honest, it looks . . ." Viola frowned. "It looks like a stone wrapped in chains and resting atop a much larger rock."

"Aye. That is exactly what it is."

She jerked her gaze to his in surprise, a startled laugh on her lips. "Truly?"

"Aye," he repeated.

And indeed, when they stopped before the lot, that was precisely what Viola found: a roundish rock—wrapped round and round in a length of metal chain—resting on top of a much larger boulder embedded in the soft grass.

Malcolm nudged the chained stone with a booted foot. "This rock is a symbol of why I should be more guilt-ridden over keeping Ethan in the dark with regards tae yourself."

In all of this, Viola had never really pondered the brothers' close relationship. How much her presence was perhaps driving a wedge between them.

Though how a stone wrapped in chains relayed to guilt . . .

"Tell me about the stone then," she said. "At the moment, it only seems rather . . . whimsical."

He smiled faintly, just as she intended. "Ethan wrote that poem about me . . . about my grief . . ."

"*I carry with me always a weight,*" she murmured.

"Precisely. And I did. I still do some days, if I'm truthful." He looked out over the field, crossing his arms over his chest. "But it was much worse in the year after Aileen's loss. On the first anniversary of her death, Ethan dragged me out here and presented me with this chained stone."

"So . . . as I was saying . . . whimsical."

His smile broadened, touching his eyes with gentle humor. "Aye, we Scots can be a *bampot* lot. Anyway, that's how it started."

"How what started?"

"The truth throwing." Taking a step away from her, Malcolm mimed picking up the end of the chain, twirling it over his head, and releasing it. "Ethan made me throw the stone—which is right heavy, mind ye—over and over. Initially, he said it was tae literally cast off the metaphorical weight I carried. And a contest, of course, tae see who could throw the stone the farthest . . . because we're Scots and that's what we do.

"But he and I rapidly began adding words to each toss. A truth or confession or something that we needed tae set free along with the stone. A metaphorical weight that had tae be cast off before we could throw the physical one."

"What a beautiful sentiment." Viola touched her breastbone. "So what would you confess? What were your truths?"

Malcolm shrugged. "Everything. My anger and pain over losing Aileen so young. The grief of all the living she and our stillborn babe would never experience. My fury at the sheer unfairness of it, that something so vital could have been torn from me in one single afternoon. The truth-telling, more than anything, started me on the road tae true healing. Grief, when contained, only turns gangrenous and festering. Ethan was right on all counts; it needed tae be set free."

"He has been a good brother to you."

"Aye, that he has."

They both looked down at the chained stone, letting silence rest between them.

"If I were to offer you a truth," Viola said, quietly, "it would be this: I am sorry if I have put you in a position where you feel like your loyalties are divided between Ethan and myself."

As Malcolm had just done, she mimicked picking up the chain, swinging it over her head, and releasing it.

Malcolm shook his head, something soft and tender in his gaze. "Ah, lass, the decision is hardly that simplistic. My love for Ethan does not have tae be linked with my care for yourself. None of us can help where our affections lie. Why, consider your situation. It's not as if Ethan and myself were a pair of shoes, and ye simply chose the right over the left. Would ye have fallen for Ethan were I not around?"

Viola pondered that for a long moment, searching her heart.

"No," she finally said. "I think it might have taken me a bit longer to understand my own heart, but I would have arrived at the same conclusion regardless. Consider that a second bonus truth." She mimicked tossing the stone once more.

"So there ye are. It isnae as if I manipulated ye into choosing myself over Ethan."

"But will *he* see things that way?"

A long pause.

Malcolm let out a slow breath. "I fear he might not. That's my truth."

He mimed throwing the stone again.

"Let me tell Ethan." She looked up, up, up into Malcolm's warm brown eyes.

"He's my brother, perhaps I should—"

"No. It should be me. As you say, Ethan might see the issues as being connected—one, my lack of affection for him, and two, my growing attachment to yourself. I want him to understand that they are unrelated, separate things. I'll call tomorrow afternoon when he arrives home."

"Are ye certain, Viola?"

Of course she was certain. Just as certain that she adored the husky sound of her name on his lips.

"I willnae be around tae help," Malcolm continued. "Sir Rafe has arrived tae visit with Hadley, and we will be consulting on business matters for most of the day."

"I am sure. Leave it with me. I shall tell Ethan as gently as I can."

"Thank ye for caring so for my brother." Malcolm's eyes melted, the color of treacle in the sun.

"I will always do my best to safeguard those you love. That is my final truth."

Because my heart is intertwined with yours, and your concerns become my own, she did not deign to add.

She pretended to hurl the stone one last time.

A faint smile touched his lips. "How like ye, lass, tae say and do such admirable things when I cannae kiss them from your lips." He darted a meaningful glance toward Thistle Muir and the servants surely peeking out windows to watch them.

She raised an eyebrow. "Meet me tomorrow afternoon along the lane before the dinner party, and you may kiss a great many things from my lips."

And truly, Malcolm's slow spreading smile was almost as good as a kiss anyway, Viola decided.

But only almost.

17

Viola intended to keep her promise to tell Ethan herself.

Truly she did.

She stayed up far too late writing a letter, explaining everything.

Of a certainty, she should have told him the lot face-to-face. Leaving a letter was, in a sense, a craven act. And Viola disliked feeling fainthearted.

But she worried that if she attempted to tell Ethan the truth in person, her tongue would knot and her throat would close, trapping the words behind her teeth.

If she relayed the whole to him in writing . . . well, that solved her primary dilemma.

The second problem was related to the first—she couldn't bear to watch Ethan as he read the words, to witness every minute emotion flit across his face.

So she devised to leave the letter at Thistle Muir just after breakfast, well before Ethan was expected to arrive from Aberdeen. Malcolm was with Sir Rafe, and the maid and housekeeper had their day off again—

Mrs. McGregor's daughter, Isla, still hadn't had her baby, as far as Viola knew—so no one would be present to insist she wait for Ethan.

Viola would simply wedge the letter between the door and frame and allow Ethan to read its contents without an audience. It seemed the kindest thing to do.

Or perhaps, the most *English* thing to do. Avoiding confrontation was, after all, practically a national sport.

But when Viola walked up the drive to Thistle Muir, letter heavy in her pocket, she found Ethan newly arrived and dismounting from his horse.

"Miss Brodure!" He immediately strode toward her, his handsome face stretching into a welcoming smile.

Viola froze, a rabbit caught in a snare, unsure of what to do. Because apparently, no matter how many times Malcolm had praised her courage and ferocity, she was, at her heart, a coward.

Ethan's happy grin and enthusiastic greeting shattered Viola's resolve. He bowed low over her hand and even pressed a kiss to her knuckles.

She couldn't hand him her letter. He wouldn't wait to read it.

No.

Ethan would insist on devouring every word as she looked on, no matter how forcefully she demurred.

"Come in!" He waved a cheerful hand. "On the ride home, I remembered a book of translated French poetry that I hoped tae share with ye."

Still too unmoored to think properly, Viola could do nothing but follow him into Thistle Muir, mind racing through possibilities. Could she somehow leave the letter on the mantle for him to discover later?

Regardless, she sat in the quiet parlor of Thistle Muir for half an hour, declining tea and listening to a summary of Ethan's week in Aberdeen.

"My uncle likes tae make his presence known in my life, but as I owe him much, I cannot say I chafe too greatly under his care. Though I admit tae some eagerness to return tae your side, Miss Brodure." Ethan paired this comment with a meaningful glance that caused Viola's stomach to sink.

She was going to have to tell Ethan herself, wasn't she? Face-to-face. With *words*.

Her lungs burned at the very thought.

A banging at the front door startled them both.

Frowning, Ethan motioned for her to stay put.

"No need for anyone tae know you're here," he whispered as he left to answer the door.

A rush of voices followed from the hallway. Viola caught *Malcolm* and *Isla labor* and *can't find Callum*.

The front door closed and Ethan returned, expression cheery.

"I apologize for the interruption, Miss Brodure. It would seem Mrs. McGregor's daughter has finally begun laboring to bring her babe into the world. Callum, the lass's husband, needs to be informed, so I must walk down to the south fields to find him. I apologize for cutting our delightful *tête-à-tête* a wee bit short."

Hallelujah!

Relief was a giddy rush in Viola's veins.

"Of course." She stood on a smile. "I shall see myself out."

Several hours later, Viola arrived early to the swing along the lane, swaying back and forth on it as she waited for Malcolm to arrive.

Her initial relief at having avoided a confrontation with Ethan had faded. After all, the conversation still loomed before her. She had only delayed the inevitable.

As usual, Beowoof arrived a few minutes before his master, yipping in excitement and nudging at her skirts. Tugging off her bonnet and gloves, Viola buried her face in the dog's fur, the simplicity of his affection soothing the jagged edge of her nerves.

"How did things go, lass?" Malcolm's voice had her lifting her head.

And there he was.

Her Malcolm.

Shoulders wide, arms folded, eyes attentive.

Concerned for her even though he himself appeared careworn and tired.

I want to keep him forever.

The thought had her rushing off the swing and into his arms before she consciously understood she was moving.

MALCOLM CAUGHT VIOLA to him, her slight frame molding to his. Bloody hell but he liked this woman far more than was sane.

Though *liked* was perhaps too tame a word to describe his emotions for her. She inspired a heady mix of peace and exhilaration and burning adoration that felt too much like love.

Love.

His heart quaked at the thought.

The events of the past few hours had rattled him to his core.

One of his field hands had interrupted his meeting with Sir Rafe and Hadley, whispering in his ear that Callum's Isla was struggling in childbirth.

Malcolm understood only too well how dangerous bringing a babe into the world could be. Despite the ease of Isla's other births, this one had all gone sideways.

Giving Hadley and Sir Rafe his excuses, Malcolm had raced to sit with an ashen Callum, watching his friend tremble and flinch with each of Isla's screams. She labored in agony—the babe stuck within her, or so Callum relayed from the midwife.

The memory of Aileen's passing had hovered in the room. Isla's cries echoed in Malcolm's own memories until he feared he would crawl out of his skin.

Grief was utterly relentless.

He could go along just fine for weeks and months and then something would happen—a smell, a sound, an off-hand comment—and he would be propelled right back to that terrible afternoon five years past. To the tiny, blue bundle in Leah's arms, to the horrific silence that followed Aileen's screams. To the moment where his world had utterly disintegrated.

Sitting with Callum had required more courage than Malcolm knew he possessed.

Thankfully, two of Callum's brothers arrived with the doctor in tow. Malcolm had been able to ask them to send word of Isla's condition and stride out the door with dignity intact, instead of racing from the house like a demented, grief-stricken creature—*greiting*, howling, breathless.

But now . . . holding Viola . . .

The terror of facing such loss again set his hands to trembling and a panicked vise squeezing his chest.

Malcolm finally, fully acknowledged the stark truth—

He struggled to see a road forward for Viola and himself.

All paths ended in some way or another, whether with the Duke's schemes, her father's ambition, or Malcolm's own fears for her health and writing career.

There was no escape for him.

Because while sitting in Callum's wee cottage, listening to Isla's agonized cries and reliving the trauma of Aileen's death—Malcolm had realized an awful truth—

Love wasn't quite what he had thought it to be.

Loving Aileen had been a straightforward thing—happiness and sunshine, a blissful sort of simplicity.

But after suffering the heartbreak of her death, Malcolm's feelings toward love had changed. Instead of hope and felicity, the emotion now elicited a raw desperation.

For him, love equaled fear and loss.

He didn't know if he could outrun, out-think, or out-maneuver his panicked, uncontrollable reaction to it.

Och what a mess.

And still, his muscles flexed, pulling Viola fractionally closer, helpless against the onslaught of *loveterrorfear* that pummeled him.

"What happened with Ethan?" he murmured against her hair, anything to distract his increasingly morose thoughts, to banish the phantom sense that he had already lost her.

Viola sighed into his chest and tightened her own arms around him, refusing to relinquish her hold. "I wrote a nice long letter to him, intending to leave it at Thistle Muir this morning, but your brother arrived home far too early."

"Ethan returned this morning? He wasn't expected until later this afternoon."

She nodded, face pressed to his sternum. "I know, but there he was on your doorstep, so happy to see me, and I just . . . Malcolm, I panicked. I couldn't give him the letter—not then, not where he would read it in front of me. Miracle of miracles, someone came to the door needing Ethan. I was granted a reprieve and took it like the coward I am." She pulled back to look up at him. "But now I have regrets, because I *must* inform him of the reality of my affections. I should have been braver."

This woman and her *muckle* heart.

"Hush, lass. As I said yesterday, allow me tae accompany you. Let us get through dinner with Hadley this evening, and I will be at your side tomorrow when ye talk to Ethan."

But would he be at her side? *Should* he be, if he didn't intend to see their budding romance through to its logical conclusion of marriage and children?

Some days, Malcolm felt as if he were clinging to the side of a runaway carriage, knowing that every choice he made—hold on or jump—would result in traumatic injury.

Viola looked up at him then—blue eyes pools of joy, lips pink and so very kissable . . .

Desperate to silence his inner voices, he lifted her higher in his arms, lowered his head, and captured her mouth.

He adored how her body turned boneless against his, her curves flowing perfectly into his hollows. He loved the breathy catch in the back of her throat when he pressed his lips to the underside of her jaw. The hungry slide of her fingers into his hair—

"Well, I had suspected something like this," a male voice drawled at Malcolm's back, "but such an amorous display is still rather shocking."

Malcolm released Viola as if struck. Whirling, he placed his body between her and the unknown threat, an outstretched hand holding her behind him.

The Duke of Kendall stood in the path, a slight sneer on his handsome face. As usual, the man looked like a Bond Street fashion plate—an expensively-cut gray coat over a green-shot silk waistcoat and crisply-pressed trousers.

The duke spared a glance for Viola over Malcolm's arm and then raked Malcolm himself from head to toe.

"Protecting her?" Kendall asked, expression amused but eyes hard. The difference between the man's gray hair and unlined youthful face had never been more pronounced. "Bit late for that, isn't it?"

"Your Grace," Malcolm said through clenched teeth, "how may I help ye?"

He could practically *feel* Viola's panic at his back, the rasp of her breathing.

"I had called at the cottage, intending to speak with Miss Brodure about a matter." Kendall lifted a gloved hand, a sheaf of rolled papers in his fist. "Dr. Brodure sent me in this direction, declaring Miss Brodure to be a 'great devotee of a restorative afternoon walk.' Given the display I was just subjected to, I must quibble with Dr. Brodure's use of the word *restorative*. I'm more inclined toward *scandalous* or *salacious* myself."

Malcolm clenched his jaw.

Kendall appeared to be thoroughly enjoying himself.

Damn him.

"Again, how might we assist ye?" Malcolm refused to say a word about his relationship with Viola. It was none of Kendall's concern, despite how eagerly the duke played the role of village busybody.

"I wish to speak with Miss Brodure." Kendall tilted his head sideways, peering at Viola.

Malcolm turned to look at her behind him.

She appeared . . . distressed. Her chest heaved, the hollow of her throat sucking in as she tried to breathe.

"Do ye wish tae speak with His Grace, lass?" Malcolm asked. "I willnae see ye lapsing into an asthmatic fit for it."

She placed a shaking hand on Malcolm's arm, swallowing hard. But her voice, when she spoke, was stronger than he would have anticipated. "Say what you m-must, Your Grace."

Kendall brandished the roll of papers in his hand. "I have been patiently awaiting the short story you are to write for me, Miss Brodure, but waiting has been a challenge. The editor of *The Gentleman's Magazine* liked the idea of publishing a fictional story with a political bent—any political bent, it turns out—but without an actual manuscript before him, he has become somewhat anxious. So the man went hunting for another story."

Malcolm felt the very air around him freeze.

Given how Viola stilled and closed her eyes in a long blink, she also guessed what was coming next.

Kendall peered down his aristocratic nose at them. "Imagine my fury when the editor sent me a work entitled *A Hard Truth* from *The Rabble Rouser* and informed me that, if he didn't receive a story from yourself, he would run *A Hard Truth* instead—a tale which directly opposes every last political aim I hold dear. My fury only increased once I uncovered the origins of its author."

Malcolm dared a glance at Viola. She stared with desperation at the journal in Kendall's fist as if it were her own child trapped in the man's hand. When the duke abruptly slapped the papers against his open palm, she flinched.

"I see from both your expressions that a lengthy explanation is hardly needed." The duke's tone was hard and unyielding. A volcanic anger lurked under his polished veneer. "Oliver Aubord Twist? The anagram was easily deciphered. The editor of *The Gentleman's Magazine* uncovered the truth, as well. In his mind, one Viola Brodure story is as good as the next. Your father was appalled when I told him."

Viola let out a choked cry. "You t-told my father?"

"Of course, I did," Kendall snapped. "Have you *nothing* more to say for yourself, Miss Brodure?"

Viola paled further. Malcolm slid his hand into hers.

"I think *A Hard Truth* made my stance f-fairly obvious, Your Grace," Viola stammered. Her fingers trembled in Malcolm's, but his brave lass bit her lower lip and continued, voice strong. "As I said last week, I c-cannot write what you wish me to. I will not contract a sham betrothal with Ethan Penn-Leith. Both actions would be wrong."

The duke snorted. "And as *I* said last week, I do not wish to be cruel, Miss Brodure. But I cannot allow direct attacks against my own ideals to go unanswered—particularly if those assaults originate from within my own household, as it were. It is one thing to decide not to assist me in my aims. It is something else entirely to directly oppose me. You do not wish me to become your enemy, Miss Brodure."

Viola said nothing more, swaying slightly on her feet. Malcolm dropped her hand and wrapped an arm around her waist, pulling her against his side. She permitted it but didn't sag her weight into his.

Instead, she held herself stiff. As if fearful that the slightest change in direction might shatter her entirely.

"Let me be clear," Kendall said, rolling up the journal once more and pointing it at Viola. "I hold all the cards here. I will give you one week to produce a short story I can send to the editor of *The Gentleman's Magazine*. I require something tangible to persuade him against re-publishing *A Hard Truth*."

"I will n-not do that."

Kendall continued as if he hadn't heard her. "I can, and *will*, personally ruin your father and yourself if you use your limited power to thwart my political aims. If you marry"—here he shot Malcolm a particularly withering look—"I can happily see your husband ruined, too. Trust me when I say, this is not the plot you want to be living, Miss Brodure."

"*Och*, how could a man of your stature be so threatened by one wee woman?" Malcolm jumped to Viola's defense. "Surely, ye have other ways of promoting your political agend—"

"Clearly, you do not understand the influence of the lady you court, Mr. Penn-Leith. That hardly surprises me, given that you are—" Kendall paused, raking Malcolm from head to toe with what could only be described as aristocratic disdain. "—what you are. Allow me to enlighten you. Miss Brodure is one of the most well-known and beloved writers of our generation. Her stories are read by thousands the kingdom over, masses who do not know their own opinion until someone else informs them of it. *That* is why I require her compliance on this matter."

Malcolm held himself still, refusing to allow the duke's blow to land true.

But how could it not?

The gulf between Viola and himself was vast. He intellectually knew that, but the duke's words painted the differences in tangible black and white.

Malcolm could feel anxiety writhing in his chest.

"So you intend to b-blackmail me?" Viola said.

"I think *appropriate encouragement* would be a more fitting description.

You may have power in your limited sphere, Miss Brodure, but you are hardly a match for myself."

"Do ye have tae play a villain straight from a Drury Lane farce?" Malcolm couldn't stem the bitter words.

Kendall leveled him with a dark stare. The duke might be young yet, but he had already perfected an imperious gaze.

"I don't think my life is the one that has devolved into a Drury Lane farce." He looked to Viola meaningfully before fixing his gaze on Malcolm once more. "What precisely is your aim here, Mr. Penn-Leith? To drag this high-born lady down to your lowly level?"

Viola gasped at the insult.

Och, this fiery lass.

Kendall could destroy all her dreams, but if the duke took a figurative swing at Malcolm, Viola lifted her fists to fight.

Malcolm held her fast, tension coiling in his chest.

Kendall wasn't done. "Do you think to marry Miss Brodure?" His laugh was caustic and cruel. "What is she going to do? Become a farmer's wife? Set down her writerly pen and help you tend to your precious *coos*?" he said the noun on a sneer. "Grow old before her time, worn down by life on a farm?"

The duke's arrow flew so true, Malcolm barely avoided flinching.

No wonder Kendall's ancestors had become dukes. The damn man noticed the slightest chink in Malcolm's armor and instantly stabbed a rapier into it.

But knowing that did not erase the truth in Kendall's words.

Viola, of course, took in a stuttering breath and breathed out bravery.

"The r-relationship between myself and Mr. Penn-Leith is n-none of your affair, Your Grace," she said, voice trembling but strong.

"Then please, by all means, continue to make a public spectacle of yourselves." Giving them one last scoffing look, Kendall tipped his hat. "I suggest you consider your path carefully before making a choice, Miss Brodure. Your present course is charted straight for destruction. One week. You have one week to provide me with a suitable short story."

And with that, Kendall pivoted and walked back up the lane.

Malcolm turned and immediately pulled Viola into his arms. The poor woman was shaking, her breathing harsh and labored.

"Dinnae *fash* yourself, lass," he murmured. "Kendall willnae win. We'll find a solution for you, and surely your father will understand once ye explain everything to him."

Viola pushed back slightly. He expected her expression to be devastated. Instead, she nearly vibrated with rage.

"My father? I am too angry to think about him at the moment. How d-dare Kendall?" she stammered. "How dare he threaten you!"

"Of course, he will threaten me, lass. I'm a mere speck of irritating sand underneath his foot." Malcolm tried—and mostly failed—to keep the bitterness out of his tone. "Have ye considered that an association with myself may force ye tae put down your pen, if only tae let the outraged gossip settle?"

"And so? Of course I would set down my pen for a year or two if it meant being with you," she said, as if the idea were patently obvious.

Malcolm barely stopped himself from scoffing. "Nothing should come between yourself and your pen, Viola. Your words are too precious, too vital, for ye to stop writing because of me. And then how would ye spend your days? Help me with my coos? Become aged before your time? Kendall wasnae wrong about those things."

Viola recoiled, her arms sliding off his waist. "Why would you automatically assume there is no place for me in your life?"

"Because your fine talent should not be hidden away! Because ye are such a fine lady, Viola, and I am not so fine a gentleman that—"

"The Gloves. Come. Off." She neatly enunciated each word. "Just because the social level of our families does not precisely align, it's no excuse for us to push one another away."

And yet, that was exactly what Malcolm had to do—pull back before his irrational fears utterly owned him.

"I will fight to be with you, Malcolm," she continued, "just as I expect you to fight to be with me!"

And there it was.

The place where Malcolm's courage stuttered.

His heart hammered in his chest, images flitting through his mind, a kaleidoscope of warning.

Kendall's sneering condescension at the thought of Viola wedding him.

The ticking of the mantel clock in the silent aftermath of Aileen's agony.

The endless nights, walking the dark floors of Thistle Muir, lost in the bottomless chasm of his grief.

Fear tasted acrid in the back of his throat and his breathing quickened. A fine tremor shuddered through his body.

He couldn't—

It was simply too—

The silence between them lengthened, morphing into a cutting thing with sharp edges.

Viola took another step back, arms coming around her own mid-section.

"I do not like your hesitation right now," she said. "I do not like your silence, as if you agree with Kendall's assessment of us."

"I dinnae—" Malcolm began, his thinking a disordered muddle. He grabbed onto what words he could. "Kendall's opinion is telling of all the wee abuses and sacrifices ye would endure were ye to commit your life tae one such as myself."

Viola pressed shaking fingertips to her forehead.

"I would count it a small sacrifice," she said, voice so very soft. "But we need to be in this together, Malcolm. It's already enough that Kendall is attempting to force me to his will. Are you truly thinking I need to give up yourself, as well?"

And there it was.

The heart of the matter.

Because truthfully?

Malcolm's answer was *aye*.

Aye, lass, ye likely do need tae give me up.

He wanted to be with her, but that damned fear loomed before him, a vast expanse of glacial blue-white that he was too terrified to cross. The pain of plummeting into another crevasse of grief paralyzed him.

He simply could not confront the possibility of such loss again. And with *Viola*, of all people—a woman he adored and cherished and worshiped.

She didn't misunderstand his continuing hesitation.

"Well." She took a step back from him. And then another. "I guess we both have some thinking to do. I'm sure my father is beside himself right now, so I must be off. I will see you this evening."

And just like Kendall before her, Viola spun on her heel and retreated up the lane.

18

What just happened?

Viola's thoughts snarled as she rushed home along the lane, heart hammering against her breastbone.

How had everything gone sideways so quickly?

Her lungs burned, tight and unyielding.

How was she not in the throes of a full-on asthmatic fit right this instant? Her nerves had certainly experienced enough trauma today to merit one.

Though the deception with her father distressed her, and Kendall was a burr in her side, and she honestly didn't know how to resolve the situation with her writing . . .

Every jolt paled in comparison to the acidic sting of Malcolm's silence.

Though how on theme for him, really.

Malcolm Penn-Leith—Fettermill's resident stoic—would never injure with words.

No. It would be his *lack* of them that dealt the blow.

And his muted quiet ten minutes past had communicated volumes.

The hesitation in his body. The anguished indecision of his expression. The uncertainty in his dark eyes when considering a life with her.

Although they exchanged barely a handful of words, Viola felt scrubbed raw. And now, something hard and aching had taken up residence in her throat.

She had supposed, despite the rather short time of their acquaintance, that she and Malcolm shared the same page of a love story, united in their willingness to push through obstacles to be with one another.

But if he didn't desire the happiness and joy and work of a life lived together—if he was content with mere friendship and kisses—well, then . . .

Viola Brodure begged for no man's affection.

If Malcolm wasn't interested in her heart, then she would be damned if she would give it to him.

Though as she rushed up the path to her rented cottage—and the painful, likely-heated conversation with her father that awaited—she acknowledged she might be somewhat histrionic in her thinking at present.

Viola threw open the front door and crossed the hall.

Her father paced before the hearth in the parlor, eyes scarcely darting her way as she all but ran into the room.

His brows were drawn down, hands clasped behind his back, shoulders slumped. His gray hair was more askew than normal, poking out from behind his ears. The sight further twisted the pinch in Viola's chest.

"I take it Kendall found you?" he asked woodenly.

Her father's tonelessness was somehow worse than anger.

He appeared . . . defeated.

"Papa," Viola began.

He held up a staying hand.

She stood still, one hand pressed to her abdomen.

"I've spent the past hour trying to understand," he said slowly. "Why would you swear an oath to me one month—promising to wait to publish your more liberal views—and then turned around the next and published them anyway. We have always been united, you and I. Always in each other's thoughts and conversation. And yet, in this . . ." He waved a helpless hand. "I don't understand why you wouldn't have discussed it with me. Why you felt the need to deceive me."

Viola swallowed against the remorse pricking her eyes.

How could she justify her actions? He was correct.

"I should have spoken with you about it, Papa," she said, tears thick in her words. "But those days with Cousin Eloise in Manchester wouldn't let me be, and I just . . . acted."

"Yes, I understand the ache to help those in need. It's what I have dedicated my life to. We are in the midst of a war on poverty and suffering. But as any good general knows, sometimes you must give up short-term ground in order to gain the greater prize. I thought you understood that."

"Yes, in principle, Papa, but—"

"We agreed to wait." His voice began to rise. "I can accomplish more good once I'm in a position of power. As a bishop, I could be granted a seat in the House of Lords. There, I could enact *true* change with the rest of the Lords Spiritual. You know this, Viola. So why did you do it? Why not at least speak with me about this before publishing?"

"Because I feared you would talk me out of it!" Viola all but shouted the words and then winced.

She had *never* shouted at her father. This was not their relationship. What was becoming of them?

"Of course I would have!" her father shot back sharply. "Publishing such a story was a poor chess move. Not speaking with me about it beforehand was similarly ill-advised."

"Was it though? At least when Kendall confronted you not two hours past, you could honestly tell him that you didn't know what I had been doing. His judgment fell on me, not you." Viola closed her eyes, licking away the tears that trickled down to her mouth.

"Bah! That's splitting hairs. I assure you Kendall did not see it in that light. Worse, I looked an old, doddering fool. Is that your opinion of me?"

"Of course not!"

"The duke made it exquisitely clear that he now doubts my suitability for appointment as a bishop."

"Kendall is just as manipulative as his fath—"

"He is a realist, daughter! As am I!" Her father whirled to pin her with his blue gaze, eyes the same bluebell blue as her own. "This is *my* hard truth, Viola. I love you. I have gladly postponed my dreams and career for your health. It was a sacrifice I happily made. But I had assumed that you felt a similar devotion to myself."

"I do, Papa! I do!"

"And yet, in this moment, I do not believe you."

Viola flinched as if struck. Tears blurred the room into amorphous splotches of color.

"Papa," she began. "I *do* love you."

"Daughter, I don't doubt that you believe that, but your actions speak otherwise. You have betrayed my trust in the most terribly public way." Dr. Brodure turned for the door, eyes anguished and too bright. "And in the end, our actions reveal the true intent of our hearts more than words ever could."

Viola feared her own heart would crack in two.

"Papa, please."

"I need some time on my own to think." He pressed two fingers to his forehead. "Please give my apologies to Lord and Lady Hadley tonight. Tell them I am feeling unwell and am unable to attend their dinner."

Her father left the room, closing the door with a quiet *snick*.

Viola collapsed onto the sofa before the fire and poured her woes into the obliging wool of a soft cushion.

HOURS LATER AND Malcolm's thoughts were still a *fankle*. Damnation.

Aileen had never turned him inside out like this. Their relationship had been so effortlessly linear, graduating from friends to sweethearts to marriage in a gentle ascending line.

Granted, if he were being honest, he and Viola had followed a similar arc though in a fraction of the time.

And perhaps that was part of the problem.

They had moved from strangers to lovers in such quick succession that the velocity of their affections inevitably crashed into the unyielding wall of his grief and fear, of the external pressures of family and vocation.

All Malcolm could do, at the moment, was attempt to pick himself up out of the wreckage.

He still had yet to receive word from Callum regarding Isla and her babe. All anyone could do at the moment was wait.

And now, he faced an interminable evening at Muirford House, permitting Kendall to heap wee abuses on himself and watching an oblivious Ethan court Viola. Leah and Fox had sent their regrets, as Leah had a wee chill.

Thank goodness Hadley and Sir Rafe and their wives would still be in attendance. Hopefully, they would act as ballast to keep the dinner party from floundering. Though given Kendall's mood, the duke might decide that Sir Rafe, as his older half-brother, would also be an acceptable whipping boy.

Wishing to put his best foot forward, Malcolm had decided to forgo wearing his usual great kilt. Instead, he donned a well-cut suit of superfine wool that Leah had insisted he purchase on a rare trip to Edinburgh.

He was brushing the tight-fitting evening jacket when Ethan burst into his room, sheets of foolscap clutched in his fist.

"Malcolm, what would be a good metaphor for love?"

"Pardon?" Malcolm turned toward Ethan, eyebrows lifting.

"Love. A metaphor."

"Why do ye need my help with a metaphor?"

"I *always* need your help with metaphors. Ye practically breathe the things." Ethan tapped the papers in his hand. "I'm trying to write yet another sonnet for Miss Brodure, but my thoughts are still *gubbed*. I need your help until I can get my feet under my pen, so tae speak."

As usual, Ethan's mention of Viola sent a stab of guilt through Malcolm's chest.

"Why not just write what ye feel?" Malcolm suggested, setting aside his jacket. He wrapped his neckcloth around his neck and turned to the mirror with a frown. He so rarely attempted a complicated knot, he was unsure where to start.

"Yes, yes." Ethan set down his papers and stepped in, batting Malcolm's hands away from the neckcloth and grasping the ends himself. "That's all well and good, but I need a proper metaphor to capture the depth of my affections."

Malcolm looked up at the ceiling as his brother tugged on his offending neckwear.

"And how deep is your affection, precisely?" Malcolm *had* to ask it.

He was going to Hell. That was a certainty.

He would burn in Perdition for allowing this deception to carry on so long.

"My affections?" Ethan gave a soft laugh. "I'm asking ye for a metaphor about love. Doesn't that say it all?"

Oof. A horse kick to the solar plexus would have winded Malcolm less.

"Are ye sure ye love Miss Brodure, Ethan?" he asked. "Or is this more a case of being in love with the idea of love?"

"In love with love?" Ethan snorted. "As if I'm too naive to understand my own mind? Give me a wee bit more credit than that."

Bloody hell. Guilt rode Malcolm hard.

Spurred on by self-reproach, he searched his mind. What was it he had said to Viola weeks ago about taking risks?

"Well, in that case, why not something about how living without her love would be a death, that actual death isnae how we die most or some such," Malcolm offered.

"Mmmm." Ethan stepped back, surveying the neckcloth.

Malcolm waited, not sure if his brother's frown was for Malcolm's metaphor suggestion or his clothing.

"Though I appreciate the sentiment," Ethan turned back to his papers, "I fear that's a wee bit morbid for Miss Brodure. I need something more refined."

Malcolm surveyed his cravat in the mirror. If he required proof of the difference between his lot in life and Ethan's, Malcolm needed look no further than his reflection at present—his wee brother had tied the neckcloth with effortless precision.

Malcolm reached for his coat.

"The problem as I see it," Ethan continued, "is that I have been too hesitant with Miss Brodure, and therefore, I fear she does not understand the depth of my regard. She is naturally timid and reserved, and so I have moderated my passions to suit her temperament. But no more. I have determined to be bolder, starting this evening."

Malcolm froze, one arm in his coat sleeve.

Timid and reserved? *Viola?!*

Oh, for the love of—

"Miss Brodure is *shy*, Ethan. That isnae the same thing as being timid. And as with most shy people, I presume she becomes more open the more ye get to know her."

Which begged the question: in all his time spent with Viola, why hadn't Ethan come to know her better?

"Shy?!" Ethan's head reared back, nose scrunching up as if the very notion was absurd.

And then slowly, like pale dawn washing the horizon, understanding flowed in.

"Oh," Ethan breathed out. "She is . . . *shy.*"

Malcolm longed to roll his eyes right out of his head. If remorse hadn't been constricting his chest, he would have.

"When did ye realize all this about Miss Brodure?" Ethan asked.

"*Och*, from the very beginning. 'Twas obvious."

"Why didn't ye tell me?"

"Because I assumed ye were making an effort tae know Miss Brodure, to understand her quietness. After all, a gentleman should take the time to observe his lady-love. That way, he can meet her as she is, not as he supposes her tae be."

Silence rested between them for a moment.

"*A gentleman must meet his lady-love as she is . . .*" Ethan said, slowly. Eyes lit with delight, he reached for his pencil. "Hah! I knew ye would be good for an idea or two." He bent over his foolscap, scribbling.

Malcolm barely suppressed a growl. "Why must ye always pass off my ideas as your own?"

Ethan chuckled, unrepentant. "*Och*, they say creativity is simply the art of covering over the source of your inspiration—"

"Are ye sincere with this?" Malcolm placed his hands on his hips. "Why must my ideas and my musings and my soul wind their way into your work? What if I tire of being your inspiration?"

Or if ye ever learn of my deceit, ye decide you're too angry tae talk tae me anymore, he didn't add.

Shaking his head, Malcolm pivoted out of the room.

But not fast enough to escape his brother's voice.

"*My ideas, my musings, and my soul . . .*" Ethan's words carried down the stairwell. "That's bloody brilliant."

THE FEW TIMES that Malcolm had been invited to dine with Lord and Lady Hadley—usually when Sir Rafe and his wife, Lady Sophie, were visiting—he had enjoyed the evening. Good wine, excellent beef, genial bonhomie, and even better conversation were usually on hand at Muirford House.

Tonight, however, was an aberration, at least in regards to the company invited.

The guests were currently gathered in the drawing-room, talking with one another and awaiting late arrivals.

Or rather, *attempting* to speak with one another.

The Duke of Kendall loomed over the room, his icy stares chilling the atmosphere by several degrees.

Lady Hadley had been sending her husband rather telling looks for the past fifteen minutes communicating, as only the daughter of a duke could, her annoyance at His Grace's arrogant behavior. Hadley had subtly rolled his eyes in agreement, causing his wife's lips to twitch into a smile.

Malcolm longed to loosen his neckcloth, anything to ease the strain.

Worse, Viola had yet to arrive. Hadley said he had received word that Dr. Brodure was indisposed, but Miss Brodure would still attend. Was her father truly unwell? Or was Dr. Brodure's 'illness' the result of the revelations earlier in the day?

Perhaps Viola would decide she was 'unwell,' too.

A heaviness settled in Malcolm's lungs at the thought of not seeing her tonight.

Regardless, every guest who entered the drawing-room had him turning his head, looking for her in vain. Just one glance would tell him all he wanted to know, he reasoned. If her father had been understanding or condemning of her lies of omission. If their parting on the road earlier had overset her.

However, one small piece of good news buoyed his spirits. Malcolm had received word as he and Ethan stepped into the gig for the journey to Muirford House that Isla and her babe had come through the birth. Mother and baby were now resting easily and a relieved Callum had wept with joy.

The news had swept Malcolm with profound relief. *Hallelujah!* If anyone deserved a miracle, it was Callum and Isla Liston.

But now, faced with dinner at Muirford Park and no Viola yet in attendance, Malcolm was crawling out of his skin. Finally, he began to stroll slowly around the perimeter of the room, anything to stem the agitated wave of thoughts threatening him.

Lady Hadley and Lady Sophie were deep in discussion about Lady Isolde, the Hadley's eldest daughter, who was currently enrolled in a university for women in the United States.

"Isolde has two more years of study," Lady Hadley was saying, "and I don't know how I shall bear her continued absence."

Malcolm knew that the village busybodies had raised their eyebrows at a woman attempting a university degree. But by all accounts, Lady Isolde had been determined, and the United States had one of the only universities in the world that would award a baccalaureate degree to a woman.

"It is difficult when they leave." Lady Sophie nodded in agreement. "But just think of all the wonderful conversations we shall have when Isolde returns. Has she taken up mineralogy like yourself?"

"No," Lady Hadley sounded appalled. "She prefers mechanics and physics, which truly, astounds me . . ." Their voices drifted away.

Malcolm pivoted at the fireplace, glancing toward the open door to the entrance hall.

No Viola.

He paced toward the bow window overlooking the back garden.

Sir Rafe had sidled up to Kendall.

It was striking to see Kendall and Sir Rafe side by side. Any onlooker would assume them to be brothers, or even father and son.

They were nearly of a height—tall and lean—with similarly dark eyes and hair equally gray, though Sir Rafe's gray was more commensurate with his age.

Murmured words passed between them. Shamelessly, Malcolm edged closer to hear.

" . . . why are ye truly here, Your Grace?" Sir Rafe was saying, giving his younger half-brother a rather guarded look.

"Why am I here?" A tight smile touched Kendall's lips. "Believe it or not, I find this corner of Scotland somewhat diverting. The ongoing drama involving Ethan Penn-Leith and Viola Brodure amuses me. It has all the hallmarks of London's finest melodramas. I should hate to miss the final act."

"With all due respect," Sir Rafe snorted, "I highly doubt ye are a closet romantic, Your Grace."

"Perhaps I have a bit of a vested interest in the outcome of this whole affair."

Sir Rafe eyed the younger man. "Pulling strings?"

"Something of the like."

"*Och*, spoken like a true Duke of Kendall." The scathing bite to Sir Rafe's words left little doubt as to his opinion.

"And how would you know that?" Kendall's tone matched Sir Rafe's.

"More than a welp like yourself could ever understand."

"Pardon?" Kendall turned to look at his brother full on.

Malcolm pretended interest in a painting of—he glanced up—a hunting dog with a brace of pheasants, it appeared.

Sir Rafe didn't back down. "Ye be scarcely what? Twenty-three? I lived a lifetime under the cruel tyranny of our bastard of a sire. I thank God that man is now dead. He no longer plays the puppet-master. You're free. Why prolong his legacy?"

Kendall's brows drew down, his mouth opening as if to reply, but then stopped, eyes swinging toward the open door.

Malcolm followed his gaze.

Viola stood in the doorway, scanning the room.

She looked stunning in a pale pink silk gown that nipped in her tiny waist and slipped off her slim shoulders and glimmered in the candlelight.

But even from across the room, Malcolm could tell that she appeared a wee bit *peely-wally*. High color flooded her cheeks, and her shoulders sagged as if carrying a weight. He wanted to go to her, to settle her slight hand on his arm.

But she did not look his way.

And Ethan, of course, raced across the room to her side, escorting her to greet Lord and Lady Hadley.

Malcolm tried to catch Viola's eye, but she studiously avoided his gaze.

What had she said when they parted earlier? *We both have some thinking to do.*

Had she decided against even maintaining a friendship with him? Reasoning that if they did not intend to carry their relationship to its logical, marital end, then they should cease speaking altogether?

A wheezing panic settled into Malcolm's chest, as if he had taken the mountains surrounding Laverloch at a run.

Theoretically, this was the outcome he had wanted, was it not? After all, a romantic relationship was an all-or-nothing proposition. And if he felt they should be nothing to one another, then this was how things had to be.

And yet, the frantic whipping lash of his pulse implied precisely the opposite.

Had any dinner ever gone on for so long? Viola wondered.

She was quite sure she had been sitting for weeks at this table.

And yet, the clock—placed directly opposite at eye level, as if to better mock her—showed that scarcely an hour had passed.

The guests chatted and laughed. Cutlery clinked against china dishes. A lady giggled. Lord Hadley smiled politely at something Kendall said to his right. Lady Hadley and Sir Rafe were speaking with Malcolm at the other end of the table.

Viola, sitting precisely in the middle, had never felt less merry. The tense conversations from earlier in the day had cast a pall over her mood. How could they not? In the space of just a few hours, her future had hidden itself behind a foggy wall as impenetrable as *haar* rolling ashore from the North Sea.

How was she to navigate her life now? When all familiar landmarks— her father's affections, her hopes for romantic love, her desire to write on topics of her own choosing—were now shrouded and indistinct.

She fanned herself.

Light streamed into the room, the last gasp of the sinking sun. The attending footman had drawn translucent shades to block the worst of the glare through the terrace doors, but the shimmery curtains did nothing to block the heat. The room had warmed several degrees over the past hour.

At Viola's elbow, Ethan kept up a steady stream of conversation, on everything from his love of a good walking stick to the beauty of foliage in autumn.

His attentions had been more marked than usual this evening. He had raced to her side the moment she arrived and hadn't left it since. Viola fretted over the frank conversation she had to have with him tomorrow. But if anything, his eager behavior made it imperative that she curtail his affections before they progressed further.

Across from her, Mrs. Ruxton regarded Viola and Ethan sitting side-by-side, smiled widely, and abruptly exclaimed for the ninth time—yes, Viola was counting—

"I say, Lord Hadley, what a bonnie couple Miss Brodure and Mr. Penn-Leith make!" The lady's glib tongue was insatiable this evening.

Both Hadley and Kendall looked at Viola and Ethan . . . also for the ninth time.

"Indeed, Mrs. Ruxton," Lord Hadley boomed, a smile on his lips. "We have all agreed on that point, have we not?"

Kendall met Viola's gaze with a sardonic lilt of his eyebrows.

"Yes, Hadley," the duke said, words so *very* dry and monotone, "but surely it bears repeating."

Viola ducked her head, a blush painting her cheeks cherry red. Her breathing constricted.

Lord Hadley laughed good-naturedly, either oblivious to the undercurrents racing like escaped geese around the table, or more likely, choosing to ignore them like the sensible person he appeared to be.

Viola lifted her head for the briefest moment, her gaze unerringly finding Malcolm's at the other end of the table.

Forgoing his habitual kilt, Malcolm had arrived in the evening dress of a London gentleman. He wore his black evening coat and loose trousers with an easy grace, the hallmarks of a man comfortable in his own skin. To Viola's endless frustration, the sight had sent a flutter of excited butterflies skimming her stomach.

She refused to lose herself in contemplating Malcolm Penn-Leith's broad shoulders and enticing lips.

Her father's words from earlier rang in her head—

Actions reveal the true intent of our hearts more than words ever could.

What did that idea say about Malcolm Penn-Leith? Was his silence an action, in the end? Or merely a void of unsaid thoughts?

And at this point, did the distinction matter?

Malcolm's hesitation had made his feelings clear. And staring at the man would solve nothing.

Viola jerked her head away from him.

Unfortunately, the movement merely forced her eyes to Kendall.

The smug aristocrat merely tipped his wine glass in her direction, a sardonic *I-find-this-entire-situation-vastly-amusing* lift to his lips.

Oof!

Speaking of actions revealing the intent of one's heart . . .

Must Kendall *be* such an ass?

Perhaps someone needed to tell him that other behavioral selections were available. That he didn't have to wake every morning and *choose* ass-ishness.

Ethan shifted beside her, his breath tickling her ear. "You look beautiful this evening. I daresay the very angels in heaven are brought to shame by your presence."

"I am hardly as perfect as an angel of God," Viola whispered in return. "I should not like to be the cause of such blasphemy."

He leaned closer. "Adoring you could never be considered blasphemous—"

"I say, Sir Rafe, aren't they simply the bonniest of couples." Mrs. Ruxton called down to the foot of the table.

Ah. Ten times. They had progressed to double-digits it seemed.

"Most certainly, Mrs. Ruxton." Sir Rafe lifted his wine glass in a salute.

Ethan beamed. Viola bit her lip.

And still, she could feel the press of Malcolm's gaze on her.

It seemed the farther the day took her from their fraught, brief exchange, the greater it loomed in her head, until it had ballooned to mountainous proportions and Viola could see nothing beyond it.

Footmen cleared the cheese course and brought in frosted glasses of strawberry dessert ice on silver trays. Just as the last glass of ice was placed before guests, Ethan unexpectedly rose, lifting his wine goblet with him.

All eyes turned his way.

He stood confident and tall, his glass in one hand, the other hand folded behind his back. Unlike his brother, Ethan had *not* foregone his kilt for the evening. He looked every inch the Highland Poet—his wry grin charming and roguish, hair tousled as if he had just raced in off the moor.

The Viola Brodure she had been three months ago would have swooned at the sight.

Now, Ethan Penn-Leith in all his glory—clearly intent on saying *Something Important*—merely filled her with anxious worry.

"Your Grace. My lord. My lady." He nodded toward Kendall and Lord and Lady Hadley. "Esteemed guests." He gave Viola a triumphant smile. "Ladies and gentlemen." He swept his glass to indicate Sir Rafe, Lady Sophie, and the rest of the room. "Please forgive my interruption." Ethan's unrepentant expression made clear that no one ever categorized his desire to speak as an 'interruption.' "But I can sit in silence no longer. We have all been the fortunate recipients of Miss Brodure's company over these past seven weeks. I believe I speak for us all when I say that I have never met such a gracious, kind lady."

"Hear, hear!" Sir Rafe encouraged.

Kendall shot his half-brother a repressive look. Sir Rafe grinned in reply.

Viola spared a glance for Ethan. What was he leading up to?

"Thank ye." Ethan lifted his glass in Sir Rafe's direction. "I have been pondering as of late the truths of life, particularly those pertaining to love."

That got a lively laugh from the room.

For her part, Viola wanted to press a hand to her forehead.

Please say no more, she plead within herself.

But Ethan continued on, oblivious. "I have often pondered how living without love, true love, is like a death." He paused. "That actual death isn't how we die most."

Viola gasped—a startled shock of sound. Ringing filled her ears.

What had Ethan just said?!

An idea blasted its way to the forefront of her brain. Her heart sped up, and her breathing constricted further.

Surely that wasn't the case.

And yet . . .

Her eyes flew to Malcolm's. She could practically hear him saying those same words in his gravelly brogue on the path beside the folly, tree branches arching like comforting arms above them.

Literal death isnae how we die most.

Malcolm met her gaze—mouth pinched, expression drawn—and in that moment . . . she *knew.*

He served as his brother's Muse.

Malcolm was the source of Ethan's profundity.

How could she have missed this?

Understanding snicked into place.

Why she was so drawn to Malcolm instead of Ethan.

Why Ethan struck her as so much surface. Why she struggled to connect with him.

Clearly, Ethan had talent. Viola strongly doubted that Malcolm was the author of his brother's poetry. And surely not all of Ethan's ideas originated with his older brother.

But some of his ideas—their philosophical depth—

Over and over, Malcolm proved himself to be so much more than she had fathomed. So much more than he himself believed.

And, perhaps more importantly . . . why, in all their conversations and confidences, had he never given the slightest hint of this?

Just one more piece of himself that Malcolm Penn-Leith kept hidden.

How well did she know him, in the end?

Dimly, she realized Ethan was still speaking. ". . . celebrate having this lovely lady in our midst, I should like to propose a toast. To Miss Brodure. To her vision. To her modest morality."

"How delightful!" Mrs. Ruxton enthused, loud enough for the entire room to hear. "Truly the bonniest of couples."

The dinner guests laughed. Lord Hadley's voice called in agreement.

"Indeed." Kendall sent Viola another sardonic look, looking too much like a lion intent on toying with the gazelle of Ethan's enthusiasm.

It was all too much.

Ethan's words.

Malcolm's silence.

Kendall's menacing.

Everyone's expectations.

An errant ray of sunlight slipped through the filmy curtains, blinding her.

Her lungs seized.

No!

Not now. Not again.

She took a deep breath. And then another.

How she hated this feeling, the sense that she was underwater, sucking air through a small hollow reed between her lips.

Dimly, she noted Malcolm's alarmed expression, his creased brow.

Just breathe.

Why, oh why, could she not simply breathe?!

MALCOLM CLUTCHED THE arms of his chair, anything to stop himself from lurching to his feet.

Viola had gone so very pale, her eyes downcast, her cheeks a scorching red. Her bosom strained in her gown, clearly struggling to draw air.

How could everyone else at the table be so heedless of her distress?

Ethan laughed. "I should like to raise my glass to the hope of Miss Brodure seeing my humble self as more than just a sometime dinner companion."

Viola pressed a shaking hand to her chest, lungs laboring.

Did no one else see? Did no one understand?!

"Enough, Ethan!" Malcolm surged to his feet.

Every head in the room swung his way, brows puckered and puzzled. Kendall flicked his eyes up and down Malcolm with scathing condescension.

Malcolm felt every inch of his uncultured upbringing—his country manners, his thick accent, his calloused hands—all stark foils to Ethan's urbane sophistication.

Viola raised her head, gaze locking with his, those two spots of color flushing her cheeks.

Her chest heaved again.

That was all the encouragement he needed.

"Ethan—" He looked at his brother. "—ye are distressing Miss Brodure with your public declarations—"

"Truly, Malcolm?" Ethan scowled at him. "Miss Brodure is perfectly capable of—"

"She's on the verge of an asthmatic fit!"

Viola gasped, breath wheezing.

Every eye turned toward her, likely intensifying her distress. She needed to be free of these weighty stares, removed from this stuffy room.

"Asthma?" Ethan asked, and then his brow cleared, as if remembering the scene by the folly. He looked down at her, alarmed. "Miss Brodure, how can I help?"

"Aye," Hadley echoed, pushing to his feet.

Viola had closed her eyes, hand pressed to her sternum.

"Damp air," Malcolm said, moving around the table toward her. "She needs fresh, humid air."

But before he could reach her side, Ethan and Hadley had already assisted Viola to stand. She clung to each of their arms as they guided her toward the tall terrace doors. An obliging footman pulled one open, blasting them all with fading sun.

Malcolm squinted and held up a hand to block the horizontal light.

By the time his vision had cleared, Viola was being led across the terrace and down wide flagstone steps to a large, bubbling fountain. Ethan assisted her to sit on its stone edge, holding her hand and perching beside her with solicitous concern.

Malcolm filed onto the terrace with the rest of the guests—Mrs. Ruxton bobbing on tiptoe trying to see, Sir Rafe with his wife on his arm. Kendall, of course, pushed to the front of the group, sending Malcolm a bemused glance as he passed . . . the bastard.

For his part, Malcolm edged to the right of everyone, giving himself a clearer view of Viola.

"Breathe, lass," Hadley encouraged, crouching before her. "Reach deep . . . from the bottom of your lungs." He mimicked the motion, ribs expanding.

Viola's chest continued to heave, her face in profile, the hollow of her throat sucking in with each labored breath.

Lady Hadley sat on Viola's opposite side.

And Malcolm . . .

Well . . .

He stood with the other guests.

Powerless. Watching.

Helplessly observing.

Because he had no claim to be at the side of the woman he loved as she struggled and suffered.

The woman he loved.

Bloody hell.

He closed his eyes, swallowing hard.

A fine tremor of *rightness* shivered through him.

He *did* love her.

Thoroughly. Body and soul.

With the same all-consuming joy he had loved Aileen.

The emotion rolled over him, as obliterating and giddy as the first thunderstorm after a long drought.

"Miss Brodure?" Lady Hadley was saying. "Can I do anything to help?"

Viola spared a glance for the guests gathered, her gaze skimming right over Malcolm.

His heart panged.

"So m-many eyes," she murmured.

Lady Hadley nodded, exchanging a look with her husband. It was a wifely sort of look and Hadley, a long-time married man, understood instantly.

Standing, Hadley clapped his hands to get everyone's attention and then politely asked the guests to kindly follow Lady Hadley to the drawing-room for after-dinner tea.

Malcolm saw some of the tension leave Viola's body as the watching eyes turned away, people shuffling toward the house.

Of course, Malcolm himself did not leave.

His feet refused to obey him.

The *woman he loved* was in distress.

Kendall, curse his arrogant hide, stayed put, as well.

Why did he remain?

Malcolm wasn't the only one who thought it odd.

Sir Rafe glared at Kendall as he retreated inside, holding the duke's gaze with what could only be described as a *death stare*. Kendall broke off first, but he did not follow his brother.

Gritting his teeth, Malcolm crossed to stand beside the duke.

If Kendall tried to make a scene, Malcolm would . . .

He would . . .

Well . . . he would do *something*. Of that he was sure.

Thankfully, Viola's breathing appeared to be easing the slightest bit.

"Ye are doing well, Miss Brodure," Ethan encouraged, trapping Viola's hand between two of his own.

"Aye," Hadley rumbled. He patted Ethan on the back. "Your lass will come through this."

"*Your lass*," Kendall repeated under his breath on a snort, so quiet only Malcolm could hear.

It was all Malcolm could do to avoid flinching.

Because Kendall, despite his sarcasm, had hit upon a bedrock truth—

If Malcolm continued on his path away from Viola, someday, another man would claim her as his lass. Another man would soak up her laughter and clever wit. Another man would hold her in his arms and fret over her during pregnancy, rub her tired feet, and kiss her flushed cheeks.

Malcolm would spend the rest of his life observing her from a distance, reading about her life in the broadsheets.

And that thought was simply, painfully . . . intolerable.

No.

It was *unendurable*.

Malcolm could not continue to breathe, to live, to *endure* unless Viola was at his side.

And just like that, he made his decision.

The decision he should have made earlier on the lane, when Viola had flinched at his silence.

He simply could not live without Viola Brodure as his wife.

If he couldn't live without her, then he had to conquer the fear of living *with* her.

The choice in the end was truly that simple.

And as he stared across the fifteen feet currently separating them—at the fine-boned curve of her fingers pressed to her sternum, the purse of her rose-petal lips, the fluttering pulse in her throat where he adored pressing a lingering kiss . . .

Malcolm realized that he did.

He *did* have the courage.

And he chose her.

Over a duke's rage. Over a brother's heartbreak. Over his own black grief and unknown fear of the future.

Terror still pummeled him, a thousand *what ifs* winging through his veins. His own involuntary reaction to the trauma of Aileen's death had not magically disappeared.

But Malcolm thought of Callum, facing the horror of Isla's laboring, of the agonizing hours of her delivery . . .

It *had* all come right in the end.

That was life, was it not?

Nothing guaranteed.

Malcolm could die just as readily as Viola, tomorrow or fifty years from now.

Life was one constant gamble.

And Malcolm would face it all with Viola Brodure at his side, for as long as Fate permitted. If she would still have him.

Viola's breathing finally appeared to flow more easily. Her lungs lifted in a less labored fashion.

A soft snort sounded beside him. Malcolm whipped his head to the right, meeting Kendall's amused eyes.

"So much emotion in your expression," His Grace drawled. "This evening has been delightfully entertaining."

Malcolm turned away.

The man was a damned menace.

"I am f-feeling much improved, thank you, Mr. Penn-Leith," Viola was saying to Ethan.

"Excellent." Hadley nodded to Ethan. "Mr. Penn-Leith, would you please escort Miss Brodure inside? There is a comfortable chaise in the blue drawing-room where she can rest."

"Of course, my lord. I should be honored." Ethan helped Viola to her feet and settled her on his arm.

As they turned toward the house, Malcolm met Viola's gaze for the barest second.

He didn't know what he expected to see there. Anger over their words along the lane? Exhaustion with her body's frailty?

Some emotion for him to latch on to.

Instead, her face was . . . blank. As if all her lovely fire had been banked deep down.

She turned her head back to Ethan.

Dinnae go, his heart whispered. *Dinnae leave me.*

And in that moment, Malcolm knew as sure as he knew anything— he was going to grovel for Viola's forgiveness.

If she gave it, he was going to marry her.

Fears be damned.

Consequences be damned.

He loved her.

There would never be another lass but her.

Kendall snorted again at Malcolm's side.

"And to think," the duke said softly, "I was accused of enacting a Drury Lane farce earlier." The man laughed. "I can assure you, tonight has been *decidedly* more melodramatic."

Malcolm stood by the fountain long after Kendall wandered back into the dining room.

Hating that the duke, despite everything, had described the evening with unerring accuracy.

20

Viola woke the next morning to her maid, Mary, opening the shutters of the cottage bedroom, spilling cheery sunshine across the counterpane. Birds chirped merrily outside the window.

It was all so perfectly bucolic and joyful that it made Viola want to smash things.

Mary set a jug of hot water on the washstand and bent to stir the fire.

On a sigh, Viola sat up in bed, pushing her thick braid off her shoulder.

The day before surfaced from her memory, jagged shards of arctic ice threatening to slice her. Kendall's promised threats, and her father's devastated hurt. Ethan's earnest declarations, and Malcolm's frozen indecision.

The sting of Malcolm's hesitation along the lane was the cut that lingered, particularly when contrasted with the initial concern he had shown during her asthma attack at dinner. But once Ethan and Hadley had her well in hand, Malcolm had faded into the background.

As a weatherglass of his heart, the man's actions were at best inconclusive.

And what was she to do now? Was their rupture a fatal wound? Or would a small bit of patience on her part give Malcolm time to come to his senses?

Yet . . . just pondering the thought . . .

She didn't want a man who had to be cajoled into desiring her in return. If Malcolm wished to be back in her good graces, he would have to grovel.

Yes. That was it.

Stretching her arms over her head, she tried to hold on to her resolve. Truly she did.

But the thought of Malcolm Penn-Leith becoming a mere anecdotal chapter in her life, instead of the main plot line, left her feeling hollowed out and melancholy.

"Shall I fetch some tea, miss?" Mary bobbed a curtsy.

"Yes, please. Is there any shortbread to be had?"

"No shortbread, but Cook made a lovely almond cake. We got word last night that Isla Liston—she's the wife of the overseer over at Thistle Muir—finally had her babe. A wee girl. Cook was up well past dark baking away her nerves—poor Isla is a dear friend of hers and nearly died giving birth—and Cook was desperate for news. But all is well today, the Good Lord be thanked."

Thistle Muir.

The very name sent a lancing pain through Viola's heart.

She nodded and asked for some of the cake to be sent up with her tea.

But the mention of Thistle Muir eventually led to thoughts of Ethan. *Oof.*

A fraught conversation with the younger Penn-Leith loomed on her morning calendar. Perhaps she could simply rewrite her letter—omitting mention of Malcolm this time—and send it over with Mary.

Viola felt weary at the thought.

And then there was the revelation that Ethan used Malcolm as his muse.

Lying awake in bed—the Ruxton's having delivered her safely home—Viola had mentally reviewed all of Ethan's poems. She could practically hear Malcolm's words weaving through them, his unique view of the world.

But . . . why would Malcolm allow Ethan to appropriate his ideas?

Well, she supposed that answer was obvious. Malcolm adored his wee brother. He wanted Ethan to succeed.

And as Viola had already intuited, Malcolm Penn-Leith loved with his whole soul—every last piece of it—holding nothing back.

The knowledge hit her hard.

Every last piece.

Oh.

A curtain lifted from her mind.

Abruptly, Malcolm's expression from their conversation along the lane yesterday rose in her mind.

The tightness about his mouth. The cagey hesitation in his eyes.

And what had Mary just said? About Isla Liston?

How self-centered of Viola to assume that his emotions had been about herself alone.

Malcolm had to have known that his overseer's wife, Isla, was currently fighting for her life and that of her child.

Knowing Malcolm, he had likely sat with the woman's husband and family for a while as Isla labored in the next room.

Reliving the horror of yet another difficult birth, the uncertainty of it . . .

He had to have found that traumatic.

And then, after the encounter with Kendall, Viola's own conversation with him had immediately veered toward marriage.

No wonder that Malcolm had hesitated. The thought of taking another wife would have overwhelmed him in the moment.

Of course, this was all conjecture on her part.

Perhaps the more salient question would be—

Why, if the events of his afternoon unearthed traumatic memories, had Malcolm not said something to her about it?

If they were to contemplate a life together, they needed to begin it by speaking their truths. Preferably without Viola having to drag him into a grassy field first and place a chained stone in his hand.

Perhaps there was more to that stone-throwing thing than she had supposed.

But in the meantime . . . what was she to do?

Even if Malcolm were desperate to marry her, there was still the issue of Kendall and his threats toward both herself and her father. How were those to be overcome?

And could she plead a headache and stay abed all day without her father summoning the local doctor?

Viola was debating the wisdom of doing precisely that when a knock sounded—sharp and urgent—on the front door below her bedroom window.

The low murmur of voices followed.

Then, Mary's frantic footsteps racing up the stairs.

"Miss!" The maid rapped on her door. "Ye are needed downstairs immediately."

FIFTEEN MINUTES LATER, Viola presented herself—neatly dressed, her hair wrapped into a tidy, if hasty, chignon—in the front parlor.

Her father paced the floor in front of the hearth, hands behind his back, expression bleak.

She had never seen her father look so . . . . so . . . defeated. Nearly haggard. A prize fighter who had received one hit too many.

She crossed to him immediately. "Whatever is the matter, Papa?"

Dr. Brodure lifted his head and fixed his gaze on a point to the left of Viola's shoulder.

Spinning, Viola startled to see the Duke of Kendall. His Grace appeared to have raced through his toilette. His cravat was simply tied, and his gray hair lacked its usual gleaming pomade.

"Your Grace," she murmured, dipping a brisk curtsy, heart a pulse in her throat.

Kendall's presence did not bode well. The grim set of his jaw said his news was not pleasant. The gleeful gleam in his eye said he rather relished that fact.

Viola clasped her shaking hands before her.

"There is no easy way to say this, Miss Brodure, so I shall simply come to the point." The duke spoke each word crisply, his diction no doubt the product of hundreds of years of powerful men delivering bad news, often from a sword's edge.

Viola rather felt like he held a sword to her own throat currently. She dared a glance back at her father, but he avoided her eyes.

What had happened?!

Kendall did not keep her waiting.

"Twice in the past week, Miss Brodure," he began, "you were seen entering Thistle Muir in the company of Mr. Ethan Penn-Leith, right before and right after his trip to Aberdeen. Both times occurred on the servants' day off, when no one else was about the house."

To Kendall's credit, he didn't deliver the news with quite as much cheerful spite as Viola might have expected. But that didn't stop her stomach from plummeting like a stone.

"*Ethan* Penn-Leith?" she said.

Yes, *that* was the information her brain chose to focus on first.

The tiniest of ironic smiles touched Kendall's lips. It wasn't particularly encouraging.

"Indeed," he said, almost conversationally. "I find myself with a whole host of questions about your proclivities, Miss Brodure."

Viola blushed scarlet, the wash of color as scourging as a lash.

"Your Grace!" Dr. Brodure broke his silence on a gasp.

As if remembering he had an audience, Kendall sketched a polite bow toward her father. "My apologies, Dr. Brodure. I'm sure your daughter will enlighten us both as to the particulars—"

Another knock sounded on the front door.

Dr. Ruxton bustled in, handing hat and walking stick to the waiting Mary.

"Ah, I see my news precedes me." The vicar bowed to Kendall.

Dr. Brodure motioned for all his guests to be seated and then ordered *tea* to be brought in, of all things.

Honestly, Viola could hardly think straight, much less calmly pour tea. She wasn't quite *that* English, it seemed.

Particularly as Kendall regarded her with his dark, sardonic eyes, and her father continued to give her sideways glances, likely trying to determine if she was on the verge an asthmatic fit.

Her nerves were rather too stunned at the moment to react.

"Well," Dr. Ruxton began, hands braced on his knees, "this is certainly not how we all expected Miss Brodure and Mr. Penn-Leith to begin their life together, but they are hardly the first couple to anticipate the blissful state of marriage. I shall be the first to offer my congratulations."

Oh, good heavens!

Viola pressed shaking fingers to her fiery cheeks. Was it possible for one's skin to burst into flames spontaneously? Because, at the moment, she was rather thoroughly testing the scientific possibility.

"But nothing untoward has occurred b-between myself and Mr. Ethan Penn-Leith," she stammered out. "I merely dropped by to leave a note, assuming Mr. Penn-Leith to be away. He invited me in for a mere five minutes to lend me a book. That is the extent of our nefarious behavior. Where on earth did this dreadful rumor begin?"

Dr. Ruxton frowned, Viola's very real distress perhaps communicating the truth of her words.

"That is not quite the tale I heard," the vicar said.

NEVER IN HIS life had Malcolm wished for the ability to write a poem.

But facing the cool dawn after Hadley's dinner party, knowing he needed to win back Viola, Malcolm longed for words. He might provide Ethan with the occasional philosophical insight, but his brother had the gift of taking raw material and turning it into art.

And yet, Malcolm needed to help Viola understand the blinding terror and joy he felt at the thought of aligning his life with hers.

As soon as the sun climbed to a socially acceptable height in the sky, he would present himself on the Brodure's doorstep and beg to speak with her.

Malcolm had just finished breakfast when Lord Hadley and Sir Rafe rode up the lane.

They entered the parlor, shedding coats and shaking Malcolm's hand.

The men wore matching grim expressions.

"Is Ethan about?" Hadley asked. "We bring news that will impact him."

"He's still abed, having a bit of a lie in. I'll send the maid to rouse him." Malcolm stepped into the entry hall and asked Fiona to fetch Ethan before returning to the parlor and closing the door. "What the hell has happened?"

"I'll get right to the point." Hadley expelled a long breath of air. "Mrs. Buchan and Mrs. Clark saw Miss Brodure enter Thistle Muir with Ethan, both last week and this week on your servants' day off. Your brother has utterly compromised the lady."

The bottom fell out of Malcolm's world.

As if, once more, he had stumbled atop a crevasse, the ground beneath him melting away, sending him plummeting into the unforgiving depths.

"Pardon?!" he managed to croak out. "Ethan?!"

Malcolm knew bloody well it hadn't been Ethan the first week. As for yesterday, that had been Viola merely attempting to leave her letter.

"Aye," Hadley nodded. "Last week, the ladies claim to have seen Miss Brodure and Ethan engaging in what they called—"

"The tenderest of embraces," Sir Rafe supplied. "Said with fervent relish, mind you."

"Too true." Hadley looked back at Malcolm. "As Mrs. Clark tells it, your brother and Miss Brodure enjoyed a lover-like embrace in front of Thistle Muir before Ethan lifted Miss Brodure into his arms and carried her into the house."

"I believe her precise words were, 'The scene was so romantic I nearly swooned,'" Sir Rafe added.

"Aye. Both ladies described the event at length, commenting particularly on Miss Brodure's shocking lack of a bonnet, which apparently signaled the thrillingly illicit nature of the encounter." Hadley turned to Sir Rafe. "Did ye know bonnets, or the absence of them, could be so damning?"

Sir Rafe shrugged. "If fans can have a language, why can't bonnets protect morality?"

Malcolm began pacing before the cold hearth.

Of all the bloody, damn unfortunate—

Hadley wasn't done. "Thrilled by the previous week's revelations, our intrepid gossip mongers returned this week tae see if they had stumbled upon a pattern. And once more, they witnessed Miss Brodure arrive right as Ethan returned home from Aberdeen, as if their meeting were pre-planned." Hadley nodded toward the closed parlor door. "The ladies came running this morning at dawn tae tell me the whole. They said as the preeminent landowner in Fettermill, I needed to know. As if *I* have any desire tae be tangled in this mess."

"They were rather gleefully excited," Sir Rafe pointed out. "I cannot imagine anyone within a twenty-mile radius not knowing the news by luncheon."

Malcolm pinched the bridge of his nose.

Viola.

He had to get to Viola.

Had the news already reached her? Was this the final blow that would send her into a critical asthmatic fit?

"Aye," Hadley agreed, "but it's not as if Ethan and Miss Brodure were not well on their way tae the altar anyway. This will simply speed up the timeline, as it were, given that the lady's reputation has been thoroughly damaged. We're just here tae give Ethan a warning that his clandestine activities have been found out."

Malcolm only heard Hadley's words in passing. He had crossed to the parlor door, intent on his hat and horse.

His lovely, brave Viola.

She was going to find herself betrothed to one of the Penn-Leith brothers before the day's end.

Malcolm intended it to be himself.

He was reaching for the handle when the door flew open and Ethan all but toppled into the room. Struggling into his coat, his younger brother flailed one arm and nearly cold-cocked Malcolm in the process.

Grimacing, Malcolm ducked in time and then helped Ethan pull the sleeve the rest of the way up his arm.

"What has happened?" Ethan's eyes appeared wild as he straightened his jacket.

Malcolm looked at his brother, remorse churning in his stomach.

He and Viola should have told Ethan a week ago. It was just . . . they had found themselves in the middle of a courtship before even consciously realizing it. Then Ethan was gone away to Aberdeen . . .

And now . . .

. . . now it was far too late.

Something of Malcolm's dismay must have been written all over his face.

Ethan paled. His gaze darted past Malcolm to Hadley and Sir Rafe. "Has someone died? What is it?"

Sir Rafe and Hadley exchanged a glance, as if silently communicating to one another, determining who would deliver the news.

Hadley broke first, shrugging and turning to smile at Ethan. "*Och*, it's not nearly as all bad as that. Just a wee bump in the road tae your happily ever after."

A frown furrowing his forehead, Ethan cast wary eyes between Hadley's hearty words and Malcolm's surely stricken gaze.

"Tell me."

Keeping his eyes trained on Ethan, Malcolm waited as Hadley and Sir Rafe told his brother what had transpired.

Ethan listened with stoic stillness, his frown deepening with each word.

"Tae be honest, Ethan," Hadley said, "Mrs. Buchan thought that it was Malcolm here on that first day, as ye were said tae be away to Aberdeen already. But as the ladies were at some distance, they couldn't tell with any certainty. However, our village *nosy-nebbies* are nothing if not indefatigable. So they did more reconnaissance yesterday."

"Tae see if this were a regular thing, as it were," Sir Rafe added.

"Aye," Hadley agreed, "and there was Ethan, rushing back from Aberdeen, and Miss Brodure on the doorstep tae greet him."

"So, of course, then they knew it had actually been yourself all along."

Ethan's eyes drifted to Malcolm at that, reading the truth there.

The truth Malcolm could no longer hide.

It *had* been him.

He had embraced Viola before Thistle Muir and swept her inside.

Thank goodness, neither Mrs. Clark nor Mrs. Buchan had been privy to Malcolm and Viola's incandescently scandalous kiss in the back courtyard.

Nor all the subsequent ones in the scullery, along the lane, outside the south pasture, atop his childhood swing . . .

Och.

Did it matter at this juncture?

Ethan continued to look at him, with something like . . .

Like . . .

Malcolm blinked.

He knew his wee brother almost as well as he knew himself. And the expression on Ethan's face was not anger or hurt or betrayal.

But instead something softer . . .

Compassion? Concern?

Ethan nodded and squeezed Malcolm's shoulder, as if to say, *I have ye. All will be well.*

Too surprised to speak, Malcolm watched his brother turn his charismatic smile—*The Swooner*, in all its glory—on Hadley and Sir Rafe.

"Well, Miss Brodure and I had been trying tae keep our romance a wee bit private." Ethan released a shuddering breath. "But with such ruthless sleuths as Mrs. Clark and Mrs. Buchan around, nothing was bound tae be a secret for long. I'm sure ye both will be the first tae wish us a happy life together."

Bloody hell.

Malcolm closed his eyes, shoulders collapsing, misery and shame threatening to drag him through the floor.

Ethan, sure in his knowledge of Malcolm's honor and trustworthiness, assumed three rather erroneous facts:

One, Malcolm's actions with Viola—embracing her and sweeping her into his arms—were entirely innocuous and had a logical, non-amorous explanation.

Because, two, Malcolm would never stab Ethan in the back nor keep a secret of this magnitude.

And three, Malcolm feared he himself would have to marry Viola, were it known he had been the one at Thistle Muir that first week. And so Ethan was quickly shouldering the blame, accelerating his own relationship with Viola.

Because Ethan trusted Malcolm implicitly. Completely.

Why would he not? Malcolm had never given Ethan reason to *not* trust him.

Until now, that was.

Nausea rose up Malcolm's throat again. Of all the ways he could have imagined this going sideways—if he had given it much thought, which he really should have—this was hands-down the most ghastly.

He simply couldn't allow this farce to play out a second longer.

"Ethan," he began, swallowing hard when his wee brother turned to him. "May I speak with ye for a—"

The rattle of carriage wheels on the drive drowned out the rest of Malcolm's words.

All four men turned toward the bow window just in time to see Kendall's lacquered, gilded carriage roll to a stop, Viola Brodure's pale face framed in the glass.

21

O ver the past hour, the dread in Viola's stomach had grown fangs and wings and claws and was now well on its way to becoming a fully-fledged monster.

Stepping from Kendall's carriage, she looked through the large bow window of Thistle Muir to see Malcolm, Ethan, Lord Hadley, and Sir Rafe inside.

The beast in her stomach twisted and roiled.

Oh, what a tangled web we weave . . .

As Dr. Ruxton had related the whole sorry tale to her father and Kendall, Viola had sat in shock, her tongue cemented to the roof of her mouth.

After all, how could she defend herself?

She should have told Ethan when she had the chance. She and Malcolm should have been more open with their courtship.

And now, what was she to do? Her actions had compromised her virtue.

Malcolm had hesitated the day before when faced with the prospect of truly committing to her, to them, to a life together.

But she knew him—honorable, good, *stoic* Malcolm—would immediately offer for her today.

Ethan, too, most likely.

Viola refused to trap either man, or herself, in a marriage *not* of their own choosing.

It was a wonder she could breathe through her nerves. Or, perhaps, it was as she thought earlier—she was beyond nerves. Despite the emotional tumult, her breath and limbs floated in a sort of surreal numbness.

She followed her father and Kendall into Thistle Muir.

Naturally, Ethan rushed to her side the moment she stepped from the small entryway into the parlor.

"My dear Miss Brodure," he said, clasping both her gloved hands in his and looking at her with his earnest green eyes. "I regret that the news today has accelerated that happy event which we had both perhaps already anticipated."

"Well-spoken, Mr. Penn-Leith," her father looked on, his expression part relief, part parental concern.

After all, Papa knew that she did not wish to marry Ethan.

Without asking for her permission, her eyes drifted past Ethan's shoulder to meet Malcolm's gaze.

Oh.

He looked as weary and heart-sore as herself. Eyes haunted and lined with shadows. Hair askew and begging her fingers to set it to rights.

He had never looked quite so handsome.

Ethan frowned, following the direction of her eyes, pivoting to look at his brother.

"Ethan," Malcolm rasped. Defeated. Apologetic. Weary.

Just two syllables of sound, and yet . . . somehow Malcolm layered them with a world of meaning—confession, contrition, remorse.

Ethan's frown deepened.

Malcolm sighed, scrubbing a hand through his hair. "Ethan, ye ken it was myself who . . ." He paused and then continued on an exhale. ". . . *carried* Miss Brodure into Thistle Muir that first week."

Silence.

Very damning, ringing silence.

Lord Hadley and Sir Rafe both paused—Hadley folding his arms, Sir Rafe tilting his head—as they looked between herself and Malcolm.

Her father pressed fingers to his temple. Knowing she did not wish to marry Ethan was one thing. Realizing that Viola had been carrying on with Ethan's elder brother was something else entirely. Given the furrows lining his forehead, Dr. Brodure had already made the required mental jumps to arrive at the (correct) logical conclusion.

Kendall, of course, simply appeared vastly amused.

Ethan, however, stood very still.

Too still.

The sort of frozen panic of ambushed prey the moment before a killing blow was dealt.

"Pardon?" Ethan whispered.

He spun back to look at Viola.

Viola tried to hold his gaze, truly she did. But her traitorous eyes flitted back to Malcolm.

Ethan looked back and forth between them—Malcolm, Viola, Malcolm, Viola—as if watching lawn tennis. The expression on his face morphed with each swivel: dawning realization, wounded outrage, icy anger.

"I see," Ethan said the words with chilly civility. He turned from Viola and paced across to the hearth, before whirling around. "No, actually," his voice rose, accent slipping into the brogue of his youth. "I dinnae see. I dinnae understand what has been going on behind my back."

Ethan pivoted one final time, brushing past Viola and heading for the door.

"Ethan," Malcolm called, walking after him.

Spinning around, Ethan poked a finger at his older brother. "We're throwing stones. Right now. Me and yourself."

He turned and left the parlor, slapping the lintel on his way out.

But Ethan's voice carried to them from the entryway hall—

"I deserve all your truths, brother."

THE ENTIRE PARTY filed out the front door of Thistle Muir, following Ethan and Malcolm around Kendall's carriage, down the drive, through the small gate, and across the pasture to the small rise and boulder atop which the chained stone rested.

Lord Hadley and Sir Rafe seemed particularly pleased by the turn of events.

Viola found it rather alarming how quickly the Scots pivoted to the idea of throwing a chained stone. As if that were the most logical way to solve an argument.

Viola clung to her father's arm as they followed the men.

Malcolm looked over his shoulder at her, eyes hooded with concern. Viola offered him a wan smile in return.

"Throwing stones?" Dr. Brodure said at her side. "And . . . Mr. Malcolm Penn-Leith?"

Guilt flared bright. Viola attempted to smother it, but it was yet one more thing she had kept from her father.

"I should have told you," she murmured.

"Yes," he returned, expression haggard. "I've spent the past twenty-four hours feeling like I scarcely know you at all, child."

Viola flinched. She had deserved that shot.

Her lungs tightened, but she took in a slow deep breath.

Oddly, experiencing distressing events back-to-back-to-back seemed to act like a vaccine, inoculating her lungs against an anxiety-induced asthma attack.

After all the mounting stresses of the past twenty-four hours, her body simply didn't have the energy to fuss over them anymore.

"You do know me, Papa," she whispered. "But yes, I should have told you that my affections lie with Malcolm."

"*Malcolm* is it?"

"Yes. It is." And as she said the words, she felt the visceral truth of them.

It *was* Malcolm.

Her Malcolm.

She simply needed the man to *want* to claim her, too.

Confessing his guilt to his brother was an important step, but hardly the same as declaring undying love for herself.

And she would rather brave the adversity of a tarnished reputation than force him into an unwelcome marriage.

Once in the field, the four Scotsmen shucked their coats, tossing them atop an obliging stump, leaving themselves in waistcoats and shirtsleeves.

Kendall looked upon the whole with disdain but apparently not enough disgust to climb back into his carriage and leave.

Viola watched unabashedly as Malcolm cuffed his sleeves, rolling up the linen to expose muscled forearms, tendons flexing underneath his skin. Malcolm caught her staring and quirked his eyebrows into a question mark. Viola looked away, a blush surely staining her cheeks.

Ethan stepped up to the chained stone and dragged the rock onto the softer turf of the field. He kicked a small log into position to act as a toe board.

A muscle twitched in his tightly clenched jaw. The light breeze ruffled his disheveled brown hair.

Everyone stared, waiting, anticipating.

Finally, Ethan turned to his older brother.

"I trusted ye!" He thrust a finger at Malcolm. "I have always trusted ye! Ye knew I liked Miss Brodure. Ye knew I was courting her. How could ye betray my trust in such a manner?!"

Glaring at Malcolm, Ethan hefted the chain and spun in a quick circle, the shackled stone spiraling in an arc around him—once, twice—

On the third rotation, Ethan released the chain, sending the rock soaring down the field.

Malcolm's stoic expression gave nothing away. He retrieved the stone—marking Ethan's placement by stabbing a stick upright in the ground—and dragged it back to the starting line.

"I am sorry, Ethan," Malcolm said, leaning toward his brother. "Sorrier than I can say. This is not how Viola or myself wished ye tae find out."

Mimicking Ethan's actions, Malcolm spun and sent the rock flying. It landed several feet beyond Ethan's marker.

Ethan glared, as if personally offended, stomping off to fetch the stone. He marked the placement of Malcolm's throw with a second stick in the ground.

"I deserved tae know the truth," Ethan spat when he returned to the toe board. "Why didnae ye simply tell me?"

Ethan grasped the chain and spun around, hurling the rock across the field. It landed beside Malcolm's previous marker.

Malcolm retrieved the stone.

"Because I am a coward," he said, "and had never looked at a woman other than Aileen. Because the whole crept up on me so unexpectedly. Because I didnae realize my own heart until the moment of no return had already come and gone. And then ye were off tae Aberdeen. Viola and I intended tae tell ye today."

But did they? Viola wondered. Malcolm had said nothing of it.

Malcolm threw the stone, this time inching past Ethan's marker.

Growling, Ethan stomped off and dragged the stone back. "Viola Brodure is a refined, gently-bred lady. She doesnae deserve to be caught up in such ugliness. Did ye give this any thought at all before ye compromised her virtue?!"

Ethan's words were impassioned, but his throw fell short of his brother's stick.

Sighing, Malcolm fetched the stone.

"Miss Brodure is a grown woman," he said when he returned, "fully capable of making her own decisions about where and with whom she spends her life."

This time, his spinning toss landed beyond his first mark.

Viola wrapped her arms around her middle.

A sliver of her heart disliked that both men were speaking about her as if she wasn't present.

A larger sliver appreciated that Malcolm defended her ability to make her own choices, that he saw her as capable of knowing her own mind.

Was it any wonder she loved him so well?

The brothers stared at one another in tense silence for the space of seven heartbeats.

Viola knew, because her own pulse drummed in her ears.

"You're wrong," Ethan finally snapped, abandoning the pretense of throwing the stone in favor of venting his (justifiable) anger and hurt.

"Miss Brodure's natural timidity and shy nature are a credit to her sex, but such characteristics make her hesitant tae express her more delicate feelings—"

Malcolm scowled, folding his arms. "I assure ye, Miss Brodure is *fully* capable of expressing her feelings." His eyes flickered in Viola's direction as he spoke.

The double-layer of his meaning was not lost on Ethan. The younger Penn-Leith glanced toward Viola, as if only just realizing she was witnessing the entire scene.

"My apologies, Miss Brodure." He bowed to her. "I dislike that your tender sensibilities are being exposed tae this . . . this *unpleasantness*." He shot a dagger-laden glance at Malcolm.

Viola saw it clearly.

The moment Malcolm's tether snapped.

For the first time in what was likely years, Malcolm Penn-Leith— stalwart, stoic, unmovable—lost his temper.

"Timid? Hesitant? *Tender sensibilities*?!" Malcolm's voice rose with each word. "None of these words describe Viola Brodure. I'm beginning tae think ye dinnae know her at all!" He pointed his finger toward Viola. "Viola is fire and passion. Do ye know what happened tae her in Manchester last year? Do ye know the stories she longs tae write? Do ye know her hopes and dreams? She isnae a timorous wee beastie, fearful of the loud noise of life. She doesnae need to be protected and coddled, like some fussy, ornamental flower. She fair brims with mettle and courage."

Emotion pricked Viola's eyes.

Malcolm stood tall facing the other men, shoulders back, chest heaving with the force of his words.

He appeared immovable. A sentinel. A harbinger of a future Viola could not race fast enough to embrace.

If only he would have her.

"Viola is heather and gorse," Malcolm shouted, "sturdy and stalwart, able to face the harshest winds of the wild moor! She blooms in adversity and thrives when faced with opposition."

Malcolm looked at her, gaze so full of love and longing and adoration, Viola had to wipe tears from her cheeks.

"Viola is *elemental*." His voice cracked with emotion. "She has a vagabond heart and a banshee soul. She longs to wail a lament for the lost and downtrodden, to scream her truths to the world, demanding change and justice. She has only *begun* tae explore the greatness of her talent. She doesnae need me tae proclaim her truths!"

Malcolm's words echoed through the field.

She doesnae need me to proclaim her truths!

Viola was quite sure, even a decade from now, she would be able to call up an image of the tableau before her.

Ethan Penn-Leith scowling in incredulity.

Lord Hadley rimmed in golden sunlight.

Her father looking on in consternation.

Sir Rafe and Kendall wearing matching expressions of surprise.

And Malcolm—her beloved, fiery Malcolm—laying himself bare . . . a man mature enough to be vulnerable.

To defend her. To *see* her.

To shout her truths for all to hear—

Enough.

Something simply . . . *cracked* within her.

Some sense of self-consciousness that had been fueling her shyness, exacerbating her asthma. It all simply . . . fled.

Perhaps it was her fear of losing Malcolm before she had really claimed him.

Perhaps it was the weight of the moment, the sense that this was the fulcrum upon which the rest of her life would hinge.

Or, perhaps, it was simply seeing herself through Malcolm's eyes.

This man.

She has a vagabond heart and a banshee soul.

Malcolm had laid himself bare for her.

She longs to wail a lament for the lost and downtrodden, to scream her truths to the world, demanding change and justice.

If she wished to tackle the problems of the masses, she needed to start with her own life.

And so, despite her asthmatic lungs, the shaking in her limbs, Viola scanned the ground, found a sturdy stone, and picked it up.

Throwing back her shoulders, she marched toward Malcolm and Ethan.

MALCOLM WATCHED VIOLA approach.

How was it possible she became more magnificent every time he saw her?

He should have added *goddess* to the list of her attributes. Minerva in her wisdom. Or Diana on the hunt.

Spirited, fiery, passionate.

Viola was all those things and more.

And he loved her.

How he loved her.

Adoration scoured his heart as she stopped before him, eyes blazing, chin high.

Ethan took a step back, as if *this* Viola were a new person.

And in a sense, Malcolm thought she rather was.

Viola was finally allowing his wee brother to see the woman usually hidden behind shy stammers.

Malcolm smiled.

"Lass," he said, peering down at the rock in her hand.

"I can't throw that." She pointed at the stone still sitting down the field. "But I should like to join you, all the same." She hefted the much smaller stone in her gloved hand.

Malcolm grinned and swept a palm forward. "Please, lass."

But instead of replying to him, she turned to Ethan.

"I would like to publicly apologize to you, Mr. Penn-Leith," she said, gloved fingers closing around the rock. "I know that the manner of my arrival here in Fettermill gave rise to certain expectations. Though I consider you to be a consummate gentleman and talented fellow writer, I cannot say that my heart holds anything other than friendly regard for you. I am sorry if you had any further wishes for our relationship. Know that I only want the best for you and your future."

Straightening her shoulders and giving her head a toss, Viola wound her arm and threw the rock with a wee grunt.

It was utterly adorable and, also, a complete failure.

The rock flew generously . . . maybe twelve feet.

Viola scowled, as if personally offended. She directed a warning look at Malcolm. He tried to still his twitching lips.

"I still don't understand why I wasn't told sooner," Ethan said, folding his arms and facing both Malcolm and Viola.

Viola took the soft blow of Ethan's reproach with nary a flinch.

Ethan shifted a look between Malcolm and Viola. "How did this happen? When?"

"I scarcely understand myself." Viola glanced up at Malcolm. "But I have come to realize that what we *think* we want and what we *actually* want are often not the same thing. Someone very dear to me recently said, 'Literal death often isn't the way we die most.'"

At that, she leveled a hard look at Ethan. His eyes widened, and he took a fractional step backward.

He, at least, had the courtesy to understand her meaning—that she knew the identity of his poetic 'Muse.'

Malcolm took the opportunity to fetch her rock, holding it in his outstretched hand.

She waved it off and turned to the gathered group.

"I am a writer. And as such, I have a metaphor for you." She looked down at her kidskin gloves. With an exasperated sigh, she pulled them off, one finger at a time.

"Lately I have considered my life to be a hand in these gloves—protected and stifled." She held the gloves aloft, one end pinched between her fingers. "But gloves are not to be endlessly worn. I refuse to encase myself any longer." She tucked them away in a pocket. "I want to feel the cool breeze on my skin. I want to stretch and grow without a shell to confine me."

Viola held out her hand for the stone.

Grinning, Malcolm placed it on her palm. How he adored her like this—resplendent in her determination.

She fixed Kendall with a resolute stare.

"You already know that I do not wish to be your mouthpiece, Your Grace. I must begin writing stories that address the true ills in our society. Immediately. I am tired of waiting. I may not be the Viola Brodure you supposed me to be, but I am the Viola Brodure that *I* wish to be. Punish *me*, if you must. However, I ask you to please leave my father be. My decisions are my own, not his."

Lord Hadley and Sir Rafe both turned steely glares on Kendall.

The duke narrowed his eyes at her.

Viola pivoted to face the field, stone still in her hand.

"Throw it with all your heart, lass," Malcolm encouraged, unable to contain a love-struck grin.

Nodding, she wound her arm and again threw the rock. This time it soared in a graceful arc, landing with a soft *plunk*.

Malcolm whistled and hummed his approval.

Ethan stalked off to fetch both stones, picking up the smaller one in his fist and dragging the chained stone through the grass back to the tow board.

"I should like to throw something." Dr. Brodure stepped to his daughter's side.

Ethan held out the two options—wee stone or chained boulder.

Dr. Brodure only hesitated a moment before taking hold of the small rock.

"I couldn't manage that large one." He gave Malcolm a sheepishly apologetic look.

He turned to face everyone else.

"Though I am very proud of all that my daughter has accomplished, I am also worried for her future."

"Papa." Viola held out a loving hand, her face anguished.

"No, let me finish, daughter. I do not have concerns for the man you will likely marry." Here he spared a glance for Malcolm Penn-Leith.

Malcolm felt his chest lift at the admission. That Dr. Brodure, at least, would approve of his match with Viola.

"I have been doing much soul searching since our conversation yesterday." Dr. Brodure smiled wanly at his daughter. "Though you have been remiss in keeping secrets, it also pains me that you feel you must choose between my future and your own." He pressed a tender kiss to her forehead. Viola bit her trembling lip. "Believe me when I say, I would never put my own ambition above my child's happiness." He turned to Kendall. "Do what you must, Your Grace."

Dr. Brodure faced the field and, winding his arm much the same as Viola, tossed the stone.

The older man's throw was not much better than his daughter's.

He looked back to her with a shrug.

"Truthfully, this has gone on long enough." Kendall strode forward, finally shucking his coat and tossing it atop those of the other gentlemen. He cuffed his shirt sleeves and motioned for Ethan to hand him the chain.

Malcolm exchanged a dubious look with his brother. Ethan seemed just as surprised as himself that Kendall was enlisting for a throw. But then, Malcolm supposed that the duke simply couldn't sit by and watch other men flex their muscles without feeling compelled to assert his dominance.

Dukes were an incredibly competitive lot.

Wrapping his fingers around the chain, Kendall faced them all, but his gaze drilled that of his half-brother.

Sir Rafe lifted an eyebrow in response.

"I recognize that my story is well-known to you all," the duke said, bitterness in his voice. "The gossip rags have ensured that. Before my birth, Sir Rafe—or Lord Rafe, as he was known then—broadcasted my father's personal affairs to the world. This resulted in Lord Rafe and his older brother being declared bastards and disinherited. Shortly after, the king stripped my father of his governmental positions. That is the reality into which I was born. The world that formed me. One where the Dukes of Kendall were an impotent, powerless laughingstock." He looked down at the chain-wrapped stone. Without his coat, the duke appeared a gangling youth to Malcolm's eyes—an untried colt of a man. "So here is my truth. I will regain everything that Sir Rafe destroyed. I will become prime minister and avenge my father's legacy. I will not allow a few bleeding hearts—" Here he spared a scathing look for Dr. Brodure. "—to dissuade me."

With that, he turned and spun quickly on his feet, sending the chained stone sailing with an audible grunt.

Though Malcolm held no love for the duke, the man did have a credible throwing arm. The stone fell just a few feet short of Malcolm and Ethan's marks.

Malcolm retrieved the rock, marking the duke's toss with another stick in the ground.

Sir Rafe was waiting in shirtsleeves when he returned.

Malcolm handed him the chain.

Stretching his neck from side to side, Sir Rafe faced Kendall. Unlike his younger brother, Sir Rafe's arms and shoulders rippled with thick muscle—the physique of an older, physically-active man.

"I hadn't intended tae wade into this today," he said, "but as the person who was central tae the events that transpired a quarter-century past, I feel the need to say some hard truths of my own."

Kendall rolled his eyes in contempt and folded his arms.

"One," Sir Rafe continued, looking straight at Kendall, "our father's selfish, arrogant actions are what brought about his downfall. Do not attack the messenger—in this case, myself—for allowing truths tae come to light."

"You should have been loyal," Kendall retorted, "to our father, to our family."

"Any family loyalty I may have felt toward *that* man was beaten out of me at an early age." Sir Rafe's eyes hardened into agate, looking every bit as imperious and unmoving as Malcolm imagined his sire had. "Our father was a right bastard, as ye must certainly know, having been raised by him. The old man enjoyed crushing the will of every soul in his sphere as callously as one might snuff out a gnat. But perhaps ye, too, find perverse joy in such behavior."

Kendall flinched. The tiniest of twitches.

If Malcolm hadn't been staring right at the duke, he would have missed it.

Sir Rafe's volley had scored a direct hit.

"So, Your Grace," Sir Rafe continued, "will ye truly dismiss an excellent vicar who, by all accounts, has served your family and village well? Toss him aside simply because his daughter's writing isn't servile enough tae your cause? And if so, how despicable. If ye want tae restore honor to our family line—to truly best our father—work tae become a better human being." Sir Rafe looked his younger brother right in the eye. "Tristan Alexander Matteo Gilbert, Duke of Kendall, Earl of

Hawthorne, Baron Gilbert . . . if nothing else, remember these words—power isn't the only measure of success."

And with that, Sir Rafe spun in a dizzying circle, sending the chained stone soaring down the field, landing on par with Malcolm's farthest marker.

A cheer rose from the crowd, Lord Hadley whistling loudly. Sir Rafe raised a fist in triumph.

Kendall did not join in, Malcolm noted. Instead, the duke ignored his brother and focused on meticulously refastening his shirt sleeves. As if eager to bury his brother's words under a mountain of indifference.

Ethan strode after the stone. He marked Sir Rafe's throw before dragging the rock back up the field.

"You've been practicing, Rafe." Lord Hadley clapped his friend on the back.

Sir Rafe shrugged, flexing an arm. "I credit my coos. It takes strength tae wrangle them."

"*Och*, well, I guess it's my turn," Hadley said, voice affable as he held out a hand to Ethan, requesting the chained stone. "Dr. Brodure, if Kendall is foolish enough tae toss ye out because ye insist on supporting your daughter, well then, come talk tae myself. Kendall isn't the only aristocrat with power in Her Majesty's government. As I see it, the Lords Spiritual need more men who are willing tae stand up for their beliefs—to be a voice for those whose struggles should be heard. Such behavior smacks of bishop material tae me." He shrugged. "As for the rest, I say we leave Malcolm, Miss Brodure, and Ethan tae settle themselves. My Jane is waiting for me at home, and Rafe and I have thirty years of friendship tae reminisce upon over a bottle of fine Glenturret whisky. Ethan, when you're done here, feel free tae join us. Rafe and myself will assist ye in getting roaring *fou*, if ye would like." Hadley tightened his grip on the chain. "Are those enough truths for the lot of ye?"

Malcolm nodded along with the rest of the group.

And with that, Hadley seized the chain, spun around three times—his form a whirling Dervish— and sent the stone flying, landing a solid meter past everyone else.

He turned back to them, hands on his hips, and an unmistakably smug smile on his face.

"And that, my friends, is how we do it here in Scotland. Now, I say we retire and permit these three—" He gestured toward Malcolm, Viola, and Ethan. "—tae sort themselves out."

22

Not even five minutes later, Malcolm, Ethan, and Viola found themselves alone in the field. Hadley *et al.* had disappeared around the side of Thistle Muir.

Malcolm took in a breath, intent on speaking. But before he uttered a sound, Viola walked right into his arms, burying her face in his chest and wrapping her arms tightly around his waist. His arms instantly reciprocated, desperate to close all distance between them—physically and emotionally.

For everything the day had brought, Malcolm could not regret this—the freedom to hold Viola Brodure openly. To present themselves to the world as a united front.

Ethan's gaze drifted to Viola for a long moment, surely seeing how her body melted into Malcolm's, how her head sank into his sternum.

For his part, Malcolm watched his brother with careful eyes.

Ethan's anger appeared to have burned off—the flush in his cheeks gone, hands hanging loosely at his sides—but a rattled pain had taken its place. A wary tightness around his mouth, a tense hunch to his shoulders.

The pain was infinitely harder to witness than the anger, Malcolm decided.

Ethan looked away from Viola, as if the sight had overflowed some inner basin of misery and he could bear it no more.

Instead, he regarded the chained stone, nudging it with his foot.

"I really wish ye would have told me." Ethan's words were quiet and all the more devastating for it. "Ye cannot tell me you didn't have the opportunity. We both know that tae be a lie."

"Aye, I should have told ye." Malcolm agreed, hand moving to cradle the back of Viola's head.

A long silence stretched.

Ethan continued to study them with solemn eyes. Malcolm knew that expression on his brother's face—the one he wore when wrestling with some inner turmoil.

"Perhaps all of this could have been avoided had I been more aware," Ethan finally said.

"Pardon? More aware?" Viola turned sideways in Malcolm's arms, keeping one hand around his waist.

"Aye. I should have asked ye more questions, Miss Brodure," Ethan said. "I think I was rather caught up in the idea of yourself—the beauty of your writing, and, well, the beauty of your person, as well—and so, I only thought tae talk of myself. To prove my own worth, as it were. I never took the time to get tae know ye as ye are. Malcolm tried tae point that out tae me yesterday, but I think it's only now sinking in. I should have been more perceptive."

"Not that it excuses our deceptive behavior," Malcolm added.

"No. It does not. But I think ye were right. I have been perhaps a wee bit in love with the idea of being in love. It is, after all, the grand emotion that poets are best known for. I think my eagerness clouded my judgment. But seeing you two now, together . . ." He paused before asking, "Do ye love each other?"

Viola slid her hand from Malcolm's waist, down his arm to nest in his palm, a flush coloring her cheeks.

"Ask us again this evening," she said, her eyes remaining locked on Malcolm.

He understood immediately. Neither of them wanted to declare their love for the first time in front of Ethan. At least, that was what he *hoped* she meant.

"Are ye both happy then?" Ethan asked.

"Aye." Malcolm suspected the stupid-in-love smile currently blossoming on his own face matched the one on Viola's. "I didnae think it possible tae find such a feeling again. God has doubly blessed me."

Ethan studied them, eyes moving from Viola's bonnetless head to her wee hand nested in Malcolm's grasp.

"Malcolm, if this were anyone else . . . I would be angry for months, maybe years. But . . ." Ethan ran a weary hand through his hair, letting loose a heavy sigh. "I have watched ye grieve, feeling helpless to ease your pain. And though I am still furious and hurt right now—" Ethan pointed a finger at Malcolm. "—I am equally sure that I will forgive ye eventually." He looked at Viola. "Make her happy, brother."

Ethan clapped Malcolm on the shoulder. And ever the consummate gentlemen, he sketched a bow to Viola.

"I recommend avoiding me for the next several days," he said, "as I intend to take Hadley up on his offer to get blistering drunk. By the time I'm done wallowing, it would be lovely if the populace of Fettermill understood what happened between Miss Brodure and myself. I don't feel equal to explaining the situation to every village gossip who crosses my path. Just the thought of the pitying sighs, the awkward pats on my arm . . ." He trailed off, shoulders slumping even further in defeat.

"I'll make sure everyone knows tae avoid the topic of Miss Brodure with yourself," Malcolm reassured him, pulling Viola's hand closer.

Ethan nodded, and turning around, walked back across the field to Thistle Muir.

Malcolm watched him until he disappeared inside the front door.

"Did he mean all that?" Viola asked softly.

"Aye," Malcolm nodded, "though once he returns home tonight, drunk and raging, I am sure he and I will have another go. But as long as he's talking tae me, I ken we will weather this."

"I'm glad," Viola whispered, tilting her head back and fixing him with her blue eyes. "You and Ethan need one another."

"True, lass. That we do."

Tucking her hand through his arm, Malcolm led Viola out of the field and down the lane toward their swing. Viola leaned into his strength, though he caught her darting glances up at his profile.

Was she still upset over his hesitation yesterday? That he had doubted he possessed the strength to love her?

She didn't appear too distressed. Her breathing was even, and she had openly embraced him in front of Ethan.

Malcolm had experienced enough of relationships and arguments to see those things as signs of an impending reconciliation.

"Did ye mean what ye said, lass?" he asked.

"Gracious, what part?" she laughed. "I fear I said a fair lot."

"The bit about writing what ye would like from this point on, regardless of Kendall."

She sighed, hand resting more heavily on his arm. "Yes, yes I did. Am I insane?"

"Nae, lass. I admire your bravery tae strike out onto unknown paths. History never remembers the weak."

They rounded the final bend in the lane, coming to a stop before their swing.

"Write what is calling to ye, Viola." He looked down at her, noting that emotion had heightened the ring of gold circling her pupil. "Those that love you will stand at your side."

"And will you be one of those that love me?" she asked.

"Always, lass."

She smiled, her gaze turning radiant. "I ken to what ye be saying, Mr. Penn-Leith."

"That was a terrible Scottish accent, lass. Ye likely shouldnae attempt that again."

She laughed, a glorious bubble of sound. Malcolm's heart felt near to bursting.

"Yes, it was," she merrily agreed. "I fear I will have to find myself a clever Scottish lad to help me learn it properly."

"Ye will, will ye?"

"Aye."

"And who do ye have in mind?"

"There's a man, you see," she began, tracing a finger down his arm.

"Aye?"

"Aye. He's devastatingly handsome and has the most adorable dog."

"Is that so?"

"He's kind and gentle—"

"The dog?"

"The dog, too. The man is also most competent."

"Competent?!"

"Never underestimate the power of manly competence," she laughed. "It's a much over-looked quality."

She looked up at him, eyes gleaming with what he suspected was adoration.

Happiness flooded him in a single, giddy wave, champagne frothing in his veins.

Viola lifted her wee hand to cup his cheek.

"But most importantly," she continued, "I know, without a doubt, that this man perceives me as I am. Not as he would have me be, or as I feel I *should* be. But he accepts me as I am, at this very moment, with all my faults and flaws and weaknesses—"

"There is nothing weak about ye, lass."

Her eyes went suspiciously bright. "*See?!* That is precisely what I am referring to. You said I have a banshee soul! You called me elemental! Who else could be as wonderful as you? I love who I am when I'm with you. I love the woman you see in me."

"Ye paint me a saint, lass. I assure ye, I'm not quite that."

"I don't want a saint, Malcolm Penn-Leith. I simply want you."

Malcolm closed his eyes, joy rushing and cresting over his soul, drowning him in happiness.

"And I want ye, *mo chridhe*."

"You do?"

"Aye, with everything that I am."

A cloud passed over her expression. "Are you quite sure? Because yesterday, in this precise place, you seemed less . . . enthusiastic."

Malcolm straightened his shoulders. "As ye well know, losing Aileen nearly destroyed me. I never expected tae meet another woman I could adore. A woman who would become as essential tae my existence as air. So when ye came into my life—"

His voice broke at that. He swallowed and waited for the surge of love and gratitude to pass.

"When I realized how deep ye had burrowed in," he tapped his chest, "I panicked a wee bit. My life had formed around my grief, ye see. And I was comfortable in that place. The thought of truly living again—of placing my heart once more within another's frail body—when I know only too well how risky that prospect is. . . . Ye are so tiny, Viola, and I cannae imagine the danger of ye attempting tae bear a child, of being a mother—" He did break at that, dashing the back of his hand angrily across his cheeks.

Partially for the grief of all he had lost.

Partially for the realization that he would face it all again in order to have Viola as his wife.

"Ah, Malcolm. Hush, my love." Her small hand pressed to his face once more, eyes bright. "I accept the risks that come with loving you. Yes, a child would bring more love into our lives—as he or she would be our love manifest in another's tiny body. I would absolutely brave that unknown path with you . . . for you. But there is time yet. For now, let us take life one day, one risk, at a time."

Malcolm wiped his eyes again, hating how easily his tears flowed. "Aye, 'tis good advice, *mo chridhe.*"

"*Mo chridhe?*"

"My heart," he whispered. "My love."

"Oh!"

"I'm going to kiss ye boneless now," he said.

"Really?"

"Aye. I thought it fair tae warn ye."

She answered by smiling and pulling on his neck.

Malcolm was no slow-top.

His head bent down. Viola raised up. Their lips met in the middle.

Had it only been a day since he kissed her? It felt like a lifetime. How he adored the soft give of her lips against his, the sheer gift of it all.

But *this* kiss . . .

It felt like homecoming. Like sunlight. As if he had just emerged from the earth, shining and new, to find a home already prepared for him.

At her side.

In her arms.

In her heart.

VIOLA WANTED TO weep.

Why the blissful happiness racing through her could only come out as crying, she could not understand. It simply seemed the only place so much *feeling* had left to go.

Malcolm was kissing her.

She was kissing Malcolm.

Her Malcolm.

Kissing.

Openly. Together.

At last!

When he would have pulled away, she clutched his head, refusing to allow him to retreat.

"I love you," she whispered against his lips. "I love everything—"

He stole her words with his mouth, as if desperate to store them within his own chest.

She reciprocated in kind.

Silence reigned for several minutes, as Viola reacquainted herself with the heady pleasure of kissing Malcolm Penn-Leith.

Finally, she kissed him one last lingering time before leaning back against his arms around her waist.

"Ah, lass," he breathed against her mouth, "how I love ye. I dinnae want to scare ye with the force of my affections—"

"Impossible!" Viola shook her head.

"Impossible?"

"Aye. I shall never fear your love, Malcolm Penn-Leith. 'Tis mine that might send you running—"

"Never!" he scoffed.

"Then what are we to do?"

"Marry me?" he replied. "Could ye do that, lass? I ken I've shamelessly compromised ye but—"

"Yes," she whispered, licking a tear from her lip. "I would love nothing more in this world than to marry you, Malcolm Penn-Leith."

His eyes went bright. He took a slow breath, swallowing loudly. "My life is here. I cannae imagine leaving Scotland, but I also feel I cannae ask ye to abandon your life in England—"

Oh, the foolish, dear man!

"Ask me," she ordered, laughing.

He paused, regarding her with a face so serious that she had to peck his lips.

Which led to more kissing.

"Ask me," she repeated when they finally pulled apart.

"Viola Brodure," he began, "will ye leave your friends, your literary colleagues, your amusements, and every other aspect of your life in Westacre, England to marry me and move to Fettermill, Scotland, spending your life as the wife of a gentleman farmer who loves ye more than life itself?"

"Yes!" she all but shouted, startling two pigeons from a nearby tree. "I would love nothing more than precisely that."

"Truly?"

"Aye." She kissed him. "I love you, and because I love you, I adore the land that formed you. I long to be a part of it myself, to weave Scotland into my own history—the crisp fresh air, the soaring vistas, the wildness creeping in at the corners—"

"Careful, *mo chridhe*. Scotland will make a poet of ye."

She laughed in earnest, her heart on wings.

"No," she replied. "I believe one poet in the family to be sufficient. In all honesty, I think I prefer to live my life firmly in this lovely reality. The poet can remain adjacent."

"Poet-adjacent it is then." He grinned, dipping for one more kiss. "But only just."

What a whirlwind this past summer has been for literary enthusiasts! First, as dedicated readers most certainly know, Miss Viola Brodure has begun a serial novel (after the style of Mr. Charles Dickens) entitled *A Ring of Gold*. This new novel follows the misfortunes of a young woman bound to debtor's prison for losing her mistress's gold ring. Some say the topic is a stark deviation from the sentimental tone of Miss Brodure's previous works. But if the first two installments of *A Ring of Gold* are any indication, the authoress has delivered a *tour-de-force*. We predict the novel will be Miss Brodure's most popular to date.

Naturally, the change in Miss Brodure's style could be the result of her recent nuptials. The lady did indeed marry a Mr. Penn-Leith this summer. But to our puzzlement, the groom in question was Mr. *Malcolm* Penn-Leith, elder brother to the celebrated Highland Poet. How this came about, we are at a loss to explain. Regardless, Mr. Ethan Penn-Leith gave his blessing to the union and stood as best man to his brother. Both groom and brother were reported to be dashing in their full Highland regalia. Miss Brodure was radiant in a white silk gown trimmed with Venetian lace. The bride's father, Dr. Brodure, officiated the ceremony. We at *The Tattler* wish the newlywed couple every happiness.

We cannot determine if Mr. Ethan Penn-Leith is heartbroken over Miss Brodure's choice of husband, though he has tellingly left Scotland. Rumor has it he intends to take an extended holiday abroad, in Italy perhaps? His latest poem, published in this month's *Atheneaum*, will surely earn Mr. Penn-Leith a place beside the literary greats of history. In the poem—entitled *Elemental Is My Love*—Mr. Penn-Leith compares his beloved to the moors of Scotland, crying, "Her of the wandering vagabond heart and lamenting banshee soul." As one critic enthused to *The Tattler*, "Mr. Penn-Leith's comparison of his love to the battered heather and gorse of the moors positively thrums with the savage vitality of the Highlands." We also have it on good authority from Mr. Penn-Leith's publisher that his long-awaited second book of poetry should be published sometime in the spring.

If this is a taste of things to come from both our Highland Poet and Mrs. Penn-Leith *née* Brodure, we count ourselves lucky to be living in this age. Or, as Mr. Ethan Penn-Leith has said, "*Let us embrace the heather'd scent / A wanderer no more adjacent.*"

EPILOGUE

FIVE YEARS LATER

Viola tossed a copy of *The Rabble Rouser* aside in favor of looking across the parlor at her husband bathed in the soft glow of firelight. Her husband!

Mmmm, even after nearly five years of marriage, she still experienced a thrill just thinking that word. Or rather, in thinking upon Malcolm Penn-Leith as the man she married.

As usual, he sat in his favorite chair before the fire, a candelabra blazing on a table beside him, his nose buried in Mr. Dickens's popular novel, *A Christmas Carol*, despite the current date being closer to Halloween than Christmas. Malcolm was dressed casually in shirtsleeves and trousers, a loose banyan thrown over the whole to ward off the evening autumn chill.

"Enjoying your view, wife?" he asked, tone casual, but a twitch of his lips betrayed his bright mood.

"Very much, as a matter of fact." She raked him brazenly from head to toe, eyes lingering on the muscles bunched in his upper arms, the wide breadth of his shoulders. Heat unfurled in her belly.

Gracious but her husband was a finely formed man.

Malcolm raised his head, his gaze snagging on the blush currently spreading across her cheeks. His eyebrows hitched upward, as they had been married long enough for him to understand what that blush meant.

Of course, the thought simply intensified the burn of her skin.

"Careful, wife." His smile broke free. "As ye well know, I cannae resist your fair blushes. If ye keep looking at myself like that, ye might find yourself with child once more. And as we just spent the last hour wrangling our two wee hellions into bed, I can understand that ye may not be eager tae add another so soon."

Viola laughed, pressing a hand to her fiery cheeks. "I will always welcome your child, Malcolm Penn-Leith, and well you know it."

His grin turned wicked, eyes gleaming in the firelight.

Despite Malcolm's fears early in their marriage, Viola had proved a champion at pregnancy and childbirth. The birth of their two children—Kirsty and Robert—had been surprisingly quick and uneventful. Malcolm had refused to leave her side with each one, his hand trembling in hers as she pushed a new life into the world.

But the joy of watching Malcolm Penn-Leith hold his tiny daughter for the first time . . . the way he had wrapped her wee fingers around his chafed knuckle and let joyful tears dampen his beard . . .

Well, Viola nearly wept herself every time she recalled it.

As for her father, Dr. Brodure had stood by his words and defended Viola's choices. He had eventually resigned his living in Westacre and had lived for a time with Viola and Malcolm in Thistle Muir while she was pregnant with Kirsty.

However, Lord Hadley had also been true to his vow. Hadley and his good friend, the Marquess of Lockheade, had put forth Dr. Brodure's name to the Queen—along with a glowing recommendation—for appointment to bishop. Her Majesty had only been too happy to see it done. Her father had been Bishop of Ethington for nearly four years now and had done much good in his new-found role.

For her part, Viola had continued to write, even with the havoc and exhaustion and joy that came with having two small children. Kirsty was dark-haired and fearless, a whirling dervish of chaos. Robbie was blond, blue-eyed, and regarded the world with wondering caution. That is until Kirsty lured him into one of her scrapes; then, mayhem ensued.

"So . . ." Viola looked at the journal she had just set down, tracing its cover with a finger. "It *is* the servants' day off tomorrow, and I have arranged for Isla to take the children on a long walk so I can, theoretically, write. And, well, you know how empty and lonely this house is without everyone here."

In her peripheral vision, Malcolm's body snapped to attention.

"Go on," he nudged with his chin.

Meeting his gaze, Viola stood up and slowly crossed to him. Her husband grinned wider. He set down his book. Viola reached for him just as he wrapped his hands around her waist, toppling her onto his lap. Curling into his chest, Viola ran her fingers through his beard and guided his mouth down to hers.

"Ye were saying, wife?" Malcolm murmured, lips skimming down her neck.

"Just hoping you might be interested in helping me ensure the house isn't *too* quiet tomorrow." She kissed him on a giggle.

Malcolm growled and quickly stood up, easily hefting her in his arms. Viola squealed and clung to his shoulders.

"Tomorrow?" He kissed her soundly as he walked for the door. "I say we begin right now."

AUTHOR'S NOTE

I f you've reached this point, thank you for reading. I always appreciate a wee author's note at the end of a book, so here are a few thoughts about *Adjacent But Only Just*.

This book began its life as a novella entitled *A Ring of Gold*. Originally, the novella was to be a love memo to Robert Browning and Elizabeth Barrett Browning and the story of their courtship. If you don't know the details of their relationship, google it, as it's a fascinating story. Basically, the Brownings met in much the same way Ethan and Viola meet in *Adjacent But Only Just*. Browning praised Barrett Browning's poetry and they started corresponding with one another. Granted, that's where the similarities between real life and my novel end, but I loved how the Browning's love story began. That said, I did incorporate plenty of references to the philosophy and poetry of the Brownings in *Adjacent But Only Just*.

When first brainstorming my book, I didn't necessarily intend for Ethan to have a brother. Viola and Ethan would meet, it would be awkward, but they work through it and fall in love. As I outlined, however, I realized that the story would be more interesting if the unexpected happened. And so, the character of Malcolm was born (though he was originally named Lucas, until I realized that Lucas and Ethan were too visually similar to work as names of brothers, but I digress). And from the original novella of Malcolm and Viola, the whole of the Penn-Leiths of Thistle Muir series sprang.

Viola suffers from asthma. I know that asthma can have different triggers for different people, some physical and some psychological. It can also have different countermeasures, depending on the person. I obviously decided that Viola's asthma would have an emotional component, as well as a physical one.

I know I've mentioned this before, but for those reading one of my Scottish books for the first time, allow me to also comment on the Scottish language. I've used modern spellings of Scottish pronunciations and, even then, restricted myself to a few key words to give a Scottish flavor to the text. So at times, the accent as written is not perfectly consistent; this was done to help readability.

I have created an extensive pinboard on Pinterest with images of things I talk about in the book. So if you want a visual of anything—including Highland coos, my fictional town of Fettermill, etc.—pop over there and explore. Just search for NicholeVan.

As with all books, this one couldn't have been written without the help and support from those around me. I know I am going to leave someone out with all these thanks. So to that person, know that I totally love you and am so deeply grateful for your help!

To my beta readers—you know who you are—thank you for your editing suggestions, helpful ideas, and support. An extra thank you to Annette Evans and Rebecca Spencer their suggestions and encouragement.

Also, as usual, this book could not have happened without the tireless emotional and literary support from Shannon Castleton. Bless you, my friend!

Erin Rodabough, thank you for your editing insight and for being my ultimate travel buddy.

Finally, thank you to Andrew, Austenne, Kian, and Dave for constantly encouraging me to keep writing forward.

And to all my readers, thank you for continuing to read and recommend my work!

READING GROUP QUESTIONS

Yes, there are reading group questions. I suggest discussing them over lots of excellent chocolate (solid, liquid, frozen, cake . . . I'm not picky about the precise state of matter of said chocolate; chocolate in any form is good chocolate).

1. The title of the book, *Adjacent But Only Just*, comes from the poem that Ethan writes. How do you see the title playing out in the book? What different things are Malcolm and Viola "adjacent" to?

2. Viola suffers from a mild case of social anxiety. How did you relate to her struggles to navigate new situations?

3. Malcolm has understandably struggled to move on after his wife's death. He comments on the terrible irony that Aileen's death changed him so fundamentally that the Malcolm his wife loved is gone. Similarly, he is no longer the man who loved her. What are your thoughts on this? Would profound grief change you to such a degree that you are no longer romantically compatible with the person you grieve?

4. How did you feel about the Duke of Kendall in the story? Is he a true villain? Or more a product of his upbringing?

5. Was Viola disloyal to her father in writing the short story, *A Hard Truth*? Should she have waited to write it, as they had agreed? Or did the greater good justify her betrayal?

6. Malcolm clearly experiences some PTSD over the manner of Aileen's death. Was his hesitation to commit to Viola believable? Why or why not?

7. Ethan writes a poem for Malcolm, describing his grief as a weight. Is this comparison accurate? How does grief feel to you? Here is the poem in its entirety:

> I bear with me always a weight.
> It rests, a heavy knot of stone
> Upon my neck, sinking down straight
> Into the memory of you now gone.
>
> Your loss throbs, a vital limb
> Severed too soon. An unending
> Phantom agony, heavy and grim.
> The load a bleak unrelenting.

Each morn, I wake and heft once more
Sisyphus pushing stone uphill.
Plodding feet lead, heart black, soul sore
With the void of you bare and still.

8. Clearly, this book contains a lot of information about Scotland
   and Scottish culture. Did you learn something new or unexpected?
   If so, what was it?

9. Consider how this book would be as a feature film. Who plays
   Malcolm? Who plays Viola? Ethan? etc. In the movie version,
   what aspects of the book should be thrown out, condensed, or
   altered?

OTHER BOOKS BY NICHOLE VAN

THE PENN-LEITHS OF THISTLE MUIR

Love Practically
Adjacent But Only Just
One Kiss Alone (Forthcoming)
A Heart Sufficient (Forthcoming)

THE BROTHERHOOD OF THE BLACK TARTAN

Suffering the Scot
Romancing the Rake
Loving a Lady
Making the Marquess
Remembering Jamie

OTHER REGENCY ROMANCES

Seeing Miss Heartstone
Vingt-et-Un | Twenty-one (a novella included in *Falling for a Duke.*)
A Ring of Gold (a novella included in *A Note of Change.*)

BROTHERS *MALEDETTI*

Lovers and Madmen
Gladly Beyond
Love's Shadow
Lightning Struck
A Madness Most Discreet

THE HOUSE OF OAK

Intertwine
Divine
Clandestine
Refine
Outshine

If you haven't yet read *Suffering the Scot*,
please read on for a preview of this
Whitney Award Finalist for Best Historical Romance 2019.

SUFFERING
THE SCOT

E veryone knew it was an unmitigated disaster.

Some even deployed the adjectives "biblical" and "calamitous."

For her part, Lady Jane Everard simply hoped to survive the afternoon without anyone drawing blood.

She took a sip of her tea, politely listening to the women buzzing around the drawing room. Her younger half-brother, the Honorable Mr. Peter Langston, sat beside her. The black mourning band around his upper arm spoke tellingly of their situation.

After six months of full-mourning for her stepfather, the late Earl of Hadley, Jane's family had resumed afternoon at-home hours. Their neighbors had called upon them, ostensibly to lend support during their current hardship. Such concern only thinly veiled their delight in watching the Langstons of Hadley Park descend the social ladder.

Jane's mother, the widowed Lady Hadley, sat across the room, holding court over the tea tray. Lady Hadley had overcome the death of two aristocratic husbands—a duke and an earl. A few venom-tongued busybodies would not defeat her.

Though Lady Hadley declared herself a devout Anglican, Jane believed her mother's true religion was a fervent belief in her exalted station in life. The lady defended her social position with the ruthless tenacity of a medieval Crusader, carefully calibrated silences and chilly reserve being her weapons of choice.

"Gracious, what a disaster," Lady Whitcomb declared, leaning to take a teacup from Lady Hadley. "You are scarcely out of full-mourning, and the new Lord Hadley is at your door."

"Is it true what they say? That Lord Hadley is barely civilized?" Mrs. Smith asked, darting a glance up from her own cup.

"But, of course." Lady Whitcomb tilted her head, her graying curls swaying with the motion. "He is an impoverished, coarse *Scot*, after all."

Jane considered Lady Whitcomb's opinion to be slightly redundant, as all Polite Society knew the word *Scot* already encompassed *impoverished* and *coarse*.

"You have the right of it." Mrs. Burton tsked, accepting a teacup with a mournful shake of her head. "Rumor says Lord Hadley was raised in a crofter's hut deep in the wilds of Scotland."

The way Mrs. Burton pronounced *Scotland* imbued the word with a thousand years of history—the medieval battles between Robert the Bruce and King Edward, the horror of England suffering a succession of wastrel Scottish kings after Elizabeth's glorious reign, the more recent Battle of Culloden and the current Highland Clearances, all threaded through with Scotland's uncivilized behavior and loose understanding of decorum.

Lady Hadley did not react, proving again her ruthless control over her emotions. Jane followed suit, keeping her own expression polite, resting her cup and saucer on the table beside her before folding her hands in her lap with exacting precision.

Lady Hadley and her daughter were well-known for their exquisite manners. It was what made the current situation all the more horrific and, to be honest, horrifically delightful to those observing from the outside.

Peter, predictably, snorted.

Jane forgave him. What else could she do? Growing up, she and Peter had only had each other and that fact had not changed over the years. No matter what he did, she loved Peter more than anyone else in the world.

That said . . . snorting was decidedly ill-mannered.

Jane surreptitiously nudged Peter with her foot, a silent reproof.

"Indeed," Mrs. Burton replied. "Given the Earldom of Hadley's history with Scotland, the situation is decidedly . . ."

"Ironic?" Lady Whitcomb supplied, mouth pursing into a simpering moue before sipping her tea. "That the hunter has become the hunted?"

Lady Hadley replied with a taut smile.

The facts *were* decidedly ironic, Jane supposed.

The first Earl of Hadley had been raised to the peerage for, *Invaluable services to the Crown in assisting His Majesty's troops to defeat the unruly Scottish rebellion at Culloden.* In short, the first Earl had been a celebrated English war hero noted for his savagery in dealing with wild Scottish rebels.

However, his grandson, Henry—born to be the third Earl of Hadley—did not view Scots in quite the same fashion. So much so that, while on a hunting trip in the Highlands, Henry had abruptly married an impoverished local lass. (*Lass* was the kindest way Jane could describe the woman. Others used more colorful words, the politest of which were *trollop* and *light-skirt*.)

Horrified at finding himself with a low-born, Scottish daughter-in-law, the old earl had cut Henry off without a farthing and never spoke to his son again. If it had been within his power, the old earl would have even barred Henry from eventually succeeding to the title. Fortunately, Fate listened, and Henry had died before his father.

So it was now Henry's son, Andrew Langston—the Scottish lass's offspring and therefore uneducated, crude, and completely unfit—who had become the third Earl of Hadley. The very sort of Scot the first Earl of Hadley had valiantly tried to exterminate.

Irony, indeed.

"They say Lord Hadley is a veritable savage." Lady Whitcomb practically quivered in delicious excitement, her pinched face narrowing further. "He certainly doesn't mix in polite company. There has never been a whisper of him at any *ton* event." She arched her eyebrows before biting into a buttery biscuit. "My cousin, Lord Wanleigh, stated as much in his most recent letter."

Lady Whitcomb's cousin was the aging Marquess of Wanleigh—a fact no one was allowed to forget. Jane had never met the man, but she often wondered if he was as pompous in person as he sounded on paper.

"And why *should* the new Lord Hadley have mingled with Polite Society? Savages don't attend balls." Mrs. Burton pronounced her words with zealous conviction. Jane was quite sure fealty had been sworn with less fervor.

Peter angled himself fractionally closer to Jane, snorting again. "Of course savages attend balls," he muttered under his breath.

Jane concentrated on not smiling.

Do not react.

She pressed her fingernail into her palm, pressing hard enough to feel a bite of pain but never breaking the skin.

Peter leaned into her ear, clearly undeterred. "One must be nearly feral to survive the London Season. Cannibalism is the *ton*'s *modus operandi*. We thrive on devouring our own—"

Jane barely swallowed back the laughter climbing her throat. She shot Peter a quelling side-glance.

"Hush." She managed to say the word without moving her lips, for all the good it did.

Peter was determined to win this round.

It was a game they played. Peter said outrageous things, and Jane bravely refrained from reacting beyond a discreet pinch or *sotto voce* reprimand. Abruptly smiling, frowning, smirking, eye rolling, or heaven forbid, *giggling* would earn Jane a dressing down from their mother after guests departed.

After all, she had an image to maintain.

Ladies never indulge in broad emotions, Jane, Lady Hadley would say. *Emotion, if it must be shown, should be conveyed through a raised eyebrow or slight tonal inflection. Nothing more.*

Peter, of course, had no such constraints. He could make faces all he wished, and their mother would never say a word. Facts he well knew.

Thankfully, Peter obeyed Jane's quiet reprimand and sat back, crossing his arms, his black armband straining from the movement. But the smile lurking on his lips promised more harassing torment.

Her brother knew her polite, elegant manners were studiously learned; a facade she carefully donned. Unladylike behavior and rowdy thoughts lurked just beneath her polished veneer, defaults she constantly strove to quash.

In true younger brother fashion, he delighted in reminding her of these facts. Over and over again. Endlessly.

Jane forced herself to focus by pressing another fingernail into her palm, leaving a clear half-moon shape. It was a habit born years ago. She had found that the small pain channeled her emotions, keeping them off her expression. After a particularly trying afternoon, her palm would look like fish scales, the markings taking an hour or more to fade.

"However will you manage, Lady Hadley?" Mrs. Burton tsked, reaching for a biscuit. "A coarse, bawdy Highlander as the Earl of Hadley—"

"Oh, a Highlander." Mrs. Smith's gaze went wide and a little dreamy-eyed. "Like one of the heroes of a Walter Scott novel?"

"No, Martha. The man is not to be fictionalized," Lady Whitcomb admonished, much as one might reprimand an overly-eager poodle for jumping up on the furniture. "I shan't permit you to romanticize the severity of this situation."

"Hear, hear. The new Lord Hadley certainly does not belong to the Church of England." Mrs. Burton nibbled her biscuit daintily, obviously enjoying the conversation immensely. "More likely he is a pagan heathen."

Peter huffed, quiet and low.

"Or, worse," he whispered, "a Presbyterian."

He nudged his foot against Jane's.

I know you want to laugh, his movements said.

Jane pinched her lips, keeping her head determinedly faced toward their mother. *You shall not defeat me.*

She supposed most sisters would feel aggravation over such teasing. But Peter's actions showed louder than anything that he understood, that he *knew* her.

And Jane adored being known. Being known meant she was loved, accepted just as she was.

Was it any wonder she loved Peter so thoroughly in return?

The ladies continued their gossip.

"Indeed," Lady Whitcomb agreed. "A pagan Scotsman might do for a novel but place such a man in an English drawing room . . ." She drifted off, giving a violent shudder.

In that moment, Jane nearly pitied Lord Hadley. The man would be walking into a hornet's nest of expectations and rigid etiquette rules he clearly did not understand, crofter's hut or not. He was in for a brutal time of things.

Lady Hadley offered a restrained smile, expression politely arctic. "It has been a dreadful shock. Thankfully, we have the care of kind friends to buoy us up."

Her mother delivered the words with dripping sweetness. Lady Whitcomb did not miss their venom, her lips pinching in response.

Jane longed to roll her eyes and lounge back in her chair, posture slumping.

She took another sip of tea instead.

The Langston family had already survived four Scottish kings, three German ones, and pink powdered wigs. It would surely outlast this catastrophe.

Jane herself was no stranger to disaster. Her father, the Duke of Montacute, had died when Jane was still a babe. When Jane was a toddler, her mother had remarried, this time to the widowed Earl of Hadley. Lord Hadley had not been a cruel stepfather to Jane. He had simply never acknowledged her existence beyond the occasional polite nod or word.

Jane might have taken offense at this, but the old earl treated everyone that way—his wife, relatives, his deceased son, Henry . . . even Peter, his only child with Jane's mother. No one mourned when, after years of poor health, the earl had finally passed on six months ago. Only his lordship's creditors and immediate family considered his death a calamity.

No, the true horror came in the aftermath of his lordship's funeral.

Jane vividly remembered the palpable gasp in the room as the family solicitor politely informed them that the old earl had made a series of unwise investments, leaving the earldom heavily in debt and on the verge of bankruptcy. Lady Hadley would receive her dower portion, as was legally required, but no other allowances had been made.

Peter, his lordship's *English* second son—the spare, not the heir—had received nothing.

Instead, what little remained had been left to his lordship's Scottish grandson, the new Lord Hadley.

Laws of primogeniture being what they were, the title *had* to pass to the eldest son of the eldest son—the Scot, Andrew Langston.

But . . . the ailing estates, lands, and investments were not currently entailed. Some portion of them—or all, quite frankly—could have been left to Peter. Yet, for some unfathomable reason, the old earl had utterly cut his second son from his will. The question was why?

The old earl had been ill for years before his death. Had he simply neglected to update his will in a timely fashion? Or, had he truly been so uncaring of Peter? Regardless of the old earl's finances, to deny his son any inheritance whatsoever seemed excessively callous.

Peter had borne it all with a stoic, white-lipped silence—the same wretched, suppressed fury with which he greeted all information about the new Lord Hadley. Having spent her whole life concerned for her brother's welfare, Jane found it physically painful to witness.

The disorderly heart of her—the inner wild self she kept contained and thoroughly battened down—raged at the injustice. *That* Jane wanted to raise the old earl from dead, just so she could send him to his Maker again. This time in a more painfully lingering fashion.

Of course, such thoughts merely underscored *why* she kept her inner self thoroughly contained. No one wanted a lady who behaved in such a manner. Her past had proved this most cruelly.

"When do you anticipate his lordship's arrival?" Mrs. Smith asked Lady Hadley, interrupting Jane's thoughts.

Though Lord Hadley had immediately petitioned Parliament for a Writ of Summons, he had waited six months before making an appearance in Sussex.

The previous week after Sunday service, Mrs. Smith had the audacity to muse that it was to his lordship's credit that he had waited until the family was out of full mourning before visiting them. She was immediately silenced.

"His man-of-affairs said to expect him in three weeks' time," Lady Hadley replied.

"The earl did not write you himself?" Lady Whitcomb was all astonishment.

"No."

Silence greeted Lady Hadley's curt response. Unspoken assumptions hung in the air—if Lord Hadley hadn't written the letter himself, was his lordship even literate? However, he *did* employ a man-of-affairs, so perhaps opinion was divided on that score?

Smiling stiffly, Lady Hadley motioned toward the tea tray. "Would anyone care for another biscuit?"

Eventually the ladies rattled through their gossip about the new Lord Hadley and took their leave.

"Well, I cannot say I missed afternoon calls when we were in full mourning," Peter said as the door closed on the last of them. He stood, walking over to the fireplace. "I'm quite sure my ears are bleeding from their lacerating witticisms."

"You acquitted yourself well, Peter, as usual," Lady Hadley smoothed her lavender skirts, before turning to Jane. "You were far too quiet, however, Jane. You need to speak more."

"Of course, Mother." Jane gave her reply automatically. If she had said more to their visitors, her mother would reprimand her for speaking too often.

Jane pressed her fingernail into her palm. *Half-moons*, she thought. *Concentrate on making half-moons.*

"Why are you harping on about Jane's manners, Mother?" Peter rolled his eyes and snorted, sarcasm dripping. "The new Lord Hadley will not notice one way or another."

He pronounced *Lord Hadley* with a hostile wince, as if saying the man's very name hurt his mouth.

Jane shot Peter a grateful look. She could see them both reflected in the mirror above the mantel, their heads nearly touching, Peter's tousled blond overlapping her brassier auburn. Symbolically always beside her.

"Hadley . . . perhaps not." Lady Hadley glanced her way. "But I've had another letter from Montacute, Jane, and your brother is hinting, again, at you joining him and his duchess in London for the Season. If that happens, we must focus on perfecting your behavior."

Jane narrowly avoided a wince herself. Only the biting pain of her nail into her palm stopped her reaction.

Her other half-brother, the current Duke of Montacute, had exacting expectations of her. Words from his latest letter rattled through her skull:

> You must ever be mindful, sister, of the honor your name does you. You are the daughter and sister of Montacute. Your every breath should reflect the exalted circumstances of your birth.

Nearly twenty years her senior, Montacute had always been a menacing figure, more stern father than brother, truth be told. Jane revolted at the thought of living with him and his duchess in London, forced to interact daily with their caustic selves. Worse, it would separate her from Peter.

Her mother continued, motioning toward Jane with a languid hand, "Montacute has increased your pin money since the old earl's death, Jane, but with the earldom on the brink of bankruptcy, I do not know how much longer you will have a home here. It all depends on what the new earl decides when he arrives. Unmarried, you are simply a drain upon both Hadley and Montacute."

As was proper, Montacute had assumed financial responsibility for Jane since her stepfather's death and provided her with a monthly allowance. But her mother's words were true—unmarried, Jane was nothing more than dross.

Peter moved to sit, sprawling in the chair opposite, shooting her an understanding look. While neither of them was enthusiastic about having to tolerate the new Scottish earl himself, they genuinely dreaded the consequences of his choices.

"Well, we are *all* drains on Hadley now, Mother," Peter said, again distracting Lady Hadley's attention. "He holds our purse strings, such as they are. We are all reliant on his good-will for our every need. I consider it prudent to politely avoid the man as much as possible."

Given that Peter could scarcely say the man's name without grimacing in distaste, her brother was far more troubled than he let on. He was justifiably angry that Hadley—uncouth, unrefined, and currently unknown—now held Peter's future in his hands. The hurt of being abandoned so thoroughly by his sire ran deep. Peter had been cut adrift, floating away from her, and Jane felt powerless to bring him back to shore.

Jane sat straighter in her chair.

"I agree with Peter," she said. "We shall simply endure Hadley's coming the way all English have faced Scots over the centuries—with impeccable manners, reserved politeness, and sardonic verve."

Peter grimaced and saluted her with a raised eyebrow. His expression mirroring her own sense of impending doom.

Visit www.NicholeVan.com to buy your copy of
Suffering the Scot today and continue the story.

ABOUT THE AUTHOR

THE SHORT VERSION:

NICHOLE VAN IS a writer, photographer, designer and generally disorganized crazy person. Though originally from Utah, she currently lives on the coast of Scotland with three similarly crazy children and one sane, very patient husband who puts up with all of them. In her free time, she enjoys long walks along the Scottish lochs and braes. She does not, however, enjoy haggis.

THE LONG OVERACHIEVER VERSION:

AN INTERNATIONAL BESTSELLING author, Nichole Van is an artist who feels life is too short to only have one obsession. In former lives, she has been a contemporary dancer, pianist, art historian, chore-ographer, culinary artist and English professor.

Most notably, however, Nichole is an acclaimed photographer, win-ning over thirty international accolades for her work, including Portrait of the Year from WPPI in 2007. (Think Oscars for wedding and por-trait photographers.) Her unique photography style has been featured in many magazines, including Rangefinder and Professional Photographer.

All that said, Nichole has always been a writer at heart. With an MA in English, she taught technical writing at Brigham Young University for ten years and has written more technical manuals than she can quickly count. She decided in late 2013 to start writing fiction and has since become an Amazon #1 bestselling author. Additionally, she has won a RONE award, as well as been a Whitney Award Finalist several years running. Her late 2018 release, *Seeing Miss Heartstone*, won the Whitney Award Winner for Best Historical Romance.

In February 2017, Nichole, her husband and three crazy children moved from the Rocky Mountains in the USA to Scotland. They currently live near the coast of eastern Scotland in an eighteenth century country house. Nichole loves her pastoral country views while writing and enjoys long walks through fields and along beaches. She does not, however, have a fondness for haggis.

She is known as NicholeVan all over the web: Facebook, Instagram, Pinterest, etc. Visit http://www.NicholeVan.com to sign up for her author newsletter and be notified of new book releases.

If you enjoyed this book, please leave a short review on Amazon. com. Wonderful reviews are the elixir of life for authors. Even better than dark chocolate.

Made in the USA
Las Vegas, NV
21 June 2023

73719056R00173